Praise f

MW00770530

A WILD FRIGHT IN DEADWOOD

"A WILD FRIGHT IN DEADWOOD—quirky, hilarious and downright brilliant! Take a wild ride with Ann Charles. You'll be so delighted you did!"

~**Robyn Peterman**, New York Times Bestselling Author

"A highly entertaining mystery with a dash of sizzle, a splash of spooky, and a huge helping of fun."

~**Chanticleer Book Reviews**

"Part Laugh-Out-Loud Funny and part Read-With-The-Light-On Scary, WILD FRIGHT IN DEADWOOD is a definite page turner you don't want to miss!"

~**Kim Hornsby**, National Bestselling Author

"Ann Charles' Deadwood series is an intriguing mixture of humor and suspense all blended into a complex world a reader can get lost in."

~**Diane Garland**, Owner of Your WorldKeeper

"Full of humor, sarcasm, spooky excitement, steamy moments and old friends. Ann knocked this one out of the park!"

~**Mary Joyce Avery**, Freelance Artist

"Just when I thought Ann couldn't add anything else to the story, something new popped in and surprised me. A WILD FRIGHT IN DEADWOOD is loads of fun!"

~**Dave Smithwick**, Helpdesk Support Agent

For more on Ann and her books, check out her website, as well as the reader reviews for her books on Amazon, Barnes & Noble, and Goodreads.

Dear Reader,

Once upon a time I was going to write a book about a real estate agent from Deadwood who was struggling to make ends meet while raising two children and running into trouble with oddball clients and peculiar houses. Now, seven books later, I feel like I opened a chest full of treasures, at least from an author's point-of-view. With quirky characters, memorable locations, and humorous hijinks just for starters, there is so much more of Violet's story yet to come.

A WILD FRIGHT IN DEADWOOD is the longest novel I've written so far—three more chapters than usual thanks to Violet's crazy life. It's also the fastest novel I've written to date. I think I burned off my fingertips in the rush to relocate the story from my brain to the page.

I've included a good friend of mine in this book: bestselling author Terri Reid. For those of you who have read Terri's Mary O'Reilly Mystery Series, you might remember that Terri included my mom and me in the 16th book in her series. I thought it was fun to be in Terri's story as "Ann Charles" so I decided I needed to include "Terri Reid" in my series. (By the way, Terri loved meeting Violet on the page. I hope you get a chuckle out of the sections mentioning her.) If you haven't checked out Terri's books, you're missing some fun and addictive paranormal mysteries.

I hope you get some laughs and frights and everything in between out of this latest segment in Violet Parker's ongoing adventures and mishaps.

As old man Harvey often says, "Never kick a cow chip on a hot day."

Ann Charles

www.anncharles.com

A WILD FRIGHT IN DEADWOOD

ANN CHARLES

ILLUSTRATED BY C.S. KUNKLE

For Justin

You will always be old man Harvey in my imagination. I wish you'd stuck around long enough to see if I have Harvey spot-on with Bessie and all of the crazy dames.

You will be missed.

A Wild Fright in Deadwood

Copyright © 2016 by Ann Charles

Cover Art by C.S. Kunkle
Cover Design by Sharon Benton (www.q42designs.com)
Editing by the Grammar Chick (www.grammarchick.com)
Formatting by Biddles ebooks

E-book ISBN-13: 978-1-940364-44-5
Print ISBN-:13: 978-1-940364-43-8

Acknowledgments

This book is long! Because I blathered on so much in the story, I'm going to keep this short and sweet. Thank you to my husband, kids, family, friends, graphic artist, artist, editors, first draft readers, local expert, world keeper, beta readers, promotion team, and ornery cats. Thanks also to my brother, Clint, who has been making me roll my eyes for almost four decades now with his nutty antics.

Special thanks to Robyn Peterman, Chanticleer Book Reviews, and Kim Hornsby for your wonderful quotes.

Thank you to all who support me and my books by reading and sharing them with friends, family, local librarians, and complete strangers in line behind you at the liquor store and food truck.

Many thanks to the bookstores, tourist stores, and other venues who help me by selling my books.

Thank you to five wonderful friends from Deadwood and Lead who have helped Violet and I succeed over the years in many ways: "Chip" Tautkus from Chubby Chipmunk Chocolates, Kim Rupp from Executive Lodging of the Black Hills, Karen Everett from the Lead Deadwood Arts Center, Janell Andis from Custer Crossing, and Sue Stone-Douglas (my local expert). I cherish your friendship, generosity, kindness, and support!

Finally, a big thanks to YOU for reading Violet's latest calamity. I hope you get some laughs and chills. If I keep you up late into the night and you're tired at work the next day, feel free to email me with curses and love.

Also by Ann Charles

Deadwood Mystery Series
Nearly Departed in Deadwood (Book 1)
Optical Delusions in Deadwood (Book 2)
Dead Case in Deadwood (Book 3)
Better Off Dead in Deadwood (Book 4)
An Ex to Grind in Deadwood (Book 5)
Meanwhile, Back in Deadwood (Book 6)
Deadwood Shorts: Seeing Trouble
Deadwood Shorts: Boot Points
Deadwood Shorts: Cold Flame

Jackrabbit Junction Mystery Series
Dance of the Winnebagos (Book 1)
Jackrabbit Junction Jitters (Book 2)
The Great Jackalope Stampede (Book 3)
The Rowdy Coyote Rumble (Book 4)
Jackrabbit Junction Short: The Wild Turkey Tango

Goldwash Mystery Series (a future series)
The Old Man's Back in Town (Short Story)

Dig Site Mystery Series
Look What the Wind Blew In (Book 1)
(Starring Quint Parker, the brother of Violet from the Deadwood Series)

Coming Next from Ann Charles

Dig Site Mystery Series
Title TBA (Book 2)

Deadwood Mystery Series
Title TBA (Book 8)

Cast

Violet Lynn Parker (1,2,3,4,5,6,7)—Main heroine of the series, Doc's girlfriend, Aunt Zoe's niece

Willis "old man" Harvey (1,2,3,4,5,6,7)—Violet's sidekick and so-called bodyguard

Dane "Doc" Nyce (1,2,3,4,5,6,7)—Violet's boyfriend, main hero, medium

Detective "Coop" Cooper (1,2,3,4,5,6,7)—Deadwood and Lead's detective

Zoe Parker (1,2,3,4,5,6,7)—Violet's aunt and mentor in life

Layne Parker (1,2,3,4,5,6,7)—Violet's nine-year-old son

Adelynn Parker (1,2,3,4,5,6,7)—Violet's nine-year-old daughter

Natalie Beals (1,2,3,4,5,6,7)—Violet's best friend since childhood

Jerry Russo (4,5,6,7)—Violet's boss, owner of Calamity Jane Realty

Mona Hollister (1,2,3,4,5,6,7)—Violet's coworker and mentor in realty

Ray Underhill (1,2,3,4,5,6,7)—Violet's coworker and nemesis at work

Benjamin Underhill (1,2,3,4,5,6,7)—Violet's coworker

Cornelius Curion (3,4,5,6,7)—Violet's client; so-called ghost-whisperer

Reid Martin (2,3,4,5,6,7)—Captain of the fire department, Aunt Zoe's ex-lover

Jeff Wymonds (1,2,3,4,5,6,7)—Violet's client; father of Adelynn's best friend

Prudence (2,3,4,5,6,7)—Ghost who resides at the Carhart house

Zeke and Zelda Britton (2,4,5,6,7)—Owners of the Carhart house in Lead

Wanda Carhart (2,3,4,5,6,7)—Previous owner of the Carhart house in Lead

Katrina King-Mann (7)—Ex-wife of Douglas Mann

Tiffany Sugarbell (1,2,3,4,5,6,7)—Violet's rival Realtor; Doc's ex-girlfriend

Susan Parker (1,2,3,4,5,6,7)—Violet's evil sister; aka "the Bitch from Hell"

Quint Parker (1,2,3,4,5,7)—Violet's supportive brother; Layne's hero; giver of her famous purple boots

Freesia Tender (5,6,7)—Owner of the Galena House

Stone Hawke (5,6,7)—Cooper's ex-partner; detective called in to solve cases

Rex Conner (3,4,5,6,7)—The biological father of Violet's children

Dickie Dowdin (5,6,7)—Host of TV series called "Paranormal Realty"

Honey (5,6,7)—Dickie's assistant

Rad (6,7)—Reality series cameraman

Rosy (6,7)—Reality series camerawoman

Eddie Mudder (3,6,7)—Owner of Mudder Brothers Funeral Parlor

"Such ingratitude, after all the times I saved your life."

~from *The Good, the Bad and the Ugly*

Chapter One

Saturday, November 10th
Lead, South Dakota

"Hell hath no fury like a high-steppin' heifer who's been downright scorned," old man Harvey told me as I steered along the back streets of Lead.

I frowned across the console of my new-but-used SUV at my self-proclaimed bodyguard and partner in troublemaking. "First of all, you know how I feel about being compared to a cow." I poked him in the ribs to emphasize my feelings on that matter. "Second, I'm not high-stepping. I can barely raise my boots off the ground most days."

As a single mom with almost ten-year-old twins ruling my world, I was usually dragging my raggedy pride behind me wherever I roamed.

Harvey rubbed his side, grunting. "I'm not talkin' 'bout you, Sparky."

"Third, how many times do I have to tell you to stop calling me *Sparky*?" It was bad enough that most of Deadwood's fire department and half of its cop-shop were now calling me that. "My name is Violet Parker. Period."

"*Spooky Parker* is more fittin' these days, don'cha think?"

After some of the freaky shit Harvey and I'd been through lately, he had a point.

"Better yet, *Killer Parker*. Ya gotta admit, that has a real nice ring to it."

I aimed another rib poke his way.

Harvey held up his hands. "Fine, plain ol' Violet Parker it is."

"That's better."

A snort came from his side of the vehicle. "It's no fair. Ya let Doc call you all sorts of names besides *Violet*."

I also let Doc Nyce see me naked whenever life allowed us a moment alone, and I often encouraged him to touch me in territory outlawed to the rest of mankind. "That's different."

"Because you two are knockin' your low-steppin' boots?"

This time I pinched his thigh.

He howled. "Dang it, girl, ya sure got yer horns out this mornin'."

He didn't know the half of it. I'd woken up fighting with my pillow in sweat-soaked sheets again. Over the past week, while the flu held me hostage, my nightmares had returned in full force. The legendary cast of my nocturnal imaginary world ranged from white-haired juggernauts to snarling bone crunchers and face-melting demons. I'd been slain in my sleep more times than I could count thanks to their ghoulish choice of weaponry.

But my nightmares were my problem, not Harvey's.

A glance his way found his blue eyes narrowed, watching me. "If you're not talking about me high-stepping, who then?" I asked. I slowed, easing as far right as I could on the narrow residential street to allow a jacked-up pickup to pass going the opposite way. "One of your old flames?"

Harvey had so many old flames burning around the Black Hills that I couldn't go to the grocery store without getting singed.

"Nope. Yer boyfriend's ex."

The mere thought of Doc's ex-girlfriend made me clench the steering wheel until my knuckles turned white. "I don't want to talk about Tiffany Sugarbell!"

Or her flat stomach.

Or her perky boobs.

Or her gorgeous red hair, especially after trying to wrangle my blonde curly mess into submission today only to have it spiral out of control as soon as I'd stepped outside.

He blew out a low whistle. "Yer like sittin' next to a box of ol' TNT today. You need to breathe easy for a bit, spitfire."

"I can't help it." I peeled my fingers off the wheel, trying to shake the tension out of one hand and then the other. "You and I both know that bitch is nuts."

Harvey nodded. "That's how the cow ate the cabbage."

"The cow ate what?" Was that another bovine comparison?

He waved off my confusion. "That woman's banjo ain't been tuned right since you came to town."

It wasn't my arrival that sent Tiffany spinning out of control; it had been Doc cutting her from his life. That had been when she'd started filling up his phone with text messages and voicemails.

"I'd like to shove her banjo where the sun doesn't shine." Or better yet, take a sledge hammer to it now that she'd decided that wooing back my boyfriend wasn't enough and had begun seducing my clients, too.

I slowed and turned into the gravel driveway leading up to the Carhart house. The arched and gabled Gothic-revival style dwelling loomed in the windshield. Dark clouds threatening snow painted a gloomy backdrop.

Speaking of a lack of sunshine ...

I killed the engine.

"There she sits in all of her hair-raisin', blood-stained glory." Harvey stared out the windshield along with me.

"It's a beautiful house." I stuck to my original observation from back in August, but my tone was more anxious than in months past.

The old place was the picture of elegance and calm on the outside, a wood and nails version of a classic Hollywood starlet. My gaze climbed up past the first two stories, faltering when it reached the attic window. The gauzy white curtain hanging there swayed even though the window was closed. If only the ghost living within the house's graceful bones would stop scaring the bejeezus out of me every time I crossed the threshold.

"It's time to batten down the hatches." Harvey's voice had a smidgen of unease rippling through it. "Things are gonna get ugly."

I dragged my focus away from the attic window. "I heard we're supposed to get several inches of snow by nightfall."

"I'm not talkin' about the weather." He pointed at the house. "I got a notion tightenin' my innards."

"I told you at breakfast that I was done talking about glitches with your bodily functions for today." Frankly, I didn't have the stomach for that discussion. I loved the old codger dearly, but I couldn't afford to be *off my feed*, as Harvey liked to put it. With Deadwood winters being long and cold enough for my fellow cows to give ice cream, I needed to make sure my extra layers of fat remained gelatinously in place to keep me good and warm.

"This ain't about *my* problems, it's about yers."

"You volunteered to be my bodyguard, remember?" Harvey and his companion, Bessie, which happened to be a doubled-barreled shotgun, had the job of making sure I retained life and limbs at all times. "How is this going to work if my problems aren't yours, too?"

He scratched under his beard. "You got too many wasps in yer outhouse, girlie, especially with that scorned she-devil sharpenin' her pitchfork."

"Tiffany can kiss my ass."

I was done festering about Doc's damned ex. It was time to go play hide-and-seek with Prudence the ghost.

I shoved my door open, wincing as a frigid blast of cold air whipped past me and slammed the door shut behind me. "You can pucker up, too, Mother Nature." I shook my fist at the dark sky. Tucking my head inside of my collar like a turtle, I clutched my coat lapels and plowed through the wind toward the house.

Harvey caught up with me at the porch steps. "There's a shitstorm comin' yer way."

My laughter didn't travel far thanks to the gust of wind that blew it toward Lead's cavernous Open Cut next door, tossing it over the side into the 1,250 foot deep pit mine. "I've been mired in one shitstorm after another since I moved up to Deadwood last spring."

A sharp-clawed ex-girlfriend and an unnerving ghost were only two of my many problems. These days, I chewed my knuckles more about all of the other terrors hiding in the shadows.

"Yeah, but yer belly's showin' now," Harvey said.

I glanced down at my stomach, which was visible through my open coat. The sight of loose threads where two buttons formerly had been sewn distracted me for a moment, making me want to strangle a chicken. Not just any chicken—my daughter Addy's pet hen that she'd named Elvis. That damned bird was obsessed with stealing buttons and burying them in her cage down in the basement.

"Not that belly." Harvey jammed his hands in his coat pockets. "Yer other one."

"You mean because word has spread now about my real job as an …" I still couldn't get my tongue to participate on cue when it came to saying the word aloud.

"Executioner," Harvey finished for me.

"Shhhh."

"Why are you shushin' me, girl? There's nobody here but you and me and yer wacky ghost buddy inside."

"Nobody that we can see." I pulled him up on the porch, lowering my voice. "And Prudence is not my buddy."

"According to her, yer from the same killin' breed."

Behind Harvey, a black Ram truck rolled into the drive, easing around my SUV. It was time to play real estate agent extraordinaire.

"They're here." I pasted a smile on my face as the pickup came to a stop. "No more talk about all of this weird stuff going on until we leave," I warned through my teeth.

He watched along with me as the new owners of the Carhart house hopped down from the tall truck. "Woo-wee! That boy is a regular

Sherman tank."

That was a spot-on description of Zeke Britton. Larger than life from his round bald head down to his clown-sized shoes, the man was a former professional wrestler. After years of pounding bodies into the mat, he'd left the ring to be an independent surveyor.

Zelda, his wife, was about a third of Zeke's size. She'd tucked her auburn hair under a black stocking cap decorated with a big yellow daisy on the front. Our shared love of the happy-faced flower was one of the reasons I'd liked her the first time she'd walked into the Calamity Jane Realty office back in August. That and the way her smile made her green eyes sparkle. I'd never have guessed she had such a passion for books from the way she'd been draped from head to toe in biker leather. A career librarian, Zelda knew books like Harvey knew ranching. It was in their bones.

Realty, on the other hand, barely scratched below my skin's surface, and my executioner role floated beyond my fingertips most days. If only eating chocolate mixed with peanut butter were a legitimate profession.

"What am I doin' here again?" Harvey asked out of the side of his mouth.

"Protecting me from Prudence."

"I mean what was that tale you were gonna tell these two?"

"You are here with me because we're going house hunting after we leave."

"Gotcha." He glanced my way. "You might wanna dial that ghoulish grin of yers down a few notches before you scare the birds away."

"Zip it, old man." I left the porch and met Zeke and Zelda halfway up the walk, welcoming them with a hug. "Congratulations, you two. Your new house is all ready for you."

At least I hoped it was. I'd been too scaredy-cat to go inside and inspect the haunted house by myself after the housekeeping service had called to tell me they were done. Instead, I'd paid extra to have them place a few flower-filled vases around and make sure the place looked inviting for the new owners.

Another frigid blast of wind urged us up onto the porch where Harvey stood waiting, his grin wide enough to show off his two gold teeth.

"Zeke and Zelda, this is my client, Willis Harvey. I hope you don't mind that he tagged along. We're heading out to shop some potential homes as soon as we leave."

"Not at all," Zelda said, shaking Harvey's hand after her husband. "Brrrr, your hands are cold, Mr. Harvey. How long have you two been standing out here?"

"A few minutes," I told her, unlocking the front door. "We wanted to let you two be the first to step inside your new home."

Not to mention that the less time I spent within the walls of the Carhart house the less I needed adult diapers to cope with its overactive ghost.

I followed Zelda and Zeke through the door, soaking up the warmth inside the narrow foyer. The place smelled like vanilla, the same as always. Prudence must be partial to that scent.

"It's just as amazing as I remembered." Zelda trailed her hand lovingly along the silk wallpaper and then touched her fingertip to one of the Tiffany style stained-glass wall sconces. She caught her husband's hand and towed him into the kitchen. "Oh!" she cried out in happiness. "Look at the bouquet of lilies, poms, and magnolia tips. How perfect!"

The sound of the door closing behind me gave me a start.

Harvey patted my back. "Yer actin' like a hen in a coyote den."

"I can't help it," I whispered. "This place messes with my head." Prudence always had a way of sneaking up on me even when I was ready for her.

"It sure is a purty home. You'd never know all of the murderin' that's gone on in here."

"Let's just hope that its gory history stays in the past."

The Brittons joined us again and then wandered into the sitting room, admiring its birch floor covered with cream-colored shag rugs. Wanda Carhart had sold the house to them as is, including the burgundy leather furnishings, which was nice for the new owners. However, I would have preferred a total remodel to erase my own bloody memories of the place.

After more coos of happiness, the Brittons headed for the wide stairwell. I motioned for Harvey to stay put and then followed them up the stairs, wanting to make sure Prudence hadn't carved any words into the walls or played any other pranks to get my attention.

We traversed the house, Zeke and Zelda all smiles and glad-eyes while I cringed and winced at every turn, anticipating Prudence turning Zelda into her personal ventriloquist dummy. I breathed a sigh of relief when we returned to Harvey, who was still waiting in the foyer.

At his raised bushy eyebrows, I shook my head.

"Well, you two," I said to Zeke and Zelda, "if you're happy with the place and ready to enjoy it on your own, Mr. Harvey and I will take our leave."

"I hope you'll come back soon." Zelda hugged me for about the tenth time since we'd entered the house. "You've been such a joy to work with. I'm so glad we chose you to be our Realtor."

My cheeks warmed at her compliment. "It's been my pleasure."

"There's just one more thing." Zelda looked around. "Where's my purse?"

"You left it in the kitchen, baby," Zeke said.

Zelda zipped into the kitchen and back again. "We want you to have this." She handed me a jewelry box.

"You two didn't need to get me anything," I said, frowning down at the box.

"Open it," Zelda urged.

Inside was a leather necklace with a white, arrowhead shaped trinket surrounded by beads. I lifted it out of the box.

"It's an alligator tooth," Zelda explained. "Some cultures believe alligator teeth bring good luck while gambling. Since you live in Deadwood, I thought of you when I saw it."

Considering that I'd been gambling with my life more often than not lately, I was happy to have any good luck charms that came along. "Thank you both. It's very sweet of you."

"Here, let me help you put it on." Zelda took the necklace from me and slipped it over my head. "There, now you're ready to go out and win."

I'd settle for going out and not dying.

"We'd like to have you come over for a thank-you dinner sometime, too, if you don't mind."

Dinner with Prudence the ghost? I didn't know how I'd be able to keep from hiding under the table the whole time. "Sure," I said, trying to mean it. "Give me a call and we'll pick a date."

"Deal." Zelda followed us to the door while Zeke disappeared into the kitchen. "And please don't be a stranger. I feel like you and I are two old souls who have been waiting to meet up again."

I stared at her with my breath held, wondering if that was Prudence talking or Zelda. Usually Prudence's melodic mid-Eastern Atlantic accent took over when she played puppet master, but maybe Zelda would be different. After all, I was pretty sure that she was the "librarian" Prudence had demanded I bring to the house on several of my past visits.

Harvey elbowed me in the spine, nudging a reply of, "Yes, old souls, definitely," out of me.

I fingered the alligator tooth hanging from my neck. If Zelda and I were going to continue spending time together, I was going to insist it be outside of this house more often than not. Otherwise, she was going to quickly figure out what a nut case I was and hide when I came knocking.

Zelda opened the door for us. "Who's that?" she asked, looking at me. A frown clouded her usually sunny demeanor.

Harvey and I shared a wide-eyed look.

"Where?" I asked, afraid to move in case Prudence was standing behind me.

She pointed out the door. "Sitting in your Honda."

What? Sure enough, someone was sitting in the passenger seat. I could have sworn Harvey and I had come alone.

I stepped out onto the porch, trying to see who it was. "Harvey, did you leave your door unlocked?"

"Of course. This is Lead, not Los Angeles."

True. Come to think of it, I had, too.

"It looks like a woman." Zelda joined us on the porch, shivering in the cold breeze.

Who in the hell was in my vehicle?

"We'll be on our way now," I told Zelda, taking Harvey's arm and dragging him down the steps with me. "Call me," I hollered over my shoulder.

Zelda disappeared back inside, closing the door behind her.

Halfway to the SUV, Harvey tugged free of my grip. "You tryin' to pull my arm off, girlie?"

We drew close enough to get a good eyeful of our visitor through the windshield and stopped.

"She looks familiar," I whispered. Something about her high collared shirt—or was it a dress—jogged my memory.

"What's that dark stuff on her neck?"

"It looks like ..." The rest of my words trickled out in a wheeze. I gulped. "It's Prudence."

I'd seen her picture once in an historical book Doc had shown me. She'd been married to a local doctor. His position in town had given her clout in Lead's historical records. News about the horrifying murder of her family had made its way into the book as well.

"I thought the ol' gal never left the house," Harvey said.

"Me, too." This was a first. Usually I was safe outside of the walls of the Carhart house. The chills that now peppered my body had nothing to do with the wind.

"We might as well see what she wants."

"You go. You're my bodyguard."

"My job is to guard you from the livin'." Harvey pointed at Prudence. "That one there is long dead."

A stronger blast of cold air rocked us. This time my goosebumps were from the wind. If we kept standing out here, we'd turn into popsicles.

"Fine, I'll go." I took a step forward, then glanced back. "But you stick to my heels."

"Deal." He locked onto my shoulder instead and we crept up to the driver's side window together.

Prudence stared straight ahead out the windshield, seemingly oblivious to our noses pressed against the glass. Her regal profile appeared blurry around the edges, her creamy complexion softened, almost glowing, as if there were a filter between us.

"Now what?" Harvey asked.

How in the world had Prudence made herself visible to Harvey and me … and Zelda? Or was it Zelda's presence who'd given Prudence the extra boost she needed for this feat?

"I don't know. I'm new at actually seeing ghosts." My specialty was more along the lines of running the other way when I was told they were sharing the room with me.

"You're an executioner."

"Exactly. I deal with living beings, and usually not of the human variety. Doc's the one who dallies with the dead." That was one of his specialties, along with a handful of other sixth sense abilities. I was still learning how many tricks of the trade he had up his sleeve.

"Well, yer stud's not here at the moment, so we need to improvise."

"Okay. How about you make the first move?"

"How about you knock on the glass." He grabbed my hand and lifted it toward the window.

I yanked it back. "You knock first."

"No way. She's your kin."

"We are not …" I looked in the window. Prudence stared straight at me. My breath caught. "She's looking at me," I whispered.

"Are her eyeballs supposed to be all white like that?"

"How in the hell am I supposed to know, Harvey? This is the first time we've actually met face-to-face."

As we stared through the window, Prudence raised her hand and gave me a come hither gesture with her index finger.

My blood froze.

Harvey pointed at his own chest. "You want me?" he called through the glass.

She shook her head slowly and pointed at me.

"Winner winner chicken dinner." He smirked at me. "Yer lucky alligator tooth necklace is striking gold for ya already."

I shot Harvey a worried look. "What am I supposed to do?"

"I'd start with gettin' inside the vehicle."

"I don't want to be in there with *her*."

"Yeah, well I don't want to keep standin' out here in the wind. My nuggets are frozen. Another stiff breeze like that last one and they'll break right off. How about I climb in the back seat so yer not alone."

I nodded, reaching for the door handle. Seconds later, we were all three inside, snug as bugs in a rug.

I sniffed, noticing the faint scent of roses. Her perfume? Or was this the olfactory indication Doc often noticed when ghosts came around?

The back of my seat jerked like it had been kicked. Harvey cleared his throat.

I glared back at him.

"Say something," he spoke out of the side of his mouth.

Wasn't he just loaded with advice? Move over, Dear Abby. I'd bet he'd be a little more shy if he were the one face-to-face with a ghost whose eyes looked like white gumballs.

"Hello, Prudence." My voice started out rusty. "Is there something you want from me?"

"Wanda needs you," she said, only her lips didn't move. Instead, her voice had come from the back seat sounding more garbled and scratchy than usual.

I shot a surprised look at Harvey.

One of his hands was covering his mouth. His eyes were as wide as silver dollars.

"Did that come from you?" I asked.

He nodded so hard his earlobes wobbled.

Frowning at this new take on Prudence's usual ventriloquist act, I focused back on my ghost passenger. "Why does Wanda Carhart need me?"

"A cloaked stranger visited the house last night." Prudence's voice was muffled thanks to Harvey's hands covering his lips. "A hunter searching for a treasure believed to be in Wanda's possession."

Wanda's treasure? Did Prudence mean the money willed to Wanda from her aunt? Had someone intended to rob her but showed up one house sale too late?

Tucking my cold hands into my armpits, I tried to stop trembling. Prudence's phantom-like presence a mere arm's reach away from me was as unsettling as the idea of someone sneaking around the Carhart house in the dark.

I glanced at Harvey again. Both of his hands now blocked his mouth from view, reminding me of the speak-no-evil monkey.

"Who came to the house?" I asked, not sure if I should look at Prudence or Harvey when I spoke.

Harvey won my attention. He was a lot less creepy looking than a dead woman with a bloody throat.

"An assassin." I watched as Harvey fought to control the muscles of his face and lost as Prudence continued to use his mouth and vocal chords. "Wanda must return the missing pearl."

"A pearl?" From a pearl necklace her aunt had left her? Was that the treasure? Or was Prudence once again being metaphorical?

"The assassin made no sound," the ghost continued, ignoring my question. "But its foul stench spoke the truth."

What truth? I sighed in frustration. "Prudence, stop being so damned cryptic. What did the assassin look like?"

Harvey gave up fighting her and lowered his hands. He sighed and crossed his arms over his chest, looking up at the ceiling as she spoke through him. "One of the Others."

At the word *Others*, my stomach fluttered.

"YOU MUST GO TO WANDA NOW!" The sudden intensity in her voice made Harvey flinch in surprise.

I let out a surprised squeak.

When I turned back to the dead woman in my passenger seat my limbs tingled with adrenaline. "I need more information, Prudence."

The ghost leaned toward me, so close that I could see the air swirling on her pale cheeks, blurring all fine lines. She looked so real, yet vapory at the same time. For a split-second I thought I smelled the metallic scent of blood on her dress. Fighting the urge to recoil, I held her white-eyed stare.

"*Scharfrichter.*" Harvey spoke the German name for executioner from the back seat.

The ghost in my face reached her finger toward my chest. I held still. My heartbeat revved as she came nearer. Would I be able to feel her touch?

Her finger hesitated over my sternum. "Your job is to protect. Not question."

"How can I protect when I don't understand?"

I looked down, watching my chest rise and fall quickly.

"Do as I say!" She thrust her whole hand inside of me.

Heat seared my lungs in a flash, burning so hot my eyes watered. Her ghostly face lunged toward mine, her mouth gaping wide and dark as it came at me.

I screamed and retreated back.

Then in a blink she was gone, along with her burning touch.

Clutching my chest, I turned to Harvey. "What should I do?"

He made a weird croaking sound, then cleared his throat and tried again. "Change your underwear." His tone was higher than normal.

"Right." I clasped my hands together, trying to stop the trembling. "And after that, what should I do about Wanda?"

"Call Coop." Harvey worked his jaw a couple of times, as if Prudence had over-tightened the joints.

I hesitated, my heart still running in the red.

Detective Cooper and I had a rocky relationship on our good days. My breaking his nose hadn't helped, nor had the phone calls I'd made regarding the dead bodies I'd found in his jurisdiction.

This time was different, though. This would be a warning call, no body parts or shriveled up heads to discuss.

I pulled my phone from my coat pocket, almost dropping it with my shaky hands. Pulling up his contact info, I took a calming breath and touched the call button for his cell phone. It went straight to voicemail, so I tried his office number.

"Put him on speaker so I can hear," Harvey said.

Cooper picked up on the third ring. "I'm busy, Parker," he snapped. "What do you want?"

What I wanted was to reach through the line and whop him upside the head. Instead, I held my course. "I need you to pay a visit to Wanda Carhart."

I heard the sound of a chair squeaking, only it was slightly tinny. Our connection must not be the greatest.

"Why's that?" his voice came through with a hint of an echo.

"I think she might be in trouble."

"What kind of trouble?"

I could tell he was being purposely obtuse. I snarled down at my phone in frustration. "Like death trouble, Cooper. You want me to come to your office and draw you a freaking picture?"

There were some scuffing sounds and then a bit of static from his end.

"Cooper, did you hear me?"

"We both did," a voice said that was definitely *not* Cooper's.

Son of a bitch!

I knew that voice. It belonged to Detective Stone Hawke, Cooper's partner in crime-solving. The same detective who suspected I was somehow involved in several of the past deaths I'd stumbled upon. The same jackass who had an ongoing theory that I was a witch and not the pretty Samantha from *Bewitched* kind.

Before my big mouth said anything else, I hung up on the two detectives.

"Now yer in a pickle."

"Shit! Shit! Shit!" I pounded on the steering wheel with each curse. I was still beating up the wheel when my phone rang.

I scowled down at it. "It's Cooper."

"Course it is. Hangin' up on him like that only makes him more ornery."

Worrying my knuckle, I looked at Harvey in the rearview mirror. "What should I do?"

"Ya better answer it. You know how curly lipped he gets when he has to track ya down."

Wincing, I answered via speakerphone. "Hello?"

"You have the worst fucking timing, Parker!"

Uh oh. It was never good when Cooper shot out of the gate swearing at me.

He huffed through the line. The big bad wolf had nothing on Deadwood's ace detective. "You got a serious problem now."

"Actually, Detective, I have several serious problems." Including him and his new partner.

Harvey snorted in agreement.

"You shouldn't have called," Cooper continued.

"Why's that? Were you and Detective Hawke busy painting each other's fingernails?"

He cursed at me under his breath. "Because we already checked on Wanda this morning."

"You did?" Had Prudence alerted Wanda about the break-in before I showed up and convinced her to contact the police? If so, what was with the freak show a moment ago in my front seat? "For once Cooper, you and your police pals seem to have your act together."

"Would you shut the hell up for a minute, Parker?"

Sheesh! If his sphincter twisted any tighter, his spine was going to crack. "Why are you so pissed? All I did was make a phone call."

"Because Wanda's dead, Parker. Congratulations, you managed to link yourself to yet another death."

For several blinks, his words ricocheted throughout the different lobes in my brain before penetrating and sparking a reaction. I hit the disconnect button, not wanting to incriminate myself any further before I found out how Wanda had died.

Harvey's open-mouthed expression in the rearview mirror matched mine.

"Wanda's dead," I told him.

"I heard."

"What do we do now?"

"Get the hell out of Dodge."

Chapter Two

"Wanda's dead," I repeated, staring out the windshield at the house where she'd spent so many years.

The house where her husband and son both had died violent deaths.

The house where I'd almost been sliced and diced thanks in part to her wacko daughter.

Dead.

Damn.

I'd seen Wanda a couple of days ago to give her the check for the sale. She'd smiled often during that meeting, brimming with plans for what she would do now that she no longer had this place tying her to the past.

The check? Was money the "treasure" Prudence had been talking about?

"Are you just gonna sit there and spin, girl?" Harvey asked from the back seat.

I looked up at the attic window. How was Prudence going to take this news? Would she be sad?

"That's it!" I heard a door open, and then a blast of cold air hit me. Harvey filled the doorframe. "Move it. I'm drivin'."

Before I could get one leg over the console he was aiming pinches at my backside, hurrying me along.

"Ow! Dang it, Harvey, that hurts." I settled into the passenger seat, rubbing one of the stinging spots on my lower back.

He buckled up. "Stop bein' such a big baby. Yer givin' all of the other executioners a bad name."

Harvey didn't mess around behind the wheel. We were heading down the road lickety-split.

I stared out the window, watching the buildings along Lead's main drag slide past, still grappling with Cooper's news. Wanda had gone from living to dead in a blink of an eye, leaving a gaping hole in my world.

Harvey nudged my leg. "Yer phone's ringin'."

The Harlem Globetrotters' theme song played from my coat pocket.

My boss, the ex-professional basketball player, was calling.

I shook thoughts of Wanda from my head and answered, "Hi, Jerry."

"Violet, do you have a minute? I need to fill you in on some upcoming plans for next week."

Had the assassin Prudence warned me about killed Wanda? Cooper hadn't explicitly said someone had murdered her, but what were the chances of her keeling over out of the blue? Wanda was no spring chicken, but she had seemed healthy enough.

"Violet? Are you there?" Jerry's voice cut through my rumination.

"What?"

"I need to talk to you."

"Now?"

"Preferably, unless you're busy."

Not busy, just scatterbrained. "I'm on my way to the office."

Harvey shot me a frown.

I shrugged back. "Can it wait until I get there?" That would give me some time to get my head back in the game.

"Sure. I'll see you in a bit." Jerry hung up.

I lowered my phone to my lap, feeling lost at sea. I needed a vacation from all of this murder and mystery bullshit. "Harvey, how do you feel about Mexico this time of year?"

"Bikinis in the sunshine make my ticker do loop-the-loops."

I was thinking more along the lines of tequila in the moonlight. "What am I going to do?"

"First ya need to take care of this business with yer boss. As soon as you can tuck tail and run, slip next door to Doc's office. The three of us will put our melons together and figure out how to patch this hole in yer chicken fence."

Doc. Right. He'd know what step to take next. At least I hoped he did, because I felt like I was standing in the middle of a circle of land mines. No matter where I put my foot, something was going to blow up in my face.

"I saw a ghost, Harvey." Until today, I'd been a dud when it had come to the specter world. "What does that mean?"

"Keep in mind that ol' Prudence isn't yer typical spook."

"Do you think I'll be able to see all sorts of ghosts now?"

"If so, you'll be the Mayor of Nutter-ville by Christmas."

Ten minutes later, he parked my Honda behind Calamity Jane Realty next to the Picklemobile, Harvey's old green pickup. Since I was no longer in need of the exhaust belching beast, Harvey had loaned her to Doc to drive during the winter. Doc's sexy 1967 Camaro SS now sat safe and sound in storage.

"He's really cleaned her up," I said to Harvey while looking at the old pickup.

"You should hear her purr now," he told me, pushing open his door. "Doc knows his way around under the hood. The boy has magic hands."

He sure did, I thought with a small grin.

Harvey waited for me while I collected my purse and tried my best to tuck away my bewilderment about Wanda's death for the time being. We rushed through the lot, the wind whipping about our loose ends. Since Doc's office was in the building next to Calamity Jane Realty, we headed in the same direction.

At Doc's back door, Harvey handed me my keys. "You gonna be okay in there?"

I nodded. The freezing air had bitch-slapped me back to life. "I just needed to downshift for a moment, but I'm up to speed now. I'll join you two as soon as I can."

He patted my shoulder. "I like the grit in yer gizzard, girl."

I started toward the back door of my office but then stopped. "Are you okay, Harvey? Prudence was pretty heavy-handed with you back there."

"I feel like I got my tongue caught in my eyeteeth, and I couldn't see what I was sayin' there for a bit." He stroked his beard. "But I'm comin' back to my usual way of thinkin' now."

"That's too bad," I joked but then sobered. "Thank you for coming with me this morning."

"Just doin' my job, Sparky." After dodging my pinching fingers, he pushed inside Doc's door.

A blast of chilly air chased me into Calamity Jane's.

"Violet?" Jerry called from out front, where I usually sat along with the three other real estate agents on his payroll.

I kept my coat on since I hoped not to stay long.

My boss appeared to have relocated to Mona Hollister's desk. His paperwork filled the area where her laptop usually reigned. His extra-long, ex-professional basketball player legs stuck a few feet out the back of the desk, and his elbows extended to the sides. If Thor were to get an office gig, this was what I imagined he'd look like stuffed behind a desk.

What the heck? Where was Mona and why was Jerry working from her seat? He had a nice office of his own down the hall with a large desk and fancy leather chair that fit his oversized body perfectly.

"Hi, Jerry." I dropped my purse on my desktop. "Is Mona okay?"

"Sure. She took the day off, so she won't be lacing up and hitting the court with us today." Jerry spoke fluent Sport-u-guese thanks to spending over half of his life suffering from acute basketball-itis.

He eyed me up and down, as usual. "That outfit looks nice. Those boots really make a statement with your red coat."

"Thanks." I waited for the "but" that I was certain would follow.

"But you might want to dress it up with a wool peacoat that still has all of the buttons next time."

There it was. "Buttons, got it." Stupid chicken!

Jerry had taken it upon himself to be in charge of my wardrobe. Every day he gave me his opinion of the ensemble I had selected, whether I wanted it or not. Knowing his intent was to help my career kept my temper in check when I wasn't dressed to his standards, but that didn't stop me from wanting to kick him in the shin periodically.

"What did you need to talk to me about?"

He sat back. "You want to take your coat off first?"

I shook my head. "I dropped off the keys at the Carhart house—or rather the Britton house."

"Congratulations again on making that sale." His proud smile made me feel like I'd scored a winning basket for the team.

I dipped my chin, acknowledging his words, and then continued. "I need to run over to Detective Cooper's place and make sure it's ready for the viewing tomorrow."

That was a mix of lie and truth.

Truthfully, I had an appointment in the morning with an older couple from Pierre looking for a second home in the Black Hills. I had my fingers crossed that Cooper's bungalow might be the sort of place they were looking for since they preferred something smaller that wouldn't take a lot of upkeep.

Not so truthfully, Cooper's house was already in tiptop shape and ready for potential buyers. I'd seen that for myself when I'd picked up Harvey earlier, who was temporarily staying at his nephew's house for the winter ... or until I sold it.

Helping Cooper get rid of this home and move on to his next had become one of my top priorities since the nosy detective was bunking at Doc's house now, interfering with my love life. Role-playing with handcuffs wasn't nearly as titillating when followed with a stay in a dirty jail cell.

"Okay, I'll get right to the point then." Jerry clapped his big hands together, which sounded like a balloon popping.

I jerked slightly, strung too tightly for loud noises after Prudence's game of show and tell.

"The Paranormal Realty television crew will be back this week to pick up where they left off filming before everyone came down with the flu."

"Great." My reply sounded hollow, but Jerry didn't seem to notice. "I look forward to getting back in front of the camera."

Being filmed was right near the top of my things-I-hate list, located one notch below having my hoo-ha examined while a group of resident physicians observed and took notes.

"I like your attitude, Violet. You're a team player through and through."

Not really. I just wanted to do whatever I could to avoid the unemployment line.

"We still need to film in The Old Prospector Hotel, along with a few other haunted locales."

I grimaced on the inside. The Old Prospector Hotel was the home of several creepy ghosts, including a little blonde girl who wanted to have me over to share some invisible tea and temporary insanity.

"I want you to talk to the Deadwood police," Jerry continued, oblivious to my mental heartburn. "See if we can grab a few takes out at Willis Harvey's ranch, too. His house is one of two rural locations that we have on the docket. I think it adds more color to the mix."

Did he mean more red color, as in blood? Because Harvey's ranch was a regular body part depository these days. In the last few months alone, an ear with part of the scalp attached, a decapitated corpse, an old boot with a dried up foot still inside, and a faceless body all had been found out at Harvey's place. Unfortunately, I'd been present for the last two sightings and wasn't really anxious to head out there and stumble upon anything else—especially after the visitor I'd encountered in Harvey's family graveyard a week ago. Its milky eyes and sharp teeth had guest starred in my nightmares almost every night since.

"Jerry, I think the police might be more willing to let us film at Harvey's if you ask." My history with the Deadwood Police Department involved multiple threats of incarceration and one broken nose, not cookies and milk. I had a feeling he'd at least be able to make it through the station's front doors without anyone tasering him.

Honestly, though, I didn't think it mattered which one of us asked, because I was ninety-nine percent sure that they would come back with a firm, "Hell no!" There was too much trouble out at Harvey's place these days to allow a camera crew on the premises.

Jerry's brow creased as if he were considering my suggestion. "No, I think you have more clout with the folks in charge there."

A laugh bubbled up my throat. Me? Oh, dear Lord, if he only knew how few crumbs of this so-called clout I had with the lead detective working on the case. But Jerry had made up his mind, so now I had to figure out how to do as he asked without actually following through.

Maybe I could write Detective Hawke a note and have Doc pass it to Cooper to deliver. Something like, *Can we film out at Harvey's?* ending with a *Circle Yes or No* option.

More laughter bubbled up, making me swallow a couple of times to keep it all down. "I'll see what I can do," I told Jerry. "Is there anything else?"

"There was something else. Let me think for a second."

Was it something to do with why he had commandeered Mona's desk?

I looked through my purse for some lip gloss while I waited and then double-coated my freeze-dried lips. My stomach growled, reminding me that I'd skipped breakfast this morning due to nerves. Going to the Carhart house had given me a solid case of indigestion, but now my hunger had returned tenfold. Apparently, facing off with Prudence was more troubling than learning of Wanda's death.

"Oh! Now I remember." Jerry shuffled through the papers on Mona's desk, finding a business card and holding it out to me.

"What's this?" I took the card.

Jerry answered before I had a chance to let the name on the card register. "Rex Conner stopped by earlier. He's back in town and really needs a place to rent."

I glared down at the name on the business card, waiting for my hair to catch on fire.

Rex Conner was my children's sperm donor and a no-good, rotten son of a bitch. After our last showdown in this very office, I was amazed at his audacity to show his face yet again. I was going to have to follow through on my last threat and leave him kidney-less in a bathtub full of ice.

"Something wrong, Violet?"

"No." I dropped the card in my purse. "Nothing I can't handle ..." *without some castration snippers.* "I'll be back later."

"I may not be here when you return. I have an appointment down in Rapid. Nobody else will be here either."

"Where's Ben?" Ben Underhill was my equivalent at work in the male form, only he played with balls better than I did.

My lips twitched. Then again, Doc might disagree on that point. I quietly groaned at my own joke. I'd been hanging around Harvey way too long.

"He's in Hill City. There are a couple of vacation home properties down there that a friend of mine is considering putting on the market. Ray went with him. He has a client there who is interested in acquiring some more land."

Ben's uncle, Ray Underhill, held the World Record for most consecutive sexist offenses. He and I shared a garden abloom with dislike and watered our loathing daily while glaring at each other across the office. I'd lost count of the number of times I'd wished for a voodoo doll of him to tear limb from limb.

As much as I detested Ray's stinging insults, he had nothing on Rex Conner's venomous bite. Rex seemed to keep forgetting about those papers he'd happily signed after the kids were born. The ones where he agreed that he'd have nothing to do with his offspring, which included a pass on paying child support. Now that he was in need of a fake family to land some job promotion up at the old Homestake Mine turned science lab, my children and I were suddenly a prize worth claiming.

Oh, the irony that was my life.

Jerry watched me sling my purse over my shoulder. "Drive safe, Violet. We're supposed to get snow tonight."

"I heard they're calling for a few inches."

He looked out at the dark sky. "It could be even worse."

Ha! It usually was in my case.

I left via the back door and hopped on over to Doc's office, shutting out the cold behind me.

For a few moments, I let the door hold me up while I breathed my way through the choking bout of rage clogging my throat. I let my purse *thump* onto the floor.

What was I going to do about Rex? Nobody at work knew our history and I wanted to keep it that way. The fewer who were in on that secret, the less of a chance the truth might slip out in front of my kids.

Addy and Layne needed a real father, not someone who was going to use them only for his own gain. In spite of Rex's threats to reveal his role in their conception, he had no intention of actually following through and playing daddy. He was simply using his position as leverage to try to control me.

Somehow, I needed to make him go away for good. Too bad killing him wasn't going to work. Detective Hawke was already printing up wanted posters with my picture plastered on them. I didn't want him to up the bounty for my hide.

Movement at the end of the hall interrupted my internal blustering.

"Can I help you with something, Miss?" Doc leaned his shoulder against the wall. His gaze slid over me, brushing away all thoughts of Rex Conner in one smooth stroke.

I tried to give Doc a smooth stroke back, but my eyes kept hitting snags on the way up, starting with the well-worn blue jeans hanging low on his hips. His black thermal hugged his ribs making his shoulders look solid and broad. I was going to need those shoulders shortly to help me carry the load of emotional baggage I'd picked up during my trouble-filled milk run this morning. His dark brown hair looked finger plowed, making me wonder how much Harvey had told him about our visit with Prudence.

I arched one eyebrow. "What do you have to offer, Mister?"

"Let me see." He patted his pockets, first front and then back. "Seems like I have something somewhere around here in case a gorgeous blonde wearing purple cowboy boots walked in my back door."

"Give her yer lollipop," Harvey hollered from behind Doc.

"Harvey, you're ruining the moment," I shouted back.

"Here it is." Doc offered his right hand, palm up and empty.

I often enjoyed being touched by that hand. He could do all sorts of wonderful tricks with it when it came to making me levitate off his bed. "With the way things have been going since I left my pillow, I'm going to need two of those."

"Throw in a fifth of whiskey for me," Harvey interrupted again. "That damned ghost got me good and boogered."

"Come here, Boots." Doc's voice had that sexy, gravelly growl that made my heart gallop off into the sunset.

I closed the distance between us, taking his outstretched hand, moving into his arms. He smelled woodsy and fresh, his aftershave making me want to burrow deeper under his covers and forget about the world and all of its creepy "other" crawlies.

"I've missed you," I whispered, trying to keep the nosy Nellie out front from being privy to our few seconds of hallway foreplay.

"My diabolical plan to make you a smitten concubine is working." He studied my face, zeroing in on my eyes. "Got something you want to tell me?"

"About my day?"

"About your nights."

Doc was too observant for my own good. He must have noticed the red lines road-mapping my tired eyes. "My nights? Well, let's see. To start with, you haven't been there next to me."

"That's your fault." He leaned down and stole a kiss.

There was no need to steal. I would have given him a whole bundle for pennies on the dollar.

"Are you feeling better?"

I nodded, easing back so that I could look up at him without craning my neck. "The quarantine order has been lifted."

I'd insisted Doc stay away while I went through the nasty bout of illness for two reasons. First, I didn't want him to catch it. Second, I didn't want him to pass it on to Cooper, who I figured might shoot me in his high-fevered state for adding fits of coughing to his pain. The detective's ribs still had to be sore from that sharp-toothed beast pouncing on him in Harvey's family cemetery last week.

"What are you doing tonight?" Doc asked.

"Hanging out with my kids in front of the TV while my aunt plays catch-up in her workshop."

Aunt Zoe had gotten behind on several blown-glass orders due to helping me out during the flu. Tonight she was planning an all-nighter with her glass furnace and block tool.

"Is there room for me on the couch, too?"

"Sure, on one condition."

"Name it."

"You don't bring your roommate."

"Poor Coop," Harvey spoke up again, still eavesdropping. "Yer gonna make the boy feel like a porcupine at a nudist colony if you don't start invitin' him to play in your treehouse, too."

Doc chuckled. "Other than our weekly poker game, Coop's too busy playing detective most nights to have a normal life."

I envied Cooper. Playing detective in the dark hours would be better than running from ax-swinging juggernauts. I wondered if Prudence had ever experienced chronic nightmares when she had been alive. Was it part of the job for an executioner, or was I just a big wuss? Or had awakening the killer inside of me somehow broken that part of my brain? If so, what was next? Madness? My ghostly predecessor hoarded human canine teeth as trophies. That didn't exactly speak of a sound mind.

"Violet?" Doc's voice lowered with concern. He must have picked up on my sudden mood shift. He lifted my chin, his brow wrinkling at what he saw on my face. "What is it?"

I shrugged, avoiding eye contact. "Nothing."

"Tell me."

I'd rather my boyfriend not know that I was courting insanity, so I started offloading my baggage instead. "Wanda's dead."

"I heard."

"Prudence sat in my passenger seat."

"I heard about that, too."

"Rex is back."

His gaze narrowed. "*That* I hadn't heard."

"He's using Jerry to manipulate me."

Doc swore under his breath.

"I'm sorry," I said, hating how contagious my problems were when it came to him.

"Violet, this isn't your fault. Conner wants you back. He's willing to fight dirty." He raised my hand to his lips, kissing my knuckles. "I can't say I blame him when it comes to you."

I stared into his brown eyes. The outside world and all of its problems faded. My vision tunneled, my pulse racing with its skirt held high.

Tell him.

"Doc," I started. The words *I love you* hovered on the tip of my tongue. I'd practiced saying them in the mirror several times over the last week, hoping to find the right moment to perform live for him.

"Come on you two horny toads," Harvey called out. "I'm gonna be pushin' up daisies by the time you finish ruttin' around back there."

Shut up, Harvey! I just needed a moment to rev my engine a few times before I hit the gas. I wetted my suddenly dry lips.

Doc raised his brows, waiting for me to finish what I'd started.

"Doc, I …" My engine stalled out again.

Oh, come on. Was I really this big of a chicken shit? They were three little words. I said them all of the time to my kids.

But Doc wasn't of my flesh and blood.

What if he'd been goofing around on Halloween night when he'd whispered that he loved me? What if he started laughing when I told him I was drawing little hearts with his name inside of them on my notepad at work? What if he didn't say those three little words back this time? How would I recover from that emotional car wreck and the cheek-burning awkwardness that would follow?

Criminy! I snatched the damned bullhorn from the fear-mongering imp in my head and whacked the little devil over the head with it. This was why I was in my mid-thirties and still single.

"Violet?" Doc was starting to look worried.

Ah, hell. Rather than bumble along like a fool any longer, I looped my arms around his neck and body-slammed him into the wall.

He blinked in surprise, grabbing me by the hips to steady both of us.

Going up on my toes, I kissed him good and proper. Well, maybe not so proper considering the way I pressed my soft parts against his hard edges, showing him what I really wanted to do.

"Wow," he breathed after I'd stepped back and straightened my sweater.

I could still taste him on my lips. "How come you taste so sweet?" Seriously, there was something sugary there, a hint of molasses maybe. My stomach got growly just thinking about it.

"Willis brought me a bag of homemade cookies."

"What!!? And he didn't give me any?" They must have been what he'd tossed in my back seat when I'd picked him up at Cooper's place.

"I'll share my cookies with you." Doc ogled the front of my sweater. "But it will cost you some more sugar later."

"Deal."

Doc led the way out front where Harvey sat waiting with a smartass smirk above his crumb-covered shirt. Doc pointed toward his desk chair. "Have a seat and tell me about Prudence."

I settled into the soft, warm leather. I grabbed a molasses cookie from the plastic storage bag, and then changed my mind and grabbed two. "Didn't Harvey give you the lowdown already?"

He turned the Open sign in his front window to Closed, and then took up residence on the corner of his desk "Only his version. I want to hear yours."

After swallowing a bite of molasses goodness, I rehashed my morning's adventure. Harvey butted in now and then to add more color to my tale. When I reached the part where Prudence shoved her hand inside of me, Doc stopped me.

"What do you mean she reached inside of you?"

"She stuck her hand straight into my chest." I tried to show him with my own hand. "I felt this burning sensation for a moment. Then she disappeared and the pain went with her."

Doc's expression looked even stormier than the snow clouds darkening the sky outside his windows.

"What do you think that means?" I glanced at Harvey, who was picking at the crumbs on his shirt. "Was she messing with me or testing out her abilities or what?"

"I don't know." Doc rubbed his jaw. "But I'd rather Prudence kept her hands to herself around you."

Me too. I continued with my recount, rushing through the part about calling Cooper and having Detective Hawke listen in unbeknownst to me. Damned Cooper for making me feel like a first-rate idiot. What was he thinking when he put me on speakerphone for the whole damned police station to hear?

Doc was still rubbing his jaw when I finished with Cooper's announcement about Wanda's death.

"So," I took another cookie from the bag. "How much trouble do you think I'm in this time? I mean, I wasn't interfering with any police business, right? I was just trying to give them a heads up."

"Maybe you should ask Coop," Harvey answered.

I swallowed a mouthful of molasses dough. "I'd rather face off with another albino juggernaut than talk to that man."

Harvey snorted. "You better get yer war paint on then, because he's crossin' the street and comin' right for us."

Crap! I stood up, looking around for a place to hide.

"He'll chase you if you run," Doc said, reading my mind.

The detective paused outside of the door, peering in through the glass. His gaze darted from Doc to Harvey before narrowing on me. When he rapped on the window, Doc waved him in.

Closing the door behind him, he blocked the exit, his arms crossed over his chest.

Detective Cooper was a chip off the old block … of granite. Like the Tin Man, he was always stiff and cold, but in place of his missing heart was a ball of rusted barbed wire. The only thing he had going for him was his James Bond looks—as in the Daniel Craig version of 007. Many women found his abrasive personality sexy and fantasized about what he was like in the sack. I had sack fantasies about him, too, only mine involved burlap and ended with a deep shaft and splash of water far below.

Cooper glared across the office at me.

I glared back.

Our silent standoff went on for several huffs.

"Well, Coop," Harvey broke the tension, "are you going to tell us what's on yer mind or just stand there with yer stinger stickin' out?"

His steely eyes stayed locked on me. "You really fucked up today, Parker."

"No, you fucked up, Detective," I shot back, not feeling like having my ass handed to me after my morning's excitement.

"Violet," Doc warned, standing along with Cooper and me. "Let's hear what the detective has to say about how things are going over at the station."

Cooper snorted. "I'll tell you how things are going. Parker here has managed to win the top spot on Detective Hawke's suspect list."

"Why is there a suspect list?" Doc asked.

Cooper didn't seem to hear him. "What is it with you two?" he barked at Harvey and me. "You're like Shaggy and Scooby-Doo, always up to your necks in trouble."

Did he mean I was Scooby-Doo or Shaggy? Never mind.

"We didn't do anything wrong, Cooper." We hadn't been anywhere close to the body this time. "Or is it illegal now to make phone calls to the cops about someone who might be in danger? Silly me, I thought that was one of the purposes of 911."

"Not illegal, but it's suspicious as hell when we receive a warning call about someone who'd been found murdered not eight hours prior."

"Murdered?" I repeated, getting stuck on the word. It was as I'd feared. Wanda wasn't just dead, she'd been murdered.

"Yes, murdered." He watched me closely, searching for who knew what.

I frowned over at Doc. The storm clouds were back on his face. I had a feeling I had a tornado brewing on mine.

Memories of Wanda flickered behind my eyes like I was watching from the backside of a movie screen. Guilt sat heavily on my chest. Regret and frustration followed, joining the sit-in. I lowered my head, blinking through an onslaught of tears.

Wanda had saved my life several times, but when the day came to return the favor, I hadn't been there for her, damn it. Someone was going to have to let Prudence know that I'd failed to do my job. That my bungling attempts to figure out my new lot in life had most likely caused the premature death of an innocent woman whom I was supposed to protect.

"How was Wanda killed?" Doc asked.

Cooper hesitated. A muscle in his jaw ticked.

My guilt grew heavier. What did the killer do to her?

"That's police business," Cooper finally answered.

"Coop," Harvey scolded. "Our friend is dead."

"I'm not at liberty to discuss it."

Anger stoked the furnace in my belly. "Yet you're at liberty to stomp over here and rake me over the coals for making a single phone call to try to help Wanda?"

"The coroner hasn't delivered his report. Until then, procedure doesn't allow speculation with the public. I already said too much by telling you three she was murdered."

Knees a little wobbly all of a sudden, I fell into Doc's chair. "So, what now?"

"We start rounding up suspects and interrogating them."

Starting with me. I snarled at him. "You shouldn't have had me on speaker phone, damn it."

He bristled. "That wasn't my doing. I was in a meeting with Hawke. He saw your number pop up on my desk phone and hit the speaker button."

Detective Hawke knew my number by sight alone? That couldn't be good. "Still, you could've warned me."

"How was I to know you were going to open your big mouth and incriminate yourself?"

"Why else would I call you? To talk about guns and motorcycles?" Or any of Cooper's other favorite topics outside of murder?

"How about to tell me you'd found a buyer for my house?"

Oh, yeah, my regular job. I bit my lip and turned away.

"How much trouble is Violet in this time?" Doc's hair was even more finger plowed now.

"Hawke wanted me to locate her and bring her to the station immediately. I convinced him that he was moving too fast and needed to collect more facts first."

In other words, Cooper had temporarily saved my ass. "Thank you for buying me time." It hurt my tongue to say that.

"Don't thank me yet, Parker. This is only temporary. Hawke really wants to string you up."

"The feeling is mutual." My love for that toe-stomping, overbearing gumshoe could fit through the eye of a needle—and a very tiny needle at that. Like the needle a flea would use to stitch its flea circus tent.

"I hope you have an alibi for the last forty-eight hours."

I did. A nasty cough left behind from the flu had been keeping me company in bed, but I doubted that would hold water with Detective Hawke. I should have sneezed all over him when I had the chance.

"Are there any other suspects?" Doc asked.

"Nobody as interesting as your girlfriend. Wanda has a few family members who benefit from her death, but that's it for the list so far."

I sighed, resting my head in my hands. "All I did was make a stupid phone call."

"What prompted that call?" Cooper asked.

Before I could answer, Doc cut in. "Is this on the record or off?"

"Off."

I looked at Harvey. "You're going to have to back me up on this, you know."

"You want me to share yer noose?"

"If it comes down to it, maybe Mr. Bodyguard."

With a nod, he turned to his nephew. "Prudence did some chin waggin' with Violet and me this morning over at the Carhart place."

Cooper's steely gaze leveled on me. "You mean your ghost pal?"

"She's not my pal." More of a disgruntled ex-coworker.

"We ain't foolin' around, boy. I was there with Violet."

I could see Cooper's jaw work, like he was chewing on Harvey's words some more, trying to swallow them without choking. "What did Prudence the ghost have to say today?"

I ciphered through the cryptic stuff Prudence had told me. "That Wanda was in danger," I told him. "Someone recently broke into the Carhart house looking for something Wanda supposedly had, but they came up empty. Prudence was worried the culprit was going to hunt down Wanda next."

Not surprisingly, my answer added a new topcoat of granite to Cooper's expression. "Let me get this straight. You called me this morning to talk about Wanda because a ghost told you that she might be in danger?"

I knew it sounded hokey, but, "Prudence was quite insistent about it."

"But your ghost pal didn't know Wanda was already dead?"

I shook my head.

He smirked.

"What? She's a ghost, not a soothsayer."

Cooper frowned at Doc. "This doesn't help your girlfriend's case."

Doc shrugged. "Maybe not with Detective Hawke, but it explains why she called you."

"And you believe her?"

"Of course," Doc said without hesitation.

"Hello," I waved at the detective. "I'm sitting right here you know."

Cooper sighed, scrubbing his hand down his face. "You all must realize that I can't use a warning from a ghost as part of any defensive strategy down at the station. Nobody will believe you or me, and I'll probably be suspended on indefinite psych leave."

I sighed. "Of course you can't." Was this what the musicians on the Titanic felt like when icy water had lapped at their feet? "Now what?"

"Stick around town and try not to do anything else wrong." Cooper glared at me. "And answer your damned phone when I call."

I flipped off the big jerk.

He wrinkled his lip in reply before opening the door. He shot Doc a glance on the way out. "I'll be home late tonight, Nyce, thanks to your girlfriend's screw up."

I scowled at the detective's backside, wishing I were close enough to plant my size 8 boot in it. "I didn't kill Wanda Carhart!"

Cooper paused on the other side of the threshold, squinting back in at me. "Oddly enough, Parker, I believe you're innocent. But I'm not the one you need to convince this time."

Chapter Three

I'd learned at a young age that when shit hit the fan, there was no better place to lie low than my Aunt Zoe's kitchen. The fresh lemonade in her refrigerator and sweet goodies in her Betty Boop cookie jar always helped me to choke down a long day chock-full with bitter pills.

And boy oh boy had today been one of those days. I had acid indigestion coming out my ears.

"Violet," Aunt Zoe's voice interrupted my pity party. "Wanda's death is not your fault."

I blinked out of my daze and looked across the kitchen table into her all-seeing dark blue gaze. Aunt Zoe always had been able to read me like an eye doctor chart. Since childhood, I'd distracted most who looked my way with my big, bold E's and F's on the surface. Only she had known to squint and peer lower, zeroing in on my tiny, troubled O's and C's.

My focus dropped to the last couple of toast bites smothered with chipped beef in white sauce that were now cold. I shoved them around the plate with my fork.

"Prudence would disagree with you," I told her.

Aunt Zoe leaned forward, her long silver-lined hair pulled back in a loose ponytail tonight. Her red glass earrings, a product of her own crafting, looked pretty fancy compared to her faded plaid work shirt and jeans.

"Violet, you may share a vocation with Prudence, but your stripes are different. Remember that the next time you compare yourself to her."

"What do you mean?" Doc asked from where he stood by the sink, drying the big saucepan Aunt Zoe had used to make Layne's favorite dish.

The kid had plowed through three helpings of what my dad always called *shit-on-a-shingle*, snarfing down bite after bite before asking to be excused to go watch *El Dorado* in the living room. One would think the nearly ten-year-old was fresh in from driving cattle up the Chisholm Trail or something, sheesh.

"Just as your talents and abilities as a medium vary from another's," she told Doc, "Violet's skills might include elements that Prudence's didn't or vice-versa."

He put the pan on the counter and pulled the ladle from the drain rack. He still wore the same jeans and black shirt from earlier and sported the same finger plowed hair, too. However, in the soft yellow surroundings of my aunt's kitchen with snowflakes falling outside the window, he sort of hypnotized me with his pulse-palpitating good looks.

It took several slow blinks and a head-clearing shake to realize that maybe it was just the sight of a man doing housework that had my motor revving. If Doc grabbed the broom and started sweeping, I might have to ask Aunt Zoe to leave so I could have my wicked way with him on her clean wooden floor.

"Zoe, have any other executioners in your family's lineage had the ability to see ghosts?" Doc asked, unaware that I had moved on to a fantasy involving him folding socks and towels.

Aunt Zoe turned to me, staring pointedly.

I left Fantasyland Doc in the midst of ironing my shirts and frowned back at present-moment Aunt Zoe. Why was I getting *that* look from her? After my kids had been excused from the table, I'd filled her in about my episode this morning with Prudence. Had I forgotten something important?

"What?" I asked, sticking a bite of cold toast in my mouth.

"Have you finished the book?"

As much as I'd have liked to pretend I didn't know what book she was talking about, I knew she'd yank on my ear if I played dumb.

"Almost."

"Violet, that's your key to unlocking the possibilities of what you can and can't do."

"I know, but reading long, handwritten tomes isn't exactly my strong suit." Unlike my son, who carted around college-sized history books on the ancient Maya in case he had a spare moment to fit some reading into his day. At her narrowed gaze, I held up my hands. "Besides, it's not my fault. I can't find the book."

"What do you mean you can't find it? I thought I told you to keep it safe up in your room."

"You did, and it's somewhere around here. I'm sure of that because I didn't take it anywhere else."

"How could you lose *that* book?"

"I was reading it when I was in bed sick and fell asleep. When I woke up, it was gone." At her growl of unhappiness, I stuck another bite in my mouth, mumbling, "I'll find it, I swear."

"Did you look under your bed?"

"Of course I did, and in my closet where I'd been keeping it tucked away. I've checked everywhere. I must have sleepwalked and left it somewhere else around here." My subconscious probably had made me hide it, trying to protect my kids from learning the truth about who we were.

"What's in this book?" Doc was drying a plate now.

I kept telling Aunt Zoe we needed to invest in a dishwasher, but she preferred to hand wash dishes. "Doc, why don't you let me finish those later." I felt guilty about him coming over to clean up after us.

He waved the dish towel at me. "Answer my question."

"The book has information on my family history."

"Not only your family history," Aunt Zoe chastised, fiddling with her coffee cup. "It's a volume full of writings from various *magistrae* throughout our history about the executioners under their charge. Some accounts include lists of kills, others define abilities and disclose experiences along the way, and some give details on what method was used when executing different enemies."

Doc's brow rose. "But didn't you say that what has worked in the past might not work for Violet? That she has to figure out how to kill each different species of these *others* on her own?"

"I did." Aunt Zoe shot me a stern look. "But in addition to possible skill crossovers, which has happened in the past, she needs to read it to understand what else could potentially be out there waiting for her."

Doc hung the towel over the cupboard door below the sink. "Zoe, how do you feel about me reading this book?"

He walked over and picked up my plate, holding it out for me to take the last bite. I stabbed it with my fork and popped it in my mouth. I handed him the fork, too, thanking him after I'd swallowed.

Doc was a definite keeper, if only I could find some sort of invisible shackling device that didn't involve a wedding band. Marriage was a topic I'd avoided around him ever since finding out he might be allergic to having a wife. And if that were the case, his gaining my two children in the matrimony deal would probably send him into anaphylactic shock.

"Or would me reading this family memoir be against the rules?"

Aunt Zoe shook her head. "There are no rules, just warnings and plenty of dangers." She sat back, crossing her arms over her chest. Her lips were pinched as she focused on me. "Unfortunately, until we find the book, nobody can read it."

"There's no second copy of it anywhere?" I asked, knowing the answer to that from her scoff alone.

"I can't believe you misplaced the book."

"It's not my fault. I'm telling you, it was there when I fell asleep."

"Why didn't you mention it was missing before now?"

"I didn't want you to look at me the way you are right now."

Doc chuckled. "Now you sound like Addy did earlier."

It was unfortunate that he'd had to witness my harping at my daughter at the dinner table about something else that had gone missing as of late— my water pick. When Layne had taken a moment to breathe in between his first and second helpings, he'd tattled on his sister. According to him, he'd witnessed Addy using my water pick to rinse off Elvis the chicken during the bird's weekly bath. While I didn't condone snitching, Addy knew better than to use my personal hygiene appliances on that damned chicken. We'd been there and done that before, with "grounding" consequences. So her claim not to realize I'd be upset about her using my water pick to blast the poop off Elvis's tail feathers didn't fly with me.

It was bad enough to lose my buttons left and right and to find eggs laid in my shoes. The water pick fiasco was the final straw, especially after my shitty day. I didn't care if scrubbing a chicken caused feather breakage. How many times had I used my water pick since Addy had started cleaning off poop with it? When I asked that very question, she didn't have an answer for me—or maybe she wisely knew better than to admit the truth. Needless to say, Addy was grounded yet again and had to split the cost of a new water pick with me.

I grimaced across the table at Aunt Zoe. "Do you think it's safe to use bleach to rinse my teeth tonight?"

Doc laughed outright.

Aunt Zoe's face softened, her grin making an appearance in spite of my losing track of the family archives.

I mock glared at Doc. "Laugh it up, funny guy, but consider this—how many times have you kissed me since Addy started using my water pick on that damned chicken?"

He wrinkled his upper lip, but his shoulders kept shaking with hilarity.

The doorbell rang.

I stood, pretending to threaten him with my finger. "Consider yourself saved by the bell."

Aunt Zoe was laughing along with Doc as I left the room, heading for the front door.

I was still shaking my head about the damned chicken when I pulled open the door. The sight of our evening visitor knocked me back a step. Before either of us could speak, I slammed the door shut and deadbolted it for good measure.

On the rush back to the kitchen, I grabbed Doc's leather coat from the peg on the wall and plucked his keys from the glass bowl on the side table.

I tossed his coat at him. "Here." There was no time for an explanation.

He caught it without dropping the plate he was drying. "What's going on?"

"Aunt Zoe," I pointed my thumb behind me, "there's a demon spawn from Hell at the front door."

I grabbed the dry plate from Doc's hand and the damp dishtowel, setting both down on the counter. "You're coming with me, lover boy." I dragged him behind me out the back door.

"Violet, what are you doing?" He dropped anchor, stopping me short at the bottom of the steps.

Snow fell around us, coming down fast in big flakes. Shivering in the freezing air, I pointed at his coat. "You should put that on."

"Why?"

"I'm sorry, but you have to leave." His face was all shadows and ridges in the pale light coming from Aunt Zoe's kitchen windows. I took his coat from him and held it out, sleeves ready and waiting.

"Why do I have to leave right now?" He took his coat back from me and slid one arm into a sleeve. "Who's at the door?"

I hugged my arms tight, shivering as snow coated my hair. My sweater was more for decoration than actual body heat retention. "Someone I don't want to see you."

He shrugged his coat over his shoulders, his gaze darting up to the house. "Rex?"

"No."

"Because if it is, I assure you I can control my temper in front of your children."

Doc had roughed up Rex the last time they'd run into each other, trying to teach the bastard to keep his hands off of me. An act I still appreciated deep in the warm, fiery cockles of my heart where I'd like to go to heat my hands for a bit.

"I wish it were only Rex." My teeth started to chatter. "Tonight's visitor is worse than Rex Conner."

He cocked his head to the side. "Who's worse than the kids' absent father suddenly showing up on your doorstep?"

"Their evil aunt." I grabbed him by the coat sleeve and led him over to the gate, tiptoeing through it to peek around the front. "The coast is clear," I whispered. Aunt Zoe must have allowed my sister, Susan, to cross the threshold.

"Violet, why don't you want me to meet your sister?"

"She's the Bitch from Hell."

"So I've heard."

"She's a man stealer."

Doc grabbed me by the shoulders, staring down at me. "I know all about Susan and Rex. You can trust me. I'm not going to end up in bed with your sister."

With the snow falling softly around us, we were one spawn of Satan away from a Hallmark movie moment.

"I do trust you, Doc." I grabbed his lapels and pulled him down for a kiss to underscore my words. My cold nose bumped his as another round of shivers rocked me.

He warmed my cheeks with his palms. "Then let's go back inside and get this over with." He kissed me back with the same motive.

I was tempted, partly because my ass was about to freeze solid and fall off onto the driveway. However, memories of past back-stabbings came to mind. I shook my head. "You don't understand the demented psychopath that is now walking around inside of that house. But I do."

I led him to the Picklemobile.

He took the keys from my cold fingers. His sigh steamed the air between us. "I can't believe you're kicking me out in the cold snow."

"At this point I have two choices. I can either send you on your way with a kiss and promise to make up for this another day and know in my heart that you are safe from Susan's sharp claws, or …" I thought I saw a movement out of the corner of my eye. I checked the front porch quickly, making sure Susan wasn't hiding there in the shadows or peering out through the front curtains, before focusing back on Doc.

"Or what?" he prompted, brushing a snowflake from my cheek. We were back to that Hallmark moment.

Sort of.

"Or I can go back inside the house and poison her to death." I tried to smile, but my cheeks were too cold to obey. "I bet that would give Detective Hawke some good ammunition for his Violet-the-Witch theory."

"Okay, Killer, I'll go home." Doc enveloped me in a warm hug. "But you do realize that your children are still inside there with her, don't you?"

"Shit, you're right." I gave him one last kiss. "I'm going to go find

Aunt Zoe's stock of hemlock and snakeroot."

He chuckled.

I didn't.

"Night, Doc. I'll stop by your office tomorrow and fill you in on the deadly details."

* * *

Sunday, November 11th

According to what I had learned in my college psychology class, psychopaths could appear normal, even charming, while underneath they lacked the ability to empathize or have remorse, often showing a total lack of conscience.

My sister, Susan, aka the Bitch from Hell, was a walking, breathing, scheming example of a psychopath.

My mother disagreed, of course, claiming I was being too hard on my baby sister. That Susan's eagerness to either destroy or covet what was mine was simply my sister being "a squeency bit jealous." I was of the opinion that my mom had dabbled in a *squeency bit* too much acid in her younger years and ever since had seen life through blurry, rose-colored glasses.

Susan had been stalking me since toddlerhood. She'd cut the head off my teddy bear, fed my Barbie through a meat grinder, burned holes in my favorite sweaters, and screwed my children's sperm donor in my own bed. Now call me kooky, but in my world that made Susan crazier than a sack full of rabid wolverines.

According to Aunt Zoe when I'd joined her back in the kitchen last night, Susan's visit had a legitimate purpose—to drop off some new snow boots that my mother had bought for the kids as an early birthday present. Unfortunately, the falling snow had made Aunt Zoe feel the need to allow Susan to spend the night on the couch.

Tension had crackled plenty between us straight out of the gate, starting with her snide remarks about the make-believe boyfriend she'd caught wind of from my kids. I didn't try to convince her otherwise.

As I finished the dish drying job Doc had started, Susan went on to make several acidic stabs about my winter weight and messy hair. I thought about breaking Aunt Zoe's dishes over her long, straight-haired brunette head and sitting on her stick insect body until she promised to move to the furthest space station, but I heeded Aunt Zoe's recommendation not to claw Susan's eyes out while the kids were in the house.

Instead, I lit her on fire and danced with joy around her burning body. Or maybe I just fantasized about that and instead escaped to the living room to enjoy watching the Duke take on a greedy land baron.

As soon as the movie wrapped up, I decided to have a slumber party with my kids. I dragged covers and pillows into my bedroom and told ghost stories until Addy and Layne fell asleep. Before drifting off to nightmare-ville, I locked my bedroom door and pushed my dresser in front of it for good measure. It was that or worry about waking in the darkness to find Satan's spawn standing over me with a carving knife.

By the time I'd gotten out of the shower this morning, Satan's bride was gone. Aunt Zoe told me that Susan had been unusually quiet during her breakfast of half a grapefruit and coffee, not bragging about her latest job or man-eating reputation even once. *Unfocused* was one of the words Aunt Zoe had used when telling me about Susan's strange behavior as I chowed down on a cheese omelet. I ate an extra piece of bacon in honor of whatever had her pouting and hoped the source of her trouble stayed sunk in like an Alabama tick.

I called Doc before leaving, but he didn't answer. Nor was the Picklemobile in the parking lot when I arrived at work.

When I'd finally had a moment on my own last night after the kids had fallen asleep, we'd shot a few texts back and forth—him to make sure my sister hadn't planted her pitchfork in my heart, me to apologize again for rushing him out the door. He hadn't mentioned anything about an appointment this morning, but then again I wasn't his secretary.

I parked between Mona's SUV and Ben's Subaru and hustled through the slushy aftermath of last night's not-quite two inches. The weatherman had been off on snowfall totals, but I was happy to forgive him since his error was in my favor.

I caught whiffs of Mona's jasmine perfume as I hung up my coat. The sound of her clacking fingernails on her keyboard echoed down the hall.

I walked straight to the coffee pot, saying my good-mornings to Mona and Ben as I poured brain juice into my cup. The nightmares had been in the bedroom along with my kids last night. Lucky for the three of us, I hadn't woken up mid-scream as I had two nights prior.

"You look nice today, Violet," Ben told me. Unlike Jerry, when Ben gave a compliment, it was just that—a plain old compliment. No advice on hair styles, suggestions on color coordination, or talk about including buttons on my ensemble.

I smiled across at him as I sat down behind my desk. "Thanks, Ben. I like that color of blue on you. It looks nice with your eyes." Usually, Ben's eyes were two different colors, but today he had his blue contact in place. It was hard to believe he shared DNA with a horse's ass. His brown hair appeared to have been trimmed lately and neatly combed with a hint of gel.

"Are you ready for another week of filming in haunted houses?" Ben and I would be taking turns standing in front of the camera when the crew from Paranormal Realty came back to town.

He glanced toward Jerry's empty office. "Not really," he grinned and added, "but I'm looking forward to seeing Honey again."

I did a double take. "Only Honey?" Unlike her name sounded, Honey wasn't blonde and super sweet. She reminded me more of Cher back when Sonny was singing at her side, only with less rainbow and sequin-covered clothing.

Ben smirked, reminding me a little of his uncle. "I guess Dickie, too. And that buff camerawoman, what was her name?"

"Rosy." As in The Riveter. At least that's how I remembered her and her beefy arms from lugging that camera all over the place.

"Isn't Honey involved with Dickie?" Mona asked, tucking a loose wave of her red hair behind her ear. Her chignon this morning looked stylish, along with her yellow mohair sweater and green silk scarf.

With a shrug, Ben said, "She didn't act like it the night we went out for drinks."

"Interesting." I wondered if Dickie knew about Honey and Ben's drink date. "He acted like she belonged to him on set." Or maybe I'd misread the way he bossed her around.

"Not everything is always as it seems, Vi." Mona said as she clacked away.

Something in Mona's tone gave me pause. "Are you referring to yourself and someone with really big shoes?"

The clacking stopped.

Several weeks ago I'd walked into Jerry's office and caught him in the midst of bending Mona backwards while the two of them were temporarily attached at the lips. The heat between them prior to that day had often made my curls smolder. The sparks since their steamy kiss nearly singed my eyelashes off whenever I got too close to the flames dancing around the two of them.

These days, however, both seemed to be cooling off in a pool of denial, avoiding touching each other to the point of it being almost comical.

Mona's eyes narrowed above her rhinestone-rimmed reading glasses. "I'm referring only to Honey, little Miss Busybody."

I chuckled.

The three of us delved into our work then, happy as shoe-making elves until Ray Underhill joined us.

Ray was looking extra Oompa-Loompa-like this morning with his fake tan a seemingly brighter shade of orange than usual. His brown hair matched his personality—slick and greasy.

"Morning, Ben," he said to his nephew as he stepped into the front office. "Looking tight in that sweater, Red," he gave Mona and her curve-hugging sweater a thumbs up. As for me, I received a wrinkled upper lip and an eyeful of sneer.

Ray and I shared plenty of sparks, too. Only ours were followed up with rude gestures and crude insults.

His lack of love was fine and dandy with me this morning. I had two clients who'd be arriving shortly to check out Cooper's place and a few other potentials. I'd rather not be foaming at the mouth when they walked through the door.

"Where's Jerry?" Ray asked, plopping down in his chair. He kicked back and rested his fancy Tony Lama cowboy boots on his desk. With the boss away, Ray was off the leash.

"How should I know?" Mona snapped, surprising the three of us into silence for a couple of clock ticks.

"Whoa, there Red. You better dial it back a couple of notches before the big boss man arrives." He snickered, digging between his teeth with his pinkie nail. "You're starting to sound like Jane used to when husband number three had her panties twisted up tight about banging that younger woman in her bed."

The white board hanging on the wall behind Ray fell off with a loud crash. I jerked in surprise, sloshing coffee on my desk. Before I could register what had happened, Ray tipped backward so far in his seat that his chair flipped over, sending him tumbling across the floor into the baseboard.

"Uncle Ray!" Ben was the first to break the silence that followed. He rushed over to help his uncle stand. "Are you okay?" he asked, brushing off Ray's back.

I pinched my lips together, trying not to laugh.

"What in the hell happened?" Ray asked, kicking at his chair like it had bucked him on purpose. "What did you do to my chair, Blondie?"

"Me?" A giggle escaped my lips when I opened them.

"Violet didn't touch your chair, sunshine," Mona said, barely holding back a grin of her own. "You can blame gravity for that."

"It wasn't gravity, Red." Glaring at me, Ray pulled his chair out and sat in it, gingerly tipping back, testing. "I wasn't anywhere close to tipping over. It was like somebody came up behind me and yanked on it."

I held up my hands. "I was sitting here the whole time, I swear."

His scrunched face looked even uglier than usual. I waved off his nonverbal accusation.

"It's like the screws were ripped out of the wall," Ben said, checking out the white board that had crashed to the floor before Ray had joined it. "Look, it even took chunks of plaster with it."

Since the building housing Calamity Jane Realty had been built sometime back in the late 1800s, the walls were made of old plaster and lath. I joined Ben by the white board, dodging several crumbles of plaster spread across the floor.

Back when Jane, our old boss and Jerry's ex-wife, had been alive, she'd had two white boards fastened to the wall side by side. I'd knocked the other one down by throwing a stapler at it months ago, but it hadn't torn plaster from the wall when it had fallen.

"See what I mean?" Ben pointed at the top of the white board. "It's even a little bent right here." He glanced at his uncle and then Mona. "Do either of you happen to know if it was bent when Jane first hung it, whenever that was?"

Mona fiddled with her glasses' chain. "It was brand new, remember, Ray? You gave Jane trouble about having two white boards, making a bet with me that you'd be the first to fill it with your sales."

Ray chuckled, his gaze lost in yesteryear. "Yeah, Janey-girl reminded me of that bet many times over the years."

I ran my fingers over the slight crease in the aluminum edging. What if … I frowned, thinking back to a couple of weeks ago when Doc had been in here with me. He'd sensed a presence in Jerry's office that wasn't the normal nasty ghost, the one that always made Doc pale and sweaty when he hung around Calamity Jane's too long. He had told me Jane was back, and I'd believed him in a "Sure, if you say so" sort of way.

Now my gaze traveled from one corner of the office to the next. Had Jane been responsible for the white board's demise and Ray's tumble? Hadn't Ray been criticizing Jane right before the whole crash-and-roll happened?

Was Jane's presence in the building why Jerry had been working at Mona's desk yesterday? Had something happened in his office, driving him out under the bright fluorescent lights?

I dragged my eyes from the coffeemaker area and found Mona watching me with a searching gaze. Mona saw too much most days. I wasn't sure how she'd take my announcement that the ghost of Jane was roaming the office, so I pinned a smile on my cheeks.

"Hmmm, that's kind of odd," I said to nobody in particular, heading back to my chair. For the next minute or so, I shuffled papers, keeping my focus on my desktop until my three coworkers returned to their usual routines.

My clients from Pierre walked through the front door five minutes early, but I was ready to escape with them. We left their car in the parking lot behind Calamity Jane's, and I drove them up to Cooper's blue bungalow in Lead. Harvey had promised he'd be gone when we got there and would leave fresh baked goodies in his wake, and he'd delivered on his word with blue-ribbon brownies.

We left a crumb trail as we toured room to room, admiring the black leather furniture, wood accents, and clean white walls. Harvey had been kind enough to remove all of his nephew's gun-related magazines and art so as not to let them know how obsessed the current owner was with his firearms.

After the initial walkthrough, I stepped outside to let the friendly couple get a feel for the place without me in it. I was shivering on Cooper's front steps when a familiar black Jaguar pulled to a stop at the curb out front.

A double-take later, I stormed down the sidewalk to the man climbing out of the fancy car.

"What in the hell are you doing here?" I spit out, doing my best to zap Rex Conner clear to Mars with my glare.

The wind rippled through his blond hair. A casual passerby would never guess what a heartless bastard was hiding behind Rex's classically handsome looks. His tan wool coat probably cost a month's worth of child support, his ritzy leather shoes more like two or three.

He ignored my growling and pawing at the ground. "Did you get the message I left with your boss yesterday?"

I didn't answer, jutting my chin at him instead.

"I'll take that as a yes."

"You need to leave."

"But I just arrived."

"I mean leave the Black Hills."

"Sorry, sweetheart, but I can't. I'm here on a grant. Our project is going to take at least a year up at the lab."

Son of a bitch! It sucked that the Homestake Gold Mine here in Lead was such a prime location for scientists from all over the world to congregate. Why couldn't someone dig a deep hole somewhere else for them to perform their underground experiments? It was just my luck that Rex would be one of those scientists.

Rex's career specialty was a mystery to me. I didn't bother to ask for details on his profession, because I didn't want to know anything about his life. Anything at all. In fact, I preferred to be on an "Is he still breathing or not" level of information and that was it. Unfortunately, the jerkwad was standing three feet away from me, breathing without a problem.

I stepped closer to him. "I'm not your sweetheart. Call me that again, and I will relocate your testicles to the back of your throat right behind your uvula."

He had the gall to smile, the asshole. "I really like this new Violet. She's so feisty and hot, nothing like the shy virgin I deflowered back in college."

I sighed in disgust. "Newsflash, dickhead. I hadn't been a virgin for years by the time I met you, so you can flush that deflowering fantasy of yours down the toilet."

One blond eyebrow raised. "You acted virginal."

"It was called role-playing. It went with the stupid outfits you insisted I wear."

His smile widened. "That's right. My sexy young assistant in a lab coat and horn-rimmed glasses."

Before he could finish that sordid flashback, I interrupted him. "Find a different Realtor."

He faked a pout. "But I want you."

"I'm not available."

"According to your boss you are."

"He's confused."

His face tightened. "Violet, you know I'll leave you be as soon as you follow through on the favor I requested."

"It wasn't a request, more like emotional blackmail."

The sound of his phone ringing interrupted his reply. He pulled it out of his coat pocket and read the number, then answered.

I stepped away to give him some privacy, hoping he was being called away on an emergency at the McMurdo research station down at the South Pole. Before I'd made it too far away, he hung up and pocketed his phone.

"Violet."

"Go away, Rex."

"I told you, that's not an option."

"Then we have nothing left to say." I started toward Cooper's house, fingers crossed my clients hadn't been watching the fireworks display going on outside of the front window.

"You will find some legitimate housing options for me," he said to my back. There was an underlying threat in his tone.

I turned to glare at the pompous jerk. "Or what?"

"Trust me, Violet. You don't want to find out."

Chapter Four

The thing about Deadwood was that in the century-plus since Wild Bill, Seth Bullock, and Calamity Jane had strolled the streets, the town hadn't changed all that much. Sure it had evolved into the modern age with indoor plumbing and electricity, but the gambling halls, saloons, and street fights still kept the town rootin' and tootin'. While visitors now shopped the souvenir stores instead of the brothels, and slot machines lined the floors once dotted with faro and poker tables, the local character remained as true blue as the mile-high sky. Even better, there was plenty of hard liquor to smooth the sharp edges when a no good, low-down, egotistical bastard came riding into town packing lies and threats.

Unfortunately, I was still about an hour away from the bottle of tequila sitting on top of Aunt Zoe's fridge, and Rex's parting shot had blown my inner calm all to hell.

Giving my Pierre buyers a moment alone to chat about the final stop on my tour of potential homes this afternoon—a quaint pink house with fancy gingerbread gable ornaments and shutters etched with ribbon-curls—I stepped outside and pulled my phone from my coat pocket. I needed to talk to the girl who'd had my back since second grade when my front teeth had come in big and ugly, and Bradley Jedinski had kept calling me *Bucky Parker* in the recess yard and pulling my pigtails. That was the year Natalie had taught me how to land a punch. It was also the year I'd learned how easy it was to break a bully's nose.

Natalie picked up on the third ring. "Beal's Mule Barn."

I chuckled and played along. "I need to talk to the head ass."

"Are you looking to do some ass kissing or ass kicking?"

A horn honked long and loud, drowning out my answer. I looked toward the end of the drive and groaned at the sight of a white Deadwood Police SUV idling there. "Speaking of asses."

The passenger side window rolled down and Detective Stone Hawke waved me over.

"Shit." I blew out a cloud of steam in the chilly air. First Ray, then Rex, and now Detective Hawke. "Today must be bring-an-asshole-to-work day."

"What's going on, Vi?" Natalie's voice came through the line.

"Hold on a minute," I said, taking her with me to heed Detective Hawke's beckoning. "I want you to hear this in case I need a witness at the trial."

"What trial?"

"The one I'll be attending after I finish assaulting and battering our favorite detective."

"What's Coop doing now?"

"Not Cooper. The other *bigger* pain in the butt."

I'd reached the SUV. "I'm busy, Detective." I pointed my thumb back over my shoulder. "My clients are inside. What do you need?" Besides a haircut and a frontal lobotomy?

"Detective Cooper is looking for you," he shouted through the open window.

I wasn't sure I believed him. If Cooper wanted to talk to me, he would have called my cell phone and barked me up a tree. "Why is Detective Cooper looking for me?"

"You're a suspect in a murder case," he hollered even louder.

Jeez-o-peets! Why didn't he bring a megaphone along so he could yell that loud enough for the tourists down on Main Street to hear?

"Shhhh!" I glanced back toward the pink house, making sure the bozo hadn't just lost me my potential buyers.

"You need to stick around town," Hawke told me what I already knew from my previous adventures as a Usual Suspect on Cooper's case board.

I rested my forearms on the window sill, staring in at his pork chop sideburns and wary eyes. Detective Hawke often reminded me of that old show, *The Rockford Files*. He'd have fit right into the cast with his bulky shoulders, seventies era hairstyle, and outdated corduroy suit jackets.

"Why?" I purposely played dumb, calling his bluff.

"I need to know your whereabouts the night of Wanda Carhart's murder."

Ah ha! That's what this little visit was all about. Detective Hawke hadn't listened to Cooper about playing the waiting game before coming at me with his suspicions. I'd expect a detective who'd been around a long time to know better. Then again, I knew the truth about Hawke's climb up the career ladder, which included backstabbing Cooper, aka his ex-partner, more than once when they had worked down in Rapid City.

If Hawke was going to come around to mess with me, I was going to give him something to remember me by. "You have a stain on your tie."

He lifted his wide, red and blue striped tie. "Where?"

"Not you," I smiled down at the empty passenger seat. "I'm talking to your police buddy here."

Detective Hawke's gaze narrowed. "What buddy?"

I pointed at the head rest. "The one right here."

Last month, I'd told Detective Hawke I was a medium, going so far as to carry on conversations with empty walls and doors in order to screw with his mind. In our little pissing match I'd called him on his "witch" accusation and raised him a "medium" claim, laying down a straight ghost flush to take the upper hand.

"Be quiet for a second," I silenced Hawke when he started to speak. I cocked my head to the side, pretending to listen to the fake ghost. "Does Detective Hawke know about that?" I asked the thin air.

Hawke's bushy black unibrow wrinkled at me. "Knock it off, Ms. Parker."

I ignored him, speaking again to the empty headrest. "He did what with key evidence?"

"I'm not playing games here."

"What about the murder weapon?" I continued, ignoring the blusters coming from the detective's side of the vehicle.

"Keep it up, Violet, and I'll arrest you."

"What's that?" I asked the headrest. "Detective Hawke can't arrest me without probable cause?"

Hawke revved the engine. "Get out of here or I'll run over your pointy toes."

Pointy toes? Ah, we were back to witches. I let out a loud, cackling laugh and wiggled my fingers at him. "I'll get you, my pretty," I said as he shifted into gear, "and your little dog, too!"

Detective Hawke spit gravel at me in his haste to leave my witchy side. What a jerk.

I held my phone to my ear. "Did you get all of that, Nat?"

"You're sending your flying monkeys after the self-righteous blowhard, aren't you?"

"I can't. They're out on another vengeful mission."

"Oh, yeah? Tell me more. Who else are we venge-ing today?"

"Rex."

Silence came from the other line, followed by the sound of something crashing.

"Rex Conner," I clarified in case she hadn't heard me.

"I heard you the first time but had to hit pause so I could kick something."

That explained the crash sound.

"What is good ol' Rex up to today?"

"The bastard stopped by Cooper's house while I was showing it to some potential buyers and threatened me."

"That son of a bitch!" She growled and hissed, or maybe our connection was breaking up. "I'm gonna kill him."

"Can I watch?"

"No. It sounds like you're already at the top of the suspect list for Wanda's death."

I'd texted her after leaving Doc's office on Saturday, keeping her apprised of Cooper's news about Wanda's murder.

"But I'll tell you what," she said, "I'll bring you a trophy after I'm done."

"Deal." That reminded me of Prudence and her trophy teeth.

I rubbed the back of my neck where my tension was knotted and double-knotted. "You're coming to Aunt Zoe's tonight for supper, right?"

"Are you cooking?"

"No, Harvey is."

"Then I'll make sure to be there."

"He's making baked barbecue chicken."

"Please tell me you didn't kill Elvis."

"Not yet, but I give no promises. Doc will be there, too."

"Good! He and I need to make plans on how to make Rex's life complete and utter hell until the rat-bastard skips town again."

"Unfortunately, he's not going anywhere soon. He told me he's here on a year-long grant, working in the research lab up in Lead."

She sighed. "Do you think if I slept with Detective Hawke, he'd look the other way when I kill Rex?"

"Probably not. You could give it a shot with Cooper, though."

"Nah, he's not into the local crop of girls."

Not usually, but I was pretty sure he'd make an exception for Natalie. However, Cooper's current fixation with my best friend was my gem of a secret. And Doc's, too, since he'd figured it out the same night I had. And Cooper's secret, of course. Oh, and I had a suspicion Harvey might know as well. But that was it as far as I knew. Normally, I didn't like to keep secrets from Natalie, especially after the last time I'd kept my lips sealed up tight.

This new crush, for lack of a more mature word, that Cooper had going for Natalie was different. First of all, I wasn't sure how long it would last, so why open the door to yet another heartbreak if Cooper grew bored of the chase and moved on to his next prey. Secondly, Natalie had spent her life bouncing from one shitty boyfriend to the next. This summer, after limping away from another heartbreaker, she'd taken a sabbatical from men. Things had been bumpy at the start thanks to an initial attraction to Doc, but after she'd found out he and I were an item, she'd flown the straight and narrow, keeping her heart to herself.

Over four months had passed since going on her sabbatical. Four months in which she'd been rebuilding her self-confidence and growing a stronger, less love-prone heart. It was because of this new, happier Natalie that I didn't want to tell her that the steely-eyed detective who'd shot down her flirting attempts in the past had apparently changed his mind.

The sound of a door closing made me glance back at the pink house. My clients stood on the porch waiting for me.

"Nat, I gotta go. I'll see you tonight." I hung up and joined my clients, leading them to my SUV.

Two hours later I was back in Aunt Zoe's kitchen washing up some dirty cups and coffee mugs, while Harvey spread another layer of his homemade, secret-recipe barbecue sauce over a glass baking dish full of chicken. A sweet, tangy scent filled the air. It was a good thing I was standing over the sink or there would've been drool all over the floor.

Layne skidded into the kitchen. "Doc's here," he announced and then dashed back out again.

My kids were starting to warm up to the idea of my having a boyfriend, but there were still nail-biting moments for all when it came to Doc. Layne seemed to have found some common ground on the book front, since Doc was an avid history buff, too. Addy still wanted her best friend to be her sister, though, which matched me with Jeff Wymonds, whom I liked in a father of my kid's friend sort of way, but that was it. For the time being, however, Addy had eased up and was now talking to Doc instead of giving him—and me—the cold shoulder.

As for me, I kept waiting for the day Doc stood up from the kitchen table after witnessing yet another round of my kids pounding on each other with me screaming at them from the ropes, grabbed his car keys, and wished us all a good life. For a guy who'd been a bachelor for thirty-nine years, he was settling into family life with only a few grimaces.

I glanced at the clock. Natalie should be here soon, too.

Doc joined Harvey and me, setting a small white box down on the table. "Hey, Willis," he nodded at Harvey, and then came my way, looking comfortable in his black jeans and maroon, long sleeve shirt. His lips were cool when he kissed me hello; his hands were even colder when they playfully slipped under the hem of the T-shirt I'd thrown on after getting home.

I screeched at his freezing touch on my stomach and danced out of his reach, snapping him with the dish towel when he tried to follow me around the table.

"Be good," I told him, giving him a mock glare.

He held up his hands in surrender. "I'll be good if you promise to let me stay longer tonight."

"Cross my heart. Satan's bride has left the building."

"When was yer sister here?" Harvey asked. He'd met Susan once before and put up with my ranting and raving long after she'd left.

"Last night." I was sort of worried about her driving off this morning without any parting jabs. That wasn't normal Psycho Susan behavior, and I wasn't naïve enough to believe she hadn't planted any poison apples around the house.

I pointed at the box Doc had brought. "What's that?"

"Willis told me to bring dessert." He rubbed his hands together to warm them, joining Harvey at the stove. "That smells great."

What kind of dessert comes in a small box? It was too small for a pie or cake and not cold enough to be ice cream. I opened the lid and gasped in excitement. Chocolate truffles!

"You're my hero," I told Doc, licking my lips. I reached for one of the truffles with a coffee bean stuck to the top. Kahlua and cream if I remembered right. A perfect reward after an asshole-filled day.

Harvey came flying out of nowhere and smacked my knuckles with a wooden spoon.

"Ouch!" I cradled my hand against my chest. "What'd you do that for? I was just going to touch it a tiny bit."

"Don't be saddlin' horses that ain't yer own." He threatened to whack my knuckles again, his gold teeth gleaming through his bearded grin. "Them there are my favorites, especially the ones with red on top. They're called a 'Hot Mama' and have three differ'nt kinds of peppers in 'em."

"Yum."

He snickered. "I like my truffles how I like my women."

"Sweet *and* hot?"

"Soft and messy."

The memory of a certain plaid suit jacket stained with strawberry scented love goop surfaced. I frowned over at Doc. "I shouldn't have asked." I reached for the box. "I'll put them up so the kids don't sneak any."

"The kids." Harvey gave me a squint. "Right."

I stuck my tongue out at him and then placed the box on top of the fridge for later, grabbing the bottle of tequila for now.

"Where's Zoe?" Doc asked, taking the beer I'd grabbed for him from the fridge.

"Out in her workshop. She should be in soon."

He pointed at the tequila. "Are you celebrating or drowning?"

"The latter," I said. "You want to sink with me?"

He shook his head. "I'll watch you thrash around from the beach. What happened today?"

The doorbell rang before I could answer him.

A quick wince flashed across his face. "Someone's here."

"That should be Nat."

"Let's hope your sister hasn't returned," Doc said. "I don't want to miss Harvey's barbecue chicken."

"Addy," I hollered. "Can you get that?"

"I'm washing my chicken," she yelled back.

That damned bird took more baths than Addy did, especially now that my old water pick had Elvis's name on it. I wasn't joking. Addy had written it with black permanent marker so nobody got confused—or grounded again—when my new one arrived in the mail later this week.

"Layne, get the door." I didn't bother asking this time.

"Come on, Mom!" He pounded down the stairs. "What am I? Your butler?"

"He'd look adorable in a little suit and tie," I whispered to Doc, and then hollered back, "You're the one who wants to be the man of the house. So be a man and get the darn door."

"Better watch it, Doc," Harvey warned while crumbling the leftover bacon from breakfast into a saucepan of green beans. "She's rough on the men in her life. Always huntin' trouble with a big gun."

"Rough and ornery." Doc chuckled and then took a sip of beer. "That's how I like *my* women." He winked at me.

I blew an air-kiss back at him and grabbed a small glass out of the cupboard. "I thought you liked me soft."

"Only to the touch," he shot back with a glint in his eyes.

"Hubba hubba," I joked and cut the tequila with some lime juice and a sprinkle of sugar.

"So what happened today, Tiger?" Doc asked again, leaning back against the counter next to me as I stirred my drink.

I hesitated, hating to ruin supper before we'd even started.

"Natalie's here," Layne called from the dining room.

The first sip of tequila burned a little going down. "I'll tell you in a minute."

Natalie strolled into the kitchen with a cocky smile on her full lips. Judging from her black yoga pants and faded orange sweatshirt with a cutoff hem, she must have come straight from the Rec Center. Her hair was pulled back in a crooked ponytail, her face makeup free. With my vampire skin and curly blonde rat's nest I had always envied her olive skin and rich brown waves.

"I have something for you," she told me and set a side mirror from a car on the table. The glass was shattered into a spider web of cracks.

Leaving my tequila on the counter next to Doc, I joined her at the table and picked up the mirror with care. There was a sizeable dent in the casing, the black paint flaking off all around it. "What's this?"

Harvey joined me, tapping the casing with his wooden spoon. "It's a car mirror, girl."

"I know that." I snatched his spoon from him and smacked him on the shoulder with it before handing it back.

Harvey smirked at Doc. "See what I mean 'bout her? Like a wasp with two stingers."

"But they're sexy stingers." Doc took another swig of beer.

"I meant *why* is Nat giving me a broken car mirror?"

We both turned to Natalie, who picked up my glass of tequila and leaned against the counter next to Doc.

"Well," she paused to toss back some of my drink, "it sort of fell off a certain black Jaguar parked up at the research lab when I rammed it with the front bumper of my pickup."

"A black Jaguar, huh?" Doc aimed a frown at me. "Does this have something to do with tonight's tequila?"

Nodding, I looked down at the broken mirror and then back up again, my love for my best friend warming me inside and out. "Did you really hit Rex's car?"

She held up her hand, her index finger almost touching her thumb. "Just a teeny bit."

"Nicely done, Beals." Doc held out his beer toward her, which she toasted with my shot glass.

"You better hide that somewhere," Harvey told me, heading back to the stove.

"From the kids?"

"From Coop."

"Coop?"

"Yeah," he glanced up at the clock. "The boy should be here any minute now."

What?!! "Who invited Cooper?" I glared at each of them in turn. All three had a soft heart when it came to that damned detective. Call me silly, but I preferred my barbecue chicken without a side of snarling law-dog.

Harvey pointed his wooden spoon at Doc. "*Your* boyfriend."

I turned to Doc with my mouth open in a silent shout.

"I couldn't let him stay home alone tonight." Doc reached out and snagged my hand, reeling me in. "Besides, Harvey's chicken is one of Coop's favorites."

"Fine." I leaned into Doc's side as his arm snaked around my waist. "But I don't have to be nice to him do I?" I stole my glass of tequila from Natalie, or what was left of it, and gulped down the last few drops.

Doc kissed my temple. "Just promise me you won't bite."

"What if he bites first?"

The back door opened and Aunt Zoe stepped inside, taking off her coat. "Hi, Doc and Nat." She was wearing a worn, holey shirt and matching holey jeans. She patted Harvey's shoulder on the way to the sink. "That smells wonderful, Willis."

"Should be ready in ten more minutes. I just put the final veneer on 'er."

She soaped and rinsed her hands. "What's with the broken mirror on the table?" Aunt Zoe didn't miss much, especially when it came to me and the kids. Her gaze landed on Doc as she towel dried. "It's not from your Camaro is it?"

He shook his head.

"It's from a certain black Jaguar," I said.

She laughed, catching on immediately. "What happened?"

Doc glanced down at me. "I've been wondering that since Violet got out the tequila."

Glancing into the dining room to make sure the kids weren't near, I kept my voice low and told them what had happened in front of Cooper's house, leaving out Rex's name in case any young ears were eavesdropping.

When I finished, Aunt Zoe grabbed Natalie by the shoulders and planted loud kisses on both of her cheeks. "Have I told you how much I love you lately, Natalie?"

Natalie grinned. "Oh, I'm just getting started."

"Just be careful." I grabbed the mirror from the table and took it inside the pantry, tucking it behind a box of pancake mix. "Cooper has a handcuff fetish."

"Handcuffs can be fun," she said, making a woo-woo face.

"Sure, if they're fur-lined, but Cooper's are wrapped with barbed wire."

"Make that razor wire, Parker," Cooper said, barging into the kitchen and jarring me out of my happy post-tequila haze. "But those particular cuffs are reserved only for troublemakers like you."

The detective apparently had left his coat by the front door. His hair looked extra spikey tonight, his tan shirt sleeves rolled up to his mid-forearms, his skull tie loosened at the neck. He must have come straight from work. I bet he still smelled like the police station, too, which was a scent that made me shudder after spending hours in one of Cooper's cells. As he greeted everyone, my eye got all twitchy about how at ease he seemed in Aunt Zoe's kitchen, aka my private lair.

"Razor wire cuffs, huh?" Natalie grinned at Doc. "It's a good thing Vi likes it rough." She crossed to the refrigerator. "Want a beer, Coop?"

"Sure."

Natalie had her head in the fridge, so she didn't notice Cooper sneaking peeks at her butt in those yoga pants. But I did, and so did Harvey, who shook his head as if Cooper were walking the plank.

Natalie handed him a beer with a smile, which faltered under the intensity of his stare. After several silent seconds, she asked, "Is there something on my face?" and looked over at me with raised eyebrows.

"Yeah," I answered. "A nose."

She wrinkled said appendage at me. "Smartass."

"You look as beautiful as always," Aunt Zoe said, taking the stack of plates on the counter and handing them to Natalie. It was going to be a tight fit around the table tonight, so we decided to let the kids use TV trays in the living room.

"You're biased, Zoe." Natalie shoulder-bumped Aunt Zoe.

"She is but I'm not." I grabbed silverware from the drawer, shooting Natalie a grin. "You're so ugly the tide wouldn't take you out."

She laughed. "Yeah, well you're so ugly that a cannibal would take one look at you and order a salad."

I pretended to stab her with a fork, but she blocked me with a plate.

"Sorry about that, Natalie," Cooper said after we'd settled down and he'd planted himself at the table. "Your lack of makeup threw me for a moment."

I grimaced at his explanation. Somebody needed to school him on things NOT to say to a woman—well, a woman that he's interested in for reasons other than dragging her off to jail.

"I just came from a swim workout at the Rec Center," she told Cooper. She handed him a plate. "I could dim the lights if that would help."

A lack of lighting wasn't going to help Cooper on that front.

Doc and I exchanged knowing looks as I finished setting the table.

Cooper started to say something and then stopped, pinching his lips tight. He shook his head and focused on his beer, scratching at the label.

I had the feeling he was either trying to figure out how to remove his foot from his mouth, or he wanted to say something but was having second and third and fourth thoughts about letting the words fly. How many times had I been there and done that with Doc? Hell, I still bit my lip when it came to saying the L-word to him.

Unable to watch Cooper's train-wreck pile up any longer, I laughed. It came out sounding sort of flat. "We've tried dimming the lights before, Nat, remember?" I handed Cooper a set of silverware, giving him a get-it-together look. "But you still stink even in the dark."

She chuckled. "Damn. You're on fire tonight, babe." She patted Cooper on the back as she passed behind him. "She's saved your ass twice now, Coop. You better be nice to her for a while."

It was time for a change of subject, and I knew just the diversion. "I'm on fire because Detective Hawke lit my fuse this afternoon and scampered off without putting it out."

Cooper snapped back into cop mode, his steely gray eyes locking onto mine. "I warned you about playing up the witch angle."

Detective Hawke must have told him about our face-off outside of the gingerbread house.

"I couldn't help it." I gave everyone a quick recount of the detective's visit, wrapping up with my Wicked Witch of the West send-off as Harvey set the platter of steaming chicken down in the middle of the table.

"Has something changed with the case?" Doc asked Cooper as he pulled out a chair for me, taking the seat next to mine. "Something to cause Detective Hawke to jump the gun when it comes to approaching Violet?"

"Well, sort of."

"What?"

Both of my kids came pushing and shoving into the kitchen, fighting about who made it there first. Our conversation took a brief hiatus as I dished up their plates and Aunt Zoe went with them to make sure they were all settled in front of the TV.

Until she returned, we passed the serving bowls and dished up. Harvey removed his apron and took the seat to Cooper's left, leaving the seat to his right for Aunt Zoe.

Aunt Zoe returned, and after making sure everyone had what they wanted to drink, she sat down and laid her napkin across her lap. "Where were we?"

"Coop was gonna tell us what changed." Harvey dragged us back to the topic of Wanda's death.

Personally, I wouldn't have minded waiting to hear what Cooper had to say until after the truffles. More times than not the detective's news came with a bonus of nausea—once it even induced vomiting. I frowned across the table at his tie, pretty sure that was the very tie I'd tossed my cookies all over.

"We went back through Wanda's stuff and we found some notes," Cooper said around mouthfuls of food. "Several notes actually, but they all said the same thing."

That sort of reminded me of *The Shining*. What was it Jack had typed repeatedly in the midst of his craziness? Something about all work and no play made him a dull boy?

"Were they signed by anyone?" Natalie asked.

Cooper shook his head and then took a bite out of a chicken breast.

Aunt Zoe wiped her mouth with her napkin. "How many notes are we talking here?"

He held up five fingers.

Five notes that all said the same thing. That was sort of odd. "I suppose you're going to tell us that what the notes said is police business." I stabbed a forkful of green beans and stuffed them in my mouth. "Oh, man," I looked over at Harvey. "You used real bacon grease in these, didn't you?"

The old buzzard wiggled his eyebrows at me. "I don't share my cookin' secrets."

Cooper took a swig of beer, setting his bottle down while glaring across at me. "We want what belongs to us."

I paused, my fork midway to my mouth. "Come again?"

"You wanted to know what was on the notes. That's what each one said. Those six words were handwritten on paper. Sound familiar?"

Holy shit! My fork clanged onto my plate. I knew those words too well but for a different reason, one I'd not told Cooper last month when we'd been in the morgue behind Mudder Brothers. It was time to let the detective in on another secret.

"Violet," Aunt Zoe's voice cut through the rush of noise in my head. "What's wrong?"

I pushed to my feet, holding my hand out when Doc started to rise with me. "I'll be right back."

I took the stairs to my room two at a time. Inside my bedroom, I tore through my dresser drawers and then went through the pockets of my coats hanging in my closet.

Not there or there. Where in the hell was it? I made myself slow down. Breathe. Now think.

Oh yeah. I lifted my mattress and pulled out my old diary.

Flipping open the cover, I frowned down at the slightly crumpled note. There it was.

Back down in the kitchen, Harvey had dished up a second helping on his plate. Everyone else seemed to be holding off, waiting for my return.

Doc stood as I drew near. I handed him the crinkled piece of paper. Recognition made him nod, but his face was crisscrossed with lines when he handed it back.

"These notes you found at Wanda's place," I said to Cooper, who was watching me like he was trying to read the tag on the back of my shirt. "Did the handwriting look like this?"

I handed him the note I'd received back in September right after Doc had bailed me out of jail. The note had been stuffed into my purse, which had been locked away in evidence while I had been ranting and raving behind bars.

Cooper stared down at the note without blinking. When he looked up at me, his squint was full of distrust. "Where did you get this, Parker? From Wanda? Because if memory serves me right, those six words were left with your business card in the morgue when that body disappeared. If you somehow sneaked in the Evidence cage and—"

"It's mine," I interrupted Mr. Suspicious Pants.

"What do you mean it's yours?"

"I mean someone put it in my purse, Detective." When he continued to doubt me with his eyes, I jammed my hands on my hips and squinted right back at him. "Someone who works at the Deadwood Police Station with *you*."

Chapter Five

S o, what do you think?" I asked Doc and Natalie later that evening as we stood on Aunt Zoe's front porch. Deadwood was quiet tonight, the cold keeping everyone inside all locked up and snug.

"I think it's freaking freezing out here." Natalie shivered, pulling her sheepskin lined coat tighter around her. "Why can't we talk about this in the house where it's warm?"

"I don't want to risk the kids hearing."

"They're in bed."

"That doesn't mean they're sleeping." Especially Addy, whose young ears could pick up the sound of ants walking across the carpet some days. "They tend to eavesdrop more the later it gets."

Doc leaned his shoulder against the porch post, staring down the street to where Mr. Stinkleskine was letting his little bark-a-matic do his business on a light pole one last time tonight. "What do we think about what?" he asked.

"Does Cooper believe the handwriting on that note isn't mine? Or is he going to run and tattle to Detective Hawke so the two of them can tag-team on my ass and ensure the next time I'm behind bars I stay there for a lot longer?"

"I think he believes you," Natalie answered first. "Especially since Doc was there to witness you pulling the note from your purse."

I glanced at Doc. I had fudged on my alibi a bit. Doc actually hadn't been standing there next to me that day I'd found the note in my purse. He'd been inside the police station talking to Cooper while I waited outside at his Camaro. But we'd driven straight to Aunt Zoe's place from the station and I'd shown him the note, so it was only a smidgen of a lie.

"He sure didn't act like he believed me."

The detective had glowered through the rest of supper and passed on dessert, opting to take my note with him and return to the station to compare the handwriting to the other notes. He wanted to be certain it matched. I had a sick feeling in my gut that it would.

"Cooper sees the bigger problem here," Doc said, his gaze shadowed when he looked my way.

I did too, but I wasn't keen on voicing it, not even inside of my head. "You heard Aunt Zoe," I told him. "We can't be sure that whoever killed Wanda is the one responsible for sending those notes. It could be a coincidence."

I really hoped that was the case, but I was relatively certain I was screwed here.

"Is that better or worse?" Natalie asked. "If they aren't one and the same, then you may have two whack jobs after you."

"They can get in line." There was an albino juggernaut and another milky-eyed bone cruncher in front of whoever had written that damned note.

"What do you think the note's author is talking about?" Natalie asked. "What's worth killing Wanda for?"

Doc jammed his hands into his pockets, pulling his shoulders inward. "It's too soon to tell. When I followed Cooper out, he mentioned that they were still sorting through the crime scene."

"Did he happen to tell you how she was killed?" I asked, wondering if there was any weapon left behind like there had been with Jane.

"No, but I didn't ask. He'll tell us when he can."

Doc had a lot more patience than I did.

Natalie's teeth started to chatter. "I can't quite wrap my mind around it all tonight." She pulled out her truck keys, jingling them. "I think I'll head out. I have to go down to Rapid in the morning, so I need to hit the hay early tonight."

I walked her to the bottom of the porch steps. "Thank you for the trophy mirror." I smiled in spite of the creepy note business. "I wish I could have seen Rex's face when he realized it was gone."

"I have big plans for your ex. I'm just getting started." She gave me a quick hug goodbye and then strode toward her truck, saying over her shoulder, "See you later, Doc. Keep her out of trouble."

"I'll do my best, but I'm only mortal."

She laughed. At her pickup, she tossed back, "Call me tomorrow if anything exciting happens."

"Don't be surprised if it's a collect call and you hear Cooper snarling in the background."

With a wave, she slid behind the wheel of her pickup. I watched her drive off before climbing back up the porch steps.

Doc had moved. He stood back in the shadows now, leaning against the house. "Come here, Boots," he said quietly.

I stepped easily into the safe circle of his embrace, resting my cheek against his sternum. I'd wanted to do this since I'd learned about Wanda's five notes, but I'd held myself in check while under the watchful eye of Aunt Zoe and Cooper. Executioners weren't supposed to want to hide in someone's arms, were they?

His heart thumped steadily in my ear. "How are you doing?" he asked.

"I'm better now."

"Hold on a second." He reached down and unbuttoned my coat, and then pulled me against him, settling me between his legs. My chest flattened against his, body heat doubling. "There, now we're both better."

I chuckled and went up on my toes to kiss the underside of his jaw, feeling a slight scratch of stubble on my lips.

"You want to talk about it?" he asked.

"Not really."

"Okay."

But then I changed my mind, because I'd rather speak my fears and worries while here with Doc than toss and turn and fester about them alone in my bed until the wee hours. "Whoever wrote that note wants the book on Kyrkozz enough to murder for it, don't they?" I whispered.

I could feel his warm breath on the top of my head. "That's my guess."

Back in August, I'd taken a book about a demon named Kyrkozz from the Carhart house. It had belonged to a crazy, demon-loving bitch named Lila who'd tied me to a chair and had planned to use the book to raise a demon so it could borrow my womb to procreate. Thankfully, Wanda Carhart had shown up before the demon had arrived and she'd helped me escape. After a night of hair-raising moments, Wanda and I had made it out alive, and I'd procured the book as a parting gift. My reason for taking it was simple—if Lila had succeeded somehow and Kyrkozz came looking for me to finish what she'd started, I might need what was written on the pages to save those I loved from something much worse than a crazy, demon-loving bitch.

"What should I do?" I asked.

"You mean what should *we* do?" Doc's hand rubbed up and down my back. "You're not alone in this."

"You sure you don't want to take this opportunity to run the other way?" I joked, but there was a serious question hidden in between the words.

"Are you kidding? And miss out on all of this fun? No way, Killer. I'm not going anywhere without you."

When he said stuff like that, I was his slave to do with as he pleased—whips, chains, thumbscrews, the rack, even Harvey's favorite strawberry love goop. I didn't care. Although I drew the line at cooking.

"I think we should see what Cooper comes back with before doing anything on our own."

I nodded, conceding to the police on this one. "I remember him telling me that Lila was part of a group out of Yankton who had some tie to demonology. You think they are the "WE" in the messages?"

"Maybe. But how did that note get into your purse at the police station?"

"They must have members here in Deadwood." I burrowed my nose into his soft shirt, breathing in the woodsy scent of his cologne. As usual, the smell of his skin made my pulse start to skip and whistle.

"Have you seen anyone else with that goat-melting-into-a-pig tattoo Lila had?" he asked.

"No. But I'll start keeping an eye out now."

"I'll do the same at the Rec Center. Tattoos are very visible there between the exercise room and pool."

I looped my arms around his neck. "Of course you'll only look for these tattoos on the men."

He chuckled. "Of course." His hands moved up my ribs, the heels of his palms brushing along the sides of my bra. "I don't want to leave you tonight."

That made two of us. "Why do I hear a 'but' in there?"

"But I have to head down to Hill City in the morning for work, so I need some sleep."

This wouldn't be a problem if we moved in with Doc. He wouldn't have to leave me until morning light. But how could I begin to broach that subject when I couldn't get up the nerve yet to tell the guy I was in love with him.

"You could stay in my bed, wake up early, and then go home to shower and shave before hitting the road."

"Tempting." He leaned down and kissed me, taking his time about it, like he was in no rush to finish any time this evening. When he finally pulled back, I hung from his neck like a weak-kneed groupie.

"Where did you learn to kiss like that?" My lips pulsed still, pumped up and ready for more.

"I took an online course."

I giggled and fanned myself, trying to lasso my heart and drag it back into its stall. "You must have seduced a lot of women in your time with those lips."

I knew a certain redhead who couldn't stop obsessing about him. The longer I was with Doc, the more I understood why. Had he kissed Tiffany that way?

"Not really." He traced my jawline. "You inspire me, Boots."

"Yeah, well," *I love you,* "better a great kiss than some mediocre poetry."

"What? You don't want any sonnets extolling your beauty?"

"I'd rather have more kisses."

"Me, too. That's why I can't stay in your bed tonight. There's no way I'll get much sleep and we both know that. It's been too long since I've had you all to myself."

"What good is sleep? I'm saving it for when I'm dead." I let out a short, hard laugh. "Which could be sooner rather than later at the rate I'm going."

"That's what scares me, Killer." His tone was suddenly serious.

This time when he kissed me, there was more urgency. His touch was rougher, more demanding. His hands spanned my hips and then gripped me tight, his body hard against mine, aggressive and demanding.

I let him mold me against him, moaning when his hands slipped under my shirt and moved northward. "Doc," I gasped up at the porch ceiling. "Take me to bed."

"We can't." His thumbs stroked over the front of my bra. "You said yourself that your kids have big ears."

"I can be quiet." At least I could try.

He groaned at the press of my hand at his zipper. "I can't."

"But I want you to touch me." I whispered in his ear where and how and then nibbled my way down to his collarbone.

He pulled back like he'd been burned and grasped my shoulders, pushing me back a step. His ragged breathing matched mine. "You're making it damned near impossible to say no."

"So don't." If this relationship was going to continue into something more serious and long-term, we'd need to find a way to play around under the same roof as the kids. Other parents somehow managed; we could, too.

"If I didn't have a box of paperwork to go through tomorrow, I'd take you up on your offer." He raked his fingers through his hair, looking out toward the street. "Are you going to be okay here on your own tonight?"

Not really, and that had nothing to do with wanting to have sex with him. The night stretched out before me long and exhausting, promising plenty of worry fueled nightmares, but I couldn't bring myself to push for him to stay. He had clients relying on his clear head. He didn't need his scaredy-cat girlfriend screwing up his livelihood.

"I'll be fine." Because that sounded weak I added, "More than fine. You're right, you should go home and get some sleep."

"Violet, look at me." When I did, he searched my face from top to bottom, returning to my eyes at the end. "I could sleep on the couch."

"Yes, please." It came out in a gush of relief. Having him in the house with us would keep me from hiding under my covers when the walls and floors creaked and settled for the night. "But only if you think you can get enough rest sleeping on the couch."

"I'll make do." He toyed with one of my loose curls. "You know, Boots, all you have to do is ask and I'll come running every time."

"I don't want you to think I'm some wussy girl."

His chuckle was low and husky. "I've watched you take on some burly monsters almost twice your size. You're no wuss."

"So why do I feel scared about being alone most nights?"

"You may be an executioner, but you're still human."

"Am I? Do we know that for sure?"

"Well," I could hear the grin in his tone, "I've checked out pretty much every inch of you, and from what I can tell, you're human all right."

That made me laugh, easing some of the anxiety that had my guts tight about the notes, the nightmares, and the monsters still hiding out there in the shadows.

Then I sobered, licking my lips. Even though he'd already agreed, I looked into his eyes and asked, "Doc, will you stay the night with me and my family and watch over us so that I can sleep with both eyes closed for once?"

He caught my hand and laced his fingers through mine. "I'm your huckleberry." With a tug he led me to the door, holding it open for me to go through first. "But it'll cost you a breakfast."

"You mean you want me to actually get up early and cook food that's edible?"

He stepped inside after me, locking the door behind us. "I was thinking more along the lines of you spending the night with me sometime soon and letting me have *you* for breakfast." He leaned back against the door, stroking his chin as he ogled me up and down. "Although I do have this fantasy."

I stepped closer. "Oh, yeah?" I whispered. "Do tell."

His voice lowered to match mine. "I wake up in the morning and find you down in my kitchen wearing nothing but your purple boots and …"

A zing of lust gave me goosebumps. I went up on my toes and kissed him, silencing him except for the groan that came from his throat when my tongue teased his to come out and play.

When I stepped back, I raised my brows. "You were saying something about my purple boots?"

"Damn." He sighed, his brown eyes dark with want. "It's going to be a long night."

* * *

Monday, November 12th

The Old Prospector Hotel had a long-standing reputation for housing the ghosts of the prostitutes who'd once lived and worked there. This morning I was there to see the man who claimed he could hear these ghosts. I needed to set up a date with him for Paranormal Realty to film a piece inside of the building later this week. I rode the elevator up to the third floor, where I knew Cornelius Curion would be waiting for me and the protein shake I'd agreed to bring him as an entrance fee into his suite.

Being in the elevator reminded me of the last time I'd paid a visit to the hotel, which led me to wondering how things were going for Cooper down at the station with my note, which led me to smiling about the note that Doc had left under my cell phone: *You owe me breakfast, Boots.*

He'd even made coffee before he'd slipped out of Aunt Zoe's place long before I'd started stirring.

I'd give him his so-called breakfast and then some for helping to keep the boogeyman away last night.

We'd stayed up too late, lying on the couch together, falling asleep to one of Layne's favorite movies, *Jaws.* I'd slept hard, waking up with a sore hip. If my nightmares had come I didn't remember them. Maybe the shark had eaten the monsters and demons before they could get to me.

Aunt Zoe's couch was made for one. Poor Doc had been pinned between me and the back of it sans the cushions all night. I'd be happy to massage away any stiffness resulting from his sleepover. I chuckled at my own pun and then grimaced. Harvey and his dirty mind were really starting to wear off on me.

The elevator dinged and the doors opened. I stepped out into the hallway and glanced around. Not much had changed on the decorating front. The hall was lined with foot-worn carpet and wallpaper that hadn't looked new for a generation, maybe two. I closed my eyes to see if I could sense any ghosts. After a few seconds, I sniffed like Doc often did, smelling the stale scents of years gone by but nothing out of the ordinary.

I snorted at my own silliness. Who was I kidding? I was still a dud when it came to ghosts. Prudence was a special case. Aunt Zoe had confirmed that this morning when I'd joined her in the kitchen after I'd stood under a steaming hot shower to work out my stiffness.

"You doing okay?" she'd asked as I poured the coffee Doc had made.

"Sure, why?"

"Doc spent the night."

I glanced at her while adding milk to my cup. "We didn't do anything." She had to have noticed when she came in from her workshop that we were both fully clothed after falling asleep.

She waved me off. "That's not the point. Doc usually only spends the night when you need him to be here for some reason. So, why did you need him last night?"

I shrugged and carried my coffee to the table where she sat stirring hers. "Sometimes the fear of what happened to Prudence and her family grows too big for me to handle on my own in here." I tapped my temple. "Last night I wanted Doc to hold my hand and make me forget for a while about what might be waiting for me out there."

"You're not Prudence."

"Of course not." I gave her a toothy smile. "I'm a lot nicer than she is."

Aunt Zoe grinned at me over her coffee cup. "Smartass. I mean that you can't keep comparing yourself to her. She's a special case."

"Special how?" Was this about Prudence's ability to turn people into walking and talking puppets?

"She's not like most executioners. She's the first I've ever heard of who has post-mortem abilities."

"Maybe that's one of the abilities that comes with her bloodline."

"Maybe, but I want you to stop trying to measure up to her because you can't."

"Because I'm too new at this executioner gig?"

"Because you're not the same as her."

"We're both killers."

"That doesn't make you identical twins. Trust me on this. It's important to your success. Your skillset is different. The only thing you two share is your occupation."

"And its hazards."

"Unfortunately that too."

The kids had joined us then, bickering as usual.

Before I'd left to take them to school, Aunt Zoe had kissed my forehead and reiterated, "Trust me, you're just as strong, only different."

And so I did trust her, and would continue to. I had to, because Aunt Zoe was guiding me through the ins and outs of what I was and what I needed to do.

For now, however, what I needed to do was get the date set for filming in The Old Prospector Hotel this week so that I kept my boss happy. Why couldn't this executioner gig come with good pay and health insurance?

Cornelius's suite was at the other end of the hall. I made it to his room without running into anyone else—alive or dead. My cell phone buzzed in the pocket of my corduroy skirt as I lifted my hand to knock.

Doc?

I pulled it out.

Tiffany Sugarbell's name showed on the screen. My first reaction was to delete it and then throw my phone out the nearest window.

Instead, I tapped on the screen, reading her text: *I have a buyer interested in the Rockhurst Ranch property out on 14A.*

I texted back: *That's not my property. Mona Hollister is the listing agent.*

She replied: *My mistake. Thanks.*

Bullshit. I doubted Tiffany made such mistakes.

I wrote: *Welcome.*

Then I waited for a few seconds, watching the screen. Nothing. I started to put my phone away and it buzzed again. I looked down.

I suppose Doc told you he loved you, too.

I stared down at those words, my heart beating a bass drum loud in my ears as I read them three more times.

Her supposition was correct. Doc had told me he loved me, but I hadn't been sure at the time if he was acting the part of Gomez Addams or being serious, since we were decked out for Halloween and flirting in Gomez and Morticia fashion at the time.

What did she mean by that one sentence? Had Doc told Tiffany he loved her at some point in their relationship? Was that why she'd started talking about marriage to him? And then he'd left her high and dry after that?

Or was this a new kind of game she was playing with me? Trying to screw with my head since she couldn't get through to Doc anymore due to his ignoring her texts and voicemails.

Images flashed through my mind. First came Tiffany smacking Doc right in front of me, spitting fire at him about breaking up with her without saying goodbye. Following on the heels of that memory was one from the night in the Purple Door Saloon after I'd had too much tequila in spite of Cooper's attempts to stop me. Tiffany had shown up and started poking me with her barbed tongue. *What makes you think he won't get bored with you, too, Violet?* she'd said, all fangs and venom, while Doc stood right there with us. *Even curls and curves get boring for a guy with Doc's appetites.*

I leaned my head on Cornelius's door, trying to stop my fears and insecurities from ganging up on me.

Doc had warned me more than once that if Tiffany came calling, I had to keep her from getting into my head and stirring things up.

She was definitely trying to stir things up with that text.

Or was Doc staying one step ahead of her because he'd played this game before and knew how to keep me on the hook in spite of his ex's warnings?

No. Doc wouldn't do that. He wasn't a game player.

Right. *Right??*

I sighed. I didn't need this, not with another murderer possibly zeroing in on me. Playing the does-he-love-me game with daisy petals was for love-sick girls who weren't being hunted down by a handful of blood thirsty killers.

Whether or not Doc was truly in love with me, he seemed to really like me at the moment. The guy was even trying to win over my kids. Who in their right mind would subject themselves to my loving little holy terrors just for kicks?

I stuffed my phone in my pocket and decided on a new policy—I would not reply to Tiffany unless it was business related.

Now, back to the matter at hand, which was setting up a filming date in The Old Prospector Hotel with the hotel's eccentric owner, Cornelius.

Per the instructions Cornelius had given, I knocked three times hard, then lightly three times, and then three more hard. This was his version of SOS. He preferred I start my voicemail messages for him in the same style, only humming instead of knocking. I preferred beating him over the head with a rubber chicken.

The door opened and Cornelius, my Abe Lincoln look-alike pal, stood there with bloodshot eyes and even paler skin than usual. In place of his black stove-pipe hat and long wool jacket was a yellow robe that hung loosely over a stained T-shirt and striped boxers. "Violet, thank God. I thought you were someone else."

"Someone else who knocks in Morse code?"

"No, someone who's dead."

Well, I was dodging the grim reaper more often these days.

I closed the door behind me and followed him into his suite. The place was a mess. Shirts and pants were strewn everywhere, covering several of his expensive computer monitors and paranormal activity equipment. Empty cups and half-crushed takeout boxes cluttered every available surface, and the window blinds hung askew.

I sniffed, wrinkling my nose at the underlying scent of spoiled food in the room along with something else I didn't want to try to identify. I moved to the window and lifted it in spite of the freezing cold morning air that seeped inside.

"What are you doing?" he asked from where he'd collapsed onto one of his computer chairs.

"Letting the evil spirits out." I spoke his vernacular, having been around him long enough to know that would get me further than a rational explanation. "If we're going to film here this week, we have to make sure the air is clear of malevolent manifestations and ectoplasmic proteins."

"What are ectoplasmic proteins?" he asked.

Something I'd made up, but it sounded good. "That's not important. We need to get you up and moving." And preferably showered and dressed. Those boxers appeared to have been used as a napkin a few too many times.

He took a sip from the protein drink I'd brought him. "I'm glad you're here, Violet."

"Why's that?" I collected several used food containers, noticing that many were mostly full yet, and carried them over to the trash. We were going to need a lot more trash bags from housekeeping to clean up this sty.

"I need your help," he said.

"You need a maid, not a Realtor."

"I'm not talking about help on this plane of existence."

Cornelius was one of the few people in town who understood some of my executioner abilities. He had terms for things I was able to do during a séance, most of which I couldn't remember. But that didn't mean I liked to dabble in the paranormal world with him. More times than not when the two of us worked together, I ended up hiding under my bed for the next week.

I picked up his one-horned Viking helmet that he liked to wear during séances, frowning at the broken horn tip. What in the heck? "Your helmet is broken."

"It's her fault."

"Whose fault?"

"She won't leave me alone."

"Who won't leave you alone?" Was Tiffany filling up his voicemail, too?

"I can't sleep. I can't eat. I can't focus beyond the sound of her hate-filled whispers." He buried his face in his hands.

He should try being on the receiving end of Tiffany's texts.

"She's going to be the death of me, Violet," he said through his fingers. "Or worse."

I lowered myself onto the chair next to him, noticing his hands were shaking. "Who are you talking about?"

"A ghost. I need your help getting rid of her."

"I don't know how to help you get rid of a ghost." I killed things that were still alive, not those already dead. Doc would be a better choice. He was way more knowledgeable about this kind of thing.

He held the heels of his hands over his ears. "She keeps saying I have to kill the one I love," he yelled, seeming to forget that I wasn't plugging my ears, too.

Wait a second. I knew exactly which ghost he was talking about now. My breath log-jammed in my throat for a few seconds.

"It's the little girl ghost again, isn't it?" I asked when I could breathe again. Wilda Hessler was not leaving without a fight.

He nodded, brushing at some crumbs stuck to his terry cloth robe. "She's making me crazy, Violet. She says all kinds of macabre things day and night. I'm afraid that if I can't get her to leave me alone, I'll start doing some of the grisly deeds she's telling me to do just to make her stop."

Chills peppered my forearms. Wilda had driven her brother mad with her constant haunting. He'd ended up killing many in his efforts to shut her up, but nothing had worked. Nothing except his death apparently, because now she'd latched onto Cornelius.

He stared down at his hands, as if suddenly realizing they were trembling. "Will you help me get rid of her?"

This was a side of Cornelius I'd not seen before. Usually he was full of confidence, strutting around with his paranormal gadgets, eager to play with the dead.

The idea of facing off with Wilda again made me want to run away screaming. The first time she'd almost won our battle of life and death.

I frowned at Cornelius, fully seeing the shadow he was becoming because of Wilda. He looked as if he'd aged years since I'd seen him last, which had been a little over a week ago. I wondered if the little bitch somehow fed off the energy of the living, like a soul-sucking parasite.

Before I agreed to anything, I wanted to confirm one suspicion. "Who is the ghost telling you to kill, Cornelius?"

He lifted his gaze, his bloodshot eyes locking onto mine. "For starters—you."

Chapter Six

I didn't make any promises to Cornelius about helping him shake Wilda's ghost. I couldn't—I was an executioner, not an exorcist. At least I didn't think I could, which is what led me to call Calamity Jane Realty after leaving the hotel to tell Mona that I wouldn't be back in the office until after lunch.

There was only one person who might know for sure if I could do anything to get rid of Wilda and if so, how. I just hoped that she didn't need our family history book to figure out the answer.

"Aunt Zoe," I called as I stepped inside the front door.

Silence.

Her pickup was out front, though. I called her name a few more times before heading out the back door and along the stone path to her glass workshop. A peek through the window found her sitting at her worktable with a pencil in hand and design pad spread out in front of her.

I joined her inside, closing the door behind me. Her workshop hadn't changed since I had been a kid. Block and metal tools hung from a pegboard on the wall over her workbench. Next to the currently unlit furnace sat a basketful of heat resistant sleeves and mitts. Glass pieces of different shapes and designs were strewn everywhere on flat surfaces throughout the room.

The place smelled like cinnamon thanks to the air fresheners Aunt Zoe used to offset the odors that came with her line of work. Willie Nelson's voice played through her stereo speakers, singing about being a highwayman. If I closed my eyes, I could be ten years old again, visiting for the summer.

"Violet," Aunt Zoe's surprised voice interrupted my trip to the past. She checked the clock over her workbench. "It's a bit early for lunch, isn't it?"

"I'm not here to eat." I hopped up on her worktable next to the sketch she was drawing. "Is that a new vase?"

"Yes." She crossed her arms. Her chair creaked as she leaned back.

"Why are you here?"

"What are those?" I pointed at some designs on the side of her vase drawing.

"Ribs."

"Vases have ribs?"

"Violet Lynn, answer my question."

I looked up from the drawing and held her blue gaze. "Wilda Hessler wants Cornelius to kill me."

A storm of emotions crossed her face, from eye-widening shock to dipped brows of confusion to lip-tightening worry. At the end, vertical wrinkles of anger were left in the storm's wake. "Boy, as if that little brat hadn't wreaked enough havoc when she was alive. Who'd have figured she'd be worse after death?"

"She's trying to drive Cornelius crazy with her constant malicious whispering. He said that he's afraid he'll start following her commands soon just to shut her up." I rubbed my arms, feeling a chill where there wasn't one. "Wolfgang said something along those lines that last night we were together."

Only he'd already done several grisly deeds per her bidding and those hadn't satisfied her vindictive lust.

"Cornelius is serious? He's not just playing this up for drama's sake?"

I understood why she'd ask that. Cornelius was known around town and down at the cop shop for his eccentric garb and odd actions. "No, he was more of a scared and honest Abe this morning than an eccentric Ghost Whisperer." I told her about his messy suite, stained robe and boxers, and bloodshot eyes.

"Did he out-and-out say that Wilda wanted him to kill you?"

"Yep, me for starters was how he put it. I'm on her A-list."

Aunt Zoe sighed. "You can't catch a break, can you, child?"

I shook my head. Not with Wilda, nor with Tiffany. I was turning into a well-hated woman around town.

"So, what do you think? Can I do anything to help Cornelius?"

Aunt Zoe chewed on her lower lip. "Executioners usually deal with the living."

"That's what I thought."

"But not always."

I kicked my feet. "You mean like demons?"

"No, demons infect a living body and take it over, which allows you the opportunity to kill it—although it's not as simple as stopping the heart."

"It's not?"

"No, but that's a discussion for another time." She gave me the stink-eye. "When we have the book back."

"I told you it's around here somewhere, I'm sure of it."

"You'd better be right about that."

"I'll find it, I promise."

Aunt Zoe nodded once.

"If not demons, what were you referring to when you said we don't always deal with living things?"

"Take Prudence, for example." Aunt Zoe picked up her pencil and started doodling on her sketchpad. "She's a ghost, clearly not living, and yet you are interacting with her."

"More like she's forcing herself upon me."

"And then there's Willis's great grandfather."

"You mean Grandpappy?"

She nodded. "You were able to talk to him and he's long dead."

"Yes, but that was only with Doc's help."

"So you say, but the point is, you—an executioner—talked to him—a ghost."

And I talked *for* him as well as evidenced by the audio recording Cornelius had taken of that séance. While Harvey and Cooper had been asking their long lost relative questions, I had been answering away unbeknownst to me while I was lost in the past. Actually, I wasn't answering for Grandpappy, merely repeating what his ghost said to me as I stood there next to him in the dark on their family's ranch. It all still made my head spin, but Doc and Cornelius had long, strange paranormal terms to describe what had happened, so apparently it made sense to them.

"So, you think that with Doc's help, I could actually talk to Wilda?"

"Maybe."

"Hmmm."

"You don't sound happy about that answer."

I laced my fingers together and frowned down at them. "What if I don't really want to talk to Wilda?"

"Why not? I thought that's what this conversation was all about."

"Because she scares the dickens out of me."

Aunt Zoe rested her hand on top of my laced fingers, her skin warm and comforting. "She can't hurt you."

"Do we know that for sure?"

"Don't you think she would've by now if it was possible? Why do you think she uses others to do her bidding?"

She had a point. "What if she uses Cornelius against me when I'm in the midst of reaching out to her?"

"Do you think he's that far gone already?"

"I don't know."

"Well, maybe you need to have your bodyguard there to protect you from Cornelius."

"Harvey?"

She shrugged. "Couldn't hurt."

Then again, maybe it could hurt ... as in Wilda hurting me, Cornelius, even Doc. I hopped down and paced in front of Aunt Zoe. "What can I possibly say to Wilda to make her stop trying to kill me?"

"Let me think on that a little more."

"Wouldn't it be best if I could figure out a way to make her go away for good?"

"Of course, but that's not your job."

"I could give it the old college try while she's standing in front of me."

"And potentially expose yourself to something worse."

"What's worse than a psychotic little girl ghost trying to make my friends kill me?"

"A psychotic little girl ghost whispering in your ear to make you kill your family and friends."

"Jeez, Aunt Zoe." I stopped pacing and shivered. "That's really creepy. I'm probably going to have nightmares about that now." I was serious about that. My mind seemed to be collecting new nightmare fodder left and right.

"You're the one who asked."

I pointed at her. "Remind me *not* to have you tuck me in and tell me bedtime stories anytime soon."

She chuckled but then sobered quickly. "Truth be told, Violet, I don't know if you confronting Wilda is a good idea, let alone safe. Opening doors that are usually closed can lead to unwanted visitors coming through."

"I can't let her do to Cornelius what she did to her brother."

"I understand, but you need to make sure this is a charge you want to lead."

"As opposed to what?"

"Letting Doc try his hand at it."

"Wouldn't that put him at risk for Wilda to possess him?"

"Possibly."

"And he's more susceptible to ghosts than I am." We'd proven that several times during visits to Prudence and others. How strong was Wilda if she set her sights on Doc?

I returned to pacing the floor, unable to hold still.

"You'd know that better than me."

"I need to put a stop to that little bitch's reign of terror."

Aunt Zoe frowned at me. "There's something else."

Her tone alone gave me pause. "What?"

"Isn't Cornelius's suite where you saw Kyrkozz?"

I stopped my memory from replaying that ghastly scene before the film could get rolling. "Yes."

"I thought so."

"Why do you have that worried look in your eyes?"

"There's a possibility another unwanted guest could appear there again."

"Such as Kyrkozz," I whispered.

"Or worse."

What could be worse than an orange-eyed, black pustule-covered demon who liked to make an entrance via breaking out through my ex-boyfriend's skull?

"True," I rubbed my clammy palms together. "But at least this unwanted guest might be one I could actually kill."

"Sure." Her eyes darkened, a cloud passing behind them. "Unless it kills you first."

* * *

Unless it kills you first.

With those words echoing through my head, I returned to work and tried to focus on the exhilarating world of real estate. When that didn't keep me from chewing my knuckles about Wilda and Wanda, I claimed I had an appointment to meet a potential client up in Lead and escaped to my SUV.

Doc was not going to be thrilled about another séance in Cornelius's hotel suite. The last time we'd tried it, Doc had been bombarded with thirteen ghosts wanting to take whatever he could offer, which wasn't more than a brief chance at inhabiting a living body once more.

He was going to be doubly unthrilled to hear it was with Wilda that we needed to mix and mingle. She had "passed through" him one time before, knocking the wind out of him. I doubted he'd enjoy another visit with the freaky child who'd poisoned her father and possessed her brother to the point of insanity.

But I couldn't do this without his help. I wouldn't want to do it without him, either. The two times I'd reached out into the darkness when Doc wasn't there had resulted in what Aunt Zoe had warned about—opening the door for unwanted, terrifying guests. Doc had ways of playing bouncer at these so-called doors, controlling who went where during séances, using abilities that boggled my mind.

Me? I just tried to kill what needed to be killed and hoped I lived through it.

Since I was out and about, I decided to run over to Central City and pay a visit to Jeff Wymonds's house, one of my listings. He and I had an open door policy, which meant that anytime I wanted to stop by his place, I was welcome inside even when he wasn't there.

Jeff also had let me know once upon a time that if I wanted to drop by while he was there and play a little hokey-pokey in his bedroom, possibly filling my oven with one of his baby buns, all the better. Although last I'd heard he had a girlfriend and was practicing his baby bun baking in her oven, so I was probably off the hook for impregnation by the friendly but testosterone-flooded bozo.

Wymonds's truck wasn't in the drive. That didn't surprise me since it was the middle of the day on a Monday. He should be at work for a few more hours, which was why I wanted to drop in now. With worries about Wilda weighing on my brain, I wasn't in the mood to listen to Jeff's R-rated comments about his experiences with his new girlfriend's pierced tongue.

Since he wasn't home, I didn't bother ringing the doorbell. Instead, I opened the lock box and let myself inside. The whole time I kept thinking about how Cornelius had pleaded with me before I'd left his suite to help him get rid of Wilda. It was so out of character for him to beg, and that's what really spurred me to bring in the cavalry.

I needed to get a hold of Doc and see if he was coming to supper tonight. If so, we could step outside again and talk about Cornelius's ghost problem and what Doc thought could be done to help get rid of the little brat.

As I scooped up four Realtors' cards from the bowl I'd left on the dining room table, I realized I wasn't alone.

Someone was breathing in the kitchen.

And moaning.

My heart shot off the starting line at a full-on sprint.

Slowly I turned around to face whatever was waiting for me in the kitchen.

The sight of Jeff's thong-flossed butt cheeks at the counter made me recoil in surprise. My gaze lifted to the bare-chested, tattoo-dotted woman on the counter in front of him with her head tipped back and her nipple rings bouncing while Jeff worked hard at filling her baby oven.

"Oh my God!" I wheezed, dropping the business cards.

"What the hell!?" Jeff looked over his shoulder at me without breaking his stride. His angry brow smoothed at the sight of me standing there with my jaw on the dining room floor. "Oh, it's you, Violet Parker."

I covered my eyes, but my hand was too late. I'd seen too much to ever return to the happy land of Swiss mountains and twirling nuns.

"I'm almost to the end zone here," Jeff reported in from the playing field. "I'm driving in for a touchdown any second now."

His girlfriend cheered, "Go, Big Daddy, go!"

Dear Lord, it was football sex.

That was it. My poor brain split in half, both sides flopping around and gasping like dying fish. There was no way on earth that I was sticking around for the post-game show.

With the peanut butter sandwich I'd eaten back in Aunt Zoe's sex-free kitchen threatening to come blasting up and out through my pie-hole, I raced out the door. I didn't stop until my SUV was parked several miles away at the Piggly Wiggly in Lead.

Why, dammit?

Why did they have to pick today to have a nooner?

Why had there been no cars in the stupid drive?

Why did I have to see the father of my daughter's best friend with his pants around his ankles?

And why was Jeff wearing what looked like a woman's lacy red thong?

I had a gut-rollicking feeling that the sight of those bouncing nipple rings on his girlfriend's tattooed chest was going to stick with me until death did us part.

Hey, there was an upside to being murdered after all. I wouldn't have to spend the rest of my life having that scene replayed in my brain every time I saw Jeff Wymonds.

Sighing, I rested my head on the steering wheel.

How was I going to do walk-throughs of that house after today? I could hear the play-by-play that would go on in my head every time …

To your right is the kitchen. Notice the beautiful maple cupboards and tile countertops on which the previous owner had football-themed sex with his girlfriend while she wore the gold nipple rings he bought for her back in October.

I banged my forehead on the wheel, wishing I could remove the sordid sounds and images from my memory.

I'd learned a lesson today. No more open door policies with my clients. If I ever walked in on old man Harvey having sex, I'd undoubtedly turn into a pillar of salt.

My cell phone rang.

I looked down and saw the name *Jeff Wymonds* on the screen.

"Oh, hell no." I sent it to voicemail and went inside the grocery store to wash my eyeballs in the bathroom sink.

When I came back outside, Deadwood's Fire Captain—otherwise known as Aunt Zoe's old flame—was leaning against my driver's side door.

"Hey, Sparky," Reid Martin's dark blue eyes twinkled, his lips smiling along with his salt-and-pepper mustache.

Reid looked like a mid-fifties version of Sam Elliott, deep voice and all. He'd broken Aunt Zoe's heart years ago and it had taken her a long time to glue it all together again and move on with her life. But now Reid was back, willing to face off with her shotgun if it meant having a second chance at winning her love. He swore he wouldn't run from commitment and wanted the opportunity to prove it, but Aunt Zoe had built an impressive fence around her mended heart. It was going to take a lot of climbing for Reid to get inside. Time would tell if he had the stamina to make it over the top and back down the other side, but he seemed pretty damned determined these days.

"Good to see you, Reid." And I meant that, especially since he had his pants on and no lacy thong showing. I looked around the lot, seeing his red dually fire department pickup sitting a few rows over. "You shopping for food for the rest of the crew or just grabbing a late lunch?"

"Lunch. I saw your vehicle when I came out." He glanced around and then stepped closer, lowering his voice. "I need to talk to you. Do you have a few minutes?"

"Sure." I took a drink from the bottle of water I'd bought to help wash away the bad taste of catching Jeff in mid-sex. "What's going on?"

"I need to talk to Zo."

"She's out in her glass workshop today. She'll probably be there most of the night, too."

"Did she have a big order come in?"

"Yeah. The owner of that fancy gallery over in Jackson Hole is opening three more in some upscale resort towns in the Colorado Rockies. He needs her glass pieces by the first of December before the ski season really kicks off."

His eyes narrowed. "Is that the same guy she went to Denver with last month?"

I grimaced. "Yes."

And the same guy whose place she'd stayed at for a night during that trip, but Aunt Zoe had insisted each time I'd prodded for details that their friendship was purely platonic. It seemed the gallery owner was recently divorced, and Reid had taught her all about getting burned by newly divorced men. She wasn't going to make that same mistake twice, even if the gallery owner looked a bit like George Clooney.

Reid kicked at a stone. "I'm glad she's keeping busy." He didn't sound very glad at the moment, but I was relatively certain it had to do with who was buying her pieces, not the work itself. "Is she taking the shipment over to Jackson Hole?"

"Seems like she said he'd be stopping by at the end of the month with a trailer to pick it all up."

I couldn't tell by his guarded expression whether that was good news or not. "How about you invite me over for supper tonight?"

I snorted. "Now you're trying to get me shot, too."

A grin warmed his cheeks. "You can help me wrestle the shotgun from her."

"No way, I have to sleep under the same roof with her." I swirled the water in my bottle. "Why do you need me there?"

"Because when you're with us, she actually talks to me. When you're not around, she won't even let me in the door."

How ironic. Now I was channeling communication for the living as well as the dead.

I wanted to help Reid, but … I blew out a breath. "You know I don't love being a third party to your private conversations, right?"

He nodded once.

"Is this going to be one of those intimate deals where I stand there blushing and wishing the floor would swallow me up?" I asked.

"No."

"Good." I took another swig of water.

"At least not at first, but I'm always hoping for a change in the tide."

"Fair enough." I capped the bottle. "Hey, Reid, how about you come over for supper tonight? I was thinking of making pizza—the takeout kind. Six o'clock work for you?"

His moustache twitched with mirth. "Sounds great, Sparky. Why don't you let me bring the pizza? Pepperoni okay?"

"My kids like black olives, too."

He clapped me on the shoulder. "Thanks. I owe you one."

"Yes, you do, because I'm going to get a major ass chewing after you leave, so you better make your payback a good one."

He left me standing there wondering what was so dang important that he was willing to risk getting shot by Aunt Zoe.

With a shrug I climbed into my SUV and keyed it to life. I'd find out soon enough.

My phone rang. The area code wasn't familiar. A new client?

I answered. "Violet Parker speaking."

"We want what belongs to us," a voice whispered, then the line went dead.

Chapter Seven

It took a few seconds for the flood of fear to wash over me. During those seconds, I sat in my SUV staring blindly out the windshield. The caller's whispery voice played over and over in my head.

We want what belongs to us.

We want what belongs to us.

We want what belongs to us.

Then the flood rolled in and I realized that I was panting.

"Get a grip, Violet," I told myself aloud. "You've handled a hell of a lot worse."

True, but that initial gut-wrenching bombshell was a real breath stealer.

I looked down at my phone, contemplating my options. Ignoring my yellow-belly's winning vote to run home and hide under the bed, I pulled up Doc's number. He'd know what I should do. I hoped he had cell service wherever he was working down in Hill City.

I waited through six rings and then received the message that his voicemail was full.

Tossing the phone on the dash in disgust, I pounded both fists on the steering wheel. "Damn you, Tiffany Sugarbell!" The nut-ball kept filling up Doc's voicemail box with who knew what neurotic, broken-hearted messages.

"Okay, breathe," my calmer, left brain spoke up. When my tunnel vision cleared, I grabbed my phone and selected another number.

Cooper took his sweet-ass time answering. "This better be worth interrupting a meeting with the Chief, Parker."

"Am I on speaker phone again?"

"No."

"Good. Meet me at Bighorn Billy's ASAP."

"What?"

"A.S.A.P.," I spelled it out slowly. "That means As Soon—"

"I know what that fucking means, Parker."

"Good. I'll see you there shortly."

"No, you won't. If you need to talk to me, get your ass down here to the station."

"I'm not going near the police station unless I'm dragged there kicking and screaming."

"You really need to get over this police phobia of yours."

"It's your freaking fault I have it, Coop."

Well, maybe only partly his fault. Besides the fact that the sight of a policeman now gave me hives—for which I blamed Cooper, someone at his station was batting for the bad guys' team. Someone who liked to stick threatening notes in my purse.

"That's Detective Cooper to you."

"You really need to get over my calling you *Coop* like everyone else does."

He growled, low and menacing. "What do you need from me, Violet?"

I growled back, not quite as low but more exasperated than threatening. "It's frustrating when someone calls you and bosses you around, isn't it, Detective?" I emphasized every syllable in his title.

"Parker!"

Suddenly, I remembered that I hadn't called Cooper just to fight with him. I had bigger problems than a snarly detective.

"If you want to know more about Wanda's killer," I said in a level, calmer tone, "meet me alone in the parking lot of Bighorn Billy's in ten minutes."

"Or what?" he challenged.

I was done with our fun and games and hung up on him.

Eight minutes later I was sitting in the parking lot of Bighorn Billy's Diner with my doors locked and windows rolled up tight. The diner only had a few other customers this afternoon, which didn't surprise me since lunch had come and gone. Per Mona, the restaurant had shifted into its wintertime schedule recently. According to the sign posted on its front door, it was about to close for the day.

Late fall through early spring meant slower evenings in the Black Hills. The skiers and snowmobilers breathed life into the economy each winter, but they weren't as long-winded as the summer tourists who enjoyed tooling around on cool evenings after hot sunny days.

A Deadwood police Durango with the stagecoach and horses emblem on the side skidded into the parking lot, locking up its brakes next to my SUV. When the cloud of dust passed, Cooper glared at me through his window, waving for me to come to him.

I shook my head, pointing at him and then my passenger seat. For one thing, I didn't trust that someone hadn't bugged his police vehicle. For another, I was determined to win this pissing match with him.

He slammed his door so hard the Durango rocked slightly. With a jerk and a grumble and another slam he was sitting next to me. His glare could've stripped the paint off a Boeing 747.

"This had better be fucking good, Parker. It wasn't easy getting out of that meeting without answering a shitload of questions about where I was going and why I had to leave all of a sudden."

"What did you tell them?"

"That's none of your goddamned business." A muscle pulsed in his jaw.

Okay, point taken, he was annoyed with me. Well, so what. I was scared, and according to Doc, Cooper wanted to help me keep the boogeyman away. If we were going to work together going forward, one of us needed to bend a little now and then and not go ape-shit all over the other's innocent ass.

Being the bigger person, I started again. "Thank you for coming on a moment's notice, Detective Cooper. How are your ribs these days? Still sore?"

His eyes narrowed a fraction further in distrust. "My ribs are just fine. What do you have for me about Wanda's killer?"

I held out my cell phone for him to take.

He lowered his gaze to it, his expression wary. "What's this?"

"It's a cell phone." At his exasperated lip curl, I added. "You need to look at the recent calls list."

He snatched the phone from my hand and tapped the screen, then looked up at me. "What about it?"

"The third down on the list is a call that came in from Wanda's killer."

His forehead crinkled up. "How do you know?"

"Because when I answered, she whispered, 'We want what belongs to us,' and then hung up on me."

He did a double take. "You sure it was a she?"

"Mostly."

He focused on the screen again. "Fourteen minutes ago," he said under his breath, then rubbed his forehead crinkles. "You called Nyce before me?"

"Yeah."

"Did he tell you to call me?"

"No. I got his voicemail."

"Did you leave him a message about the phone call?"

I shook my head. "Tiffany Sugarbell keeps filling up his voicemail box."

That earned me a raised eyebrow. "Obsessed much?"

"Her or me?" Doc had a way of turning women into rabid stalkers.

"True." He blew out a breath, leaning back in the seat. "You got a pen and paper?"

I dug in my purse and then handed him both. He scribbled the number and time of call.

"How is it you didn't try calling the number back?"

"Contrary to what you may think, Cooper, I do not always carry balls of steel around in my purse. Today I happened to have left my balls at home tucked away in my underwear drawer."

That earned me a little less of a frown from him. Thankfully he didn't actually smile or I probably would have keeled over from the shock of it.

"Do me a favor, Parker."

I waited without agreeing to his favor request.

"Keep this to yourself until tonight."

"What's tonight?"

"I'll stop by after I check into it and let you know what I find out."

I nodded. "Supper is at six. Reid's bringing pizza with pepperoni and black olives."

"Reid Martin is coming over?" At my nod, he added, "Is your aunt going to be there, too?"

I nodded again.

"You better hide her shotgun or I'll have to bring some of my police pals to the crime scene with me."

Aunt Zoe's feelings about Reid sneaking 'round her back door were no secret to anyone in Deadwood who knew both of them. "We're going to surprise her with Reid tonight."

"You're playing with explosives there."

"It was his idea."

"Not one of his brightest." He handed back my phone and pushed open his door. "Remember, keep this under your hat until I get back with you tonight."

"I heard you the first time. Would you like me to pinkie swear with you?"

"Not even a single word to Nyce."

"He's in Hill City all day probably out of cell range with a full voicemail box."

"Knowing how crazy you and his ex are, that's probably on purpose."

I flipped him off.

One side of his mouth bowed upward for a blink, then he stared at me and his lips thinned again. He held up the paper with the phone number on it. "This isn't good, Parker."

"I know."

"I could arrange for a unit to sit outside your house 24/7 until we get to the bottom of Wanda's murder."

"No way. Knowing Hawke, he'd have me watched for a whole different reason."

"What do you have to hide?"

"That's *not* police business."

"That's what I'm afraid of, Parker. I'll see you tonight." He started to shut the door but then paused. "Who else will be at your aunt's place tonight?"

Not Natalie. "Just Reid and you, maybe Doc if he gets home early enough."

"Got it. Keep your big mouth closed until I see you again." He shut the door instead of slamming it this time.

A minute later I was still sitting there, speculating how much shit I was in now when my phone rang.

Warily, I looked down at the screen.

Tiffany Sugarbell was calling again.

"You've gotta be fucking kidding me!" I sent her to voicemail, put my phone on airplane mode, and shut it in my glovebox.

* * *

The rest of the day dragged on and on and on.

Not telling anyone about the phone call I'd received meant I had to sit on all of the theories that kept billowing in my mind about who could be behind the notes and call. By the time five o'clock hit, my head had filled up like a hot air balloon, my feet barely touching the ground as I floated across the parking lot in a semi-daze.

At home, I headed straight up to my bedroom. I changed out of my corduroy skirt and blouse into a pair of black velvet leggings and a soft fuzzy sweater, seeking warmth and comfort to offset a night that might be filled with Aunt Zoe's cold shoulder and Cooper's sandpapery tongue. Needing to keep a clear head, I stuck with hot tea in place of mind-numbing tequila and rounded up my kids to help pick up stray socks and gloves and toys before company arrived.

Aunt Zoe stayed out in her workshop until ten minutes before the magic hour arrived. Magic as in when Reid was supposed to appear at the door out of the clear blue with a pizza in hand. She was washing her hands in the kitchen sink when the doorbell rang.

"That's probably the pizza I ordered," I said and headed for the door. How much yelling was there going to be when she found out I'd invited Reid over? I wiped my damp palms on my pants before reaching for the door handle.

I was wrong about who was behind Door Number One.

"You're early," I told Cooper through the screen.

He frowned at me. "Is that a crime?"

"Probably in your book."

We stared each other down, taking turns seeing who could squint the longest.

"Are you going to let me in the damned house or not, Parker?"

I stood back, waving him inside. As I shut the door behind him, I whispered, "Don't say anything about Reid."

He slipped out of his coat and hung it on a peg. "You haven't told her yet?"

I shook my head.

"Why not?"

"Because I'm a big chicken when it comes to Aunt Zoe."

Leading the way into the kitchen, I offered him a glass of lemonade.

Aunt Zoe's mouth opened in surprise at the sight of Cooper. "Hey, Coop," she glanced around his shoulder. "Your uncle change his mind about coming over tonight?"

"No," I answered for him. "Harvey has a hot date. I invited the detective over for pizza."

"*You* invited him?"

"Yep."

"Hmmm." She grabbed some paper plates from the pantry.

"Parker and I need to talk about something that happened today," said Cooper.

Aunt Zoe's eyes widened. "Something involving the law?"

"Sort of," I said, giving Cooper a can-I-tell-her-or-not look.

"Violet Lynn," she started, only to be interrupted by the doorbell.

Cooper and I exchanged pinched brows. "I'll get that," I said, racing out of the room. Reid was right on time, which was good. Unfortunately, Cooper's early arrival had already set Aunt Zoe on edge. I glanced over my shoulder before opening the door, checking to see if she was watching from the archway into the kitchen, but it was empty.

I was wrong about who was behind Door Number Two.

"Doc!" Smiling in relief, I opened the screen and practically dragged him inside. My life raft in a stormy sea was here. I didn't even give him a chance to take off his coat before wrapping my arms around his torso and tree hugging him.

"Damn, you're better to come home to than a lonely puppy." His dark eyes searched mine when I loosened my hold so he could step back and shuck his coat. "Why is there a Deadwood Police vehicle parked at your aunt's curb?"

"Cooper's here."

He hung his coat next to Cooper's. "I figured it was him."

"I invited him for supper."

That gave him pause. "Who are you and what have you done with Violet Parker?"

To be honest, I hadn't felt like myself since ... I had to search back through the day's events. Wow. Had the whole Cornelius and Wilda episode been only this morning? That seemed like days ago.

Rather than bombard Doc with my cringe-filled day, I caught his hand and laced my fingers through his. "I'm glad you're here. How was Hill City?"

He lifted our entwined hands and kissed the back of mine, his lips soft and warm. "Good try, Boots. Now tell me what's going on."

The doorbell rang.

I grimaced. "Here we go."

I was right about who was behind Door Number Three.

Doc held the screen open for Reid while I grabbed the two pizza boxes from him so he could take off his coat and stay awhile—at least until Aunt Zoe chased him away with her shotgun.

"Does she know?" Reid said quietly to me.

"No." In reply to Doc's raised brows, I patted his chest. "I'll explain after we eat."

With a wave for both to follow me, I led them into the lion's den. Doc brought up the rear, followed by two bouncing and cheering pizza lovers. Sheesh, my kids could at least act a little sad that I wasn't cooking their supper tonight.

"Look who's delivering pizza now on the side," I joked with a big, dopey smile as I stepped into the kitchen.

Aunt Zoe was in the midst of carrying silverware to the table when her gaze hit Reid. She faltered. I waited with clenched teeth for the fireworks to start booming.

Instead, her voice was oddly calm when she eyeballed me and asked, "Did somebody call in a fire?"

Cooper snorted. "I doubt Martin would do you much good if somebody had." He leaned his hip against the oven door, watching the show with a hint of a grin. "He can't even put out old flames."

Aunt Zoe's focus shifted to Reid. "Good thing I can."

"Kiss my ass, Coop." Reid took the pizza boxes from me and set them on the table. "Hey, Zo." His stare traveled down over her pink button-down shirt and torn blue jeans like she was wearing a little black dress and sexy heels. "I hear you have a big order to fill by the end of the month."

When she looked my way again, I got busy serving up pizza to the kids, making sure they had plenty of napkins.

"Did Violet and you plan this little get together to talk about my glass business," she asked, "or is there some other reason you've stopped by?"

"Some other reason." Reid pulled out a chair for her to sit. "But first, let's eat."

Cooper took the seat on the other side of Reid, next to Doc. I used the kids as a buffer between Aunt Zoe and me, dodging her stink-eye as we ate. Doc kept shooting me questioning glances when the conversation turned toward mundane topics like school and a new casino coming to town. I nudged my chin toward the kids, shaking my head.

When Layne and Addy's bellies were full, I had them thank Reid for saving them from another one of my kitchen concoctions, and then I excused them from the table to go up to their rooms and get busy on their homework.

As soon as the pounding of their footfalls overhead indicated they were safely out of earshot, I turned to Cooper. "Well?"

He finished off his crust and swallowed. "Well, what?"

"Did you check on the number?"

"Of course."

"And?" When he looked pointedly at Doc and Aunt Zoe, and then Reid, I picked up my fork. "I swear, Cooper, after the shitty day I've had, if you give me that freaking 'police business only' baloney, I'm going to plant this in your forehead."

"That would be aggravated assault, Parker."

"What are you two talking about?" Aunt Zoe reached across the table and took my fork from me.

"Are you going to tell them, Detective, or am I?"

Cooper pulled his napkin from his lap and set it on the table. "Parker got a call today on her cell. The caller whispered the same words that are on the notes Wanda received."

"Then the line went dead," I added.

"After Parker told me about this," Cooper stood, "I asked her to keep quiet about the call until tonight, giving me time to look into it."

Doc's palm warmed my thigh. "You okay?" he asked quietly.

I shook my head. "It was a banner day all around."

He kissed my temple, starting to make it all better.

"So that explains why you invited Coop to supper," Aunt Zoe said to me, nodding as the pieces fell into place. "But not Reid," she added, which earned her a smirk from her old flame.

"No amount of arm twisting could get Parker to come to my office, so I had to come to her."

"I don't trust the police," I challenged Cooper, but he shrugged me off. "There's somebody working with you who is part of the 'We' in those notes."

"What are these notes you keep mentioning?" Reid asked.

Aunt Zoe filled him in on Wanda's death and the notes she and I had both received, while Cooper finished off his lemonade over at the sink.

"What did you find out about the phone number?" Doc asked Cooper when she'd finished.

"I tried calling it several times and kept getting a message saying the person I was trying to reach was not available." He leaned against the counter, crossing his arms over his chest. "It was a burner."

"What's a burner?" Aunt Zoe asked.

"A pre-paid cell phone," Doc answered. "Whenever you're done with it, you can throw it away."

"They're untraceable because there is no name or information attached to them," Cooper added. "Once they're ditched, there's not much chance of finding out who was using it."

Throughout the long, long afternoon, I'd held onto a single flame of hope—that Cooper would be able to find whoever had called me and drag them to the station for questioning. That flame blew out.

"And this phone was ditched." I wasn't asking, because I knew clear down in my gut where this was heading.

"Most likely they destroyed it," Cooper confirmed.

"Which means we aren't any closer to Wanda's killer than before." I shoved my empty plate away, my fists clenching at the helpless feeling of being prey with no way of telling from which direction the hunter would shoot next.

Doc squeezed my shoulder. "Did Wanda receive phone calls as well as notes?" he asked Cooper.

I looked up at the detective, wondering if he'd share what was surely police information this time or not.

"There were several untraceable calls from different phone numbers over a three-week period on her last phone bill," he told Doc with a frown.

"Fuck," Doc said under his breath.

I leaned forward, hiding my face in my hands.

"You should have someone keeping an eye on Sparky 24/7," Reid said. "And her family, too."

I peeked out between my fingers. "I don't need any cops monitoring me." At Aunt Zoe's exasperated sigh, I added, "We don't know who's safe and who's crooked at this point."

"Besides Cooper," she said.

I studied the detective for a few seconds, wondering …

"Parker, don't even look at me like that. Trust me, I wouldn't be messed up in this shit with you if I had a choice."

"Violet," Aunt Zoe started, her gaze lowering to the necklace visible at my neckline. It was a charm-like piece she'd given me to wear months ago as a form of protection, and I hadn't taken it off since. "If we're dealing with what I think we are here, I don't know if I can protect you. Not with charms or anything else."

She was referring to the various protective wards, mirrors, and other tricks of her trade that she had set up around the house to safeguard the kids and me from the "others" who might come for us. Regular old humans were a wild card in our business.

"She needs a bodyguard," Reid said to Aunt Zoe.

"The one I have is plenty."

"You mean Uncle Willis and his shotgun?" Cooper smirked. "He'll end up shooting the mailman again."

I lowered my hands. Harvey had shot the mailman before? Wasn't that a federal offense?

"I can sleep on the couch as long as you'd like," Doc offered, looking from Aunt Zoe to me.

This was not how I'd hoped to make the bridge from us periodically taking turns spending nights together, to his being with me and my kids on a more permanent basis. I'd rather that he wanted to shack up with us because he couldn't live without me anymore instead of just making sure I'd keep breathing.

"I can help keep an eye on the place," Reid's gaze dared Aunt Zoe to buck. "And Sparky's kids, too."

Lowering her eyes to where her hands were fidgeting with her fork, Aunt Zoe nodded once, accepting his help.

Cooper walked over and leaned on the back of his chair, his steely eyes on me. "I'm going to have to let Detective Hawke know about the phone call. Otherwise, I'm withholding key information in this case, and I could catch a ration of shit if something more comes of this."

"You mean *when* something more comes of this." I sat up straight, a rush of anger suddenly stiffening my spine. I'd be damned if I was going to let a bunch of prank calling, sons-a-bitches turn me into a scared mouse. If they wanted what they believed belonged to them, they needed to come and get it, damn it. Enough of these childish games.

The detective's squint returned as he measured me up. "We still aren't one hundred percent sure that the notes are tied to the murderer, Parker."

"All of us sitting here at this table have little doubt that I'm next on the hit list, Detective. There's no need to sugar coat the truth. Besides, you and I both know it's not my first rodeo."

"What are you talking about?" Reid asked. "Do you mean what you went through that night up at the Carhart house?"

Reid didn't know about my other job as an executioner. He knew that Zoe dabbled in the paranormal, but he hadn't been privy to what Doc and I had experienced via séances and more, nor anything close to what Cooper had experienced with us earlier this month.

"Something like that," Cooper told Reid.

"So, what's the plan?" Doc asked.

"For starters," the detective pointed at me, "you keep her under control." When I started to object, he interrupted, "Come on, Parker, do you think I met you yesterday? I see that look in your eyes. You're mad now, and you're going to fight back, which is the worst idea there is at the moment. You need to let me do my job."

"But I—"

"No buts, damn it. I can't put my energy into finding the killer if I'm too busy chasing you around and cleaning up your messes."

I bristled, rising out of my chair, but Doc's grip on my arm held me in check. He shook his head slightly, which I grudgingly heeded and sat back down.

"You'll let us know tomorrow how this goes over at the station?" Doc asked Cooper.

"I'll be in touch," he frowned at me, "undoubtedly more than Parker would like."

Done barking his orders at us, Detective Cooper thanked Reid for the pizza and the rest of us for the company. He said his goodbyes and let himself out.

"Damn," Reid said when the ripples smoothed out after Cooper's wake. "You Parker girls sure know how to get a guy all steamed up."

Doc chuckled, pushing out of his chair, collecting forks and paper plates. "They're real pros."

"Thanks," Aunt Zoe said as she handed Doc her plate, and then turned to Reid. "What are you doing here tonight, Reid?"

The sparkle in Reid's eyes dimmed. "It's about the Sugarloaf Building."

My ears perked up. This was the second time I'd heard Reid mention that place.

Months ago, my ghostly former boss, Jane, had asked me to gather historical information for her on the Sugarloaf Building. That was back before she'd ended up dead at the bottom of the Open Cut in Lead. While I'd done as she'd asked, I really hadn't paid attention to what I'd found, just handed over the copies I'd made. I'd been a little busy at the time trying to figure out who was kidnapping little blonde girls around Deadwood, if memory served me right.

"I thought I warned you to stay out of there," Aunt Zoe said.

"You did, but it was too late by that point."

She shoved her chair back from the table. "Damn it, Reid. You're dabbling with something that could permanently scar you inside and out. Or worse."

"Ah ha!" He grinned. "I knew that you still cared about me."

She rolled her eyes. "Just because I don't want you back in my bed doesn't mean that I want you dead."

"What's wrong with the Sugarloaf Building?" I asked, eager to focus on something besides my own troubles for a while. "Let me guess—it's haunted." I spoke in jest, being that every other building and house in Deadwood and Lead were rumored to have ghosts.

She stood and moved to the sink, pouring herself a glass of water from the faucet, staring out the window into the darkness beyond. "It's not the building so much as the man who had it built back in the late 1800s."

Doc returned to the table. "I haven't read much about the Sugarloaf Building," he told me, settling back into the chair next to mine.

That was surprising having perused the books in Doc's bookcases, as well as knowing that the South Dakota history room at the library was his home away from home.

"His last name was Cukorsüveg, which from what I understand translates into Sugarloaf. If I remember the story correctly, it was believed that he came to Lead with the wave of Central European miners in the early 1890s. He was Hungarian and claimed to be a ... what's the word?" She looked up at the ceiling. "*Táltos*, which is another name for a wise man." Her eyes returned to the window and the darkness. "Like a shaman. But he was also a doctor of general medicine, except the Slavs avoided going to him, which should have been the first clue about good old Dr. Ottó Sugarloaf being not-so-good."

She turned around and focused on Reid, leaning back against the sink as she sipped from her glass of water. "Ottó had a problem, according to rumors among the Slavs. Back in Hungary, he'd removed a curse from a young girl, but things hadn't gone so smoothly and it turned out it wasn't really a curse, more of a malicious, otherworldly creature that had latched onto the girl. Ottó hadn't protected himself properly during the removal procedure and ended up as the new host. Within a short time, the creature had caused enough problems for Ottó that he was driven from his home country and hitched a ride with the miners over here to Lead. Now Ottó is gone, but his building is still here, and so is the *lidérc* he left behind."

"The *lidérc* is the creature?" Reid asked.

She nodded.

"That's the thing that I saw?"

She nodded again. "That's the thing that saw you, too, unfortunately."

They stared at each other in silence for several ticks from Aunt Zoe's Betty Boop clock on the wall.

"I have to go back inside that building," he said, rubbing his jaw. "Is this watchband going to keep that thing from attaching to me like it did good old Ottó?"

"I don't know. I'm not real fluent on my Hungarian Middle World mythology. I pieced together what I know about the Sugarloaf Building through some old newspaper articles I found on it years ago."

"Why was it in the newspaper?" Doc asked.

"That building has made headlines off and on over the years. Every time a new owner comes along, they try to open up a business in it or convert it to a boarding house or apartments. That's when things go awry."

The tone in her voice made the word "awry" sound spooky, giving me chills. "What kind of things?"

"Things that nine times out of ten leave someone dead."

Those weren't good odds.

"But not always?" Reid pressed.

She shook her head slowly, honing in on him. "No, not always. If what's in the Sugarloaf Building doesn't kill you, though, it will drive you insane."

Chapter Eight

Several hours later, Reid was gone and Aunt Zoe had returned to her shop to work on her glass order. Although judging from some of the glares I'd received from her while Reid hung around after supper, I suspected she'd left partly to escape her meddling niece, too.

While I herded the kids to bed, Doc drove home to grab clothes and his shaving kit since Aunt Zoe and I were keen on his sharing quarters with us another night. As soon as he returned, I dragged him into the laundry room and closed the door behind us.

Huh. I hadn't remembered the laundry room being so narrow. Then again, his six-foot-plus, wide-shouldered frame wasn't usually in the room with me. I kicked aside a basketful of dirty clothes and pushed back several shirts waiting to be ironed that hung on the rack next to the door.

"Is this where I'm sleeping tonight?" he joked.

He'd changed into jeans and a T-shirt when he'd gone home. I tried not to let the urge to ogle him distract me. "I need to talk to you about something."

His dark brown eyes glittering with devilry, he leaned back against the washer. "Is this your secret clubhouse?"

"Maybe, wise guy. Or maybe it's the only room in the house that I'm pretty sure is safe from nine-year-old eavesdropping ears."

"Ah, so the bit about the anonymous phone call wasn't the real juicy stuff?"

"Only part of it."

"Let me have it."

"Wilda is haunting Cornelius."

Doc's grin slipped a few notches. "Haunting how?"

"I went to see him this morning to confirm a date for filming Paranormal Realty later this week. He was a mess, wearing a stained robe and boxer shorts, his face sallow with dark circles under his eyes. His suite was a sty too. He said Wilda won't leave him alone and keeps trying to convince him to hurt others. He even went so far as to beg me to help him get rid of her."

"Beg?"

"Yeah. He was nothing like his usual odd duck self."

Doc crossed his arms over his chest. "Hurt who? You?"

"Starting with me, yes." I wrung the hem of my sweater, my palms damp at the idea of dealing with Wolfgang's evil sister. "She wants him to kill me. I guess she's still miffed because her brother didn't finish the job."

He blew out a breath, rubbing his forehead. "You're becoming quite popular it seems."

"Wilda scares me, Doc."

"Because she's obsessed with you?"

Obsessed was a more fitting term for nutty ex-girlfriends who filled up voicemail boxes. This was a step further, taking things beyond the grave. "No, because I've witnessed up close and personal what she can do to a mere mortal. She drove her brother to madness."

"You think Cornelius will follow in those footsteps?"

I shrugged, and then changed my mind and nodded.

"I talked to Aunt Zoe about this at lunch. She isn't sure that I can do anything about Wilda since she's only a ghost."

"You still think you're a dud?"

"I don't know what the hell I am." I grabbed a plastic hanger from the rack and started fiddling with it, keeping my hands busy. "Aunt Zoe is also concerned that if I try to help Cornelius, especially if I'm in his suite, I might open the door for unwanted visitors who can do more than just whisper in Cornelius's ear." I swallowed, my mouth suddenly dry. "Like Kyrkozz."

When Doc continued to stare at me without saying anything, I added, "She suggested I talk to you to see if anything can be done before Wilda pushes Cornelius over the edge."

He took his time answering, his focus lowering to the hanger in my hands. "That depends on what you want to accomplish."

"I can tell you what I don't want to accomplish."

He lifted his gaze back to mine, his brows lifted.

"I don't want Wilda to choose you next for her Let's Kill Violet campaign."

I was hoping he'd laugh off my worry. Instead he frowned. "There is that possibility."

"Has it ever happened to you before?"

"No, but I haven't met a ghost like Wilda before."

He'd said something similar about Prudence. What was it about the ghosts in the Black Hills that made them so damned special?

"I don't want Wilda to destroy Cornelius," I bent the hanger almost to the breaking point. "He's an eccentric man with his weird hats and paranormal fetishes, but he's a good egg overall."

"You're willing to face off with an entity that has the ability to direct its hatred into a human and corrupt their energy, in order to help someone who likes to have sleepovers with ghosts in jail cells?"

I held his stare. "Cornelius is my friend."

"Your friend."

I nodded.

He took the hanger from me and hung it back on the rack. Then he hooked his finger in the neckline of my sweater and pulled me closer. "I missed you today, Boots," he said when the tow line slackened. "How come you didn't call me when you got that creepy phone call?"

"I tried, but your voicemail was full."

His upper lip curled in what looked like disgust or frustration or both. "I cleared her messages as soon as I had cell service again."

"Did you listen to any?"

He shook his head.

I opened my mouth to tell him that Tiffany had also texted me this morning but hesitated. Knowing my big mouth, things would take an awkward turn right off the line and end in another one of my infamous crash and burns.

"What?" he asked, taking my hands in his and lacing our fingers together.

"I ... uh," I licked my lips. "Never mind."

"Tell me."

After the day I'd had, I wasn't in the right place mentally to go down that particular rabbit hole, so I hopped to a different one that was also awkward but much safer.

"I stopped over at Jeff Wymonds's house today to do a sweep of the place. You know, check for other Realtors' business cards and make sure the property was still show-ready. I didn't see his truck in the drive, so I let myself in without knocking." I made a face. "But someone was there."

"Who?"

"Jeff. I walked in on him and his girlfriend having sex."

"No!" Doc's jaw gaped.

"Yep. They were in his kitchen. She was on the counter while he ..." I made some hip thrusting gestures. "You get the picture."

"Not as clearly as you apparently did." His mouth twitched.

"She had lots of tattoos. Oh, and those nipple rings he showed off to us in Aunt Zoe's backyard."

His grin broke the surface. "You *saw* the nipple rings?"

I scowled in reply. "Jeff's pants were around his ankles and he had on this lacy red thong. I'm pretty sure it was something you'd find in the women's department."

Doc chuckled under his breath. "Oh, Boots, I'm so sorry." His chest shook with silent laughter.

"That's not all."

"It isn't?" he said, as if he couldn't believe there was more.

I wished that had been it. I wished I were the only one who knew I'd walked in and witnessed the scene.

"Jeff caught me watching them."

"How long were you standing there?"

"Only seconds, but I said something in surprise and he heard me."

Doc covered his mouth, trying to hold his amusement inside.

"He even said my name." I scratched absently at the back of my neck, feeling itchy to run again at the mere thought of what had happened. "Then he just kept going at it, telling me over his shoulder that he was almost in the end zone. Or was it that he was driving in for a touchdown?" I shuddered at the sordid memory.

He lowered his hand to ask. "What about his girlfriend?"

"What about her?"

"Did she say anything?"

I shook my head slowly, as if in a trance. A horrible, embarrassing, brain numbing trance. "She just cheered him on, nipple rings bouncing and bouncing and bouncing."

Both of Doc's hands now covered the bottom half of his face. His eyes were peeking over his fingertips, shining extra bright.

"It's not funny, Doc." Well, maybe for him since he wasn't standing in my boots. "How am I going to ever look Jeff in the face again?"

"You could …" he paused to laugh, "skip looking at his face and …" more laughter, "have him turn around and drop his pants again."

A volley of laughs escaped his mouth at my glare.

I punched him in the shoulder, which only spurred him to double over and really let the guffaws fly.

"I'm sorry … Violet." He swallowed a few times and tried to collect himself, but hiccups of laughter chirped out a few more times. "So, did you … wait around and cheer for him to make a touchdown?"

"No, Mr. Giggle-Pants, I did not. I raced out the door and drove up to the Piggly Wiggly, which is where I ran into Reid." I squeezed the bridge of my nose. "Jeff had called when I'd pulled into the parking lot, but I didn't answer it. I couldn't. It was all still too fresh and sticky."

"Damn." Doc wiped at the outside corners of his eyes. "You really had one hell of a day, didn't you, Tiger?"

At my nod, he grabbed my shoulders and turned me around, pulling me back toward him. His hands pushed aside my mass of curls and settled onto my shoulders, massaging out the day's knots. I closed my eyes and let my head hang down, groaning as he worked out one angst after another.

"Was there anything else?" he asked, the laughter gone now.

"You mean with Jeff?"

"No, in general."

The text from Tiffany moved back to the front of the line. It bounced a few times on the end of my tongue, prepping to dive off into the deep end. But I wasn't sure I was ready to hear his answer. If he had told Tiffany he loved her, how would that change things for us? Maybe it was better not to know the truth and let myself hope that when he'd said those three words to me that night in the haunted brothel, he was serious.

"That was it," I answered.

"Tell me something," he said while rubbing on a sore muscle bunched up under my shoulder blade.

I grunted in agreement.

"Are you really going to let Coop and Detective Hawke figure out who's sending those notes? Or are you going to start digging on your own?"

"I'll do whatever you want me to do, Doc."

He snorted in disbelief.

"I'm serious," I said. "If you're willing to help me with Cornelius and Wilda, I'll do as you say when it comes to Wanda."

"Okay." I felt his lips brush over the back of my neck and shivered.

There was a long moment of silence as he squeezed and rubbed, broken only by the sounds of my moans and groans. My body began to thrum, electricity building.

"Doc?"

"Yes?"

"Where are you sleeping tonight?"

"I thought we agreed I was staying here."

"No, I mean where are you sleeping in the house?"

"I figured on the couch, why?"

I turned in his arms. "Because I want you."

"Is the massage seducing you?"

"No, you are." I went up on my toes and kissed him. "I want you to make it all go away for a while. Wilda, Wanda, the phone call, Jeff." *And Tiffany's words.* "Take me somewhere else."

"But what about—"

I didn't let him finish, kissing away any "buts" until he was too focused on kissing me back to come up with more excuses. When we paused to catch our breaths, we were well on our way to steaming up the small window that looked out into the backyard. Thankfully the curtains were closed, because somewhere in the process of convincing him to have his wicked way with me tonight, my bra had slipped off and Doc's hands had taken its place.

"You want to stay in my room?"

He groaned deep in his chest, his body obviously in favor of a slumber party in my bed. "That's a bad idea."

"Yeah, but there are these to consider." I lifted my sweater to show him what I had to offer.

He sucked a breath in through his teeth, his eyes locked below my chin. "Your kids might wake up in the night."

I lowered my sweater. "How about if I didn't actually sleep in there with you?"

His gaze lifted to mine. "Am I reading between the lines correctly?"

My fingernails scratched down his shirt, heading further south. "We could lock the door and make it a quick hour of debauchery."

"You keep touching me like you are right now, Boots, and we won't even need to leave the laundry room."

"Really?" I pressed the heel of my palm into him. "Tell me more."

"How about I show you?"

I reached behind me and hit the lights, shrouding us in darkness. The faint glow of moonlight seeped through the curtains, shadowing his face.

"Okay, Doc." I breathed in the semidarkness. "Show me."

"Wait," he stopped my hand. "What about your aunt?"

"She's working out in her glass shop until late tonight." I unbuttoned his jeans. "You're out of excuses, big boy."

"Tease," he whispered and slid his hands inside the back of my velvet pants, his palms cupping me, hauling me against him. His lips came down on mine, hungry and fierce. The whirlwind of lust that came with his kiss made me dizzy. His heated touches made my whole body tremble in anticipation.

"Doc," I gasped at the ceiling when he rubbed me just right. "I ... I

…" I was trying to tell the man that I loved him, but the delicate stroke of his fingers blasted the words from my brain.

The laundry room door creaked open, the light from the kitchen spotlighting us. Doc grabbed a shirt hanging from the rack and shielded us from view, while my brain tried to yank on the brake handle and stop my body from finishing what Doc had gotten rolling.

"Hot damn!" Old man Harvey's voice cut through the fog of lust in my brain, sounding the alarms. "Looks like I caught me a fox in the henhouse."

"Willis, would you please close the door for a moment," Doc said, since my red face was currently hiding in his chest.

"How about I go see a man about a mule and come back when my prostate finishes its usual drippity-jig?"

The door closed. The room was dark again, thank God.

I sighed, frustrated and mortified at the same time. "I'm going to put a lock on the laundry room door."

"Good thing I wasn't wearing my lacy, red thong tonight." Doc chuckled when I pinched his stomach.

Five minutes later, clothes intact, we were in the kitchen keeping our hands to ourselves when Harvey moseyed back into the room. His grin reminded me of an upside-down rainbow, which matched his colorful suspenders. His beard looked combed and crumb free; his hair was slicked back.

"What are you doing here, Harvey? I thought you had a big date tonight."

"I did. She wasn't in the mood for hanky panky—unlike you two, so I dropped her off early and came to see if the rumor is true."

"What rumor?" Doc grabbed a beer from the fridge. He offered me one, but I shook my head. Harvey took it instead.

"The one Coop was tellin' me about when he stopped by earlier to grab some fresh clothes and his other Colt .45."

"What's wrong with the gun Cooper carries already?" Did that mean one wasn't enough these days?

"Nothing. He's lending it to Doc."

I hit Doc with a set of raised eyebrows.

Doc shrugged and then took a swig of beer. "He wants me to keep it handy until they find whoever killed Wanda."

"Don't you have to have some kind of permit to carry?"

"Coop's taking care of that for me."

Harvey pointed his beer bottle at me. "So, did you really get a call from the boogeyman like Coop said?"

"It was more like a boogey-woman."

"Sounds to me like a job for your bodyguard."

"What do you think Doc is doing here?"

Harvey snickered. "Judgin' from that peepshow in the laundry room, I'd reckon his plan has more to do with playin' with your body than guardin' it."

Doc's grin had GUILTY stamped all over it. "I was planning on multitasking when it came to Violet's body."

"Me, too. Only mine included watchin' a movie while I guarded it. Who's game for the Duke tonight? After catchin' you foolin' around in her henhouse, I got an itch for some *Rooster Cogburn*."

* * *

Tuesday, November 13th

Harvey was still around come morning. He'd fallen asleep in Aunt Zoe's recliner. Whether or not he'd stayed there, I wasn't sure because I went up and fell asleep in my bed around midnight, knowing the film crew might show up the next day and beauty rest was a must when the cameras were rolling.

Doc had still been down on the couch when I'd gone to bed. In the morning, the pillow next to me had an indent and smelled like him. The covers looked like someone had slept on top of them, but there were no other signs of him, not even down in the kitchen. Harvey confirmed Doc had left early to go to the Rec Center and asked the old goat to give me a message—I still owed him breakfast.

That painted a happy face on my heart that lasted until I drove into the parking lot at work and my cell phone rang. The number was local. Warily I answered, "Hello?"

"Is this Ms. Parker?" Detective Stone Hawke asked.

I made a face at the sound of his voice. I'd almost rather the call had been from Wanda's killer again.

"Who's calling?" I purposely played dumb.

"Detective Hawke." Even the sound of his breathing through the phone made me bristle. "You know, the policeman whose calls you've been avoiding."

"Your name rings a bell."

"You might want to write it down then, Ms. Parker, with your spotty memory and all. Or have you broken all of your pens in another one of your estrogen-fueled rages?"

Ahhh, the dense cretin was still sore about that stupid pen of his I'd stomped into pieces. "Have you called to harass me, Detective, or is this a social call to compare outfits today?"

That gave him pause. "I see that your sarcasm is just fine this morning in spite of your claim to have received a call from Wanda Carhart's killer."

My claim? I ground my molars. Cooper must have told him about the call and Detective Hawke had taken it upon himself to poke holes in my story. "Is there a purpose for this call, Hawke?"

"That's Detective Hawke to you, Parker."

"That's *Ms.* Parker to you, Hawke."

Judging from the intensity of his exhalations, his nostrils had to be flaring wide enough to fill with ping-pong balls. "Has anyone ever told you that you're difficult to work with, Ms. Parker?"

"Detective Cooper might have implied it once or twice."

"Do you realize that your defensiveness makes you seem suspicious?"

I was in no mood to analyze my personality this morning with Detective Hawke. "Do you realize that your grandstanding makes you seem like an asshole?"

He hung up on me.

I stared at my phone in surprise. How in the planets had I managed that? I must have woken up with magical powers this morning.

Collecting my purse, I headed toward Calamity Jane's back door. Apparently, my magic quit working when I got inside, because Detective Hawke was waiting for me at my desk. He must have run across the street as soon as he hung up on me. Wonderful. Just wonderful. He really needed to use cologne that was less nose burning.

Mona shot me an inquisitive look. Her SUV had been the only one in the lot, and I crossed my fingers and toes that we stayed the only two in the office until I could shoehorn Detective Hawke from the building.

"Morning, Mona," I said, avoiding eye contact with the surly detective standing at my desk. "That color of red makes your hair really shine. Is that cashmere?" I nodded at her sweater.

"Let's try this again, Ms. Parker," Detective Hawke interrupted my morning pleasantries. His sideburns seemed extra bushy today, his eyes as beady as his namesake. "Maybe we can be more civilized in person."

I doubted it knowing me and my history of friction around alpha males. The mere sight of his mustard corduroy blazer had me gnashing my teeth on the inside, and his condescending smile was like a magnet for my size 8 boot. But if Detective Hawke played nice, and that was a Mount Rushmore sized *IF*, I might be able to resist face-planting his smug mug on my desktop.

"Okay, Detective Hawke. How are you this morning?"

"Resolved."

I stuffed my purse in my drawer. "About what?"

"You and that film crew will not step foot on Willis Harvey's ranch."

Ah, so he had received the request I'd delivered per Jerry's instructions. "You do realize that since Willis Harvey is my client, I have his permission to be on his property."

"Fine, you can go, but if I find out any filming was done, I'll file charges against you for obstruction of justice."

I blew a raspberry. "Good luck making that stick."

I'd be sure to let Jerry know the Deadwood police's answer to his filming request as soon as possible. For once, I was happy with something that had come out of Detective Hawke's mouth.

Hawke's square jaw jutted. "I'm also curious."

I walked over to the coffeemaker so that I could do something other than look at the doofus. "Curious about what?"

"If the phone call you claim to have received yesterday is legitimate."

"Why would I make up such a thing?"

"To add cement to your alibi and throw the investigation off track."

I poured extra sugar in my coffee, crossing my fingers that the sweetness would work on my personality as well as my blood. "So, you think I fake-called myself from a burner phone?"

"It's a possibility."

As was dumping my cup of hot coffee in his lap. "If we're playing your game, then I also put the note in my purse that day Detective Cooper had me locked up behind bars."

"We have no proof you didn't."

I glanced at Mona on my way back to my desk, my steaming, caffeinated weapon in hand. She was pretending to type, her brow pinched in a worried frown when she looked my way. I knew how she felt.

"Okay, you think I faked the threatening call yesterday and the note. What else, Detective Hawke?"

"What do you mean what else? Isn't that enough?"

"Nope." I lowered myself into my chair. "I need more coffee in my system to understand your police subtlety. How about you spell out your purpose for being here with me today?"

He shot a quick frown in Mona's direction. "Maybe we should step outside."

"Don't worry about Mona," I told him, although I'd have preferred she'd heard none of this because as my friend and mentor, she now had a whole new reason to chew me out for not sharing this bee's nest of a secret. "You've already let the cat out of the bag. Besides, I have nothing to hide from her." Which was a big fat lie, but I didn't want to show Detective Hawke any weakness.

He shrugged and settled into the chair, making himself comfortable. "I think you have a hand in all of this, Ms. Parker."

"By 'all of this' you're referring to Wanda Carhart's death?"

A small gasp from Mona told me that she hadn't heard the news yet.

"Yes and more."

"More what? Deaths?"

He leaned forward. "Don't you think it's odd that you've been involved one way or another with so many of the case files sitting on Detective Cooper's desk?"

"I thought the files were on *your* desk now."

His beady eyes hardened, his glare accusing. "You may have Cooper fooled," his voice sank into a menacing growl, "but I see you clearly for what you are."

I raised one eyebrow. "A real estate agent and mother of two?"

"That's your disguise." He knocked twice on my desk and stood. "I'll be in touch again, Ms. Parker."

"I'm sure you will. They say herpes never fully goes away."

Mona made a small, high-pitched sound in her throat, and then her nails clacked louder on the keys.

It took a couple of seconds for my insult to sink into Hawke's thick skull. Then his lip curled and he planted his hands on my desk. "Watch your back, Ms. Parker, because I certainly will be."

I hooked my boot around the leg of my desk and pulled. The desk slid toward me and Detective Hawke stumbled forward, his knee slamming hard into the metal side.

"Oops. This desk bucks like that all of the time." I shot Mona a fake frown. "We really need to talk to Jerry about getting some of those sticky pads so it'll hold still."

I stood and walked over to the door, holding it open. "Take care of that injury, Detective. A knee will go out on you when you least expect it." I spoke from experience after too many knee-buckling scares.

He limped across the wooden floor, bumping me with his broad shoulder as he passed over the threshold. Detective Hawke had a history of colliding into me whenever he was near. That wasn't part of his intimidation act usually; it was merely an uncoordinated trait of a buffoon who didn't understand the rules of personal space.

"You need to start answering my calls, Ms. Parker," was his parting shot.

"I'd hate to fall into a bad habit, Detective." I shut the door behind him and locked it, leaning back against it. *Whew!*

"What's going on, Vi?" Mona nailed me with a piercing stare, her reading glasses dangling from her neck.

I could tell by her expression that there would be no dodging her question. "Wanda Carhart was found dead last weekend. I somehow managed to," *thanks to Prudence the ghost*, "get all tangled up in her murder investigation."

"Somehow, huh?"

I shrugged, returning to my desk. "It didn't help that Wanda was receiving creepy notes, and I happened to have received one myself."

"What!?" Mona clutched her chair arms. "When? Since Wanda's death?"

"No, mine came a couple of months ago."

Her gaze narrowed. "What did the cops say when you received it?"

"Nothing because I didn't tell them."

"Why would you ..." she paused and then shook her head at me. "Vi, you need to get over your dislike for the Deadwood Police."

"It's nothing personal. I just avoid the cops whenever possible." Especially Cooper and now Hawke.

"What happened in your past to give you such a strong aversion to the law?"

I waved her off. "Let's not go there today."

She harrumphed but nodded. "So why is Detective Hawke nipping at your tail?"

"We started off bad."

"Like how bad?"

My lips twisted in scorn. "I took his pen and stomped on it with my boot during our first meeting."

"That's it?"

"And then I threatened do the same to his testicles if he didn't give me some space."

A short snort of laughter slipped out, which she quickly covered with her hand. "Oh, dear."

"Our professional relationship has never quite been able to get past that initial," I pinched my thumb and forefinger together so they almost touched, "little skirmish."

"What did he mean about a threatening call yesterday?"

I told her about the phone call and how Wanda had received calls from untraceable numbers before her death.

"You think it's the same person?"

"Unfortunately, yes. Although Detective Hawke apparently thinks I'm faking it all."

Mona's eyes were rimmed with concern. "What are you going to do, Vi?"

"Nothing. I promised Detective Cooper I'd keep my nose out of it and let him handle this."

"We need to let Jerry know."

"No!" At her surprised flinch, I scooted my chair over to her desk. "Sorry, I didn't mean to yell," I kneaded my hands together, "but I really don't want Jerry to know about this unless we absolutely have to tell him."

"Why not?"

"I still have one foul in his playbook from landing in jail back in September." Although now that I thought about it, he had said that if I sold The Old Prospector Hotel, he'd remove that foul. I continued with, "I don't need any more fouls."

She took my hands in hers, squeezing them. "This isn't your fault, Vi. You're a victim here."

"Not according to Detective Hawke, and he may be the one in charge of this case. So, let's keep this between you and me for now, and if it blows up bigger," or I get killed, "we'll involve Jerry. Deal?"

She rubbed her lips together for a few seconds. "Fine, deal. But you need to keep me in the know on what's going on with the investigation and if you receive any more calls. Deal?"

I hated to involve her in my problems, but it was a good idea to have someone in the office who could cover for me, if needed. "Yes."

We didn't spit and shake, but the contract was binding nonetheless.

I rolled over to my desk and blew out a breath, trying to get my head back into the world of real estate. Mona's fingernails began to clack away on her keyboard.

"Oh, Vi." The clacking halted. "Detective Hawke's sudden appearance this morning made me forget to tell you that you received a phone call right before you arrived." She carried a small note over and handed it to me.

I read the name on the note. "Who's Katrina King-Mann?" How did I know that name? There was something familiar about it.

"She's Douglas Mann's wife. Actually, I think they are in the process of a divorce now, but with him in prison it's slowing down the proceedings."

Clink! It all fell into place in my head. Douglas Mann was the ex-lover of Lila Beaumont, aka the crazy, demon-loving bitch from my Carhart funhouse days. Like Wanda's daughter, Millie, Douglas Mann had landed in prison after that ugly night of betrayal and bloodshed in the Carhart living room. I couldn't remember the exact charges that had put him behind bars, but I was pretty sure it went deeper than screwing around on his muckity-muck wife with a demon junkie.

"Why would Katrina King-Mann call me?"

Mona headed back to her desk. "She mentioned something about being interested in the Sugarloaf Building up in Lead and you representing her."

"The Sugarloaf Building," I repeated, almost struck dumb. It couldn't be a coincidence that Reid was over last night asking Aunt Zoe about it and saying he had to go inside of the building again, could it? And why would Katrina want me as her Realtor? Hadn't she heard about my ghost-loving reputation?

Or maybe she had.

Clueless that she'd knocked me completely out of the water, Mona squinted at her computer screen then slipped on her glasses. "Didn't Jane have you look up information on that building?"

"Uh, yeah." I picked up a pen and wrote the names *Jane* and *Reid* on the note with Katrina's information. How were those three tied together? Was there a connection, or was this some weird happenstance? Lead was a small town, after all. "She said it was for sale."

"That's funny," Mona said, looking across at me. "I don't remember it ever showing on the commercial MLS listings. You sure she said it was actually up for sale, or was the owner just flirting with the idea?"

"I believe she said it was for sale, but I never asked for any details."

Mona focused back on her computer.

"You wouldn't happen to know who the current owner of the Sugarloaf Building is, would you?" I asked

"Let's see." Her fingernails clacked, and then she leaned forward to take a closer look. "According to the records, it's owned by D. Masterson of Lead."

"D. Masterson? As in *Dominick* Masterson?"

She looked over at me, a frown wrinkling her brow. "Probably. Didn't he leave town recently and not come back? Seems like the rumor was he packed up and left in the middle of the night."

He sure did, right after he ran straight through a wall in the Opera House. Apparently, Cooper had done a bang up job of burying Cornelius's and my statements about Dominick's wall-breaking exit.

"Yeah, something like that," I told her, making a point of pretending to read my computer screen.

Mona's phone rang, thankfully.

I pulled out my cell and texted Doc: *Feel like taking a field trip to the Sugarloaf Building with me?*

A few seconds later he replied: *Not after the story your aunt told us last night. Why?*

After a glance to make sure Mona was still preoccupied, I wrote: *Something is rotten in the state of Denmark.*

I quoted one of the few lines I remembered from our high school's production of *Hamlet*.

The pause was several seconds longer this time, then he wrote back: *Did you have tequila for breakfast again?*

The back door of Calamity Jane opened. I heard the sound of Jerry's booming laugh followed by a female voice, one I hadn't heard in almost two weeks. The Paranormal Realty crew had returned to Deadwood.

I typed: *Gotta go. Coach is in the locker room.*

I shoved my phone in my desk drawer and returned to the business of pretending to be a real estate agent while my brain fretted about the Sugarloaf Building and the names now connected to it.

As much as I tried, I couldn't shake the feeling that my name was going to be added to that list soon.

Chapter Nine

Aunt Zoe's house was oddly quiet when I arrived home from work. I shed my coat and tugged off my black boots, and then headed upstairs to change from my dress pants and satin blouse into yoga pants and a lightweight sweatshirt. The chance of my doing yoga moves tonight was pretty slim, but I could definitely see me eating ice cream and stretching out on the couch.

"Addy? Layne?" I called out as I stepped back into the hallway.

Nothing. I checked their rooms. Their backpacks were there but no kids. Hmmm. A few fingers of worry tickled down my spine, but I told myself everything was fine and headed downstairs.

Aunt Zoe was pouring herself a glass of water when I walked into the kitchen. I sized her up while her back was to me. Her braid was fraying, silver and brown strands popping out this way and that. So were the threads of her old green work shirt. Her jeans had a few burn marks along with some black smudges.

"Workin' hard or hardly workin'?" I asked.

She turned toward me, a tired smile on her mouth. "Both."

Her eyes looked weary as well—too many late nights toiling away in her shop. She'd even closed down her store on Main Street for a week so she could focus on getting this order done in time.

"Are my kids out in your workshop bugging you?"

She shook her head. "Doc came earlier and got them."

"He did? Why?"

"He said the three of them had a date at the Rec Center. He assured me he'd have them back in time for supper, which he planned to bring with them."

I fell into a kitchen chair, stunned. "He didn't mention it to me."

One of Aunt Zoe's eyebrows lifted. "Is that a problem?"

"Not for me, but they might be for him. Those two can be a handful."

"They behave well for others. You get the worst of it."

"I hope so, or he may dump them off and run far away, never to be seen again." I was sort of joking but sort of not.

Aunt Zoe picked up on my teeter-tottering. She pulled out a chair and sat across from me. "If this thing between you two is going to develop into something long-term, you have to give him some opportunities to build relationships with Addy and Layne without you in the picture."

"But I worry."

"About the kids' welfare?"

"No, I know he'll protect them and treat them well. The thing is, if I'm not there with them, things could be said that might paint the future or past in a different color than I'd like."

"You mean like him and the kids talking about marriage?"

"Yes, as in him not marrying me, like he told them last month."

"Violet, you don't know how that conversation went. You're hearing one side of it, which was filtered through nine-year-old ears. If his telling the kids he wasn't going to marry you still weighs on your mind, you should ask Doc what was said. You need to hear his side of the story."

I shuddered. "No way." Especially not after receiving Tiffany's text about the L-word. "I'd rather keep working on pretending it didn't happen."

"Of course you would. Didn't you once tell me that same thing right after you found out you were pregnant with the twins?"

"Maybe." Yes, and I'd wanted to avoid reality then, too.

"And how is that pretending business going for you a decade later with two half-grown kids?"

I wrinkled my nose at her. "Point taken."

She finished her glass of water. "Talk to him."

"No way. There are too many 'what ifs' that make my mouth dry and my palms clammy."

"Take it from someone who has loved and lost, kiddo. Enjoy the good stuff while it lasts, because you might bottom out when you least expect it."

"But Reid's back."

She traced the rim of her empty glass. "Yeah, but how do I know he's not here again because he's bottomed out somewhere else?" She pushed up out of her chair, walking over to the sink. "How was work?"

A complete change of subject. It appeared we were done focusing on Reid for now. "Okay, I guess. The film crew is back in town."

"When are you on camera next?"

"Thursday. We'll be at The Old Prospector Hotel."

"You think Cornelius is up for that?"

I blew out a breath. "I hope so. When I called him today, he said he'd make sure the place was camera ready." I wasn't sure exactly what that meant, but I had my fingers crossed it didn't mean he'd have sheet-made ghosts hanging around like a haunted house.

"What did Doc say about the Wilda situation?"

"He wants to read up on a couple of things first, but we're going to try to help Cornelius."

She frowned over her shoulder at me.

I agreed with her nonverbal assessment, but I didn't know what else to do to help Cornelius.

When I'd called him today, he'd begged again for my help, saying he hadn't slept in almost two days. He'd even tried staying the night at a different hotel, but Wilda had followed him there.

Doc had once called Cornelius the Pied Piper of ghosts. According to what Doc experienced while working with him on the ghost-front, Abe Jr. had a way of drawing ghosts to him. The problem was Cornelius didn't seem to realize he was attracting them. He mistook his ability as only being able to hear ghosts. He also had no experience with making the ghosts leave his side.

This crowd of specters always following Cornelius made it tough for Doc, because as soon as the dead realized Doc could "receive" them, they would swarm him, which pretty much knocked him out with the sudden rush of energy. At least, that's how I understood it all.

"Please be careful, Violet."

The tension in Aunt Zoe's voice tugged me back to the moment at hand. "I will certainly try."

That was the best I could do since I had no idea what in the hell I was doing when dabbling with the paranormal world.

It was my turn to change the subject. "Do you know Katrina King-Mann?"

"Sure. Her family has been prominent in Lead since Phoebe Hearst's era of influence. Why?" Her gaze narrowed. "Is this about Douglas Mann and that mess up at the Carhart house that you were dragged into?"

"I don't think so. Katrina called and asked for me today. I made an appointment with her secretary for tomorrow morning. According to her initial message, she wants to meet with me to discuss a certain property that's for sale in Lead."

"Which one?"

"The Sugarloaf Building."

Aunt Zoe's mouth widened for a second. "What's with so much

interest in that old building all of a sudden?"

"I was hoping you might know that answer."

I heard the front door open and close. "Vi? Zoe?" Natalie called from the dining room.

"We're in the kitchen."

She joined us, her face alight with a grin, her eyes sparkling. The knees of her jeans looked wet and dirty, like she'd been kneeling in the mud. Her pink T-shirt had a smiling R.V. on it with Dancing Winnebago R.V. Park written across her chest.

"Aren't you cold?"

Her cheeks matched the color of her shirt, wind-blown from the look of them.

"No, I've been running hot all afternoon for some reason. I think it's my socks. They're those thick, extra-warm suckers Gramps gave me. They're supposed to be good for working outside in the winter." Her grandfather had been a contractor for decades before he retired and headed down to an R.V. park in southern Arizona and married the owner—as in the R.V. park that happened to be on her T-shirt. He must have given her the shirt, too.

"Isn't your grandfather up here in the hills with his new wife for a short visit?" I remembered her mentioning something while I was sick about him coming north.

"Yeah. I had supper out at his place the other night." Natalie stood over me, her lips quivering like she was about to burst. "I have another gift for you."

I rubbed my hands together, playing along. "I hope it's one of Rex's testicles."

"In time, my queen. For now, you'll have to settle for this." She placed something shiny on the table in front of me.

I picked it up. "A jaguar?" Then it registered. "Is this Rex's hood ornament?"

She nodded, biting her lip while she giggled.

My mouth fell open. "How did you get it off his car?" I turned it upside down. "It was bolted on, wasn't it?"

"The Internet is a wonderful treasury of information."

"Was he at work again?"

She shook her head. "He was parked outside of his hotel room."

"You know where he's staying?"

"Oh, honey," she patted me on the head like I was being dense. "I know lots about your piece of shit ex. My diabolical scheme is in its infancy stages. By the time I'm finished with that no-good bastard, he'll rue the day he stepped foot in Calamity Jane Realty."

I held the shiny jaguar up in front of me, wishing I could see Rex's face when he realized it was missing.

"Natalie, you are one in a million." Aunt Zoe joined us, admiring the jaguar. "I'm going to make you some dark chocolate brownies as soon as I finish with this glass order."

"My favorite!" She hugged Aunt Zoe. "What's for dinner? You want me to whip something up?" She glanced around. "Wait, we're missing a couple of kids. Did somebody ship them off to a French boarding school when I wasn't looking?"

"Doc's bringing dinner," Aunt Zoe said, adding for Natalie's benefit, "He took the kids to the Rec Center."

"Really? What's wrong with that man?" She tugged on my hair playfully. "He's hot for your bod and he likes your kids. He must be one of those 'others' Zoe keeps talking about. There's no way he's human."

"He certainly feels human all over," I joked.

"When you say all over," Aunt Zoe said, her face softened with mirth, "are you referring to when you give him a physical under the covers on the couch or up against the washer in the laundry room?"

My instant blush made Natalie and Aunt Zoe hoot in laugher. "I'm going to cram Natalie's thick socks in Harvey's bucket mouth."

Natalie grabbed two hard ciders from the fridge, setting one down in front of me and joining me at the table. "Hey, I've been reading these books by Terri Reid. You ever heard of her?"

I shook my head. "In case you haven't noticed," I waved my hand around, "I'm a little busy raising twins while trying to make enough money to keep them fed and clothed."

"You read. I've seen romance books next to the tub."

"Those are therapeutic, along with the bubbles and the glass of wine. Their Happily-Ever-After endings give me hope that I will make it through raising two kids and still have a life after they are gone."

"Addy insists she's going to live with you forever," Aunt Zoe said, shaking a couple of aspirin into her hand.

"We'll see if she feels that way when she hits high school and I 'ruin' her life on a daily basis."

"Anyway," Natalie continued, "Terri's books are about this woman who can talk to ghosts. She works with them to figure out why they are sticking around and helps them on their way."

"Sounds fun."

"They are, *and* there's a handsome cop in the series, too."

I wrinkled my upper lip. "Cops aren't my thing."

"I know, but this cop is really sweet and very charming."

I thought of this morning's moment of indigestion with Detective Hawke, and all of the ass-chewings Cooper had given me since we'd first crossed paths months ago. "A sweet cop? Oh, that is soooo fiction."

"You need to knock that chip off your shoulder. Anyway, my point about Terri's books is that I think they'll help you deal with your real job."

"The one where I'm supposed to kill nasty beings?"

"Yes, Ms. Executioner." She used her Vincent Price voice.

I rolled my eyes. "My targets aren't ghosts, remember?"

"Yeah, but Wilda is. Weren't you saying last night when I called that you guys have to figure out a way at the séance to make Wilda go away?"

"Yeah, but—"

"No buts, no coconuts." She used one of our childhood sayings to shut me down. "I'm going to study Terri's series since it deals with the paranormal and see if there are any ideas that I can use to help you at the séance."

"You want to be there when we talk to Wilda?"

Natalie nodded, her face dead serious. "You need me there."

Aunt Zoe frowned.

I took Aunt Zoe's side. "I think that's a bad idea."

"Didn't Cornelius once tell you that you need four to make a stronger bond or something like that?"

Yes, he had, and I'd told Natalie about that when I'd filled her in on what had gone down during our séance at Ms. Wolff's apartment. I was surprised that she remembered that detail.

"Well, I'm your fourth."

"I don't think—"

"I know you don't," she interrupted with a kidding smile and then took my hand and squeezed it. "Please, Vi. I can help you. I always have and I always will. Let me be part of this."

The doorbell rang.

"I'll get that," Aunt Zoe said and left.

I stared into my best friend's eyes, the same eyes I'd made promises to and shared secrets with for decades. The last thing I wanted was for something bad to happen to her, but how could I tell the woman who'd been there for me through hell and high water that she couldn't help this time. For all I knew, maybe she could.

"Okay, but you have to do what Doc says. He's running this show, and if he says you can't be there for whatever reason, then you can't."

"Got it." She squeezed my hand again. "We're going to kick that little bitch's ass."

"Who's kicking whose ass?" Cooper's voice was like an icicle jammed into our heartwarming moment.

I flinched in surprise. What was he doing here again? And what had he done with Aunt Zoe? Locked her up in the back of his cruiser?

Before I could ask the detective why he'd shown up on our doorstep tonight, Layne came zipping around Cooper and made a mad dash for the fridge. "Hi, Mom," he called in passing.

"What am I?" Natalie joked. "Chopped liver?"

Layne came back to the table and dropped a kiss where she pointed on her cheek. "Sorry, Auntie Nat. Doc said I needed to get drinks for everyone." He eyeballed Cooper, as if measuring him by his khakis and black shirt. Cooper must have slipped off his tie before coming inside. "Are you eating with us, too, Detective Cooper?"

"When I'm in your home, Layne, and you're *not* in trouble with the law, you can call me Coop."

My jaw hit the table. I shot a what-the-hell look at Cooper.

He held my stare, his expression deadpan. "You're always in trouble with the law, Parker."

Layne giggled, apparently under the illusion that Cooper was joking. "So are you staying for supper, Coop?"

The detective's gaze was still locking horns with mine. "I wasn't planning on joining you for supper. I need to talk to your mom about something that occurred today."

Ah, Hawke must have scuttled back to the station and tattled on me again.

"But now you're here," Natalie seemed to spring from her chair. She was at Cooper's side in a flash, taking him by the elbow and tugging him toward the sink. "So you might as well join us."

Join us? Had the rats in her attic eaten away the rafters?

She shot me a pointed look over her shoulder, which only made me scratch my head more. "It's your turn to set the table, Coop." She opened the cupboard doors. "The plates are up here and silverware is in the drawer over there." Without waiting for him to agree, she returned to the table, pretending to brush crumbs off of it into her hand. Giving me that pointed look again, she knocked the Jaguar hood ornament into my lap.

Oh, crap! In my surprise at seeing Cooper walk into the kitchen, I'd forgotten about the jaguar Nat had swiped from Rex's car. With a quick nod, I stuffed it in the front of my pants.

"I need to go grab some …" I started to say as I stood, but then I ran into Cooper's all-seeing eyes as he carried plates to the table. Suspicion shined crystal clear in their silver depths. "To grab some … uh …"

"Underwear that's fun to wear?" Natalie supplied, quoting an old marketing slogan for our favorite underwear as kids.

Layne snickered from where he was lining up glasses for lemonade.

When I nailed her with an astonished scowl, she made a production of acting innocent.

A sweep back in Cooper's direction found his frown now bouncing back and forth between the two of us.

"Right, underwear."

I turned to make a run for it and found myself staring at Doc's chest.

The glint in his gaze confirmed that he'd heard the bit about my needing underwear. His gaze dipped down over my front side, one eyebrow raised as his focus returned northward. "Missing something?"

"Yeah, you." I took the bags of takeout food he'd brought and set them on the table. Then I grabbed his hand, pulling him into the dining room. As soon as we were safe from Cooper's view, I pulled the jaguar out from the front of my pants and showed it to Doc.

It took a beat for him to register what I was holding, and then he let out a bark of laughter.

I covered his mouth with my hand and then pulled him down to my level while pretending to kiss my way over to his ear in case we had an audience. "Cooper can't know," I whispered.

He nodded and then pulled back. His hand roamed down over my backside, his gaze darkening as he stared down at me. "So, do you need help with your underwear predicament?"

"You're hopeless, you know that?"

"When it comes to your underwear, yes I am."

Chuckling, I pushed him toward the kitchen and dashed up the stairs, hiding the hood emblem in my underwear drawer. *Screw you, Rex, and your fancy-schmancy expensive car!*

How much money could I get for Jaguar car parts on the sly?

When I returned to the kitchen, the table was set and Addy was dishing up fried rice from a take-out tub. Layne was placing glasses of lemonade around the table. I grabbed Natalie's and my hard cider and set the bottles in the fridge for later.

Natalie sat between Cooper and Aunt Zoe. The scene made me smile to myself as I took one of the empty seats between Aunt Zoe and Doc.

"Would you like some fried rice, Momma?" Addy asked in her sweetest voice. I knew it was her sweetest because I was usually on the receiving end of her most sour tones.

"What's going on?" I asked, wondering if I'd passed through some invisible doorway into an alternate reality.

"We brought home Chinese food from that new restaurant up in Lead," Addy explained, dumping a spoonful of rice on my plate.

"No, I mean what's with you and your brother being so helpful?" I hit Doc with a wary look. "Did you take my kids to a cloning factory this afternoon? Where are the real Addy and Layne?"

He dished up some chicken covered in an orange sauce. "They're your kids, Tiger. I just gave them a little motivation."

"What is this black magic you speak of?" I took the container of chicken he handed my way and smelled it—sweet and tempting. My mouth watered. "You must teach it to me ... or is this the dark side of the Force at work?"

"Mom," Layne chided, carrying a chair in from the dining room so we could crowd seven people in at Aunt Zoe's table. "Quit being so silly."

I made room for him to sit next to me, but Layne parked his chair between Cooper and Doc; Doc scooted closer to me to make room. Layne sat up tall in his chair like someone had a helium balloon tied to the top of his skull. Then I realized he'd made a place for himself between the other "men" at the table. When he mimicked Doc by placing his napkin on his lap, a task I usually had to peck at him to do, my eyes sprang a leak.

Inconspicuously swiping away my sappy mom tears, I focused on Addy as she finished up with her rice-spooning duties. She planted herself on a chair that she'd butted between Aunt Zoe and Natalie. We were missing one—Harvey, who had another hot date tonight.

I glanced around the table. A surge of empowering energy washed over me. This was *my* family, and I would do whatever it took to protect what was mine from cold-blooded murderers, deranged ghosts, and other hellish beings. Well, my family except for the hardheaded detective who was eyeing me suspiciously yet again.

I stuck my tongue out at him and then focused on the food on my plate. Those damned tears threatened to return when Layne reminded me that tomorrow was garbage day and insisted he'd take care of the trash duties tonight. Criminy, was I hormonal or what? The dead executioners in my lineage undoubtedly rolled over in their graves at my sentimentality.

For the rest of supper, conversation hovered around the kids' school projects and Christmas wish lists. My tear ducts finally straightened up and stopped being big babies.

"What did you guys do at the Rec Center?" I asked, trying not to seem nosy.

Doc, Addy, and Layne all froze for a split second, exchanging looks over forkfuls of rice and chicken.

"Swam," Addy said at the exact same time Layne spit out, "Exercised." Guilt dotted their cheeks with pink circles. Both suddenly had an intense need to concentrate on their plates.

I hit Doc with a questioning glance. He was holding in a grin, I could tell. "What about you?"

"I swam and exercised, too."

Something was going on with the three of them. A warning squint from Aunt Zoe convinced me to drop the subject.

A half hour later, the kids were upstairs working on science and math homework in their bedrooms. Aunt Zoe had returned to her workshop while Cooper helped Natalie with the dishes.

I kept catching myself staring at Cooper, unable to get over the sight of him with a dishtowel in his hands. The picture didn't add up in my head. There should be a gun in place of the towel, maybe even a small cannon.

"Are you actually washing these?" Cooper asked, holding a plate out to Natalie, a smile hovering on his granite hewn cheeks.

She snatched the plate from him, dumping it back in the dishwater. "Smartass," she muttered to him and then glanced over her shoulder at me. "Looks like Detective Cooper solved the Case of the Dirty Dish."

I grinned. "And he didn't even have his sidekick to help sniff out the criminal this time."

"Who's his sidekick?" Doc asked, finishing off his lemonade.

"Ol' Red," Natalie said the name of Harvey's old yellow dog, and then flicked Cooper with dish suds in jest.

The detective wiped the suds off his cheek and started winding up the dishtowel, his smile widening, threatening to fracture his whole face. I stared, mesmerized by the sight of Cooper without a stick jammed up his ass.

"No you don't," Natalie warned him, holding up her finger.

Snap!

She squealed and danced out of reach when he wound the towel again. "Police brutality! Somebody call the tabloids."

"That's what you get for insisting I stay for supper." He snapped again, purposely missing her.

Natalie's eyes danced with mischief as she flicked soap his way again. I hadn't seen her so comfortable with a man since my brother, whom she'd been friends with forever and a day, had been home last winter and horsed around with her.

Poor Cooper. He didn't stand a chance when Natalie was this at ease, treating him like an old friend, not knowing how beautiful she looked in her damp pink T-shirt, dirty-kneed jeans, and wind-ruffled hair. He was going down faster than the Edmund Fitzgerald on that stormy November night.

Been there, done that, I thought, touching Doc's thigh under the table. "How was your day?" Had Tiffany filled his voicemail again?

"Interesting. Your pal from the Planet of the Apes called."

My eyebrows must have hit my hairline. "Cornelius called you?"

He nodded. "I'm going to pay him a visit."

"When?"

"Tomorrow."

"Why?" Natalie asked, her hands back in the dishwater.

"He's got a little problem."

"If this is about Wilda," Natalie said, "I know all about it."

"Wilda who?" Cooper took a clean, dripping plate from her.

I glanced at Doc, unsure if we should say more.

"Wilda Hessler," he answered. "Or rather, her ghost."

Cooper scowled but said nothing.

"Doc," Natalie stole Cooper's towel and dried her hands, then tossed it back at him as she joined us at the table. "I want to be the fourth. Vi said you have to okay it first, though."

"The fourth what?" asked the professional interrogator in the room.

Doc drew circles on the table top with his empty glass. "Natalie, this ghost is not like Coop's ancestor. Wilda is far from tame. Homemade moonshine and pretty blondes won't keep her in line."

"I understand. I grew up with Wolfgang a few grades ahead of me in school. He was sweet to me in study hall, always the gentleman. His sister destroyed that in him, though, killing the kindness and replacing it with an ugly madness."

Cooper came closer. "A fourth what?"

"Now she's out to destroy Cornelius," Natalie continued. "He may be a bit peculiar, but he's a nice guy under all of his kookiness." She leaned forward, imploring Doc with her clear gaze. "But most importantly, Wilda wants him to hurt Vi, and there's no way I'm going to let that happen. I want to be there when you three talk to that evil little bitch."

"You're going to hold another séance," Cooper answered his own question, his expression hard and jagged again.

Doc nodded once.

"Who's going to protect Vi while you're dealing with Wilda?" Natalie pushed.

I sat up straighter. "Who says I need protection?"

A smirk curled Doc's lips. He patted my hand that still rested on his thigh. "Down, Killer. Natalie is trying to use how I feel about you to convince me to let her join us."

"Come on, Doc," Natalie pressed. "You know I've had Vi's back since we were kids."

He shot me a raised brow. "You're okay with Natalie taking this risk?"

"Not really, but she'll pester me like Wilda is doing to Cornelius if I tell her no."

"Hey," Natalie said and lightly backhanded my shoulder.

"Okay," Doc laced his fingers in mine. "She's the fourth."

Cooper growled under his breath. "This is a bad idea."

He was saying that only because one—he was a cop; and two—he had the hots for Natalie.

"Why?" Natalie asked him.

Cooper turned his focus on me. "Because Detective Hawke is already up Parker's ass about the load of case files on my desk. If anything happens in that suite to one of you and Parker walks out in one piece again, he'll come up with some reason to throw her in jail, no questions asked."

We all sat on that for a moment. Aunt Zoe's Betty Boop clock ticked and ticked and ticked.

"Then maybe you should be there, too." Doc broke the silence.

"That's a *really* bad idea," I told him.

Doc lifted my hand from his thigh and kissed my knuckles, his gaze asking me to trust him. "You never did finish telling me what brought you here tonight, Coop."

Cooper pointed at me. "I needed to give Parker a message."

"What message?" Natalie asked.

If Cooper was the messenger boy, I didn't think I wanted to hear what he had to say.

"Hawke wants her to come to the police station tomorrow."

"Why?" I had a feeling I already knew the answer.

"To answer some questions about her role in the death of Wanda Carhart."

Chapter Ten

Wednesday, November 14th

I dreamed about Jeff Wymonds having sex with his girlfriend. Only his girlfriend wasn't the nameless, nipple-bouncing babe I'd seen on his kitchen counter; she was Lila Beaumont, the black-haired demon-loving bitch who'd torched my Bronco. And instead of watching Jeff drive in for a touchdown, I stared in horror as a tattoo-covered Lila raised the knife with which she'd come at me in the Carhart house and buried it in Jeff's back over and over, blood splattering and spilling everywhere while alarm bells rang in my head.

I awoke drenched in a cold sweat with my alarm going off on my nightstand. Sitting up, I held my hand over my thrashing heart until it stopped panicking and returned to a normal beat.

A shower rinsed off the sweat, while shampoo washed the remnants of the horror show from my head and restarted my worries about facing off with Detective Hawke this morning. Aunt Zoe had already volunteered to make sure the kids made it to school since I'd be sitting in Cooper's office around that time, going head-to-head with two detectives. Well, maybe one and a half, since Cooper had promised Doc before he'd left last night that he'd play the "good cop" role for once.

The smell of bacon lured me into the kitchen a short time later. Harvey was at the stove, cooking eggs and bacon in a cast iron frypan. He was a little early for the kids, who were still upstairs sleeping.

"Morning, Harvey." I poured some coffee in a mug, glancing his way. He wore a faded daisy covered apron over his bright red suspenders this morning. His beard and hair looked like he'd rolled out of bed and finger combed both on the way over. "When did you get here?"

"At the changing of the guard."

"What time was that?"

After kissing Doc goodnight and leaving him to watch Kurt Russell wielding a flamethrower in *The Thing*, I pretty much had fallen onto my pillow and spiraled into a coma-like sleep until Jeff and Lila had woken me up.

"Five-thirty."

"Did Doc head to the Rec Center again?"

"Yup. Coop called me last night. He said you have an early mornin' appointment with him and Hawke."

A glance at the clock said I had about an hour yet until I was supposed to meet Cooper at Doc's office before heading over to the police station.

Harvey dished up a plate of eggs and bacon and set it down on the table. He pointed his spatula at me and then the plate. "Eat up."

I wrinkled my upper lip. "I'm not really hungry this morning."

"If yer gonna face off with Hawke, you need somethin' in yer belly to give you some gumption." He pulled out the chair and waited for me. "Now sit and eat."

Rather than risk the wrath of his spatula, I sat down and dug in. Turned out he was right, I was hungry and finished the plateful of food in no time.

The old buzzard sat down next to me with a cup of coffee in his hand. "I'll take the kids to school this morning."

"Thanks. Aunt Zoe will appreciate it, too." I swallowed down the rest of my go-go juice in one long gulp. "She's been working long hours and could use her sleep."

Harvey frowned at my red blazer. "You need to change."

"What?" I looked down at my blazer and paisley skirt. "Why? Are we supposed to get snow today?"

"Everyone knows that red is a fightin' mad color. If yer gonna circle and snarl with Hawke this mornin', you need to wear somethin' hard-hitting and hold yer cards close to yer vest."

"Oh, really? What do you suggest? A buffalo hide? A pair of ram horns?" I'd borrow Cornelius's one-horned Viking helmet, but it was broken.

"Ya need to throw him off his game right out of the gate. Remember in that movie when that blonde-haired looker was naked as a plucked goose under her white dress at a police interrogation?" He crossed one leg slowly over the other, giving a demonstration of a sexpot.

I laughed. "Harvey, I'm wearing my underwear during my interview this morning. This is not *Basic Instinct* and I'm no Sharon Stone."

"Of course yer wearin' your skivvies. My point is ya gotta be a long way from ordinary and knock him off his fence post."

Actually, that wasn't a bad idea. Detective Hawke was probably polishing his badge right about now, all sure of himself when it came to this morning's ass-gnawing.

"What do you suggest?"

"I saw just the thing last month in Zoe's trunk up in the attic when yer kids were playin' dress-up." Harvey slurped down the last of his coffee and led the way upstairs.

Forty minutes later, I let myself into the back door of Doc's office. I could hear the drone of male voices coming down the hall from the front office. Cooper must be here already.

My spurs clinked with each boot step along the wooden floor. The conversation out front stopped when I was halfway down the hall. Taking a deep breath, I strolled out front. Doc and Cooper were both watching and waiting for me.

Doc stood up from his desk chair at the sight of me. He looked freshly showered and wrinkle free in his khakis, blue shirt, and damp hair. "What are you ..." he laughed in disbelief as he looked me up and down. "Are those real spurs?"

"I reckon so," I said in the scratchy voice I'd practiced on the drive in. I straightened my poncho and then leveled my fedora. "Ready when you are," I told Cooper.

The detective hadn't moved from his chair, except for the narrowing of his eyes as he stared at me. He didn't look very good-cop-like in his black shirt and pants. What were those little things dotting his tie? Bulldogs?

"What in the hell are you doing, Parker?"

"I'm going to an interrogation."

"It's not a costume party."

"This isn't a costume. I was cold this morning and thought I'd wear a poncho to work."

"And spurs?"

I shrugged. "If the boot fits."

Doc walked over and lifted up the front of my poncho, flipping it over my right shoulder. "Black bandana around the neck and sheepskin vest, too." His dark eyes danced with laughter. "Lookin' good, Blondie. Are Tuco and Angel Eyes coming, too?"

I winked at him.

I'd hesitated at first about Harvey's idea for me to dress up like Clint Eastwood's infamous Man with No Name character, but then we'd snickered about the fun I could have with Detective Hawke while in disguise, and I decided to go for it. Lucky for me, Aunt Zoe had been invited to a movie-themed costume party a few Halloweens ago and forked out for a high quality costume.

"Parker, what's with *The Good, the Bad, and the Ugly* getup?"

"You didn't mention a dress code when you told me I needed to be at the station for this morning's body cavity search."

"She has a point," Doc said, lowering my poncho and straightening my hat.

Cooper scowled. "Are you really going to follow through with this charade?"

"Looks like it, Detective." According to what he'd said last night, I didn't have much choice in the matter short of demanding a warrant and hiring an attorney. If I had to walk into that damned station, I was going to do it in spurs and a poncho.

"Did you come up with this foolishness on your own?"

"Your uncle thought my red blazer and paisley skirt weren't fitting for this morning's interrogation."

Cooper cursed under his breath. "I should've known."

Doc circled me, chuckling. "You have to admit, Coop, it's pretty ingenious. If this doesn't throw Hawke off his game, not much will."

"I don't know that I'd use the word *ingenious*." His steely glare examined my costume again. "You're going to get another nickname if you're not careful."

I shrugged. "Sticks and stones."

The whistling theme song to *The Good, the Bad, and the Ugly* rang out from under my poncho.

"You've gotta be fucking kidding me." Cooper shook his head in what looked like disbelief.

Doc chortled, sitting on the edge of his desk.

I pushed the coarse fabric aside and pulled my phone from my pocket. "Not yet, Harvey. Give me about twenty more minutes."

"10-4. Over and out." The line went dead.

"Do I want to know what you two have planned?" Cooper asked, standing.

"It'll just make your face get all scrunched up and your nostrils flare."

"That's what I figured." He shot Doc a chagrinned look. "You owe me double for putting up with this, Nyce."

Doc's eyes were still dancing with merriment. Apparently, he wasn't too worried about Cooper's threat. "You think you could record it for me?"

"Don't push your luck." Cooper strode over to the door. "Parker, wait a few minutes then come on over. Try not to trip on your poncho on the way up the stairs." He opened the door and then paused. "And remember, no matter what, do not fuck this up. I can only protect you so far. If you and your big mouth land in a deep hole, I may not be able to pull you out."

He left, striding across the street toward the cop shop.

"Come here, Monco," Doc said, using the last name of Eastwood's character in his spaghetti westerns.

I clinked over to him. How in the world did cowboys sneak up on anyone while wearing spurs? It was like wearing a collar with a bell on it.

Doc took my hat off and set it on his desk. "You be careful with Detective Hawke this morning."

"You think he'll bite when I yank on his chain?"

"It's not his bite I'm worried about. I've seen you tear into Coop's hide before. You have sharp teeth."

"I thought you liked it when I bite." I played coy.

He tipped up my chin, his hands framing my face. "Immensely," he whispered and kissed me, soft and slow. "But I won't be there to carry you out if Detective Hawke tries to lock you behind bars."

"I'll keep my claws tucked away, I promise." I rested my hands on his sides. "You sure you want to go into The Old Prospector Hotel without me?" He was headed over to pay Cornelius a visit this morning and scope out the situation first hand before we tried a séance. "What if a bunch of Cornelius's ghostly pals gang up on you and try to drag you under for good? I won't be there to pull you out."

"Or knock me out with your elbow." He grunted when I pinched the skin over his ribs and then grinned. "I'll be okay." He tapped his temple. "I'm ready up here."

"I'll be thinking about you while playing with Deadwood's finest. Text me when you make it out of the hotel in one piece." I grabbed my hat and jammed it on my head, squishing my curls. "You left again without saying goodbye this morning."

"You were still sleeping when I looked in on you."

"How about you spend the night in my bed again tonight?"

One of his eyebrows lifted. "How do I know you won't take advantage?"

I trailed my fingers down his shirt. "You don't trust me?"

His chest rumbled under my touch. "I don't trust *me*. You have a history of turning me inside out whenever I get too close."

"What if I promise not to touch you?" I batted my eyelashes at him and licked my lips, hitting him with a double dose of over-the-top flirting.

"Where's the fun in that?" he asked, his focus on my mouth.

"Hmmm. Maybe you'd like to watch while I touch *me*."

His gaze darkened in a flash. "Damn, Boots. You play dirty."

"We could do that, too."

A groan came from his throat. "Vixen."

"Can't blame a girl for trying."

He turned me around, smacking me lightly on the rump to get me moving. "Go over there and give Hawke hell for trying to mess with you, Tiger."

I headed out, pausing in the doorway to frown back at him. "Be careful, Doc. Wilda is out for blood."

He saluted me.

My boots clinked across the street. I tipped my hat at a gray-haired man leaving the police parking lot who gaped at me from his truck window.

The cop at the check-in desk snickered at the sight of me. "If it isn't good ol' Spooky Parker. I'm glad you're here. I needed a laugh this morning."

I ignored his jiggling jowls. "I have an appointment with Detective Hawke and Detective Cooper."

Cooper appeared several jowly comments later, holding open the steel door leading further into the station. "Parker, get your spurs back here."

Fortunately, there weren't many cops in the station this early in the morning. The two by the coffeemaker stopped and stared, grins spreading wide.

"Is that Spooky Parker?" one of them asked extra loud.

"It looks like Poncho Parker to me," the other shot back.

"Hey, it's the donut patrol." I bared my teeth at them. "Is that the best you two Town Clowns can do?"

"Zip it, Parker." Cooper took my elbow, practically dragging me into his office. He pointed at the chair across from his desk. "Detective Hawke will be in here shortly. You want some coffee?"

"No, thanks. I might dump it in his lap in the heat of the moment."

Cooper's gaze narrowed. "Try to keep it under control this morning, and you'll be out of here in plenty of time to go home."

"Why would I go home?"

"To change out of that stupid costume."

I smoothed down the poncho. "Maybe I'll wear it all day. Jerry might think it's perfect for my on-camera moments."

He pinched the bridge of his nose. "Let's try to get through this without your smartass comebacks."

"I give no guarantees."

The door opened and Detective Hawke blew into the room, ruffling the papers on Cooper's desk. He skidded to a stop when his gaze landed on me. "What in the hell is this?"

"It's your seven-thirty interrogation appointment," Cooper answered, offering Hawke his chair. "She's your suspect, you take the desk."

Instead of settling in, Hawke sat on the corner of Cooper's desk. He probably figured he could brow beat me better from up on high.

"Why are you wearing that stupid costume, Parker?"

I perused his rumpled, gray corduroy blazer, blue and white striped tie, and bushy sideburns. "Why are you dressed like Detective Wojo from the *Barney Miller* show, Hawke?"

"Here we go," Cooper muttered from where he was leaning against the door, barring any attempt at escape.

"This is a serious interrogation," Hawke leveled at me. "You do understand that you are a suspect in a murder case, right?"

Please, like this was the first time I'd been a suspect in a murder case.

"I understand that *you* think I'm a suspect in Wanda Carhart's murder. I also understand that *you* are desperate to find out who actually did kill Wanda and are so busy pointing fingers in my direction that you're probably overlooking key information that would tell you who her true killer is."

Detective Hawke looked across the top of my hat at Cooper. "Is this normal behavior for this suspect during an interrogation?"

"I have found that there is no 'normal' in Ms. Parker's behavioral makeup."

"There is no such thing as normal behavior," I butted in, focusing on Hawke. "Normal is relative to the subject at hand. For example, take your choice of cheap aftershave this morning."

"Parker," Cooper warned, heading me off at the pass.

Detective Hawke and I had a mini squint-off for several seconds, and then he stood and walked around behind the desk. "Ms. Parker, where were you the evening of November 9th?"

"What day was the 9th?"

"Last Friday," Cooper supplied.

"Let's see, last Friday evening I was home with my children."

"Do you have an alibi that will back you up on that?"

"Yes, two—those same children."

"What time did they go to bed?"

I thought about that for a second or so. "Around eleven."

"Isn't that a little late for young children to be going to bed?"

His tone pricked me like a sharp needle. "It was a Friday night."

"Do you often let your children stay up so late or was this a special occasion?"

"What time my kids go to bed is none of your business!" I was starting to get loud and I knew it, but who was this jackass to question me about my parenting?

"What's with the questions about her kids?" Cooper asked Detective Hawke.

"She could've gone over to Wanda Carhart's house earlier and killed her, and then returned home and purposely kept her kids awake so she'd have an alibi."

"What kind of parent do you think I am?"

"For all I know, you could be the kind who kills innocent old women and then hides behind her kids."

I glared at him, trying to make him go away with my mind powers. Unfortunately, my mind powers sucked.

"How would you describe your relationship with Wanda Carhart?" Detective Hawke asked.

"She was my client." I thought about Wanda and the times she'd saved my life. "And a friend."

"Do you make a habit of becoming friends with your clients?"

I hesitated on that question. Truth was, I had trouble differentiating between clients and friends much of the time. Doc and I were way beyond friendship, let alone client-Realtor relations. I was about to try to help Cornelius rid himself of a ghost via yet another séance. Harvey was my backup when it came to hauling my kids to and from school and declared himself to be my personal bodyguard. And Jeff Wymonds—well, I'd rather not think about Jeff and his lacy red thong, especially after my nightmare this morning.

However, there was one client that didn't fit the bill. "I wouldn't call Detective Cooper and me bosom buddies." Although he was living in my boyfriend's house at the moment and had been to supper at my aunt's twice this week already.

"Were you aware of—"

The theme song to *The Good, the Bad, and the Ugly* whistled from under my poncho again. I let it keep playing.

"What is that?"

"Was I aware of what, Detective Hawke?"

Hawke opened his mouth and then closed it again, frowning. "Don't you hear that?"

My phone stopped suddenly. Harvey hung up, as planned. "Hear what?"

Hawke turned to his fellow detective. "What's going on here?"

I peeked at Cooper, whose face was a blank slate. "You're interrogating Parker about Wanda Carhart's murder."

"I know that," he sounded disgusted, turning on me. "These silly games aren't going to work, Parker."

I pulled a pack of candy cigarettes from the pocket of my sheepskin vest and tapped one from the pack. "Listen, Detective Hawke, I have a job to get to, so if you could keep on track here, I'd appreciate it."

"You can't smoke in here," he snapped at me.

I could see his edges starting to unravel.

"Oh, these aren't real cigarettes." I stuck one in my mouth. "It's just candy."

"Why do you have candy cigarettes?" he asked.

"Detective Hawke," I said, "I'm having trouble understanding what candy cigarettes have to do with Wanda Carhart."

I bit off the end of the candy cigarette and leaned forward to spit it into Cooper's wastebasket, mimicking Eastwood in the movie.

Cooper muttered something behind me that sounded like, "Un-fucking-believable."

Detective Hawke ran his hand through his rumpled dark hair. "Listen, Parker. This is no joking matter. A woman is dead here."

"Not just any woman, Detective Hawke. My friend is dead." I leaned forward, glaring up at him. "Do you see me laughing?"

Detective Hawke glared back at me, squint for squint.

My phone rang again, playing the whistling tune.

He jerked back at the song. "Shut that damned thing off."

I reached inside of my poncho and hit the silence button on the side of my phone. "Detective Hawke," I said, sitting back and lacing my fingers over my lap. "You know from Detective Cooper that I'm receiving the same messages that Wanda received. Why would I hurt my friend and send myself these messages when I have two kids I'm trying to raise?"

"Maybe there's money in it for you. Wanda had recently received a sizeable inheritance."

"I know about her aunt dying and leaving her a chunk of money. I know that Wanda's dead husband and his lover had plans to take that money and move to Florida. I know that Millie and Lila Beaumont had probably hoped to get their hands on that money. But what does that have to do with me? I was in no way going to benefit from Wanda's death. I'm telling you, you're barking up the wrong tree."

"Really?"

"Yes, really. Now, if you're done stomping about and pointing fingers at shadows, why don't you tell me if you have something that ties me to this murder. If not, I'm walking out of here with my spurs a-jingling."

Detective Hawke reached inside his blazer and pulled out a plastic bag with what looked like pictures in it. He tossed the bag on the desk in front of me.

"Here kitty, kitty," he said.

I frowned at the bag but didn't touch it. "Is that code for something?"

"No." He opened the bag and pulled out the pictures, shuffling through them until he came to one that appeared to suit his fancy. "Here kitty, kitty," he said again and held out a picture for me.

I took the picture and examined it. From what I could tell, the picture was of a mirror with words written on it. I realized I had it upside down and rotated it, reading under my breath, "Here kitty, kitty."

"That was written in blood on the victim's bathroom mirror."

Written in Wanda's blood? I grimaced and then repeated the words under my breath, my pulse picking up speed as another voice echoed it in my head.

"Wanda's body was in the bathtub."

"That's enough, Hawke," I heard Cooper's voice in the distance as those damned words kept echoing in my head.

Here kitty, kitty.

"The old lady was torn into pieces, just like your ex-boss, Jane Grimes, had been at the bottom of the Open Cut."

In my memory, I heard the sound of something metal being dragged across bathroom stall doors.

Here kitty, kitty.

My breath whooshed from my lungs as if invisible arms had wrapped around me and squeezed tight.

"Violet," Cooper said, standing in front of me.

"See," I heard Detective Hawke say. "I told you she'd know something. She always seems to have inside information when it comes to your case files. How you can think she's not in on this is beyond me."

My heart was pounding its way up my throat. I looked away from the picture, letting it hang between my knees, and latched onto Cooper's steely stare.

Whatever Cooper saw in my eyes made his jaw tighten. "Hawke, go get some water."

"I'm not your errand boy."

"Just go!" Cooper's tone left no room for arguing, yet Hawke bickered and tossed a dirty look our way as he left.

As soon as the door closed, Cooper pinched my outer thigh.

"Ouch!" I cried, smacking his hand away. "Damn it, Cooper, that hurt."

"Good. Now what's the deal with that mirror?"

"She's back," I whispered as if she'd hear me if I spoke too loud. "*Here kitty, kitty* was what she called when she was hunting me down that night in the Opera House."

"Parker, who are you talking about?" When I didn't answer right away, he threatened to pinch me again.

I lifted the picture, holding it in front of his face. "I'm talking about Calypso, Dominick Masterson's minion. This message on the mirror is for me."

He took the picture from me and frowned at it. "You mean that white-haired girl who used to run the tours at the Opera House?"

"Bingo. Caly's back, and it looks like she's on the hunt again."

Chapter Eleven

An hour and plenty of knuckle-chewing later, I sat at my desk in Calamity Jane's and stared blankly at my computer screen.

There'd been no word yet from Doc about how his visit had gone with Cornelius and any of his ghostly lemmings. I'd picked up my cell phone to call Doc so many times that I'd finally given the damned thing to Mona, my only coworker in the office this morning, and told her to let me have it only if someone called.

Katrina King-Mann had rescheduled this morning's appointment, moving it from nine to eleven, thankfully. I needed those extra two hours to stop my world from cartwheeling enough to handle a meeting with the ex-wife of the philanderer whose secret lover had tried to kill me.

Good old small towns and the twisted relationships tangled up in their nets.

"Are you sure you're okay, Vi?" Mona asked.

She'd checked on my well-being multiple times since I'd stumbled through the front door with my spurs jangling. After leaving the police station, I'd been so preoccupied with thoughts of Caly and what she'd done that night not so long ago in the Opera House bathroom that I'd neglected to go home and change.

"I'm fine," I told her and returned to my stare down with my computer. "I just need a few more minutes to work something out."

"You know, when something is bothering me, I either talk to a good friend or write my thoughts down on a piece of paper."

"Trust me on this, Mona, you don't want to know what's going on." I grabbed a pen and paper, taking her up on her other advice though, and started with what I knew about my current location several miles up shit creek:

—*Caly killed Wanda.*
—*Caly wants to kill me next.*
—*Caly is an "other" who belongs to the same species as the albino-like twins.*

—*Caly worked for Dominick Masterson.*

—*Dominick disappeared the night of the Opera House showdown between Caly and me.*

—*Dominick warned me, "Now it's in your hands."*

—*Dominick owns the Sugarloaf Building.*

—*Reid needs to go into the Sugarloaf Building for some reason.*

—*Katrina is interested in the Sugarloaf Building.*

—*Something dangerous is living in the Sugarloaf Building according to Aunt Zoe.*

—*Detective Hawke believes I'm dangerous and that I had a hand in killing Wanda.*

—*Detective Hawke is a thick-skulled buffoon who dresses like a 1970s private dick.*

—*Detective Hawke gets all pissy when I call him a prick.*

—*Cooper says I have to stop making fun of Hawke in front of other police officers, especially while standing in the middle of the police station.*

—*Cooper believes me about Prudence's warning to check up on Wanda.*

—*Cooper wants to meet Prudence.*

I laid my pen down and sat back, frowning down at my list. Even though I hadn't really solved anything during that ink gusher, my thoughts felt a little less chaotic for the time being.

Although that last one still had me spinning.

Cooper had sprung that request on me while we stood outside of the station. I wasn't sure how to orchestrate such a meeting since the Brittons now lived in the Carhart house with Prudence, or if it was even a good idea. Prudence was a stubborn ghost who played by her own rules. I could try to bring that horse to water, but there was no way of making her drink if she wasn't in the mood.

The office's front door opened. I forced a smile and looked up … right into Rex Conner's sneer. His disheveled blond hair matched his wrinkled shirt and crooked tie.

He stormed over to my desk. "We need to talk outside right now," he spoke low and tersely.

Mona's clacking stopped. "Is there something we can help you with today, Mr. Conner?" she intervened.

His glare stayed fixed on me. "I need to speak with Violet in private about a particular location I'm interested in seeing again."

There was no way in hell I was going anywhere with him, not after how touchy-feely he'd gotten more than once.

"We can talk here about this," I said, in no mood to boogie to his tune today. I had a revenge-crazed killer coming for me. A selfish ex-lover would have to wait for an opening on my dance card. "Mona is aware of your needs."

That was a bald-faced lie. She didn't know Rex was the father of my children. But to hell with it, maybe now was as good a time as any to come clean with her on this mess, too.

"Violet," Rex's voice grew more threatening. "Step outside with me."

I turned to Mona, who was watching the two of us over the top of her reading glasses. "She knows you're the sperm donor, Rex." With that cat out of the bag, I focused on the bastard. "Now what do you want?"

His gaze narrowed. "Leave my car alone."

"I don't know what you're talking about."

"If you think these little games of yours will derail me you can think again."

"Rex." I sat back, crossing my arms over my poncho. "Whatever you're accusing me of is unfounded. I don't have time to play these 'little games' of which you speak. I'm raising two children without any financial support, remember?"

He put both hands on my desk, leaning closer. "Stop calling me every thirty minutes and breathing into the phone."

My surprise at his words was the real deal. "I haven't called you." I didn't even know where I'd put the business card he'd left. I'd thought it was in my purse, but when I had gone to dig his card out and throw it away before my nosy daughter found it, it had been gone. "I made a point of not retaining your phone number."

His upper lip curled in a snarl. "I don't believe you."

I hooked my foot around the desk leg and yanked. Rex stumbled forward, sprawling across my desk and sending papers and my costume fedora flying. That trick was really starting to come in handy.

I stood, smiling down at him. "Gotta watch this desk. It has a way of bucking assholes."

He pushed himself back upright. "You did that on purpose."

"I think it's time for you to go."

"We're not done."

"Oh, I think we are for now." I grabbed my hat from the floor and then made for the front door. "I'd hate to have to call my good friend, Detective Cooper," I fibbed over my shoulder, "and have him throw you out of here."

He strolled toward me, chin high, back to being cock of the walk. "Is he your new fuck buddy?"

I flinched. I couldn't help it. Whenever anybody mentioned Cooper in that role it made me recoil. Cooper was way too sharp-toothed and sandpapery for my taste in bedfellows. It would be like skinny-dipping with a great white shark.

"I'm not going to justify that crude question with an answer." I raised my chin at Rex. "But to be clear, I'm still in a relationship with the guy who lifted you off this very floor and threatened to remove your kidneys."

He scoffed. "You're the one who threatened to remove my kidneys."

"That's right." I held the door for him, a blast of cold air finding the holes in my poncho. "Aunt Zoe has the perfect fish gutting knife for the task."

He paused on the threshold. "Prank call me or touch my car again, and I'll pay a visit to the kids, tell them a story or two about their mother."

"Step one foot on Aunt Zoe's property and I'll fill you full of rock salt."

He bent closer, his usually cool blue eyes flashing hot. "You don't want to fuck with me, Violet."

"You're right about that." I reached up and locked onto his nose in a Three Stooges style pinch, twisting it.

He howled, dropping to his knees in pain.

"Watch where you stick this thing, Rex." I twisted his nose the other way, toward the street. "The next time you shove it into my life, I'll break it, I swear."

With a push between the shoulder blades, I sent him outside nose first and slammed the door behind him, locking it.

Across the room, Mona was standing behind her desk, her mouth and eyes wide.

"Is he glaring in at me?" I asked, my back to the door.

She nodded.

I raised my left hand and flipped him off through the glass, then walked over to the coffeemaker and poured myself a cup of acid-inducer in case I needed to breathe fire on the son of a bitch to make him go away.

"He's gone." Mona fell into her chair. Her focus stayed locked on me as I returned to my desk and settled back into my seat. "So, that's what's going on between Rex Conner and you."

I nodded. "Now you know."

"I thought Addy and Layne's father left you when you were pregnant and wanted nothing else to do with you and the kids."

"That used to be correct."

"But now he's back."

"And insisting on me finding him a place to live."

"Oh, Lordy." She pursed her lips.

"He's working at the research lab up in Lead for the next year or so."

"If he wanted nothing to do with his kids, why is he bothering you?"

"He wants me and the kids to play 'family' with him in front of his family-oriented bosses so that he can land some big promotion."

"You're kidding."

"I wish." I sipped on the black coffee. "If I don't agree to play the part of loving wife and mother, he's threatening to tell the kids he's their father. If I do agree to play his game, we'll play family for a short time with the kids thinking he's just a boyfriend. Then he'll go on his merry way, leaving us alone again."

"What a dirty rat. Doesn't he realize how much that might mess with your kids' heads?"

"He doesn't care." Rex was one of those people who only thought of their own needs, in and out of the bedroom. Always had, always would. "I refused to go along with his family act, but he's determined to get his way in spite of my refusal."

"Is that why Doc had him pinned up against the wall that time Ben and I came back from lunch early?"

I nodded.

She smiled. "Are you really messing with his car?"

"Not me personally, no."

"Are you not personally prank calling him, too?"

"I honestly don't know anything about that."

Mona's smile turned upside-down. "You should have told me about Rex before, Vi. I could have insisted that Jerry let me take him as a client." She tapped her nails on her desktop. "Maybe I still could."

"I don't want anyone else here to know who Rex really is."

"You know my lips are sealed." She tapped her nails some more. "It all makes sense now."

"What?" I thought back to the conversations she'd witnessed in the past between Rex and me. "You mean me telling him there's nothing available to rent?"

"No, his insistence on only you helping him find a place to live no matter how much Ray tried to steal him away when you weren't here."

I rolled my eyes. "Ray is such a backstabbing ass-clown."

She chuckled. "We should make him a World's Best plaque with that title on it." Leaning forward onto her elbows, she raised both eyebrows.

"What can I do to help?"

My first instinct was to reject her help. She didn't need to get involved in one of my problems. But then the obvious came to mind. "Help me find him a place to live so he'll stop having a reason to bug me at work."

Mona nodded once. "Consider it done. Rex Conner is no longer your client. I've just stolen him right out from under you."

"I think I'm in love with you, Red," I winked at her, "and your sexy sweater, too."

She chuckled and straightened her white cashmere sweater that emphasized her chest and then some. "I bet you say that to all of the redheads in your life."

I thought of Tiffany. "Not really."

Mona returned to her keyboard, and I went back to staring at the computer screen until it was almost time to leave for my appointment with Katrina King-Mann.

Unsure if I should take any paperwork with me to our meeting, I opted for a couple of business cards and that was it. "I'm going to run home and change into something more suitable for my meeting with Katrina, then I'll head up the road. I don't know when I'll be back."

"I brought my lunch today, so don't worry about having to be back anytime soon. Since Jerry and Ray were going to be working with Ben and the camera crew, I figured I might need to run the ship most of the day."

"Thanks," I told her. "For everything."

"I'm here to help, Vi. We girls need to stick together."

I collected my cell phone from her on my way out the back door, wondering why Doc hadn't called or texted yet. I smothered the anxiety smoldering in my gut and trusted that he knew what he was doing and would call later.

Aunt Zoe's house was empty. I could see a light on in her workshop when I stopped in the kitchen to grab a yogurt from the fridge. I changed in a flash from a professional gunslinger into a boring Realtor and headed up the road to Lead.

Katrina King-Mann's office was located across the street from the Homestake Opera House in a century-old brick building. Her secretary held down the fort in the front office that looked out on Lead's main drag. As older ladies went, this one had the sort of no-nonsense stare that belonged in the watchtower of a prison yard. She smelled like she was wearing cheap men's cologne.

I cleared my throat as I approached her desk, trying my best to smile in spite of the shitty day I'd had so far. "I'm here to see Mrs. Mann."

"She goes by Ms. King now."

"Sorry. Ms. King is expecting me."

"And your name is?"

"Violet Parker. I'm with Calamity Jane Realty."

The silver haired sentry picked up her phone and hit a button. "A Ms. Parker is here to see you." She listened and then hung up. "She'll be right down. You may have a seat over there." She pointed to a couple of chairs near the front window.

I took a seat, picking up a magazine from the table nearby. I flipped absently through the pages, wondering what in the heck I was doing here. Like I had time to sit and flip through fashion magazines with Caly out there hunting me down and Wilda trying to mind-meld Cornelius into finishing her brother's botched attempt to kill me.

Staring across the street at the Opera House, I remembered the day I'd watched Dominick Masterson and Caly greet Cornelius outside its glass doors. This office had front row seats for anyone coming and going via W. Main Street. If Katrina King had relocated to the back of the Opera House, she might have been able to spy on her then-husband (like I had) while he felt up his crazy girlfriend in a parking lot a short distance down the street. As we said in the real estate business: location, location, location.

"Ms. Parker?"

I'd been so engrossed in my mental meanderings that I hadn't heard Katrina King join me.

I rose, holding out my hand toward the very tall, sleek-haired platinum blonde with the extra cake of makeup ringing her eyes. Her face looked around my age, but her neck told an older story.

"You must be Katrina King?"

She nodded, her large-boned hand taking mine in a limp-dick grip that lasted only a second, and then she let go and wiped her palm on her jacket.

Lovely. Apparently, in addition to being a potential murder suspect these days, I also had cooties.

I followed Ms. King past her stoic secretary and up a set of stairs. At the top, it opened up into a spacious loft office with a rather regal sized desk by the plate-glass windows. The desk and visitors' chairs sat on what I guessed was a very expensive Persian rug. Throughout the room were pricey vases, bowls, and statues—antiques by the look of them.

Who would have guessed such a posh place was hidden upstairs in an old brick building in downtown Lead? Although having seen pictures of what the Opera House had looked like in its heyday, this place would fit right in with the gilded luxury across the street.

"Have a seat, please," Katrina indicated one of the dark brown leather chairs across from her desk.

I sat, smoothing my red blazer and paisley skirt as I tried to get back into real estate mode.

She settled into the cushy-looking chair behind her desk. "I asked you here this morning because I need your help securing my immortality."

Hmmm. I looked down at my hands. I was pretty good at tying my shoes, but immortality might be a little out of my range.

"Are you sure you called the right office?" Maybe Calamity Jane's phone number was one or two numbers off from Mudder Brothers Funeral Parlor.

Her smile barely touched her cheeks. It was like part of her face was a frozen mask. She must have had her fair share of plastic surgery, or maybe she'd had her frown lines overly smoothed via too much neurotoxic proteins lately.

"Oh, I'm sure, Violet. You see, I'd like to purchase a particular building and renovate it, including renaming the stone façade. For that, I need you."

Well, my chiseling skills were pretty much nonexistent, but I could certainly offer assistance with the purchasing part. "Are we talking about the Sugarloaf Building?"

She nodded, her green eyes hard little crystals behind thick black eyelashes. I'd bet Harvey's left nut those spider legs on her eyelids were fake.

"It's not even up for sale," I said.

A wave from her told me that I didn't need to worry about such silly stuff. "I'd like you to prepare the necessary paperwork in order to get things rolling."

I crossed one leg over the other, buying a little time while I considered something Mona had told me recently. "Isn't that building owned by Dominick Masterson?"

Her eyes widened a fraction at Dominick's name. Had I not had my focus locked onto her, I would have missed it. "I'm not certain who currently owns the property. This is the reason I'm hiring you. I need someone to take care of these petty issues."

I got the feeling Katrina King was accustomed to having someone else make things happen whenever she snapped her fingers.

I frowned.

How did one purchase a building that wasn't for sale from an owner who seemed to have disappeared into thin air? Even Cooper and his expert criminal sniffer-outers hadn't been able to locate Dominick since that night he'd blasted out through the Opera House wall.

"Why the Sugarloaf Building?" I asked. As buildings went, it wasn't anything spectacular. Sure it was a century old brick beauty, but there were several others of those in Lead whose owners would probably be much easier to contact.

"Let's just say it holds a special place in my heart."

My cell phone rang in my purse. It was not Harvey's whistling tune either.

"Sorry," I lifted my purse from the floor. I would have silenced the ring upon arrival at her office, but I was waiting for Doc to call. "Let me send that to voicemail."

I glanced down at the screen. It wasn't Doc. It was a number I didn't recognize with a strange area code.

"Take it," Katrina ordered.

"Excuse me?"

She pointed at the phone. "You should take that. I would expect phone calls are important in your profession."

Nodding, I answered the call. "Violet Parker speaking." I sent a quick, apologetic smile across Katrina's desk.

"We want what belongs to—," a whispery voice started.

"Fuck off!" I didn't let the caller finish and hung up. I wasn't going to play these stupid prank call games with Caly. If she wanted me, she needed to come and get me, damn it.

Of course that was some pretty tough talk while sitting here safe and sound in … oh, shit! I grimaced across at Katrina, who sat watching me with her frozen face.

"I'm sorry about that." I searched for a good excuse, but all I could come up with was, "I've been getting some prank calls lately."

"I see. Have you considered going to the police?"

I shrugged. "It's a minor thing. Probably some silly teenagers." Or a killer albino decked out in leather, spikes, and a dog collar—minus the part of her arm I'd removed, of course.

Katrina stared at me several seconds. "How long will it take you to get the offer paperwork ready for the Sugarloaf Building? I'd prefer to move on this sooner rather than later."

Something about the way she was pushing me to hurry up and help her buy the building reminded me of her ex-husband. He'd been in a hurry to purchase the Carhart house, too. Turned out he had big plans to turn Lead's Open Cut into a mini-Grand Canyon tourist attraction. I wondered if Katrina's plans were as "grand" as her ex's? If she was serious about immortality, it sounded like she was trying to one-up him.

"Before I can answer that," I said, stuffing my phone back in my purse with silent mode enabled this time. "I need to do a little research on the Sugarloaf Building."

Katrina stood, signaling the end of our meeting.

Thank God, because while I'd sounded tough and hung up on who I was guessing was Caly, I was not feeling tough on the inside. I needed to talk to Cooper about the phone calls Wanda had received before getting murdered. How often had she received them? At regular intervals? Or had the calls come in more often with each week until her death?

I stood as well, hanging my purse from my shoulder, and followed Katrina down the steps to her front office. Her secretary was nowhere to be seen.

It was getting close to lunchtime. My stomach growled at the thought of food. The yogurt hadn't really cut it, and apparently a spooky phone call was no match for my appetite.

Katrina held the door for me. "I will expect a call soon regarding what you find out, Violet."

She spoke like a woman used to getting her way. If she were willing to fork out a chunk of money that would mean a sweet commission for me, I was willing to put up with her high and mighty attitude for the time being.

"I'll get to work on this as soon as I return to the office."

I had to, actually, because tomorrow I had to spend the day on camera. Maybe Mona had the bandwidth to help me with this in exchange for a percentage of the commission.

I didn't offer my hand again to Katrina. With my cooties, I was sure a second shake was out of the question. But I did remember my manners. "Thank you for this opportunity."

Katrina sniffed and shut the door in my face.

I watched her walk back toward the steps leading up to her office. When she turned out of sight, I sniffed my shirt to see if I stunk as well as had cooties. I smelled my perfume, but that was it. Maybe all of the money her family had been swimming in over the decades had made her overly sensitive to the scent of hard-up single moms.

Back in my SUV, I whipped around and headed back down toward Deadwood, swinging into the parking lot at Bighorn Billy's. A sprinkling of cars was parked in the gravel.

I was pretty sure bacon would take care of my frustrations.

Fifteen minutes later I sat alone in a booth seat, sipping on a Diet Coke while waiting for my club sandwich with extra bacon when Cooper walked into the diner.

He strode over to my table and took the seat opposite me. "Let me see your phone."

I handed it over without hesitation. "It's the number right before yours on the recent call list."

He raised his eyebrows. "You didn't call Nyce this time?"

"I'm waiting for him to call me."

"No word about his visit to The Old Prospector Hotel then I take it?"

I shook my head.

He pulled out a notebook and wrote the phone number down, then tried to call it while his steely eyes searched my face.

When he hung up, I said, "No answer I'm betting."

He shook his head and handed my phone back.

The waitress stopped by and took an order for coffee and a chicken sandwich from him. Apparently, he was joining me for lunch. With Caly on the loose, I wasn't averse to his company.

"How did your meeting go with Katrina King?"

I had used the meeting to escape Detective Hawke's hounding this morning, still thinking I had to be in Lead at nine instead of eleven.

"It was moved to eleven," I informed him, and then added, "She's old money through and through."

"What did she want?"

I shrugged. "Nothing much, just immortality."

"Immortality, huh? Is that something your marketing-savvy boss has decided to sell in addition to real estate these days? You could paint a halo or devil horns on that billboard of yours out on Interstate 90."

"Cram it, Cooper." I sipped on my drink. "Katrina wants me to help her purchase the Sugarloaf Building."

The waitress delivered his coffee and a small pitcher of cream.

"What does that have to do with immortality?" he asked, stirring in some sugar along with the cream.

"Your guess is as good as mine, but that building is owned by Dominick Masterson."

He paused in the midst of stirring. "You haven't run into him again and not mentioned it, have you?"

I rolled my eyes at his suspicion. "Trust me, Cooper. If I see Dominick, I'm calling you first thing so that he can tell you and Detective

Hawke for himself that I am in no way responsible for that mess at the Opera House in September."

That earned me a nod. "What do you do if the owner of a property is listed as missing but not dead?"

"I don't know. That's not something we run into much in the real estate business. Maybe there's someone running his estate. Mona will probably know what to do."

"So the call came in while you were talking with Katrina?"

"Yep."

"And you took it right there in front of her?"

"She told me to answer it. She said that in my line of work phone calls were important."

His eyes narrowed slightly as he stirred. "And then what?"

"I started to hear that stupid 'We want' bullshit and told the caller to … uh …" my cheeks warmed at how unprofessional I'd been at that moment. "I told her to fuck off."

Cooper's blond eyebrows crawled up his forehead. "You said that in front of Katrina King."

"It wasn't one of my shining moments."

"You have shining moments?"

I threw my wadded up straw wrapper at him. "You can fuck off, too."

He chuckled and took a sip of his coffee. "In all seriousness, I'm not sure antagonizing your caller is a good idea."

"I'm not going to play a scared little kitten with Caly."

"We don't know for certain it is Caly. Someone else could be toying with you, trying to use Caly to incite fear in you."

"If that's the case, they picked the wrong mask to hide behind." I didn't relish the thought of facing off with that spikey Chihuahua, but I'd faced off with her breed before. They were deadly, but they had a weakness. I just had to be willing to get in close and personal for some fisticuffs.

My phone dinged. I looked down to see who was texting me, breathing a sigh of relief at the sight of Doc's name.

Where are you? his text read.

"It's Doc," I told Cooper and texted where we were.

Almost there. Order something for me, pls.

I signaled the waitress and ordered a Buffalo burger and a side salad, the same thing he'd had last time we'd stopped in to eat.

When she left, I turned back to Cooper. "Did the calls on Wanda's phone from the unknown numbers increase in frequency before her murder?"

He nodded. "Right before her death, she was getting them multiple times a day."

"So the first one for me came around noon on Monday. And this one came around that same time today. Two-day intervals at the moment. We'll see if I get a call tomorrow or in two more days on Friday."

"Wanda's calls happened over a three-week period. We can't tell for certain if the threats started before that via the notes since there's no time stamp on them."

"Are you going to tell Detective Hawke about this?"

He nodded.

"Am I going to be hauled in for more questioning?"

"It's always a possibility."

"Okay. I'll start planning my next costume for the party."

The sight of Doc walking through the diner's door made me miss his reaction. I waved him over, noticing the somber lines on his face.

Scooting over, I made room for him on the bench seat. If he was surprised to see Cooper sitting with me, he didn't show it.

"What's wrong?" I asked as soon as he'd had a moment to catch his breath. "Did something happen at the hotel?"

"You could say that," he nodded a greeting across the table at Cooper.

"Is Cornelius okay?"

"For the time being." Doc's dark gaze focused on me. "But this Wilda deal is no good."

"What do you mean?"

"We have a bigger problem than I thought."

Chapter Twelve

What did Doc mean we had a bigger problem with Wilda Hessler? Was the demented little ghouly-girl hanging out with a headless Hessian in Sleepy Hollow now? Taking notes from the blood-bathing Countess Elizabeth Báthory of Hungary? Swinging an ax around like Lizzie Borden?

Or did he mean the problem with Cornelius himself was bigger? I was supposed to film there tomorrow. Maybe I should figure out a way to convince the filming crew to reschedule.

The waitress stopped by, topping off Cooper's coffee. I took a moment to quell the questions pinballing around in my head and give Doc time to explain.

As soon as she left, he derailed me with, "Your poncho is missing. How was the interrogation?"

Cooper guffawed as an answer, which earned him a dirty look from me.

"What's that for?" I asked. "I didn't bite Detective Hawke, so I'd call it a success."

"Or throw up on him," Cooper added.

I pointed at the Detective. "If you'll remember, I tried to warn you beforehand that time, but you didn't listen." I turned to Doc, lowering my voice. "Hawke showed me a picture of Wanda's bathroom mirror. It had 'Here kitty, kitty' written on it with Wanda's blood." I wasn't sure if I needed to explain more or if his memory was firing on all cylinders this morning.

He cursed. "Caly's back." All cylinders it was.

"We don't know that for certain," Cooper iterated.

"Would you look at that, Doc? Cooper has turned into Polly Positive. Did you ever think you'd see the day?"

"Pipe down, Parker." Cooper stirred more cream into his coffee. "My point is that maybe we should do more digging before jumping to the conclusion that some magical, albino biker chick covered in spikes has returned to cause more mayhem and murder."

He'd used the description of Caly I'd given for the police report after the night she'd tried to make me her pet. Except for the *magical* part.

"She's not magical," I clarified. "More like crazier than a coked-out weasel. She needs to be stopped before somebody else is killed."

Doc aimed a squint my way. "You said you'd let the police handle this in exchange for me helping Cornelius."

"I know, I know." I sipped from my Diet Coke, my gaze avoiding his. "But bullets won't stop Caly." That was where I came into the show. It was time to get mad-dog mean, that was all there was to it.

"Violet," he warned.

I held up my hands. "Listen, there is nothing I can do other than wait for Caly to come to me, right?" I aimed that question at Cooper, who nodded. "So, let's move onto Cornelius and Wilda and why we have a bigger problem."

The dang waitress returned before Doc could start, plates of food in hand except for Doc's buffalo burger. She passed the food around, promising to refill my drink and bring Doc's burger as soon as it was ready.

When she was out of earshot, I looked at Doc. "Let's have it before my heart keels over from anxiety."

He stirred his side salad around with his fork. "Wilda is growing in strength."

"What's that mean?" Cooper took a bite out of his chicken sandwich.

"From what Cornelius and I can tell, she's siphoning energy from the other ghosts that are drawn to him, as well as from Cornelius himself."

I chewed on that and my bacon-laden club sandwich for a few seconds. "To what end?"

He shrugged. "Your guess is as good as mine, but I'm thinking it has something to do with her top priority at the moment—killing you."

"You think since I'm a dud when it comes to ghosts, she's figuring out a way to get to me? Like the trick Prudence pulled last weekend with Harvey?"

"We'll find out when we do the séance." Doc stabbed at his salad. "My worry is that we'll find out too late to stop her from getting to you."

"Me? You're the one who will be opening yourself to her."

"Yeah, but you have no defenses against ghosts. Hell, most days you can't sense them when they're practically standing inside of you."

I shuddered at the memory of that moment in the dark stairwell of The Old Prospector Hotel.

"You only handle living things," Doc continued. "I've been dealing with the dead for as long as I can remember."

We ate in silence for a moment, listening to Roger Miller singing about a trailer for sale or rent in *King of the Road*. If I didn't have two kids to take care of, I might join Roger on the road to forget about this insanity that was now part of my day-to-day life. Looking back, working long hours down in Rapid City at the car dealership hadn't been such a bad gig.

"I've thought about it and I need to be at the séance with you." Cooper broke the silence.

"Why?" The idea of the growly detective sitting in during what undoubtedly would be a nail-biting event didn't sit well with my lunch.

"If anything happens, Parker will need me as a credible witness."

"You mean if someone doesn't make it back, like what happened with Cornelius's cousin?"

Cornelius had a cousin who could open doors or channels to the spirit world, like I could. According to him, she made the mistake of opening a channel too wide and something latched onto her. When he and others tried to exorcise it, his cousin ended up dead. Lucky for him, there were several witnesses who told the same story about the exorcism, so none of them were arrested for murder.

These days, Cornelius made a habit of warning me about opening channels for fear of a repeat performance. I didn't think I was anything like his cousin. In fact, I feared I was something far darker.

The waitress stopped by again, delivering Doc's food, topping off Cooper's coffee.

"It's a good idea." Doc picked up his burger. "To be honest, I'm not certain having Natalie there is wise."

"I agree." Cooper didn't hesitate to jump on that, his steely eyes challenging me to disagree.

I took him up on that challenge. "She's coming."

"Don't make this about you and me," Cooper said. "If her life is at risk, then you should listen to Nyce."

I wiped my mouth and leaned forward, lowering my voice. "Listen, Cooper, in case you haven't been taking notes in your little police notebook, every single one of our lives is at risk if we do this séance. I've had plenty of nightmares about what is out there in the darkness waiting for us when we open that channel. So, don't think I haven't considered the potential danger for my best friend, and how I'd feel if anything happened to her."

He leaned forward, matching my tone. "So why include her?"

"Because it's what she wants."

"Maybe she doesn't know what she wants. Maybe she just wants to be included and has no comprehension of the risk."

I snorted. "Come on. Natalie is no idiot. She may have been rash in the past when it came to trusting men, but in all other areas of her life, she's sharp as a tack." I took a sip of my drink. "Besides, I need her there to help me."

"Nyce will be there to help you."

I glanced at Doc, who was watching me with a frown. "He'll be busy, especially if we're dealing with a nastier ghost than normal. Nat will have my back while Doc tries to handle Wilda."

"And what about Cornelius?" Cooper asked.

I looked to Doc for that answer, who shrugged and said, "I don't know how taxing this will be for Cornelius. I haven't untethered a ghost from a human before."

"Never?" I had sort of counted on his leading the way with knowledge from past experiences.

"No. I've read about it plenty, and Cornelius went through the process with me today, but this will be my first attempt." He looked at me. "That's why I'm uncertain about Natalie's safety. I can't give any guarantees."

I sat back on the bench, no longer interested in eating. "I'll tell you what," I said to both of them. "I'll talk to Natalie again and explain the situation as we know it now. If she seems hesitant and wants to back out, I'll make sure she understands that I don't need her there to help me." I hit Cooper's gaze head on. "Even though I might."

He gave a nod of approval. "I can stand in for her and cover you."

"Your guns won't help, Cooper. Not where we're going."

"Maybe not, but the sound they make when I fire them always makes me feel better."

That made me chuckle in spite of the uneasy tension now rumbling around in my gut about this séance.

Cooper finished his sandwich and set his plate at the end of the table for the waitress to take. "Parker, I meant what I told you earlier about paying Prudence a visit."

Crud. I'd hoped he might have hit his head between this morning and now, forgetting all about that request.

"Why do you want to talk to Prudence?" Doc asked.

"He wants to question her about the person she told me she saw sneaking around in the Carhart house." Or rather, the Britton house. It was going to take me some time to edit that in my head.

Doc's eyebrows rose. "Do you think she'll talk to Coop?"

I smirked. "You tell me. You've shared a body with her. I've only smacked her around via you."

That brought a grin to his lips. "You're one hell of a bruiser in the ring, I can attest to that."

I playfully socked his shoulder. "Just wait until you see what I have planned for you the next time you go under and won't come back out."

"Can we leave your teeth out of it this time?"

"Sure." I made pinching motions in front of him. "I'll stick with my fingers."

"What are you two talking about?"

"Prudence has a way of possessing whoever she wants when she wants," I explained. "But with Doc, they basically switch places. While he 'sees' things happening in the past in her world, she moves and speaks to me through him. She's so overpowering, I've had to step in and help him come back."

Cooper's face lined with doubt. "And with others, like my Uncle Willis? Does she speak through them, too?"

"It varies. Sometimes she turns them into walking and talking puppets, moving their mouths like this." I showed him, playing a ventriloquist's doll. "With your uncle, she just took over the controls while he was wide awake. He tried to cover his mouth and shut her up, but she was too powerful for him."

"But she didn't possess him to the point of requiring your aid to escape?"

"No, not Harvey. With the others I've seen her turn into puppets, she released them when she finished and they sort of woke up, with no memory of what happened. But Harvey remembered everything." I could tell by the deep set of Vs in the detective's forehead that he was having trouble believing me. I shrugged. "You asked."

"This is so fucked up."

I snorted. "Tell me about it."

"I don't know," Doc said, tossing his napkin on his empty plate. "After a while, it becomes the norm. I can't imagine a world without dead people moving around in it." He picked up the bill the waitress had set on the end of the table. "You two ready?"

We tossed money on the table and headed out into the cold November wind. The blue sky and sunshine were deceptive, making it seem like it should be warmer than it was.

"How soon can we visit Prudence?" Cooper asked.

I shrugged. "I need to call the Brittons and see if I can finagle a way to stop by with you in tow that won't seem odd."

He nodded, glaring after a truck that sped by on the main road going much faster than the speed limit. "Let me know what you come up with, but for your sake, the sooner we see her the better. And if you get a third phone call, let me know."

"Of course." Since Doc insisted I let the cops handle Wanda's murder on their own, I had little choice.

Cooper looked at Doc. "Are we still on for poker tonight?"

"Definitely. If I don't get to beat you at cards every week, I get grumpy."

"Asshole," Cooper said with a grin and then left the diner.

Doc draped his arm around my shoulder and led us toward my SUV. "What did he mean about a third call? Did you get a second one?"

I nodded and told him about the phone call and my visit with Katrina King, leaving out the part about me cursing at Caly and hanging up. I also left out Rex's visit to the office this morning. I didn't want to add any more frown lines to his face.

"Do you want me to skip the poker game tonight and come straight over after work?"

"No. Go have fun with the boys and kick Cooper's butt for me. Natalie already mentioned coming over to hang out tonight and drool over the Duke on television, and Harvey said he'd be there later to play bodyguard."

"Okay." He pulled me closer as the wind whipped through the lot. "But if you have a bad dream about Wilda or Caly and need to talk to someone in the middle of the night, call me."

"And what if I have a good dream about you and me and naked stuff?"

He lowered his head, his dark eyes twinkling. "You should definitely call me then, Boots, and tell me every single detail."

His lips were warm on mine, his touch heating me up in spite of the cold wind. I wanted to go back to his place and warm up even more in his sheets, but it was time to return to the office.

"Violet," he whispered against my mouth.

"What?"

"There's something else about my visit to The Old Prospector Hotel that I didn't want to say in front of Coop."

I blinked, having trouble leaving lust-ville and returning to terror-town. "What's that?"

"Cornelius has words carved into his forearm."

I recoiled at the image that inspired. "You mean he's cutting himself now?"

Doc frowned at the hillside behind me. "He doesn't remember carving the letters himself. He says he woke up in the middle of the night with his arm burning, and when he turned on the light, the cuts were there and still bleeding."

"Holy shit." I'd seen that in a scary movie about demon possession once. "What do the words say?"

His focus shifted back to me, his grim expression matching the look in his eyes. "Kill her."

* * *

Thursday, November 15th

The Old Prospector Hotel looked less frightening in the morning light than it had in my mind's eye last night when I had been talking to Natalie about Doc's concerns for her well-being at the séance.

Natalie had insisted on joining us in spite of my warnings, as I'd figured she would. She'd always been incredibly stubborn when it came to taking risks for me.

I'd texted Doc the news while he was playing poker.

He'd texted back: *Cooper isn't happy about this.*

I'd downed several gulps of hard cider and sent back: *Tell Cooper he can shove his unhappiness up his tight ass next to that piece of rebar he keeps jammed up there.*

There'd been a pause and then he'd written: *Are you drinking and texting?*

I set the empty cider bottle on the counter next to the other one I'd finished earlier.

Only a little.

Natalie had taken my phone away then and we'd enjoyed some John Wayne on the small screen along with Harvey, who'd shown up with his shotgun ready for guard duty.

Harvey had still been hanging around this morning, working the spatula in the kitchen, making sure my kids didn't go to school on carbohydrates alone. Aunt Zoe had come down the stairs in her yellow, smiling sunshine slippers and matching robe right before I'd headed out the door.

"Violet." She'd caught me in the dining room where I'd been putting on my coat. She pulled the neckline of my satin blouse apart slightly, nodding when she saw the glass necklace she'd made for me hanging around my neck. "I wanted to make sure you were wearing it before you go into that hotel."

"I don't leave home without it." The necklace was one of her charms. It was more of a warning device than a protection piece and helped me sort the humans from the not-so-much humans.

After a kiss on my forehead, she'd sent me on my way.

Now here I was, riding up in the hotel's elevator with Dickie, the host from Paranormal Realty, and his Cher-look-alike assistant, Honey. Rosy the camerawoman would be along shortly with her equipment and the lead cameraman, Rad.

The lights in the elevator flickered, but the elevator continued upward without a jerk or pause. I wondered if a wire were loose. In a hotel this old, I wouldn't be surprised if it was a lot more than loose wires causing the flickering. The whole electrical panel could probably use updating.

The doors slid open. I gestured for Dickie and Honey to lead the way out into the empty hallway. My fingers were crossed that Cornelius was dressed this morning. My toes were doubly crossed that he wasn't going to kill me per Wilda's bidding while the cameras were rolling.

Taking a deep breath, I knocked on his hotel suite door. "Cornelius, we're here," I called through the door, trying to give him a heads up that he had company—the ones I'd called to remind him about last night. "We brought your protein shake."

A few seconds passed and then the lock clicked and the door opened wide. Cornelius was dressed in his usual Abe Lincoln Jr. garb, which included the stovepipe hat and a cane along with a dark wool suit. For once, I was happy to see his eccentric clothing choice. Maybe today wouldn't end with a ghost-inspired murder after all.

As we stepped inside of his suite, I sighed in relief. The place had been cleaned up and spit-shined, made ready for the camera. It even appeared that his paranormal gadgets and monitors had been dusted off.

In the morning light I studied Cornelius without being obvious, checking to see how he compared to his suite. He looked like Cornelius on the outside, but upon closer inspection, his cornflower blue eyes were slightly dilated and shifty, his skin more waxen than pale, and his movements were wooden. A life-sized Pinocchio minus the strings and telling nose. Prudence would have had fun playing with yet another puppet had she been here.

Dickie and Honey immediately kicked into high gear, scouting for good lighting locations, discussing the script, outlining where else in the hotel they wanted to shoot before the day was out. I stood back and watched, happy to have only to stand in front of the camera and talk. The sight of Ray Underhill breezing into the suite made me groan. Had it been too much to hope he'd skip his job of "coaching" me on the set today? Apparently so, because he was now eyeing my outfit with a disgusted frown on his face.

"Why are you wearing that?" he whispered when he joined me, glaring at my purple dress suit. "Jerry wanted you in pink today."

Jerry wanted me in pink every damned day. That man's obsession with pink should be analyzed one of these days. "Too bad. I got toothpaste on the pink dress." The toothpaste had actually blended in with the white polka dots, but I was happy to have an excuse to wear a different color and not look like a made-up 1950's housewife today.

"Honey is supposed to know about any wardrobe changes in advance."

"Honey told me the purple would look great on camera, so quit your bitching about my outfit and find something else to nag me about already."

When he couldn't come up with anything other than a bluster or two, I rolled my eyes and walked to the other side of the suite, joining Cornelius. "How are you feeling?"

He glanced at the TV show's host. "Ready to shine along with my haunted hotel."

"I mean how are you really feeling?" I spoke quietly through the side of my mouth.

"She cut my arm," he whispered back, pulling his sleeve up enough to show me the edge of the white bandage.

"I heard."

"First she broke my horn, Violet, and now this." His hand trembled as he sipped on his protein shake.

"We'll find you another horn."

"I've only ever read about ghosts who could cause actual injuries. I thought it was an exaggeration."

"You've never witnessed one yourself?" I was a little surprised after what his cousin had experienced.

Cornelius shook his head. "We need to take care of this soon before she grows even stronger and cuts deeper."

I agreed. "Do you think you can hold it together today?"

He didn't answer for a few seconds, and then tugged on his goatee. "The question is, can *she* hold it together being around you all day?"

"You tell me. You're the one she's chatty with."

He pushed his hat up, rubbing his forehead wearily. "I hope so. She's been quiet since you arrived."

"Is that a good thing or bad thing?"

"We'll see."

For the next hour, we tested lighting, sound, and lines. After that, Dickie started with his piece about the hotel. Next, Cornelius and I did another test run, and then we were on. I noticed a slight shake in Cornelius's hands at one point, but he seemed to regain control and play his role as the eccentric hotel owner without a hiccup. I could tell he'd played before an audience in the past.

Around noon, Dickie decided he needed to change his outfit before moving down to the second floor for more filming. Cornelius had offered Honey and him the empty room across the hall for the day and they disappeared into it along with Ray, closing the door behind them.

While Rad and his camera headed downstairs to check out the location, Rosy moved into the kitchen to review some of the morning's filming. The last time she'd filmed in town she'd lost footage while in the Carhart house and now made a habit of double-checking scenes before leaving a location.

Cornelius sat down heavily on one of his bar stools. I took the one next to him, careful not to crease or stain my outfit while chowing down a protein bar and some fruit.

"Violet," he said, opening one of the protein bars I'd offered him. He looked out the window where clouds had darkened the November sky. "I've been meaning to ask you something."

"What's that?"

"Do you like clowns?"

"Clowns? Not really, why?"

He finished off the bar before answering. "I keep having this dream about—"

"Uh, Violet," Rosy said from the kitchen. Her high, fluttery tone made Cornelius and me both frown in her direction. "You might want to come take a look at this."

I joined her with Cornelius following. "What's wrong? Am I too purple today?" I tried to joke, but the wide-eyed look she shot me made it fall flat as soon as it left my lips.

She pushed a couple of buttons on her camera and then pointed down at a display. "Watch."

I bent closer to get a good view of the screen. I was giving my lines about the role The Old Prospector Hotel had played in the past while Cornelius stood close by, adding a bit about the mirror exploding during a séance he'd had—one of his roundtable gatherings before I'd gotten into the game.

"It's coming," Rosy said from behind me.

One moment I stood alone, smiling into the camera. The next, I wasn't alone anymore.

I gasped, stepping back, bumping into Rosy.

She steadied me and then hit the pause button. She pointed at the screen. "Who's that?"

Next to me stood a hazy figure, semi-visible from the waist up. She had blonde pigtails, a white dress, and came to my shoulders.

"Wilda Hessler," Cornelius said without hesitation. When I glanced back at him, he added, "She's the girl in my dreams."

More like nightmares.

"Why is she staring up at Violet like that?" Rosy asked. "Is she trying to get her attention?"

More like kill me. Chills crept up my spine, spreading across my shoulder blades.

Cornelius held his finger over the play button. "Do you mind?" he asked Rosy.

"You think there's more?"

"I fear there will be."

I wished he wouldn't use that haunted house voice when we were talking about real ghosts.

The three of us practically butted heads as we watched the playback. Wilda stood watching me as I repeated the scripted lines Mona had written for me.

"That's sort of creepy," Rosy whispered.

More than sort of. I had goosebumps running up and down and all over town. I glanced around us. Was Wilda still standing next to me now? Was she watching the show along with us or still glaring at me?

I was trying to get over the idea of her standing next to me on the screen when she turned toward the camera. Where her eyes and mouth should have been were dark fuzzy circles, making her face look like a skeleton in pigtails.

"Holy fuck!" Rosy whispered. "She's looking at the camera."

"Or you," Cornelius said.

"That's some creepy-ass shit."

We all leaned closer, watching as one.

Wilda suddenly rushed the camera and shoved something up in front of the lens.

Rosy screeched and jerked back. I choked on my breath. Cornelius covered his eyes.

And just as quickly as Wilda had appeared, she was gone. The scene returned to Cornelius and me talking about the hotel.

I pulled Cornelius's hands away from his eyes.

Rosy hit the fast forward button and the show played on, twice as fast but still visible. Wilda didn't reappear. When the recording was done, the screen went black.

She stopped the playback. "Wow," she said, stepping back with her arms wrapped tight around her midsection like she was trying to hold something inside. "That was pretty warped. Have you two ever seen anything like that before?"

"No," I said.

"Yes," Cornelius answered just as quickly.

"What was that she shoved in front of the camera?" I asked. It had been a blur at the time, but I remembered some red and white and yellow on whatever it was.

"Do you want me to play it back again?"

"No!" Once was too much.

"It's a half-melted clown doll," Cornelius said, knowingly. When I shot him a how-do-you-know look, he shrugged. "I've seen it in my dreams. The face is half-melted off and the hair is completely gone on that side. It looks like it was in a fire."

As in the Hessler house fire? The very one I'd caused when I'd inadvertently knocked a candle over in a room filled with dead girls coated in lighter fluid? Had I burned up one of Wilda's favorite dolls? Was this rage about a stupid, damned doll? No, it had to be bigger than that, didn't it?

"I need to splash some water on my face." Rosy fanned her red cheeks and glistening forehead. "For some reason, I'm overheating all of a sudden."

I wondered if Wilda had something to do with that, too.

As soon as Rosy closed the bathroom door, I turned to Cornelius. "Is that why you asked me if I like clowns?"

"Yes. I keep seeing that clown doll in my dreams and wondered what it has to do with you."

I was afraid I knew what it had to do with me. Wilda was sending me a message with that clown, and it wasn't that she was happy to see me. I'd burned her clown and her house, and I'd killed her brother. She wanted revenge.

The urge to run out of the hotel had my feet tingling, but I owed it to Cornelius to stay the course today and as long as needed to free him from her monomaniacal fixation.

The rest of the day's filming went as planned, no more creepy little girl ghost and her half-burned doll. But I did keep watching around me, wondering if she were there. Not even Ray's nitpicking could distract me from worrying about Wilda and her macabre doll.

After we'd wrapped for the day, I bid Cornelius farewell after expressing my concern for him several times, which he waved off. He informed me he was going to sleep in the hotel across the street again tonight for a change of scenery and pushed me out of his suite with instructions to call him at precisely nine-twenty-eight tomorrow morning. I left on the comforting note that Cornelius was still his peculiar self under his tired mask.

I headed down the quiet hall, wondering if Rosy was going to show the footage with Wilda to Dickie and Honey tonight. She'd come out of the restroom earlier still pretty flushed and had seemed jumpy the rest of the afternoon, like me. As she'd packed up her equipment, I'd told her to call me if needed, giving her a look that made her nod in understanding.

I hit the elevator down-arrow, checking my phone for messages. Mona had called, so had Nat, but nothing from the cops or Doc. I was looking down at my phone when the elevator doors opened and I stepped inside, pulling up Mona's message first. When the doors closed, the lights flickered. I frowned up at the fixture just as it blinked off.

My heart rocketed into outer space, where the darkness and silence were probably similar to where I stood at the moment. What happened to the light and why wasn't the elevator moving? Were the elevator motor and the lights hooked up to the same electrical source? Then I remembered that I'd been so intent on pulling up Mona's message that I'd forgotten to hit the button for the lobby.

I turned on the flashlight feature on my phone and shined it on the buttons, tapping the one for the lobby two floors below. The button lit and the elevator started descending slowly, the motor droning in the darkness.

I shined the flashlight overhead at the dark light fixture, remembering how it had flickered earlier when I'd ridden up with Dickie and Honey. I'd have to let the front desk clerk know about it before I left.

"Violet," someone whispered in my ear, so close I could feel the poof of hot breath.

I gasped in surprise, fumbling with my phone before dropping it. The flashlight went out, leaving me in a darkness lit only by the faint glow of the first floor button.

Shit. I held my right hand over my pounding heart as my eyes tried to adjust to the dark. Had I really heard my name, or was my mind playing tricks on me?

Something bit into my forearm.

I screeched and whirled around, searching the shadow-filled corners as I clutched my arm. *What in the hell was that?*

The corners were too shadow-filled for me to see, so I moved closer to the dim light from the lobby button. Where was my phone? I tried to scan the floor for it, but it was too dark to see anything below my knees.

The elevator slowed to a stop. A rush of relief filled my legs, making them wobbly and weak. A ding sounded outside the doors. I backed up against them, keeping my eyes on the shadow-thick corners, wishing the damned doors would hurry up and open.

The lights overhead flickered on, the sudden brightness making me recoil.

Then I saw my phone. It rested on the handrail that lined the opposite wall. Next to it, with its legs splayed over the rail, was the half-burned clown doll I'd seen earlier in the video playback.

It took a second for me to remember to breathe.

Why weren't the doors opening?

I had a feeling it had something to do with that clown and the little girl who'd been holding it earlier.

Stepping forward, I reached as far toward my phone as I could without one foot leaving the doors. My hand trembled as it neared the phone. My gaze moved to that damned clown in case it decided to come to life and go all Chucky the killer doll on me. As soon as I grasped my phone, a cackle of clown laughter filled the elevator. I cried out and plastered myself back against the doors, which were now opening, thank God.

"Wilda," I said over the cackling while backing out of the elevator, "leave Cornelius alone."

The cackling stopped as suddenly as it had started.

As the elevator doors started to close, the light flickered out again. From out of the darkness I heard two words spoken in a high, scratchy voice: *Kill her.*

Chapter Thirteen

After joy-riding in an elevator with a bitter ghost and her freaky-ass clown doll, I drove straight home. I wasn't even going to try to keep from giggling hysterically in front of my coworkers for the last hour of the day and called in to say that I had a stress headache and would be in tomorrow morning.

I checked my arm every other minute on the ride home, looking for teeth marks, but nothing ever showed up—no indentations, no bruises, not even a single red mark. Maybe I was starting to crack up.

When I pulled into Aunt Zoe's drive, I groaned at the sight of Jeff Wymonds's pickup and rested my forehead on the steering wheel. "Oh, hell. Not this. Not tonight."

Before I'd even opened the door of my SUV, Harvey stepped down from the porch, followed by Jeff. The two approached, waiting for me to join them. Judging from Harvey's smartass grin, there'd be no skirting Jeff and the subject of counter-top sex.

I grabbed my purse and braced myself for the late afternoon cold breeze and Jeff's crass mouth.

"Looking good, Violet Parker," Jeff spoke before my feet touched the ground.

"Is Kelly here?" I asked, my fingers crossed that Jeff's reasoning for hanging out on my doorstep had nothing to do with his sexual escapades.

"Nope. I came to talk about what happened the other day."

So much for finger-crossing. I wrinkled my nose. "I'd rather not go there."

Harvey snorted.

"What are you doing out here?" I asked the old goat.

"Listenin' over yer back fence 'bout what happened the other day."

"I told him how you stopped by and watched me getting busy with my girlfriend." Jeff made a crude gesture with his index finger and closed fist, as if reliving it in my head wasn't enough torture. "And now you won't take my phone calls."

I wrinkled my upper lip along with my nose. "I wasn't watching you, Jeff."

"Sure you weren't." He winked exaggeratedly at me.

I resisted the urge to pop him in the eye and started walking up the sidewalk toward the house. I needed something to take the edges off of this day—fast.

Jeff caught up with me. "There's nothing wrong with liking to watch, Violet."

I whirled on him, glaring holes through his thick skull. "I was not staring at you and your girlfriend because I was getting my rocks off, Jeff. I was in shock. You weren't supposed to be home. Your truck wasn't in the drive."

Harvey joined us, his grin now bridging his earlobes.

"My truck was hidden in the garage. We like to sneak in a nooner every now and then for a little excitement." He moved in close enough for me to see a line of blond stubble he'd missed on his neck. "Speaking of making it more exciting," the glint in his eyes made my defenses raise their shields, spears at the ready. "My girlfriend said it made her really horny to have you watching us." He held up three fingers and wiggled his eyebrows.

Harvey whistled. "That's a hat trick."

"Blech!" was all I could think to say.

"We were wondering if you wouldn't mind stopping by again tomorrow say around twelve-thirty-ish for another 'surprise' visit? Maybe leave your hair down and look all wild and sexy this time."

"Oh, dear God." I scrubbed my hand over my eyes, trying to wipe away the vision of nipple rings bouncing in my head. "Jeff, please go away. I don't need this tonight."

"You could bring your boyfriend if you want, get in on some of the action."

Harvey's shoulders quaked with laughter. He was enjoying the pre-dinner show way too much for *my* own good. It was going to take a long time to live this down.

I walked away without replying. I'd rather stick my head in the toilet and hit the flusher than talk about Jeff and his girlfriend's sex-capades anymore.

"Think about it, Violet Parker. I'll park my truck in the garage again tomorrow and leave the front door unlocked."

I reached for the screen door handle. "Ask Harvey. I'm sure he'd be game."

"He won't do. My girlfriend digs blondes."

"Goodbye, Jeff. Tell Kelly that she can spend the night on Saturday if she'd like." Addy and I had agreed to a sleepover in exchange for her cleaning the upstairs bathroom yesterday.

I slammed the door shut behind me, not waiting for Harvey. Detouring straight upstairs, I changed into a long black cardigan sweater over one of my favorite old Elvis Presley T-shirts and yoga pants. I wasn't sure if Doc was coming over for supper or not, but I wasn't in the mood to dress in anything beyond the basics of comfort.

When I made it back down to the kitchen, Harvey was raiding Aunt Zoe's Betty Boop cookie jar while she fried hamburgers on the stove. My stomach growled, happy about the meat after a day of protein bars and pretzels from the hotel casino's bar.

I dropped into the chair next to Harvey and stole the cookie jar from his grasp.

"I don't want to talk about it," I told him before he'd opened his mouth to speak.

He wheezed with laughter.

"What's so funny?" Aunt Zoe asked, glancing at us over her shoulder.

"I'll tell you some other time."

"Was she wearing those fancy nipple rings he bought her?"

Yeah, and a bunch of tattoos. Something about that visual was stuck in my brain, and it had nothing to do with the actual act of sex. I blinked it away and crammed a chocolate chip cookie in my mouth.

"Shush it," I muttered, spitting a few crumbs in Harvey's direction by accident.

"Violet Lynn," Aunt Zoe said, "What's wrong with you?"

"I saw Wilda today."

Harvey's laughter fizzled out.

Aunt Zoe turned, spatula in hand. "But you can't see ghosts."

"I saw her when the camerawoman played back some of the filming we did."

Wrinkles filled Aunt Zoe's brow.

The doorbell rang.

I growled at Harvey. "If that's Jeff again, you're in trouble."

"Why am I in trouble? Yer the one playin' Nosy Parker through his kitchen window, not me."

I wish it had been through a window, then they wouldn't have heard me cry out in surprise. "He wasn't supposed to be there, dammit." I grabbed another cookie and headed for the front door, grumbling all of the way. When I opened it, Doc stood there holding a long wooden box in his arms.

His smile faded as he searched my face, turning into an all-out frown when he locked onto my eyes.

"What happened?"

"Jeff wants me to watch him and his girlfriend have sex again tomorrow because it makes their sneaky tryst more exciting, and Wilda accosted me in the elevator with a half-charred clown doll." I wasn't sure which was worse at the moment. Both gave me the heebie-jeebies in new and unique ways.

I held the door open for him while taking a bite of my cookie. He stepped inside, smelling fresh from outside, and paused in front of me to brush crumbs from my face. His kiss tasted better than the cookie, and I really liked Aunt Zoe's chocolate chip cookies.

"How about I stay over tonight and help you forget about both Wymonds and Wilda?"

When I nodded, he set the box down and stole the last half of the cookie from me. "Your aunt makes the best cookies."

"Between her treats and Harvey's mastery in the kitchen, my hips are starting to bulge."

"Mmmm, I love your hips." He ran his hand down over one, palming it.

"Flattery will get you everywhere, Mr. Nyce." I pointed at the box. "Whatcha got there?"

"I don't know. It has your initials on it."

I knocked on the wooden lid, remembering the crates I'd found at Mudder Brothers Funeral Parlor months ago. This box reminded me of them, only smaller. On the front was a rectangular piece of tin screwed into the wood. V.P. had been etched into the tin.

"What do you think it is?" I asked, lifting it. It weighed about as much as a toddler, only it was much less wiggly and sticky. Had Jeff left me a bribe? This was too big to be another set of nipple rings.

"We'll need something to pry it open." Doc took it from me. "Is Zoe's toolbox still in the laundry room?"

"I think so."

"Mom!" Addy yelled from the top of the stairs. Elvis clucked in her arms, wearing the green sweater with yellow baby chicks decorating it that my mother had crocheted for the damned bird.

"What?"

"Is supper ready?"

"Yes," Aunt Zoe answered from the kitchen. "Come and get it while it's hot."

"Put that bird in the basement, Adelynn, and then scrub your hands." I took the box back from Doc and stuffed it in the hall closet. If it was from Jeff, I certainly didn't want my kids to see it.

We followed Addy and Elvis into the kitchen with Layne bringing up the rear. I set the table with Layne's help, and then we all took a seat and dug into burgers and salad, along with some tater tots for the kids. Any talk about Wilda and Jeff Wymonds was put on hold until supper was over.

Before asking to be excused from the table, Layne shot Doc a sly look. "Are we going to go exercising again soon, Doc?"

I started to interfere, not wanting Doc to feel obligated to entertain my kids, but he beat me to the punch with, "I was thinking I could pick you two up after school tomorrow if that works for you?"

Addy nodded so fast and hard I thought her head might bobble right off.

Layne grinned. "Sure." Then he turned to me. "Mother, may I be excused so I can go upstairs and do my homework?"

"Me, too," Addy said, collecting her empty plate.

I squinted at each of them in turn. Something smelled like phony-baloney in Deadwood tonight. Getting my kids to do homework, especially Addy, usually required a lot of yelling and a good dose of threatening. "What's going on?"

"Nothing," they jinxed each other.

I looked over at Doc. He was too busy inspecting his fork to return my stare. "Fine, but put your dishes in the sink first. Addy, don't forget to clean Elvis's cage tonight. We don't want Aunt Zoe's basement starting to stink like a chicken coop." The bird didn't go outside as much since the weather had cooled.

They jumped up and rushed to the sink, giggling together as they raced out of the room.

"You know that you don't have to take them to the Rec Center if you're busy, right?" I asked Doc.

He set down the fork that had held him entranced moments ago. "I like to take them to the Rec Center."

"What do you guys do there?" I pressed.

Aunt Zoe cleared her throat, giving me a hard look.

Harvey leaned forward. "Yer makin' kitten britches for tomcats."

Doc chuckled. "I haven't heard that saying since my grandfather was alive."

"What does that mean?" I asked Harvey.

"It means mind yer own business, girlie."

"You're one to talk, you eavesdropping old man." I stood and collected plates. "Is it so wrong for a mother to be curious about what her children are up to when they're out of her sight?"

"Would you ask Wymonds what he was up to if he took them to the Rec Center?" Doc challenged.

He had me there, but that was only because I wasn't head-over-heels for Jeff, wanting him to spend the rest of his life having supper with us every night.

"Violet," Aunt Zoe cut in, "finish telling us about what happened today with Wilda."

I told my tale while I collected the rest of the dirty dishes from the table and put away the leftovers, ending with that goosebump-inducing clown in the elevator. The normalcy of my task helped keep my anxiety from bubbling up and burning my throat like it had on the way home.

"What I want to know," I directed at Doc, "is how can a ghost make a clown doll appear out of thin air?"

His frown deepened.

"I mean, earlier it was just a wispy image, like Wilda was. And then all of a sudden it was there with me in the elevator."

"Did you touch it?" Doc asked.

"Touch the clown doll?"

He nodded.

"Hell, no."

"Then how do you know it wasn't an illusion?"

"It looked real."

"Didn't you—and Harvey—say that Prudence looked real sitting there in the seat next to you last weekend?"

Harvey and I exchanged wrinkled brows. "I guess so."

"Did either of you touch Prudence?"

We both shook our heads. "No, but she touched me."

"Her hand went through you, though, right?" At my nod, he continued, "I would suspect what you saw in the elevator today was a very real looking manifestation."

"Of a half-burned clown doll?"

He shrugged. "It's better than the alternative."

"Next time you need to touch it," Aunt Zoe said.

"I'm not touching that doll."

"I hate clowns," Harvey said. "Touchin' that thing would turn my knees to puddin'."

I wet a clean dishrag and started wiping down the table. "What about the whisper and the bite? Are you going to tell me they weren't real either?"

"No," Doc lifted the bottle of hard cider I'd given him so that I could wipe under it. "I think Wilda has the ability to telepathically communicate with the living. As for the bite, she could have put that idea in your head as well and psyched you into thinking she bit you."

"But I'm a dud."

"You're not a dud."

"How come I've never been able to hear or see ghosts before?"

"You were a skeptic then, with your mind closed to possibilities. That's changed in the last five months."

"You think that's why I could see Prudence?"

"I think it might have something to do with your ability to see certain ghosts now, but that's really more of a theory. We don't know the extent of your abilities yet … or hers." He smirked. "We may never know on both counts."

"You're like a young flower," Aunt Zoe said. "Your outer petals are only now beginning to open."

"I feel more like an onion, sloughing off dead skin."

"Ya look like an onion tonight in that ragamuffin outfit, that's fer sure."

I threatened to throw the dishrag at Harvey. "For that, old man, you're coming with me and your nephew to see Prudence."

"No I'm not. That batty dead broad is bucksnortin' mean. She makes me all squirmy in my skivvies."

"I need a bodyguard."

"What do ya think Coop is?"

"Not *my* bodyguard. You gave me your oath."

"To defend you against livin' things."

"Do I need to stop down at the senior center and find another bodyguard?"

His bushy eyebrows pulled together. "Now, ya don't need to go stirrin' up hell with a long spoon."

"You're going then?"

"Well, ya sure seem to be makin' it somethin' I can't ride around."

"Blame your nephew. He's the one bent on meeting Prudence."

"Why is he so set on meeting her?" Aunt Zoe asked.

I grabbed a bottle of beer from the fridge for me, popping the top. "I kind of wonder if he thinks we're telling tall tales and wants to see her for himself."

"If she'll talk to him," Doc said, "Coop might find out a few answers to some of his unsolved cases."

I tipped the neck of my bottle toward him. "Or that."

"I think it's a mixture of both." Doc stood and left the room.

"Whatever the reason." I took a swallow of beer. "You're coming with me, Harvey."

"Why don't you take Doc?" Harvey asked.

"He needs to save up his energy to deal with Wilda. Besides, Prudence has proven that she can use pretty much anyone for a medium."

Harvey was still grumbling when Doc walked back in carrying the wooden box I'd stuffed in the closet earlier. Apparently, while it had slipped my mind, it hadn't his.

"What's that?" Aunt Zoe stood to take a closer look.

"It was outside on your front porch when I arrived earlier. It has Violet's initials on it."

I glanced at Aunt Zoe. "It's nailed shut. What do you have handy to pry it open?"

Harvey beat her to the punch, pulling a screwdriver from the side pocket in his overalls. "Ya never know—"

"When you're going to need to screw something," I finished for him. "You told us that once before."

"Spoilsport," Harvey said to me.

Doc grinned, taking the screwdriver from him. "It's always good to come prepared."

Aunt Zoe brought him a hammer. It took a minute, but he managed to loosen the lid. He turned to me. "It has your initials on it. You open it."

I chewed on my lower lip. "What if there's a half-burned clown doll inside?"

"Move aside, yellow belly." Harvey said, grabbing the lid and tugging it the rest of the way free.

Straw filled the interior.

I looked at Harvey. "Keep going, tough talker."

He stuck his hand into the straw, feeling around. Then he paused, his eyebrows turning into one long crinkly caterpillar. "What in tarnation?"

"What is it, Willis?" Aunt Zoe asked.

He pulled out what appeared at first to be a short handled ax. Upon closer inspection, I realized it was more a hammer of sorts, not an ax, and quite a bit more elaborate than a regular old hammer, having a spike on the opposite side of the face rather than a claw. A metal ram's skull decorated the center of the head while a dark leather strap wrapped down the handle, acting as a grip. The leather was darker at the far end, like it had been handled plenty. The metal head had several scars.

"What is that?" I asked.

"It's a war hammer," Doc said, taking it from Harvey to admire under the kitchen light. "I've only seen them in books and museums. Often they have longer handles so they can be used when on horseback."

"There's a note." Aunt Zoe plucked a piece of folded paper from the straw. She held it out to me.

The outside was blank. I unfolded it and read the words inside, a sinking anchor of dread hit bottom in my gut as I stared at the paper.

"What's it say?" Doc glanced up from the war hammer.

I held up the paper for him to see the words scrawled in a script that reminded me of something I'd see on a medieval scroll:

You will need this soon.

"Why am I going to need a war hammer?" I dropped into one of the chairs, resting my chin on my hand.

Doc touched his index finger to the tip of the spike. "Let's hope it's not to penetrate something coated with extra tough armor."

"Who left it for me? The war hammer fairy?" I inspected the paper again to no avail.

"I'm more worried about why it was left." Doc handed the war hammer back to Harvey.

"Whoever left it must know you're an executioner," Aunt Zoe said.

"Why's that?"

She pointed at a word branded in the wood on the inside of the lid. "*Carnifex.*"

"What's that mean?"

"It's the Latin word for *executioner.*"

* * *

Friday, November 16th

Morning came no matter how much I tried to hide under the covers and make it go away.

Doc was putting on his coat as I came down the stairs, his jaw dark with stubble, his duffel bag zipped and waiting by the front door. His gaze traveled up from my bare feet and legs to my puffy eyes. "You look soft and sleepy."

"I feel like something Layne dug up in the backyard." I paused on the bottom step, almost eye level with him. "Are you heading to the Rec Center?"

He nodded. "How'd you sleep? Any nightmares?"

"Only the usual sweet dreams. You know, killer clown dolls, angry one-armed albinos, and a bone cruncher or two." I shrugged. Such were my nights when I was left to my own devices for entertainment during pillow time. "How was the couch?"

Harvey had taken Aunt Zoe's bed since she'd planned to spend the night in her workshop, crashing on the sofa in her back room. That left the couch for Doc instead of my bed.

"I don't remember much after you went upstairs for the night."

"Any more wooden boxes left on the front porch?"

He peeked out the front window. "No. I guess one war hammer is all you're going to need."

"Lucky me." I ran my fingers through my hair, patting down a poof I'd acquired from my pillow. My first attempt in front of the bathroom mirror had barely made a dent in the tangled mess. "I should hop in the shower. Jerry wants to debrief me first thing this morning before the TV crew shows up."

He leaned back against the door, a smile on his lips. "I can't blame Jerry. I'd like to debrief you, too. Especially with your hair all crazy sexy like that."

I squinted at him. "You had your chance last night, but you passed."

"Your kids are right down the hall."

And they would be for another nine or ten years, maybe longer. We'd hit a stalemate on this one, since I wasn't going to ask him to make any kind of long term commitment and risk scaring him off, and he wasn't going to take a chance of my kids catching him under the covers with me.

"My door has a lock, you know."

He stared at me for several seconds, his expression sobering. "You do realize this isn't about your bedroom door, don't you?"

I thought on that for a moment, letting it sink into my foggy brain. No, I didn't. "Of course."

"Your nose twitches when you lie, Boots."

Covering my tell-tale appendage, I asked, "Okay, what's it really about?"

Was it me? My morning makeup-less face? My breath? Hair? Or was it something deeper, like the commitment that came with sleeping semi-regularly in a single mother's bed? Was he afraid if he had sex with me in my bed routinely with the kids down the hall that I'd think a wedding ring came next?

He picked up his duffle bag and hung it from his shoulder. "Think about it, and when you come up with a possibility, I'll be all ears." He bridged the distance and gave me a quick kiss on the lips. "Until then, beautiful, you know where to find me."

"On the couch?"

He smiled and left. I watched him close the door behind him, wishing I'd stuck with Plan A for the day and stayed hidden under the covers.

The kitchen was empty, thank the stars. I wasn't really in the mood to talk to anyone yet this morning, especially with the worries buzzing around my head thanks to Doc's cryptic reply.

And men complained that women were hard to figure out.

Oh, that was rich.

Doc had made fresh coffee. I grabbed a quick breakfast of yogurt and toast, chugged down a cup of coffee, and headed back upstairs to shower and get dressed. Harvey and the kids were stirring by the time I was ready to go talk to Jerry.

"Thanks again, Harvey," I said as he came down the stairs.

He helped me with my coat. "You owe me, girlie. How 'bout ya leave me out of the Prudence field trip in return?"

"Nope. There's no way I can handle Prudence *and* your prickly nephew on my own. You're stuck, so quit trying to weasel out of it."

Grumbling and sputtering, he waddled off toward the kitchen. I kissed each kid goodbye and threatened eternal grounding if they didn't behave for Doc when he took them to "exercise" at the Rec Center after school.

There was a dusting of snow on the ground this morning, making it look like someone had dropped a big bag of flour above the town on Mount Moriah. The streets were clear without any slipping and sliding, the ground not cold enough to keep the snow from melting.

The Picklemobile wasn't parked in Doc's usual spot, but then I was a half an hour early coming into work this morning. Jerry's Hummer was the only vehicle on the scene. I climbed down from my SUV, breathing in the fresh, cool pine-scented air as I made my way to Calamity Jane's back door.

When I stepped inside, I could hear Jerry's voice. His office lights were on but the door was shut. His voice was too clear for him to be behind a closed door. The bathroom was dark, the door open. I made my way out front and found Jerry sitting at Ben's desk, talking on his cell phone.

"Sounds good, Dickie. We'll meet you there in an hour." He hung up and smiled at me as I set my purse down. "Good morning, Violet. Thanks for coming in early. This filming business has me burning the candle at both ends."

Why him? He hadn't shown up yesterday at The Old Prospector Hotel until the afternoon, and then he'd only stayed for an hour and left again.

"No problem." I glanced down the hall toward his office. "Do you want to talk out here or in your office?"

"I don't want to go in there right now," he said, scowling in the direction of his office. "How did it go yesterday?" He leaned back in Ben's chair, his fingers laced behind his head. "Did you have any luck with the ghosts that I've heard haunt the place?"

Hadn't he been speaking with Dickie a moment ago? Surely Rosy had shown Dickie and Honey the Wilda footage. The clown doll shoved in the camera's eye? I would think that piece of film would be gold for the show and Dickie would be raving about it on the streets of Deadwood. The idea of how this piece of film would affect my reputation and future as a Realtor had been one of my middle of the night worries last night, right after my nightmare about Caly stabbing me in the eye with a broken piece of glass over and over and immediately before the one where I woke up next to that half-burned clown cackling at me with its big frozen mouth.

"I'm not sure." I played dumb, heading over to the coffee machine so my nose didn't get all twitchy about my answer. "I didn't notice anything while we were filming." No lie there.

Until Rosy told everyone about the segment we'd caught with Wilda, I wasn't going to say a peep.

"I liked your outfit yesterday. It turned out better than the pink one we'd discussed."

I stirred some sugar into my coffee, waiting for the "but" that was sure to come. When it hadn't by the time I tossed the stir stick in the trash and returned to my desk, I smiled. "Thanks. I tried to keep your clothing tips in mind when I picked it out. I spilled toothpaste on the pink dress."

A note was stuck to my desk. Mona's writing was on it, telling me she was still working on finding out if the owner of the Sugarloaf Building was interested in selling to Katrina King.

"Is the pink dress still usable?" Jerry asked.

"Sure. I dropped it off at the cleaners on the way to the shoot yesterday. They said the toothpaste should come out without a problem."

"Good. You can wear it on Monday. Or maybe the white one with cherries on it."

I wasn't a fan of either dress, but the cherry covered dress made me cringe the most. "What's Monday?"

"You're on camera again."

"I am?" I thought The Old Prospector Hotel had been my last gig.

"Yep. Ray overheard Mona making some phone calls about a place up in Lead called the Sugarloaf Building. He said it's a well-known haunt, and he was able to get permission from the management company overseeing it to film on the bottom floor."

I more or less fell into my chair. Why did it seem like someone or something was trying to get me into that building come hell or high water? "But I don't know anything about the Sugarloaf Building."

"Ray is putting a script together on it for you. He knows a little of its history and says he can come up with enough to satisfy Dickie and his crew."

"Then maybe Ray should be the one on camera."

Jerry snickered, shaking his head. "Ray's no good on camera, Violet. He doesn't shine as bright as you and Ben."

I didn't fully believe that, but I could tell Jerry had his mind made up, which meant I was stuck. "Okay, Monday I'll wear whichever dress you choose." *Please not the cherry dress.* "If you see Ray before I do, tell him I'll need a day to go through the script so I can memorize it."

"Will do." He knocked twice on the desk, reminding me of a judge with a gavel. Court adjourned, onto the next hearing. "How are things going with Rex Conner?"

Not well enough, considering the bastard was still breathing. Maybe if I threatened Rex with my new medieval war hammer he'd leave me alone. "I haven't really had time to work with him between both of our busy schedules."

"How do you feel about letting Mona help out with finding him a place?"

It took everything I had not to hop up on my desktop and dance the Charleston. Mona, my guardian angel, had stepped in to help me. "I'm okay with that."

"You're sure? I don't want you to feel like she's stealing your client."

"Oh, I don't feel that way even a little. I'd love to have her help with …" *castrating the bastard,* "… finding him a place to live."

Two more knocks on Ben's desk said we were done with that, too.

Zelda Britton answered my call after a couple of rings.

"Zelda, it's Violet Parker."

"Violet, I've been thinking about you this morning."

Really? "Is everything okay with the house?"

"Everything is wonderful."

"Good. Listen, I was wondering," I hesitated, licking my lips.

"You were wondering if you could come for a visit."

Wow, she must be able to read minds through the phone. "Yes, but I won't be alone."

"That's okay with me, but I'm not sure how Prudence will feel about company."

"Prudence?" Had Zelda actually said that name aloud?

"She is who you're coming to see, I presume."

"Uhhh," Zelda's familiarity with Prudence had me twisting in the wind for a moment, trying to get a foothold.

"It's not the house that has me thinking about you this morning, Violet, it's Prudence. She told me you'd be coming to visit."

"Did she happen to mention why I'd be coming?" I hoped Prudence hadn't opened her big ghost mouth about my being an executioner.

"Yes, she did," Zelda spoke nonchalantly, as if we were discussing the chance of more snow later tonight. "Prudence said you're going to need her help avenging Wanda Carhart's death."

Chapter Fourteen

According to Zelda, Prudence demanded my presence at her home immediately. For a woman who had been dead and loitering around the house for over a century, Prudence sure was short in the patience department. Since my afternoon was wide open, I told Zelda I'd stop by after lunch.

After I hung up with Zelda I called Cooper. The last thing I wanted to do today was have tea and biscuits with a skeptical cop and a haughty ghost who thought her family line of executioners was superior to mine, but I knew from experience that avoiding either would make them even bigger pains in my ass.

The phone rang on Cooper's end five times before he bothered to answer it. "Make it count, Parker," was his greeting. "I don't have time to listen to you prattle on about your nail color this morning."

"You know what, Cooper? Screw you." I hung up and cursed out several puffs of breath at the cold gray sky. This was the thanks I got for delivering on one of his demands?

"Lesson learned, Detective," I told my phone.

My cell phone rang. I let out one more puff of steam and then took the call. "Are you going to be nice this time, Cooper?"

"The only reason 'nice' is part of my vocabulary around you, Parker, is because it's your boyfriend's last name. Now what do you need to talk to me about?" His tone was much less snippy this time, almost friendly. Almost.

"Meet me up at the Carhart's place at one o'clock today."

"What?! This is pretty short notice."

"Oh, I'm sorry. Was I supposed to clear an appointment to interrogate a ghost with your secretary first?"

"Watch that mouth, Parker. I can still arrest you."

"For what?"

He let out a bark of laughter. "The list is long, trust me."

"Yeah, but the question is—can you or your bumbling gumshoe

partner make it all stick?" When he grumbled something unintelligible in reply, I smirked. "I thought not. Remember, this was your idea, not mine. Besides, I'm not the one who insisted we do this today, Prudence did."

"A ghost is demanding our attendance?" he asked in a much quieter voice. Had someone walked within listening range? Detective Hawke? The Chief of Police?

"No, Prudence wants to see *me* as soon as possible. She believes I'm in need of her help avenging Wanda Carhart's death. I'm merely bringing you along for your charming company as far as she is concerned."

"Listen, Parker," he lowered his voice even more, making me press my phone closer and plug my other ear. "You promised Nyce to keep your big nose out of this case. You'd better stick to that promise or things down here at the station are going to get messier concerning your status as a *Suspect*."

"I gave Doc my word and I plan to stick to it. If it wasn't for you, I wouldn't be going to see Prudence. So, don't start gnawing on me because the ghost you insist I introduce you to wants to talk to me about the death of a mutual acquaintance. And on that note, let me add up front that any snags in Wanda's case that arise due to today's visit are *your* fault, not mine."

"I'll remember this conversation when you're knee deep in Wanda's murder and calling me to save your ass."

"You save my ass? Ha! Monkeys on broomsticks will fly out of it before that happens."

"Jesus, Parker," he paused to growl in the phone. "I swear, you'd argue with a fence post most days. Why do you always have to come at me shooting with both barrels?"

"Because your stinger is usually sticking half out." I stole one of Harvey's lines. "Now quit your bawling and meet me up at the Carhart house at one. And don't be late. Prudence hates tardiness."

I hung up before he could get in the last word and returned to my desk with hopes of burying myself in my job to kill time. After several long, worry-filled, unproductive minutes, Mona returned from lunch.

I grabbed my coat. "I have a house to show Detective Cooper," I told her and headed for the door. She didn't ask any questions, so there was no need to clarify that the house was known for its notorious past or that I'd already sold it last month.

I swung by Cooper's place first to pick up Harvey on the way to the Carhart … make that Britton house. Maybe I should call it Prudence's place from now on, since the other living residents came and went over the decades while she kept on being dead within its walls year after year.

After a minute of waiting for Harvey to come out, I honked the horn. He knew I was coming. I'd texted him before leaving work.

Another minute later I was still sitting out by the curb and Harvey's grizzled mug hadn't made an appearance in Cooper's doorway. Cursing under my breath, I climbed out and stalked up the walkway. After three hard fist pounds on the door, I yelled, "Harvey! I have the key to this door, so you'd better get your butt out here or I'm coming in."

I'd learned my lesson about walking into occupied client houses without announcing my intentions. Jeff's red thong had taught me that one.

The door swung wide. "Hold yer damned horses, girl. I had to see a man about a mule." He stepped out onto the porch with me. "I wanna have my tank empty in case that old dame tries to scare the piss out of me again."

"Sorry." I started back down the steps. "I thought you were chickening out."

"I would if I could, but you'd find me and drag me along by my ear if I tried." He followed me to my SUV. "Where's Coop?"

"He'll meet us there."

"Ya think the boy is ready for this?"

"Are you?" I opened the driver's side door, climbing in behind the wheel. "Because I'm certainly never ready for an encounter with Prudence."

Harvey buckled his seatbelt. "If that ain't the truth, you can cut me up for catfish bait."

As I drove the rest of the way down one hill in Lead and up another hill to where Prudence waited for us, I told Harvey about my earlier conversation with Zelda.

He frowned under his beard. "Feels like we're parachutin' into an eruptin' volcano."

"What do you mean?"

"I'd sorta hoped Prudence would play hide-and-seek with Coop, and we could skip havin' to flap jaws with her—my jaws in particular."

"Me, too."

Cooper's unmarked sedan was parked at the curb when we pulled into the drive. He stepped out in the cold still air and zipped his black leather coat up before joining us as we made our way up the walkway in silence. Neither Harvey nor I were in a big rush, in spite of Cooper's attempts to herd us along.

"What's with you two?" Cooper glared at each of us in turn as we stepped up onto the porch. "I don't have time to waste smelling the roses all the way to the damned front door. Let's get inside and wrap this up."

"What's got you chompin' at the bit, boy?"

"The stack of paperwork on my desk isn't going anywhere unless I'm there to move it."

After a final squint in our direction, Cooper pressed the doorbell. When the door opened on the other side of the screen, he dragged me in front of him, holding me in place by the shoulders.

"Hi, Zelda," I said with a smile, as if we were there for hot chocolate with marshmallows. "I brought my friend Harvey and his nephew, Cooper, along with me." I purposely left off Cooper's *Detective* title in case that caused any friction with Zelda or Prudence. Although, Cooper had been here before to interrogate Wanda, so Prudence might remember him.

"Come in out of the cold." Zelda actually looked happy to see us. If she'd known our true reason for coming, I wondered if she'd be as smiley.

We log-jammed into the front foyer, handing Zelda our coats to hang in the hall closet. Zelda led the way into the sitting room, which still looked almost exactly as it had when Wanda had lived there, furniture and all, except for the personal photos on the sideboard and a bright oil painting of daisies now hanging on the wall. The place even smelled the same, only there was a hint of apple pie in the air, too.

"If you three will have a seat, I'll dish up some pie."

Ah ha, so the apple pie was the real deal.

Harvey licked his chops. "I'm hungry enough to eat a buffalo with the hide still on it."

After Zelda left the room, I took a seat on the end of the couch. Harvey shook his head at me when I patted the middle couch cushion next to me.

"It's safer over here." He lowered himself into the chair on the other side of the coffee table.

That left Cooper the rest of the couch, but he chose to remain standing at the end opposite me.

"You might want to sit," I told him. Prudence tended to knock the wind out of most folks.

"I prefer to stand."

"This isn't really an interrogation, you know. I was joking earlier when I said that."

"You let me decide what it is." He pulled out his hand gun and checked it before stuffing it back into his shoulder holster.

"Why did you bring *that* along," I said under my breath. There was no need to bring a gun into this house, especially with its murder-filled history. The place was hair-raising enough without the potential for bullets flying.

"I always carry it."

"I shoulda brought Bessie along." Harvey tugged on his beard as his gaze warily roved the room.

"Guns will only piss her off," I told both of them.

"The safety is on, Parker," Cooper said. "So why don't you relax and focus on playing patty-cake with your ghost buddy."

Patty-cake? Oh man, Cooper needed to keep in mind the old adage: never underestimate the power of a woman. Especially when the woman was a dead executioner who could manipulate the living.

Harvey grimaced at his nephew. "Keep talking that blue streak, boy, and yer gonna wanna hold onto yer teeth."

The old man was right. Prudence had a history of having her puppets yank out their own teeth when her feathers got ruffled.

I frowned at the sarcastic, gun-toting skeptic in the room. "I am focusing, Cooper. I'm focusing on where I can take cover so that I don't end up with a bullet in me by mistake when Prudence freaks you out with one of her surprises."

His upper lip curled. "I'm no rookie."

"You are when it comes to Prudence."

Zelda joined us again, setting a tray with four pieces of pie dolloped with whipped cream, and forks and napkins on the coffee table. "Pie anyone? I find there is something about this house that makes me want to bake, and with Zeke gone for the weekend, it would be a shame to let a warm pie go to waste."

That warm pie was going to go straight to *my* waist, since my willpower was currently nowhere to be found. I suspected my stomach had it chained and ball-gagged in a closet somewhere.

Harvey beat me to the tray, taking his pie back to his safety zone. Cooper held back, thanking Zelda politely but refusing.

No pie? It was moments like this when I returned to my suspicion that the detective was a killer robot sent back from the future to destroy mankind.

"I could get you something to drink instead," Zelda offered Cooper. "I have tea, coffee, cider, and hot chocolate. Oh, and water of course. But no ice."

I stopped with the fork midway to my lips, locking wide eyes with

Harvey for a moment.

"Why no ice cubes?" I asked Zelda, the déjà vu I'd been experiencing since entering the house was growing stronger by the minute.

"It's the oddest thing. The ice maker on the refrigerator we bought isn't working. We had a repairman out to look at it and he can't figure it out either, so the appliance store is shipping us another refrigerator this week."

I stuck a piece of warm, chewy apple pie goodness in my mouth to keep from telling her that Wanda had experienced similar problems. Maybe I should have added the no-ice-cubes disclaimer on the sale paperwork. What did Prudence have against ice cubes, anyway?

"No, thank you," Cooper said politely, holding his stiff-legged stance. I saw a grimace flash across his face before he could corral his features back into the usual hard-edged mask. I couldn't tell if he continued to stand because he was uncomfortable being there with us, or if that piece of rebar jammed up his anal cavity made it more painful to sit some days than others.

"I'd love a cup of tea," I said, more to get Zelda out of the room for another moment than to actually drink anything. After she left, I polished off the last of my pie and set the plate on the tray. Harvey did the same, and then picked up the piece Cooper hadn't eaten.

"What are you doing?" I asked him.

"Ya heard Betty Crocker—we shouldn't waste warm pie."

I rolled my eyes at him and looked back at his nephew, only to blink in surprise. Something was wrong.

Cooper's skin was turning ashen, his breathing audibly labored, his eyes red and watery. He looked like he was going to toss his cookies right there on Zelda's plush white rug.

"Cooper?" I stood as his knees started to give.

He lurched forward. I barely caught him before he timbered into the coffee table. He weighed a lot more than I'd have guessed for his rawhide frame. Maybe he really was made of granite, which would explain his chiseled expression most days.

"I need ..." he said in between gasps, "to sit."

I helped lower him onto the couch next to me. His muscles trembled under my hands, his skin felt hot through his shirt. "Are you okay?"

"Really dizzy." He lowered his head between his knees, gulping deep breaths. "Give me ... a minute."

Harvey stood across the coffee table from us, scooping bites into his mouth. "He should've eaten some pie," he mumbled in between bites.

"His blood sugar might be tankin'."

"Has this happened to him before?"

Harvey shrugged. "How should I know? I'm not his momma." He glanced toward the kitchen, then whispered, "He looks like he saw a ghost. Seems fittin' for this place, don'cha think?"

"Aren't you a little concerned about your nephew?"

"Nah, that boy can lick a chainsaw most days. He'll be right as rain soon as he catches his wind."

I tentatively touched Cooper's shoulder and then pulled away, but not before I noticed his shirt was damp. He and I weren't very hands-on with each other most days—make that ever. The last time I'd touched him had been when I'd planted the back of my skull into his nose. "Cooper, what's going on? Talk to me."

"He'll be fine," Zelda said, joining us with my cup of tea. "Prudence had a similar effect on Zeke the first time he met her." She giggled. "I think it's harder for men to handle her," she passed the steaming mug of tea to me. "Or maybe they fight her more, who knows. I hope you like blueberry tea. I thought it would be a nice chaser after the apple pie." She turned to Harvey, who was finishing off a bite of crust while staring at his nephew as if an alien might burst forth from his stomach at any moment. "Would you like another piece of pie, Mr. Harvey?"

He nodded, handing her his empty plate without taking his eyes off Cooper.

"How about I bring the whole pie out here and then we can get started?" Zelda disappeared back into the kitchen.

"Coop?" Harvey slinked behind his chair again, the big scaredy-cat. "You feelin' all right, boy?"

"No," Cooper wheezed. The back of his light blue shirt was now spotted with sweat. His shoulders started to shake more violently.

Holy crap! Something was going to hell in a handbasket here. I was used to dealing with this sort of shit when Doc was in the thick of working his ghost medium gigs but not with someone like Cooper who had no paranormal abilities. I needed to do something before he keeled over and we had to call the paramedics, and then I got busted by Detective Hawke for assaulting a police officer.

I looked at Harvey. "Maybe we should come back some other ti—"

Cooper's hand snaked out and latched onto my leg above my knee, his iron grip making me freeze.

"Cooper, what are you doing?" I tried to scoot away but his grip held tight, his long fingers wrapping two-thirds around my leg. "Let go, damn it."

When he didn't release me, I palmed his forehead and pushed his head up so I could see his eyes. His lids were still closed, but I could see his eyeballs rolling around behind them. It reminded me of someone in REM sleep. I cringed as I kept watching, waiting for his lids to open and the whites of his eyes to turn my way. That was Prudence's usual routine when she commandeered someone to use as her puppet.

"Why did you bring this lawman into my house?" Prudence's mid-Atlantic, Grace Kelly-like accent came from behind me.

I squawked and whirled around as best I could with Cooper's hold on me.

Zelda stood holding a pie pan in her oven mitts, her eyes rolled back showing only the whites. There it was. The white-eyed look I'd been expecting from Cooper.

So, if Prudence was speaking through Zelda, what was going on with Cooper? And why was his hand still locked onto my leg?

"He wants to ask you some questions about Wanda Carhart's death," I told Zelda ... make that Prudence.

The pie pan started to slide out of Zelda's oven mitts. I tried to stand to catch it, but Cooper's vice-grip on my knee held me in place, a flash of pain making me flinch.

Harvey rushed to the rescue. He caught the pie as it slid free of Zelda's mitts. Cursing, he lowered the hot pie pan to the coffee table, setting it on the book that I slid his way.

"You let her die." Prudence didn't try to hide her contempt.

I'd expected to bear some of her anger over Wanda's death, but it didn't mean I liked it. "She was murdered before you even warned me to check on her. As far as I'm concerned, it's your fault, too." I pointed up at Zelda. "*You* should have warned me sooner."

Cooper's grip on my leg squeezed hard, making me cry out and squirm under his touch. What the hell, Cooper?!! While I figured it wasn't him at the helm, it didn't stop me from wanting to sock him in the nose again. Instead of planting my fist in his face, I focused on trying to free my leg.

"You dare disrespect me, Executioner!" Prudence bit out as I struggled to pull out of Cooper's hold. "My skills remain far superior to yours."

My eyes watered from the pain she was inflicting through Cooper. "I'm sorry, Prudence," I said, tugging on his wrist with no luck.

Finally his clasp eased, but his hand stayed in place, still holding me prisoner.

Somehow Prudence was speaking through Zelda while controlling

Cooper's body. This was a first, as she usually worked only one puppet at a time. Either her strength was growing like Wilda the ghost's was, or Zelda was a clearer channel for Prudence to use than Wanda had ever been.

Meanwhile, I was stuck with a damned cop attached to my leg. I tried to pry Cooper's fingers up one at a time to no avail. How fitting for Prudence to use the detective as the tool to cause me grief.

While I struggled under Cooper's clamp on my leg, Harvey scuttled over and scooped another piece of pie onto his plate.

I gaped at him. "You've got to be kidding me."

"I was off my feed earlier." He shoveled another forkful into his mouth. "Besides," his voice was muffled with pie, "it's a shame to let it get cold." He pointed a fork at Cooper, his eyes widening. "Better watch that," he said, ducking behind the chair.

When I looked back at Cooper, he—or rather Prudence—had drawn his handgun from his holster.

"What are you doing, Prudence?" I said in a high voice, leaning away from the bozo with the loaded gun. What had I said about bringing a gun to a haunted house, dang it?

"Such puerile weapons humans use," Prudence continued to speak from Zelda's mouth.

Cooper tossed the gun onto the coffee table, where it spun in a circle like we were playing spin the bottle. The barrel came to a stop pointing at me.

Of course it did.

I huffed, glaring at Cooper-the-gun-toting puppet. When this was all over, I was going to take his gun and clock him upside the head with the damned thing.

"Prudence," I said, trying to stretch my right leg out. Cooper's grip was starting to make it tingle with pins and needles clear to my ankle. "There were several messages left at Wanda's house, all saying the same thing: *We want what belongs to us.* The lawman I brought along needs more information about who broke into the house and what you think they were searching for so he can find the killer."

"It is your duty to find the killer, Executioner. Not his."

"Times have changed from when you were alive, Prudence. I can't go snooping around crime scenes and killing bad guys willy nilly. The police will throw me behind bars and what good can I do from there? My hands are tied. I have to work with the police on cases like Wanda's." I tried a sneak attack, attempting to yank Cooper's hand free while I had her distracted.

Prudence made him clamp down hard again, bruising my bruises. My eyes watered anew from the punishment she was inflicting.

"The law cannot be trusted," she said when I stopped fighting his grip and held still.

"Not all of the police are trustworthy, that's true." I had experienced that first hand when I first received that anonymous threatening note after reclaiming my purse from evidence. "But this lawman sitting beside me is different. He knows about you and me and what we are. He respects our kind." Okay, so maybe that was exaggerating a teeny bit. "He's willing to help us no matter the consequences."

"So you say, but why should I trust him beyond your word?"

"He has a good heart."

A hard laugh came from Zelda. "He has a strong heart and an even stronger will. I can feel both as he fights me, but that does not mean he will not strike given opportunity. I put my trust in lawmen when I was alive and my family suffered. Murdered in cold blood." They'd been killed before her eyes according to Doc, who had traded places with Prudence on previous visits and relived her death. But this was the first I'd heard that the police had been involved somehow.

"Every human can be bought for the right price, Executioner, even those who vow to protect. Don't ever forget that or you may suffer the same fate as me." Cooper's fingers began to tighten again. "How do I know you haven't brought another traitor into my house?"

I looked to Harvey for help. He'd returned to his chair to watch the show. "Tell her about the doin's out back of my barn last month."

Struggling under Cooper's grasp as pain shot up and down my leg, I glared at Zelda. "Prudence, stop it and listen."

His clench held steady, not tightening further but not loosening either.

I breathed through the pain, like they'd taught me in birthing class. "You can trust this lawman because I've tested him and he passed."

"How did you test him?"

I could hear the disbelief in her question.

"He helped me kill a bone cruncher," I told her.

"Humans can't kill bone crunchers, Executioner."

"Officially, I killed it, but he distracted it." Sort of.

Actually, Doc had distracted it, but Cooper had filled it with lead and done a great job of pissing off the ugly beast before I'd stepped in to keep it from ripping him to shreds.

"You took a human with you to a kill?" Cooper's grip on my leg loosened enough for me to rest easy again. "Such an inept hunter." Her disgust was crystal clear. "It is unfortunate that your line of executioners was sent to finish the job mine started."

Yeah, well Prudence and her super-star relatives were all dead, while mine were still getting the job done, so she could take her high and mighty attitude and shove it. Although I hid that thought behind a grimace since Cooper's fucking hand was still locked onto my leg.

"You will avenge Wanda's death, Executioner." There were no ifs, ands, or buts about it in her mind apparently. "If you refuse to take up arms and do your duty, this lawman will die."

What? Was she threatening to kill him? "By whose hand?"

"It is not in his power to complete the task."

I was afraid of that, but I doubted Cooper would listen to me or a dead woman when it came to facing off with Wanda's killer. "I don't know where to find the one who murdered Wanda," I admitted.

"You must set a trap. Any good hunter knows that."

"And use what for bait? Myself?"

"You are not what they want."

"What do they want?"

"I warned you to protect Wanda."

"Do you have any suggestions on finding the killer before she finds me?"

"She? You speak as if you know who murdered Wanda."

"I might. She's, as you say, one of the undead."

The first time Prudence had called Caly and her albino-like buddies that, I'd been confused. I'd figured she meant the human actors in a zombie wedding musical that was performed at the Opera House back in October. Today, I wasn't confused.

"She and I have faced off before," I continued. "I believe she wants revenge."

"But revenge does not explain why Wanda was killed, nor why this house was searched after she had moved out." Zelda's mouth moved once or twice without sound coming out. I wondered if Prudence's strength was beginning to weaken. Cooper's hold on my leg certainly seemed to be.

"I saw something on the visitor that night," Prudence finally got out.

"What?"

"A tattoo—Half goat, half pig. It was the same tattoo worn by the men who murdered my family."

I knew that tattoo. Lila had the same one on her chest.

"I know what they want," I told Prudence, my understanding of the situation suddenly clear.

"What?" Harvey beat Prudence to the punch.

"The book."

"What book?" Prudence asked.

"The book Lila was going to use to raise Kyrkozz the demon. She had it the night she died."

"Where is this book?" Prudence asked.

"I have it." Actually, Aunt Zoe had it now, since I'd given it to her. The text was written in Latin, and since my knowledge of that written language went only as far as Pig-Latin vernacular, I needed her help deciphering it.

"That means Wanda's death is even more your responsibility. You must avenge her, Executioner," Prudence demanded.

Prudence was right. If I hadn't taken the book and hid it, Wanda might still be alive. "I will," I told Prudence and meant it.

"You will try," she corrected. "When I release this lawman, tell him the answers he seeks can be found with the timekeeper."

Ms. Wolff? She'd been slain by one of Caly's cohorts last month. "I already told you that Ms. Wolff is dead."

"There is more than one. Find the other."

Criminy! I hadn't even known the first existed until it was too late. "How will I find the other?"

"Must I do everything for you?"

"Cut me some slack. I'm new at this, remember?"

"I do not know what the other timekeeper's disguise may be, but I can tell you that timekeepers reside close together in case one is eliminated. It is crucial the other maintain the time."

"What happens if the time isn't maintained?"

Zelda's cheeks creased into a ghoulish smile. "All of Hell will break loose, of course."

All of Hell? What exactly was in Hell to break free besides Kyrkozz?

With a blink, Zelda's green eyes were back in place. "Oh dear, did I drop the pie?" she asked.

"Harvey saved it." I shot the old man a glare. "Were you paying attention to everything she said or were you too busy filling your pie-hole?"

"She who?" Cooper asked from the couch cushion next to mine. "Who said what?"

I looked at him, and then down at where his hand was still clutching my leg.

His gaze dipped to his hand as well. It took him a second before he yanked his hand back like it had been burned. "What did you do to me, Parker?" He leapt up and put several feet between us, rubbing his forearm.

"I didn't do anything. You met Prudence."

"I did not."

"Yes, you did, and you lost the battle."

"What battle?" He grabbed his gun off the coffee table, aiming a squint at me as he stuffed it back into his holster.

"The battle for control." I reached down and pulled the hem of my skirt far enough up for him to see what I could feel—five reddish-purple marks clearly made by his fingers. "Who do you think did this to my leg, Cooper?"

Zelda gasped. "Oh, my Lord. Did Prudence do that?"

"Yeah, through him."

Cooper's face paled again. I scooted further out of his reach in case Prudence wanted to get in one last squeeze before I left.

"Did she tell you why she wanted you to come today?" Zelda collected the pie plates, clattering them onto the tray along with the pie.

"Yes, she did." And then some. I had a feeling the punishment she'd inflicted through Cooper's hand was merely a taste of what she could do when angered. Why couldn't my mentor be like Glinda, the Good Witch from the North with her pretty pink dress and sparkling crown? "Thank you for allowing us to come to your home and speak with her."

"The pie was delicious," Harvey added, fishing pie crumbs out of his beard.

A lot of help he was this afternoon. Next time I'd be better off bringing Elvis the chicken. At least she might try to peck at Cooper's hand for me.

I started to stand and dropped back onto the couch. A sharp pain from my thigh down held me immobile for a moment.

Cooper reached out to help me up and I batted his hands away. "Don't touch me. Just give me a moment to get some blood back into my lower leg."

I rubbed my thigh gingerly and stretched my calf. Then I stood, testing my weight on it. The pain eased to a dull ache as I limped toward the door. Harvey handed me my coat, careful to keep his distance. I didn't blame him. Prudence didn't play nice most days.

"I'll be in touch," I told Zelda ... or maybe not since "touching" in this house tended to come with a side effect of fear or pain or both.

I followed Harvey out the door. Cooper brought up the rear, keeping his distance along with his silence all of the way out to our vehicles.

As we neared my Honda, Harvey rubbed his belly. "You know, I could use a burger."

I scoffed. "After all of that pie?"

"The pie whet my appetite, and they were small pieces. Don't you owe me a dinner?"

I owed him several, as a matter of fact. I could use something to fill my stomach, too, since I'd skipped lunch. Comfort food beckoned after Prudence's reprimand. "Bighorn Billy's?"

He nodded and rounded the front of the SUV.

"Parker." I could hear the weariness in Cooper's voice. His battle with Prudence must have worn him down around the edges. The sharp-tongued detective who'd greeted me upon arrival was gone. "I need to know what happened in there."

I pulled open my door. "You want to join us, Detective?"

"I can't. I have a meeting this afternoon."

I searched his gaze, seeing the uncertainty and conflict behind his gray eyes. Damn it. The last thing I wanted to do was feel bad for Cooper, but here I was with my heart getting soft and melty. "How about you meet Doc and me at the Purple Door Saloon later tonight. We can talk more then."

He looked back toward the house with a frown etched deep into his face. "Okay."

I started to climb into my SUV, but he caught my arm, stopping me. "Violet," he said and then seemed to realize his hand was touching me again and drew back. "I'm sorry about your leg."

"That wasn't you, Cooper."

"It was my hand that did it."

"Maybe so, but Prudence was the one squeezing me with it."

"How?" He rubbed his hand down his face. "How did she do that?"

"Doc can explain it better than I can." I climbed inside my SUV. Without a backward glance, I hightailed it out of there before Prudence decided to sic Harvey on me next.

Chapter Fifteen

My visit with Prudence left me feeling like I was up to my hips in alligators. Not even the lucky alligator tooth necklace Zelda had given me was going to help me on this count.

After a quiet, thought-filled lunch with Harvey at Bighorn Billy's, I dropped him off at Cooper's house and headed back to work. The afternoon was almost as slow as the morning, which I didn't mind after chitchatting with a bossy ghost. It gave me time to think about her advice on using bait to lure Caly to me. That was if Wanda's death really was her handiwork. The style of murder sure seemed like Caly's, but the mention of that goat-pig tattoo had me scratching my head.

"V1," Mona interrupted my cogitating. "Your phone is ringing." She grabbed her purse and headed toward the bathroom.

My phone? I looked at my desk phone. Then I heard the muffled ring coming from my purse. I'd forgotten to take my cell phone out when I returned to work.

I answered it before the ringing stopped without taking the time to look at the number on the screen. "Hello?"

"Violet, it's Rosy." When I didn't make a sound, she added, "the camerawoman for Paranormal Realty."

"Yeah, sorry. You caught me off-guard. Is everything okay over there?" They were filming in Spearfish today if I remembered correctly. I'd sort of forgotten the details Ben had mentioned this morning because of Prudence's big fat guilt bomb.

"Yeah, we're fine. Nothing crazy like what you and I saw the other day."

What? Nobody else was being haunted by psychotic little girl ghosts or their clown dolls? No fair!

"That's uh …" Rosy lowered her voice. "That's why I'm calling."

"Let me guess, Dickie wants to know all about Wilda?"

"Actually, I haven't shown him the footage." I heard muffled sounds from her end of the line like she was partially covering the speaker, or maybe just cupping her phone. "I haven't shown anyone besides you and Cornelius."

"Why not?"

"I've been thinking about it all. A lot."

Her too? I waited to hear her take on the insanity that was my life.

"If I show this piece with the ghost girl to anyone on the crew, they'll want to put it on the air and anywhere else they can place the segment, using you to increase their own celebrity status and bank accounts. Your life as you know it will be over. I've seen it happen before with other reality television shows, and with the train of fame comes a lot of bad baggage, including long-lasting notoriety."

She confirmed the worries that had had me chewing my knuckles off and on since I'd seen the replay of Wilda and me. I had plenty of notoriety around this town already. The thought of it being on a world-wide scale made me want to build an underground bunker for me and my kids to live in for a few years.

"What are you going to do?" I asked her.

"It's not what I'm going to do, it's what I've done." Again, more muffled sounds. "I deleted that segment."

Breathing a sigh of relief, I leaned back in my chair. "Won't this cause some problems? They're going to be looking for that piece with Cornelius and me, aren't they?"

"I told Honey and Rad that the footage just disappeared, like what happened that day I filmed up in that beautiful house in Lead. Honey wasn't surprised. She said that happened to her when she was there with Dickie and you."

Actually I had been the one who erased the footage on Honey's camera that day after Prudence left me a message using Honey as her puppet. But as far as everyone else was concerned, that was the ghost's doing.

"Thank you, Rosy."

"I like you, Violet. You make me laugh. I don't want to see you or your family's lives screwed up because of something I filmed. I couldn't live with myself for that."

"How can I pay you back?"

"I'll need to film you and Cornelius reading your lines for that segment again. However, I suggest we set up somewhere less likely to have that little girl ghost running around."

"Let me talk to Cornelius and we'll come up with a safe location." Although, if Wilda were truly tethered to him, that might not be doable.

"That sounds good."

I heard the bathroom door open behind me. I tried to act normal as Mona returned to her desk. When she looked at me with raised brows, I gave her a thumbs up.

"There is one other favor I need," Rosy said.

"What's that?"

"I want to buy a house."

* * *

It turned out that Rosy didn't want to buy just any house, she wanted to buy Cooper's place. Somehow in the midst of trying to lasso the paranormal chaos stampeding around me, I had roped a buyer for one of my own properties.

This was my second time representing both the buyer and seller on a sale. I'd learned how to walk that particular fence with the Carhart house sale, so now it was a matter of seeing if Cooper liked what Rosy wanted to offer while not playing favorites.

I spent the rest of the afternoon working on the offer paperwork for Rosy in between pinching myself to make sure I wasn't dreaming. I stayed late at the office to wait for her to return from the filming in Spearfish. After thanking me for hanging around for her, Rosy told me she'd be in touch soon about the house and took off.

Ten minutes later, I shut down my computer and headed home. When I pulled into the drive, the sky was beginning to spit out wet, heavy snowflakes here and there. Nothing serious, merely a few threats from the thick, dark clouds above. My fingers were crossed we'd get the few inches they'd mentioned on the news and not the multiple surprising feet that often buried the hills for days on end.

Harvey's truck was parked in the drive, but there was no sign of Doc. Were he and the kids still doing their so-called exercising at the Rec Center? If so, it was a long exercise session.

I hurried through the cold wet stuff falling from the sky and closed the front door behind me, leaning against it. I'd lived through another day at the office without coming unhinged. Life was looking up.

"Who are you trying to keep out?" Harvey asked from the archway into the kitchen. He had a cookie in each hand, and another in his mouth from the muffled sound of it.

"The boogeyman."

He swallowed. "I think yer gonna need to put on more weight to pull that off."

I heard a squeal of anger from Addy upstairs. So the kids were home, but not Doc. He must have had somewhere to go. "Did Doc come inside or just drop the kids off?"

"He cooled his heels long enough to say he'd see you later at the Purple Door Saloon." I'd texted him earlier about meeting Cooper there with me tonight, so we were apparently still on.

Harvey continued, "Yer gonna tell him and Coop about what Prudence said, right?"

"Sure." Some of it, anyway. I hadn't decided on how to share the piece about it needing to be me who hunted down Wanda's killer.

"*All* of it?"

Avoiding his heavy-browed squint, I took off my coat and tossed it over the stair banister to dry. "Didn't we go over this at lunch?"

"Yep. You were slippery 'bout it then, too."

"Where's Aunt Zoe?" She'd offered to hang with the kids tonight, wanting to take a break from working her hiney off in her shop.

"She went to the store. Said she'd bring home supper." He crossed his arms over his chest. "Yer avoidin' my question."

"Not avoiding, just pondering."

"How long will this ponderin' last?"

I shrugged. "Until I figure out the right time to bring it up." I headed upstairs but paused two steps up and looked over the railing at him. "Remember our agreement at lunch."

I was referring to the one where I'd promised not to tell Coop that Harvey had broken his couch during a raucous evening with one of his old flames in exchange for the old buzzard not interfering with my telling his nephew that finding Wanda's killer was my job, not his.

He scowled at me. "It's feelin' more like blackmail to me already." He shoved one of the cookies in his mouth and headed into the kitchen.

By the time I made it back downstairs, Aunt Zoe was home. She and the kids were eating pizza in the living room while queuing up a National Geographic special on the boob-tube. The kids smelled clean when I kissed the tops of their heads. They must have gone swimming in the Rec Center's pool.

"How was your exercising?"

"Really cool," Layne said, his face lighting up.

Addy shot him a shush-it glare. "It was just the usual stuff, Mom. Nothing major."

"What's the usual stuff entail?" Curiosity had me fishing for information in spite of Aunt Zoe's narrow-eyed look.

"Doc showed us how—," Addy started, but Layne cut her off. "Running and jumping jacks, that's all."

"Rude!" Addy reached across the couch and punched her brother in the arm.

Layne punched her back. "Stop hitting me, brat."

And we were back to normal. I pulled them apart and told them both to behave or I'd send them to a military school in the Antarctic. Addy blamed Layne for making her mad. Layne, on the other hand, informed me there were no military schools down there, only scientific research centers, along with Emperor penguins and several other species of animals that turned into *blah, blah, blah* before they reached my brain.

I grabbed a couple pieces of pizza in the kitchen, noticing Harvey was missing. "Where's the old buzzard?" I hollered. Had he left or was his plumbing giving him grief again?

"He ran home to grab some clothes for tomorrow since he's spending the night," Aunt Zoe answered. "When are you leaving?"

We'd discussed Doc and me having a night out earlier this afternoon. I hadn't told her why, only the where part. "In about a half an hour."

I had enough time to wrangle my hair into something less wild and frizzy, brush the pizza off my teeth and tongue, and then slip into something sexy that might coerce Doc to take me somewhere private and do wicked things to me … after we finished hashing out Cooper's questions. My thigh throbbed at the memory of the detective's painful grip. The bruises were a colorful abstract masterpiece of blues, purples, blacks, and a hint of green. The next time I was in his office, I was going to take the grip-strengthener deal he liked to squeeze and throw it in the trash.

Thirty minutes later, dressed in a red button-up little sweater that hugged my chest too tight to be worn to work, a black mini-skirt, thick tights, and knee-high boots, I was ready to woo one Dane R. Nyce.

Harvey whistled as I came down the stairs. "You look like a red heifer in a flowerbed."

"Is that good or bad?"

"It's good and bad for Doc. Like smellin' whiskey through a jailhouse window."

"I'm going to take that as a compliment then." I grabbed my long black wool coat from the closet. "Keep 'em safe, old man."

He grinned. "Bessie and I will do our best."

"Bessie's here?" When he nodded, I pointed at him. "Don't shoot anyone we like. And if Reid stops by, keep that gun away from Aunt Zoe."

He snickered and headed into the living room where Aunt Zoe and the kids were watching something about sharks.

"Have fun," Aunt Zoe called as I blew her and the kids a kiss goodbye and headed out to my SUV. The sky was still spitting snow, but the ground was melting it as soon as it touched down. I'd have to be careful on the way home, though.

The Purple Door Saloon was having a slow night. No doubt the threat of snow was keeping the non-locals away as well as a good number of Deadwood's finest drinkers. The bar was only about half full, if that. The grumpy, blonde-hating bartender wasn't behind the bar for once, replaced by one of the usual waitresses.

I took off my coat while I searched the booths and tables for Doc but didn't see him.

"He's playing pool," one of the waitresses said as she set a tray down on the bar. When I looked at her like she was speaking Chinese, she added, "You're looking for Doc, right?"

She knew his name, huh? What else did she know about him? If he wore boxers or briefs? Then I remembered that the owner of the place was a client of Doc's and smacked down the jealous ogre in my chest.

Thanking her, I ordered a rum and Coke on the rocks from the bartender. I was in the mood for something different tonight from my usual tequila hit.

Drink and coat in hand, I made my way through to where Doc was leaning over the pool table, lining up a shot. He looked hot in his faded jeans and gray thermal. I should probably remove them to cool him down. I was only thinking of his health, of course.

After hanging my coat on one of the wall hooks, I moved to the wall opposite him, keeping the pool table between us. I tried to strike a pose with one knee raised, foot planted on the wall, but my drink slipped in my grasp and almost dumped down my sweater.

Doc made the shot and then stood with his pool cue in hand, watching as I mopped up the dribbles on my sweater with a skimpy one-ply bar napkin. Good thing I hadn't worn white.

"So much for trying to be sexy," I said, wadding up the napkin.

"Boots, how many times do I have to tell you that you don't have to try?" He strolled around the table, his attention locked on my face. "You should put that drink down."

"Why?" I took a sip from the straw.

As soon as he was in reach, he took the glass from me and set it on the pool rack hanging on the wall next to me.

"I don't want you to spill it again."

I stared up at him, my pulse picking up at the heat in his gaze. Batting my lashes, I trailed a finger down his bumpy shirt. "How was your day, Mr. Nyce?"

"I don't want to talk about my day right now."

"Did my kids behave this afternoon?"

"Yes, but I don't want to talk about your kids, either."

I licked my lips on purpose, luring him in. "What do you want to talk about then?"

"I don't want to talk, period." His mouth came down on mine fast and hard, surprising me into submission.

I closed my eyes, enjoying the feel of his body heating mine through my sweater. He tasted sweet and lemony, a hint of liquor on his breath, blowing my libido clear out of the water. Damn, I'd missed this carnal side of him lately. I buried my fingers in his hair and held his mouth to mine as I took over and kissed him back, pressing my soft curves into his hard edges.

He groaned and planted his palms on the wall on each side of my head, imprisoning me within his arms. He pulled back enough to trail his mouth along my jawline, concentrating on the sensitive skin below my ear.

"In case you're not getting my message," he said against my neck, "I like this outfit." He grazed his knuckles down my side, ending at where my skirt flared down over my thighs. "I really like it."

"I was hoping you would."

"It makes me want to explore." His hand trailed back up along my ribcage, his fingers tickling over my curves. "And touch."

"I know a place we could go," I said, leaning my head back against the wall as his lips traveled down my neck and along my collarbone.

"Your skin smells like coconuts." His fingers moved to the buttons on the front of my sweater, toying with the top one. He ogled my cleavage, making no attempt to play coy.

I took a deep breath, arching slightly. Looking even semi-perky wasn't so easy after popping out two kids.

"Your chest sparkles," he said, undoing the top button and pulling back the fabric enough to peek down my top. "All of the way down apparently."

That was the glitter infused in my new lotion. I slid my hands along his shoulders, craving the feel of his bare skin against mine. "Not just my chest. Want to see where else I sparkle?"

"I don't want to just see, Boots." He outlined the neckline of my sweater with his fingers. Goosebumps rippled in their wake. "How was your day?"

Now he wanted to exchange pleasantries? I was having trouble controlling my tongue enough to speak in between panting and drooling, let alone make sense. "I've had better."

He leaned his shoulder against the wall next to me, his broad shoulders completely shielding me from the view of the other bar patrons, giving us some privacy. "Did Prudence behave herself?" he asked and unbuttoned a second button so that the tiny satin pink bow in the center of my black lace bra showed.

I stared down at his fingers as they tickled along the top edge of my bra. "Not so much."

"But she did actually show up to meet Coop?" He popped the third button, his dark gaze holding mine for a breath, his fingers lingering around the front of my black lace cup, making my body pulse from head to toe and every hill and dale in between.

Holy hot flash! I was burning up from his little game of public foreplay. I hoped there weren't any cameras in the ceiling back here. This part of the bar was dark in the shadows beyond the pool table lights, but not that dark.

"She definitely stopped by and left her mark," I said. Unfortunately that mark was on me, but I didn't care so much about that at the moment. I was more interested in the fourth button that Doc had undone and what he was going to do next now that my right breast was catching plenty of air. The lace covering it was little more than a gauzy veil.

"Is that why we're meeting Coop here?" he asked, his focus centered well below my chin. His thumb strummed over me, making me moan. My knees were getting loosey-goosey, threatening to give and leave me as nothing more than a steamy throbbing mess of hair and boots at Doc's feet.

"We need your help."

He popped the penultimate button. My sweater gaped, both sides of my bra now visible. He reached up and took my drink down from the pool cue rack, offering me a sip. I took it, my throat a desert from the panting brought on by his teasing.

"My help with what?" He took my drink and rubbed the cold, dew covered glass over the front of my bra. A jolt of pleasure spiraled deep into my core. The chilly dampness should have cooled the fire burning through me, but it only cranked the heat higher. Spontaneous combustion was a finger stroke away.

I tried to gulp but my mouth had dried up.

"You need my help with what, vixen?" he asked again.

What were we talking about? Oh, yeah. "Your help with how Prudence could manipulate two puppets at once."

"Let me think about that." He leaned down and blew on the damp lace. I tipped my head back, my eyes closing at the heady sensation his breath sparked. Stars dotted the back of my lids.

His hand slid down to my waist. He leaned into me once more as his mouth came down on mine. His lips were soft this time, tenderly turning me inside out, upside down, and every which way.

I kept my eyes closed, letting my other senses rule. The scent of his cologne made me quiver. His muscles tensed under my palms as I stroked and gripped, encouraging me to grow bolder, more aggressive. His breath came fast and hard, matching mine.

"Doc," I whispered when we pulled apart, my lids still lowered. "What are we doing here?"

"Playing with fire."

"Let's go somewhere private."

"We can't." His hand brushed along the underside of my bra.

"Why not?"

His knuckles bumped me again. My eyelids fluttered open. I frowned down at the sight of his fingers buttoning up my sweater.

"Because Coop's here."

A glass of ice water dumped down my underwear would have been less jarring. I knocked Doc's hands aside, buttoning up the last three buttons while peeking over his shoulder to search the room. "Where?"

"He's at the bar."

Sure enough, there he was ordering a drink. Cooper had traded his dress pants and tie for a black long sleeve T-shirt and jeans. His spine was as stiff as ever, though.

I smoothed my sweater down over my chest, frowning at my headlights stuck on bright and clearly visible through the fabric.

Doc sucked a breath through his teeth, his gaze on my headlights, too. "Damn, that's sexy. I'm going to need a cold shower tonight."

"Or you could join me in my bed."

His eyes lifted to mine. "Have you thought about what I said?"

Thought? More like obsessed about it in between worrying about Caly, Wilda, Prudence, and more. "I've thought about the things I'd like to do to you with my mouth, does that count?"

A mixture of pleasure and pain passed over his face.

"Break it up, you two," Cooper's voice interrupted us before Doc could answer. "Enough of this PDA shit."

Doc dropped one last kiss on my lips and then turned to face the detective. "Your timing sucks as usual, Coop. I hear you had some fun with Prudence today."

Cooper looked at me, his gaze dropping to my leg for a moment. "More like Prudence had fun with me." He pointed his glass of amber-colored liquid at me. "You missed a button."

I glanced down. Sure enough, the third one down was buttoned through the second's slot. Damn his detective eyes.

"Oops." Doc stepped between us, blocking me from Cooper's view. "I get all fingers and thumbs when Violet's around." I could hear the laughter in Doc's voice as I fixed my sweater.

My skin warmed again, but only on my cheeks and neck this time. It was one thing to play the sultry sex kitten when Doc and I were the only two back here. But getting busted screwing around with my boyfriend made it tougher for me to match Cooper nip for nip when it came to our usual teeth-filled banter.

"Aren't you afraid Parker will bite your fingers off?"

Speaking of teeth, I leaned around Doc and flashed mine at Cooper in a lip-curled snarl.

"Let's get a booth," Doc said, catching my hand and leading the way through the tables. With so few patrons, it wasn't hard to find a corner of privacy. I slid into the booth first. Doc followed, his right shoulder bumping my left as we settled into the seat.

Cooper finished his drink and ordered another from a passing waitress before he took the bench seat across from us.

"All right, fill me in on your visit with Prudence." Doc's right hand slid under the table, locking onto my lower thigh.

I jerked in pain, bumping the table hard enough to rattle the salt shakers and tip over a plastic menu holder.

He drew his hand back, his forehead creased. "Did I hurt you?"

"I sort of have a bruise there."

Cooper swore under his breath.

Doc crooked his head to the side. "That was more than a sort-of-bruise reaction. What happened at the Carhart house?"

Cooper and I exchanged frowns.

"That's what we need to talk to you about," I said.

Doc scrutinized our shared frowns. "Did Prudence do something to hurt you?"

"It wasn't Prudence." Cooper beat me to the punch. "I'm the one who hurt her."

"You did not hurt me," my pride snapped back.

"Bullshit, Parker. Nyce nearly sent you through the roof a moment ago."

"That bruise was not your doing."

"It was *my* hand on *your* leg doing the squeezing, remember?"

"His hand was on your leg?" One of Doc's eyebrows crept up his forehead. "You two had better be careful or you might accidentally start being nice to each other. Worse yet," he draped his arm along the booth seat behind me, "you may actually become friends."

Cooper snorted. "Not gonna happen. I'm allergic to Parker. It's probably all of that crazy hair."

I flipped him off. "It was Prudence," I explained to Doc. "She manipulated Cooper, using him as a puppet."

"Did she speak through him?" Doc's hand warmed my shoulder, his fingers stroking, calming me.

"This was different. She spoke through Zelda." I went on to tell him what had happened. However, when it came to the part about my having to be the one hunting down Wanda's killer, I kind of skipped over that—as in not mentioning it at all.

Judging from the dark clouds hanging over Cooper's brow during my playback, I doubted he'd be receptive to my butting in on his case. At least not until he had a few more drinks in him. As in a few more than the single glass the waitress brought him while I finished my tale.

Doc's fingers stilled. "I knew Prudence was strong, but I had no idea she was capable of this."

"You should feel how hard she can squeeze," I grumbled.

"How can a ghost be strong?" Cooper asked. "They're wispy and ... what's the word? Ectoplasmic."

Grinning, Doc said, "A ghost's strength is not a physical ability, like weight lifting—something we both know you suck at compared to me."

Cooper chuckled. "Fuck you, Nyce."

Doc's eyes crinkled in the corners. "It's more a combination of mental energy and its receptivity to the medium in the room."

"But you're the medium, and you weren't there."

"No, but Violet was."

"What do I have to do with Prudence?"

"I have a theory about you two," he told me, "but first, Coop, do you remember anything during that period of altered state?"

Cooper stirred the ice in his glass. "I remember feeling dizzy and queasy, needing to sit down before I fell down. Parker led me to the couch and then everything sort of faded to black." He looked up from his drink, his gray eyes hooded. "Like I was stuck in a dream. I was fighting against something that had me pinned down. No matter how hard I tried, I couldn't get up. Then it was over and I was free, sitting on the couch next to Parker. I didn't realize my hand was on her leg until she pointed it out."

"Which is why I keep saying it wasn't you who hurt me," I told him.

"So you have no memory of seeing anything during your altered state?" Doc pressed Cooper. "Any images of other people or of Prudence herself? Any voices or smells?"

Cooper shook his head. "The whole thing was a long, dark struggle." He scowled down at his glass. "I don't remember ever feeling so weak. So defenseless." His wrinkled upper lip mirrored his apparent self-disgust.

"Don't beat yourself up," Doc said. "Prudence is one of the strongest ghosts I've ever come across. Most don't even have the ability to make you aware they're standing right next to you."

"Or inside of you," I muttered, thinking of the dead prostitute in the stairwell of The Old Prospector Hotel. She'd manifested in my shoes, using my face as a mask without my knowing it.

"How is it possible for a ghost to take over someone like that?" Cooper asked.

"There are several theories on how ghosts can manipulate the living, many having to do with telepathic communication. For example, you might have felt that Prudence was holding you down, but it likely had more to do with her ability to convince your subconscious self to take control of your conscious self."

"So I was actually controlling my hand the whole time while it squeezed Parker's leg, but I wasn't consciously aware of it?"

Doc nodded. "But that's only one theory."

"Christ." Cooper tore his fingers through his hair. It looked like a sea of blond shark fins when he finished. "I'm going to need a whole bottle of whiskey before the night is over."

"What's another theory?" I asked Doc, thinking about my experiences with Prudence and Wilda.

"It has to do with what you and Prudence have in common."

I aimed a glance at Cooper. He knew about my *other* job, but I still didn't like talking about it in front of him. "You mean the executioner gig?"

"I mean you both being physical mediums."

Huh? "You're the medium, I'm just a channeler."

"We both know that's not true, Killer."

"But I can't see or talk to ghosts." Not usually anyway. "I'm a dud."

He shifted in the seat, careful not to bump my leg as he faced me. "I've been telling you since I met you that you weren't a dud. Trust me, duds don't experience what you have with the paranormal world. Just because you don't actually see or hear or talk to the ghosts the way Cornelius and I can doesn't mean you have no abilities."

"So what am I again?"

Cornelius and Doc had come up with several technical terms for what I'd pulled off with that bone cruncher that night out back of Harvey's place, but I couldn't remember them and honestly, I hadn't wanted to. I was still trying to get used to the title of "Executioner" most days.

"You're a woman with many paranormal skills, including being a physical medium."

"How is that different from what you can do?"

"I'm a mental medium. I can tune into the spirit world using skills such as clairvoyance, clairaudience, clairsentience, transference, that type of thing. Mental mediums are common in the paranormal world. What sets some of us apart is the degree to which we have honed our skills." He tapped my shoulder. "You, on the other hand, have completely different mediumship skills at your disposal—skills I probably would never develop even if I tried."

"Besides the ability to make albino juggernauts morph into a puff of smoke?" I joked.

"In addition to that, Killer."

"This shit is nuts, man," Cooper muttered, then gulped down some whiskey. "It makes no damned sense."

"Physical mediums are extremely rare these days," Doc continued in spite of Cooper's skepticism, "partly because of the bad press they received in the past when displaying their skills in public. See, when you're working your magic, anyone who is in the area—duds or not—can witness the results. It's more 'real,' *physical*. It explains why when you sit in at a séance, shit is more likely to actually hit the fan, endangering you and for that matter anyone nearby."

I touched the faint scar on my chest. "Like what happened in Ms. Wolff's apartment that night?"

Doc nodded. "And Coop's injury during our séance out at Harvey's barn."

A scoff came from Cooper's direction. "I knew it. Parker's going to be the death of me yet. The broken nose was foreplay."

I would have shot something snappy back if his words hadn't echoed what Prudence had said to me earlier about the "lawman" dying if I didn't step up and take over hunting Wanda's killer. Cooper was often a burr in my skivvies, but I didn't want anything to happen to him or anyone else on Deadwood's police force for that matter. Not even ... well ... no, not even Hawke.

I focused back on Doc. "And you believe Prudence is a physical medium, too?"

"I suspect she was one when she was alive."

"You think that it's part of the skillset that comes with being an executioner?"

"I don't know the answer to that. I've only met two of you so far—and one of you almost stopped my heart the first time we collided."

"That day in the upstairs bedroom with Prudence?"

"Who says I was talking about the ghost?" He winked.

"Ahhh, Gomez. I've missed you so, *mon cher.*" I winked back, slipping into my Morticia Addams' role.

"*Cara mía*, that's French!" Doc growled playfully and lifted my hand, kissing my knuckles. A twinkle shined in the depths of his gaze as his lips made their way up my forearm.

"Jesus, you two." Cooper groaned at us from across the table. "You're making my eyes bleed with this lovey-dovey crap. Can we get back to the fucked-up, real world shit going on here in Deadwood?"

"Technically," I told the scowling detective as Doc lowered my arm, "we were in Lead not Deadwood when Prudence turned you into Pinocchio."

"Zip it, Parker." To Doc, he said, "Why do you think Prudence was a physical medium when she was alive?"

"As I was saying before, her strength and ability to manipulate the living are extremely uncommon. If she was a physical medium back when she was alive, she would've learned these skills she's now using on the living to interact with the other beings she was meant to kill."

"You're talking about the way she can use anyone as her conduit for speaking?" I asked.

"And her use of teleportation, allowing her to join Harvey and you in your Honda." His forehead furrowed in thought. "What's interesting is that the phenomena you've experienced so far in the Carhart house seems to be more energy-based than ectoplasm-based."

He was starting to lose me. Maybe it was the rum and Coke that I'd polished off making my brain cells relax a little too much. "Ectoplasm-based?"

"Never mind. That's not important right now."

Cooper toyed with his empty glass. "So can this Wilda ghost that you two keep talking about fuck with my mind, too?"

"I'm afraid so. And Wilda's purpose may be much darker than using you to merely hold someone in place." Doc sent me a worried glance. "She wants Violet dead."

I pointed at Cooper. "That means no freaking guns and bullets when we try to talk to Wilda. I don't care if you cuddle with your gun nightly and get all teary eyed when it's out of sight." After being on the receiving end of Prudence's macabre puppeteering, I wasn't taking any chances with Wilda. I was pretty sure it wouldn't take much nudging from her to convince Cooper to point his gun at me and shoot. His trigger finger had been itchy around me ever since I'd broken his nose.

"No guns is probably a good idea," Doc agreed.

Cooper nodded, but his pinched expression didn't look so compliant.

The waitress stopped by, offering to bring more drinks. We took her up on it, including a glass of iced tea for Doc.

"How do you feel about driving me home tonight?" I asked after she left.

"I planned on it. I walked over from work."

"And spending the night?" I pressed.

"Is there any room at the inn?"

"Harvey will be on the couch, but I have an opening in my *boudoir*."

Doc's flirty grin resurfaced. He lifted my knuckles to his lips again, but before he could get a Gomez-inspired word out, Cooper interrupted with, "I swear, Nyce, if you say 'Tish that's French,' I'm going to draw and shoot you right here."

Doc's deep laughter made my nether regions flutter. That was probably thanks in part to the rum and Coke. Doc made me easy, especially when liquor was part of the equation. I needed to change the subject so Cooper didn't get gun happy with either of us.

"On another note," I said to Doc, "how are we going to find that other timekeeper Prudence told me about?"

"I have an idea on that, but Coop isn't going to be thrilled."

One blond eyebrow raised questioningly.

"I'd like to return to Ms. Wolff's apartment and have Violet take another look in that mirror."

"Why?" Cooper asked. "What's in the mirror?"

I grimaced at Doc, not thrilled with his idea for a different reason. Cooper knew we'd slipped past the crime scene tape and sneaked into Wolff's apartment for a séance back in October, but he didn't know I'd disobeyed his stay-out orders again and gone back in because of a clock that wouldn't stop cuckooing.

"You're going to have to tell him, Violet."

"Tell me what?" Cooper sat forward, his squint firmly in place and aimed at me.

I sighed, wincing in preparation for his reaction. "You remember that day we were filming for the Paranormal Realty TV show in the Galena House and you stopped by?"

"You mean that day I found you standing outside of Ms. Wolff's apartment door?"

I nodded. "You caught me as I was leaving her apartment."

"You told me you'd only stood there and listened to the clocks."

"I kind of lied."

Several curses involving my "big nose" and "stubborn ass" blasted by my ears. "What in the hell was worth risking Detective Hawke catching you in that apartment and throwing you in jail for breaking and entering?"

"First of all, I didn't break in. When I tried the door before you showed up, it was unlocked." When he didn't spit more fire at me, I continued, "I went inside Ms. Wolff's place because I could hear a clock cuckooing and it wouldn't stop."

"What do you mean it wouldn't stop? Did you wait for twelve cuckoos?"

I leaned forward. "Of course I waited for twelve cuckoos! I'm not an idiot."

"Honestly, Parker, after some of the shit you've pulled at my crime scenes, I periodically doubt your intelligence."

"You're such a belligerent butthead, *Coop.*" I purposely used the name he'd made off-limits for me, poking the bear.

"Takes one to know one, *Vi.*"

"If you two are done trading punches," Doc interrupted, breaking us up, "how about you finish your story, Violet."

I huffed a couple of more times and then returned to that day in Ms. Wolff's place. "As I was saying, the clock kept going off. I counted almost twenty cuckoos before going inside the apartment."

"I didn't hear any cuckoos when I arrived. Did you mess with the scene of the crime?"

"That's just it—*you* didn't hear the cuckoos, but the reason I was still standing there when you walked up was that I could still hear them."

"You sure it wasn't your memory playing tricks on you?"

"I'm positive."

Cooper shrugged. "So there was a broken clock. What's the big deal?"

"You don't understand. The clock going off wasn't one of those hanging on the walls in her apartment. It was one of the clocks inside the mirror."

The lines on his brow doubled and then tripled. "You're right," he finally said. "I don't understand."

"After looking at all of the clocks on the walls in the dining room, I checked her bedroom. It was louder in there, but the clocks hanging on her bedroom walls were not going off either. That's when I noticed movement in the mirror over her dresser."

"The one your son's picture was stuck to before it was stolen from the crime scene?"

"Yes, stolen by the albino's twin." But that was a problem to fret about some other time—probably in the middle of the night again. "In the mirror's reflection, I could see the cuckoo mechanism on one of the clocks going in and out of the little door. But when I turned around and looked at it in the real world, the clock was silent."

He sighed at me. Then he took a long drink from his glass, finishing it off. "You think the clock in the mirror is still going off?"

"I don't know. I haven't been back to her apartment since that day."

Cooper's focus shifted to Doc. "You think Parker will find some answers to Ms. Wolff's murder by going back in that apartment?"

"Beats me, but I remember hearing that some of the clocks are missing. Is that true?"

"Yes."

"Then there's a possibility this other timekeeper Prudence mentioned is the one who broke in and took them."

"The motive being to keep 'all of hell from breaking loose'?" Cooper glanced my way as if those words belonged to me.

"Hey, I was only repeating what was told to me. Don't kill the messenger."

"I'm not interested in killing you, Parker. But nailing you to a wall until some of these murder cases are wrapped up is awfully tempting."

"But if I'm nailed to the wall, how will any of your cases get solved? Detective Hawke certainly isn't going to figure things out until he removes his teeth from my ass and starts looking elsewhere for answers."

Wait until Cooper found out I was going to find and play executioner for Wanda's killer. Maybe I could soften the blow by approaching him with Rosy's offer letter in hand, couching my plans with some good news for once.

"How soon do you think you could sneak us into that apartment?" Doc asked.

"Let me make a quick phone call and I'll let you know." He stood, pulling his phone from his coat pocket. "Don't go breaking and entering while I'm gone, Parker."

"I told you I didn't break in."

"Maybe not, but you did enter her apartment illegally, trespassing on an official crime scene." He walked away, winning the battle for the last word ... this time.

After Cooper disappeared from view over by the pool table, Doc took my hand in his, tracing the lines on my palm. "I should have gone with you to see Prudence."

"Then she would have used you to get to me."

"Maybe so, but she might not have hurt you with me there to channel for her."

I shook my head. "I think she was making a point about her after-death abilities, showing me who I was dealing with. She has a thing about insulting my family tree, telling me how superior her lineage of executioners is."

"Only you, Tiger, can manage to get into a pissing match with a dead woman." His grin took the sting out of his words. "I want to take a look at that leg later when we're alone."

"It's a pretty bruise but nothing more. There's not much to be done about it." I wiggled my eyebrows at him. "Except kissing it better."

"I'm your huckleberry."

I leaned in to kiss him.

Something dropped onto the table in front of us, making me jerk back in surprise.

"I brought you another present, baby-cakes," Natalie said, standing at the end of the table. Her eyes were alight with mirth, her hair and leather coat glistening with flakes of melting snow.

I frowned down at the windshield wipers on the table in front of me.

"They say the gift doesn't matter, it's the thought that counts." She held up a burly-looking pair of bolt cutters. "And by my way of thinking, that son of a bitch is lucky I didn't cut off his balls as well."

Chapter Sixteen

S orry for interrupting your date night," Natalie said as she slid into
Cooper's seat, setting the bolt cutters next to her. "But your aunt said I
could find you here when I called."

She picked up Cooper's drink and sniffed it. "Straight whiskey?" At my
nod she scanned the bar. "Is Coop here somewhere?"

"He's over by the pool table making a phone call," Doc told her,
picking up one of the two windshield wipers lying on the table.

I looked down at the other. "You brought me Rex's wiper blades?"

"Not just the blades, sweetheart." Doc held out one end of the wiper
for me to see. The metal at the base of the arm had a pinched, jagged
edge. "It's the whole damned wiper." He grinned across at Natalie. "Did
you really just snip these off his Jaguar?"

Natalie shrugged. "It was quicker than messing around with a
screwdriver."

"Rex is going to be so ticked." I half-stood and leaned across the table,
dropping a loud smooch on her forehead. "You are the best, Nat. I take
back all of the bad things I ever said about your seventh grade boyfriend."

"Don't get carried away," she said as I dropped back into my seat.
"Pete was a sloppy kisser with pizza breath. I should've known better than
to let him try slipping me the tongue under the bleachers, especially with
the way he always seemed to struggle with drooling." She fished one of
Cooper's ice cubes from his glass with his straw and stuck it in her mouth.
"But live and learn when it comes to men, right?" She winked at me and
crunched on the ice.

"I'm surprised Rex didn't have guard dogs leashed to his precious car,"
I said, thinking of how pissed he had been when he'd accused me of
messing with his car.

She fished out another ice cube. "It was a little tricky to pull off. The
ass-hat has been keeping the alarm set on his Jaguar since I took the hood
ornament." She popped the cube in her mouth, crunching. "His mistake
was underestimating my abilities to get around an alarm."

Doc laid the wiper back on the table, shaking his head. "You are one hell of an opponent, I'll give you that."

"She shares blood with the Morgan sisters," I told him. "Anyone who meets those girls learns quickly not to mess with them or their family."

"You mean Marcia and Cindy Brady from the Halloween party?" At my nod, he chuckled. "That's a fight I would've enjoyed watching."

At the time, though, Doc and I had been busy upstairs ripping my Morticia Addams' dress. From the sudden intensity in his gaze, I had a feeling he was remembering what happened after my dress got ripped.

He wasn't the only one reliving the moment.

Fanning myself, I looked back at Natalie. "I wish I could have seen Rex's reaction."

"I would've recorded it for you, but your daughter filled up my cell phone with videos of Elvis strutting around Zoe's backyard wearing different baby doll sweaters."

"That damned chicken always has a leg up on me."

"You didn't miss much, just a lot of swearing and a bit of tire kicking. I watched it while hiding behind a truck across the parking lot. The bastard had to stick his head out the window to drive home. All of that wet snow and sleet couldn't be good for his car's leather interior, let alone that expensive suede coat he was wearing."

I giggled in spite of the knockdown fight this would undoubtedly inspire between the asshole and me. I drank more rum and Coke. It might be the rum talking, but fuck Rex and his threats. Maybe when I finished using that creepy war hammer on Wanda's killer, I'd plant the pointy end of it into the hood of his Jaguar. I thought about how he must have looked when he tried to use his newly cut, windshield wiper nubs and my giggle turned into a laugh.

"What's so funny?" Cooper asked.

I squeezed my lips together. Natalie and I reached for the wipers at the same time, but Cooper beat us to them. He inspected them. "Did someone cut your wipers off?" he asked Natalie, his detective skills sharp even after almost two glasses of whiskey.

"Ahhhh." Natalie licked her lips and then looked at me.

I glanced left and right, searching for an escape route.

His gaze dipped to the bolt cutters on the seat next to Natalie and then narrowed. "What's going on here?"

"Uhh ..." my rum and Coke brain scrambled. We needed something to distract the detective. I looked across at Natalie with her damp hair, flushed cheeks, and wet lips. "Nat needs someone to teach her how to play pool."

A little flirting with Cooper during pool could work in our favor.

He scoffed, crossing his arms over his chest. "Do you really think you can fool me so easily, Parker? Besides, I know Natalie is a pool shark. She and I have played together before."

Shit, that was right. It was that night years ago that Natalie had told me about. What had started out with a shared drink had moved onto shared kisses. Then Cooper had rejected her invitation to go somewhere else, telling her he didn't mix it up with locals, and walked out. Period. End of attraction … or not.

"I'll tell you what, Coop," Natalie said, setting the bolt cutters on the table next to the wipers. "Let's make a little wager over a game of nine ball."

He watched her as she took off her coat and finger-combed her damp hair, his face set in that hard-core detective mask he so often wore. "I'm listening."

"If I win, you pretend you never saw these wipers." She picked up his glass of whiskey and took a sip. "Damn," she said with a slight grimace and handed him the glass. "This could use more ice."

He took the glass and downed the last of the amber liquid, setting the glass down with a *clink*. "And if I win?"

"I'll confess."

"And?"

"And …" she turned to me for help.

I had an idea of what else he'd want with his spoils, and nothing I could offer would satisfy.

"And a kiss," I tossed out, and then blinked in surprise at what had come from my own loose lips. Damned rum!

Everyone seemed to have frozen solid except for me. I reached for my drink while three pairs of eyes nailed me to the booth. "It just kind of flew out, you know." I shrugged and sipped from my glass. "Seemed like a good idea in the heat of the moment."

One of Cooper's eyebrows rose. "A kiss from Natalie, Nyce, or you?"

"Natalie," Doc answered for me, grinning at Coop. "I'd try to kiss you myself, but you'd probably shoot me."

"There's no probably about it."

Natalie tittered. I did a double-take at the awkward sound coming from her mouth. "Coop isn't interested in kisses from local girls," she said. "But I bet he'd take me up on an all-expenses-paid trip to the shooting range."

"Sure," I agreed in between sips of what seemed to be mostly rum at the bottom of my glass. "Especially if you tag along."

I glanced up to find both Natalie and Doc giving me what-the-hell looks again. Cooper's glare, on the other hand, had more of a shut-the-hell-up smack to it.

Oh, hell. I reined in my big mouth and tried to fix my blunder yet again. "What? Everyone knows that shooting is more fun with friends." I turned to Doc. "Don't you think?"

"I think you should take a break from the rum." He took my glass from me and set it out of reach.

Natalie shot me one last questioning glance and then smiled up at Cooper. "What do you say, Coop? How do you feel about getting your butt kicked at pool?"

"It'll be like a regular ol' night at the poker table," Doc said.

"Kiss my ass, Nyce."

"I'd sooner take that bullet you mentioned a moment ago."

"Okay, Beals. I'll take you up on that bet." Cooper thumbed in the direction of the pool table. "Lead the way."

Natalie nudged her head at me to follow and then slid out of her seat.

As soon as they were out of earshot, Doc looked at me. "I thought you weren't going to tell her that Coop's interested."

"My brain says I'm not, but my lips seem to have gone rogue."

"Oh, yeah?" He turned my chin his way and kissed me, leaving me licking my lips for more when he pulled away. "They do feel a bit more rascally. You think you can control them over by the pool table?"

"I'll try, but you may have to kiss me some more if they turn into scallywags again."

"Can do." He stood and held his hand out for me. "But there are risks involved."

I stood, straightening my skirt and sweater. "What risks?"

Doc's hand slid down over my backside. "I might take advantage of you in your rummy state, especially with that cherry-flavored lip gloss you're wearing tonight."

"I double dare you to try."

Natalie was racking up the balls while Cooper picked out a cue stick when we joined them. Doc settled into a chair at one of the tall tables made for two nearby. I opted to use him as a leaning post instead of sitting in the other chair, resting back against his chest, my hands warming his thighs. If Natalie was playing up to snuff tonight, this beating shouldn't take long.

The waitress stopped by with another round of drinks, including a margarita on the rocks for Natalie. Guitar riffs started playing from the speakers in the corners of the room as Bad Company's *Feel Like Makin' Love* cranked up.

Uh oh. This song wasn't going to help cool things down for Cooper—or me for that matter. I glanced toward the front of the bar where a twenty-something in a pair of skintight jeans and black cowboy boots was swaying her hips in front of the jukebox.

"Shall we flip to see who gets to break?" Natalie asked, grabbing a pool stick from the rack.

Cooper shook his head. "Ladies first."

"What a gentleman." She stretched her shoulders back, rolling her neck, loosening up. Her smile was an equal mix of cockiness and flirting. "That's your first mistake."

"Not my first." He took a sip of his whiskey. His eyes were locked on Natalie as she bent over and slid the stick back and forth between her fingers a few times. "And not my last."

"Poor sucker is going down in flames," Doc said in my ear.

"In more ways than one," I replied after Natalie's break knocked the one ball and three ball into different corner pockets.

She strolled over next to Cooper, standing shoulder to shoulder with him as they both looked over the table. "What do you think?" she asked. "Should I take the safe shot and sink the two ball in the side pocket or try the riskier one-cushion bank shot into the corner?"

"Risky," he answered without looking at her. "Danger is more exciting."

"You would know, Coop." She stepped forward and bent over, taking aim. "Two ball in the corner pocket."

"Watch this," I told Doc.

Natalie could sink this shot with her eyes closed. In fact, I'd seen her do that once in a pool game against a tattoo-covered biker down in Sturgis. An image of Jeff's bare chested, tattooed girlfriend flashed in my mind out of the blue, making me grimace and shake it and her nipple rings out of my thoughts. What was my brain's preoccupation with that tattooed babe?

The ball bounced once and rolled straight into the corner pocket like the table was tipped in that direction.

Natalie grabbed the chalk and moved back to where Cooper still stood stiff-legged, watching. "I pocketed the three ball when I broke. That leaves the four ball." She looked over at me. "Where should I put it, Vi?"

"Let me think." I touched my cheek, pretending to ponder. "I'm leaning toward a location on Detective Cooper where the sun never shines."

Doc swallowed his tea wrong and coughed into his hand.

Cooper slowly turned my way, his gunslinger squint in place. "Next time you're in jail, Parker, plan on spending the night before I call your boyfriend to come to your rescue."

I held up my hands, trying to maintain a straight face. "Kidding, Cooper." A giggle bubbled up my throat, ruining my honest-Abe expression. "Nat, put the four ball in the corner pocket after a two-cushion bounce."

As Natalie sized up the shot, Bad Company's lusty riffs wrapped up. She moved around the table, lining up for the shot. "Four ball in the corner." She nudged her head toward the intended pocket.

The sound of cymbals came from the speakers, followed by a bass guitar and drums buildup.

Oh, shit.

I winced as the Divinyls' hot and sexy song, *I Touch Myself*, throbbed to life. What was next? The long and dirty version of *Strokin'* by Clarence Carter?

After shooting a scowl at the woman now dancing alone in front of the jukebox, I turned back to the sparks flying at the pool table.

Natalie closed one eye, her focus unwavering, and hit the cue ball. It smacked the four ball, which banked twice off the side cushions before sinking into the corner pocket as called.

"Damn, she's good," Doc said.

"Nat and her cousins have been playing pool since they were kids. The Morgans had a pool table in their basement."

Returning to Cooper's side with her drink in hand, Natalie swayed to the sultry song. "Hold this, will you?" She handed him her drink, singing along with the Divinyls about loving herself as she rubbed the chalk over the end of the pool tip.

Cooper watched her chalk up with the concentration of a brain surgeon. His chest rose and fell visibly.

"She's playing dirty," Doc whispered.

I shook my head. "Her focus is on the table. She's in the zone, sizing things up." I'd seen Natalie flirt with guys more times than I could count, and this was definitely not one of those instances. "Her mind is on winning the game, not sex."

She exchanged the chalk for her drink, studying the table as she kept swaying and singing. I danced along with her while sipping on my fresh rum and Coke.

Doc palmed my hips, lightly holding onto me as I moved to the music. "How can she not know what she's doing to him?"

"It's this damned song. It makes your hips move on their own." I spun around and sang the chorus to him about not wanting anybody else.

He watched me as I mimicked Chrissy Amphlett's sexy moves from the video, his gaze molten.

I danced closer, rubbing over his inner thighs as I swayed "See what I mean?"

"No, show me more." He reached out and popped the top button of my sweater. "Let me help you with this touching business."

I knocked his hand away, waving my index finger in front of his face. Returning my attention to the pool table scene, I backed up into Doc, still swaying against him.

He grasped my hips, pulling me back even closer. "Vixen," he said in my ear and pushed my hair aside, nuzzling my neck. Electricity crackled along my shoulder blade.

At the pool table, Natalie danced over to her next shot while Cooper scrubbed his hand down his face. Sweat glistened on his forehead.

"Five ball in the side pocket," she sang.

"Where's the challenge in that, Beals?" Cooper's voice was huskier than usual.

"Side pockets are always a challenge for me, Detective," she said, bending down to take the shot. Her v-neck shirt dipped, allowing a peek of cleavage as she focused on the ball.

Cooper flinched, looking away sharply.

The balls cracked together, the five ball nosediving into the side pocket.

She danced back over to Cooper, doing a spin on the way, singing along with the Divinyls as the song wrapped up.

"Whew," she said with a brash smile. "I'm beginning to feel like I'm playing with myself here, Coop."

He stared down at her. The heat blasting from his gaze would've turned Natalie to ashes in a flash if she hadn't been busy scrutinizing the layout on the pool table. "I'll join the game as soon as you give me the green light."

Doc and I exchanged knowing grins. "She really doesn't see the way he's watching her?" he whispered.

I leaned back and said in his ear, "He rejected her and she's accepted his rule about local girls. Aside from those two reasons, she's really taking her sabbatical seriously." I grazed my lips along his cheek. "Besides, you didn't see the way I used to watch you either."

He chuckled. "Yes, I did."

"You're just saying that."

"Remember that day at the Rec Center pool when we played Marco Polo with Addy and Kelly?"

I nodded. "You were wearing dark blue swim trunks and a lot of bare, wet skin."

"You kept sending me invitations with your eyes."

"I did not."

"You definitely did, Boots." He toyed with a curl. "I was having trouble not taking you up on them at the time, especially with you in a swimsuit."

My cheeks warmed. I must have come across as a desperate, horny single mom. "It'd been a while for me. I was out of practice." I lifted my drink to my lips.

He ran his lips along the shell of my ear, rattling my poise. "The way the water trickled down your smooth skin haunted me *all* night long."

The Divinyls self-touching finally came to an end. It was a good thing, because all of that singing about touching on top of the rum and Doc's words was not helping to cool my core temperature. Neither was the feel of his lips grazing the side of my neck.

I took a sip of my drink only to nearly choke when the erotic guitar strums of *Darling Nikki* reverberated from the speakers.

"You've got to be fucking kidding me," Cooper muttered, scowling at the woman now dirty dancing with a cowboy in front of the jukebox. I half expected him to pull out his gun and fill the jukebox full of bullet holes.

"Not a fan of Prince?" Natalie asked, moving her hips to the suggestive beat.

"Where are you going to plant the damned six ball?" he said between clenched teeth, sounding remarkably like Dirty Harry.

Natalie glanced his way, examining his granite expression. "You know, Coop, a little more of Prince's version of 'grinding' in your life might mellow you out."

One blond eyebrow crept up. "Are you offering, Beals?"

She laughed. "You're full of it tonight." She punched him in the shoulder, kidding around with him like she often did my brother, Quint. Her focus returned to the game. "How about you pick this shot?"

"Far corner pocket."

"That's too easy." She moved over to the table and sank the ball without effort. Turning, she leaned back against the table, half-sitting on the edge.

Cooper checked his watch as Prince went on about Darling Nikki's expertise in the bedroom.

"You got somewhere else to be tonight?" she asked.

"Nope." He took a swig of his whiskey. "Just getting tired of watching instead of joining in."

Natalie raised her brows. "Tired, huh? Okay." She turned and hit the cue ball so it banked around the table but didn't knock any balls into the pockets. She waved her hand over the table. "Your turn, Detective."

"I don't want a pity shot."

"No pity," she said over the sound of Prince's grinding words. "Playing alone isn't much fun."

"I agree." He leaned down next to her to take his shot. "Seven ball in the corner pocket." His arm brushed her hip.

"Did you see that?" I said in Doc's ear. "Ten bucks says he did that on purpose."

"Of course he did that on purpose. Don't you remember how many times I brushed against you?"

Cooper sank the seven ball and stood slowly, his face inches from Natalie's when she looked up from watching the ball drop into the pocket. Her gaze widened a fraction at how close he was, her eyes dipping to his mouth.

"That was an easy one," she said, her voice sounding breathy. Then she seemed to blink out of her temporary stupor. "You'd better work harder to impress me with the eight ball."

Cheap Trick cranked up *I Want You to Want Me*, picking up the beat.

"Easy, huh?" Cooper said, stepping back. "How about a two-cushion bank shot?"

Her eyebrows rose. "You sure you can handle two?"

"Watch me."

We all did as he lined up his shot, aiming for the side pocket. He struck the cue ball. It bounced twice off the bumpers and then struck the eight ball, which rolled slowly toward the side pocket, almost stopping. I held my breath as it reached a tipping point, cheering as it fell into the pocket. Then I remembered that I didn't want Cooper to win because Natalie would have to come clean about the windshield wipers.

"Ha!" Natalie clapped. She seemed to have forgotten she was playing to win, too. "What are you going to do for the last one?"

He leaned over the table. "Nine ball in the side pocket," he said and sank it without a big production, winning the game.

"Well, hell." Natalie hopped off the edge of the table. "Looks like you won, Coop."

She'd given him that win and we all knew it. But why?

Cooper walked over and took her pool stick from her, his hand brushing hers.

"See?" Doc said. "Classic."

"You let me win," Cooper told her. "It's a draw."

"What about the bet?"

"I'll forget about the wipers, but you owe me a trip to the shooting range."

She patted his shoulder in a totally friendly manner, no stroking or flirty touching. "Sounds fair."

"And Parker was right—it's more fun to shoot with a friend so I'll expect you to join me."

"I'm not as talented with a gun as I am a pool stick."

Liar, liar, pants on fire! Natalie's grandpa had taught her all about guns and shooting while she was still in a training bra.

"That's okay." He placed the sticks on the rack. "I'll teach you how to squeeze and not yank."

"What's that supposed to mean?" I asked Doc. Was it another double-entendre?

"It's a line from one of Coop's favorite movies, *Harley Davidson and the Marlboro Man.*"

"The one with Mickey Rourke and Don Johnson?"

"Damn, Boots. Killer curves and you know your action movies." Doc whistled low, flattering. "How's a guy supposed to stand a chance around you?"

I pretended to shoot him in the heart and then blew on the tip of my finger.

"Tomorrow after lunch." The sound of Cooper's voice behind me made me lower my fake gun.

"What's tomorrow after lunch?" Doc asked.

"You two meet me at Wolff's apartment." Cooper slipped on his black leather coat.

He must have had enough ghosts and girls for one night. "Are we going inside?"

His steely gray eyes met mine. "That depends."

"On what?" I would have promised to be on my best behavior, but I doubted he'd buy what I was selling.

"If I can figure out how to slip you two past the patrol unit Detective Hawke has on surveillance 24/7 outside the Galena House." He looked up at Doc. "Sorry to ruin the party, but I need a ride home."

"Have a little too much whiskey tonight, Detective?" I asked, holding up my own empty glass. I'd sure had plenty of rum.

He looked over his shoulder at where Natalie was talking to some dark haired guy over at the bar. "As Carl Sandburg once said, 'Ashes to ashes, dust to dust, if the women don't get you then the whiskey must.'" He grabbed his glass off the edge of the pool table and downed the last of the amber liquid in one smooth gulp. "Prudence got to me earlier, now it's the whiskey's turn."

* * *

Saturday, November 17th

The Galena House loomed tall and alone, looking down on the road. As I stood at the end of the cobblestone walk leading up to the porch, a single ray of sunshine broke through the clouds and spotlighted the Italianette-style Victorian building. For a moment, the old boarding house appeared almost elegant.

Almost.

But I knew that the cornices were crumbling, the shingles were worn, and the paint was beginning to peel. The old gal needed a facelift, but her owner didn't have stacks of cash tucked away in a hidden safe somewhere, so she was selling it "as is." Or rather I was selling it for her, I thought as I glanced at the Calamity Jane Realty FOR SALE sign planted in the front yard. It rattled in the cold breeze blowing in from the north.

Dark, thick snow clouds swallowed up the sun again. Gloom and doom returned as Doc and I followed Cooper up the sidewalk to where Freesia Tender waited, leaning against one of the two large columns that bracketed the porch.

A movement in the stand of pine trees off to the right of the house caught my eye. I slowed, watching the shadows, searching for any signs of … There it was again. Something white moved in the semidarkness under the trees. Then it stopped. Was that fur? A rabbit maybe? No, something larger.

I took a step toward it, veering off the sidewalk into the brown grass. My gut tightened. Something wasn't quite right with what I was seeing.

"Parker!"

Cooper's bark snapped me back to the task at hand.

The detective stood on the porch, arms crossed over his black leather jacket, jaw rigid. He'd been pricklier than usual today, no doubt thanks to all of that whiskey last night and the resulting skull cramps. "Get your ass up here before someone sees that damned hair of yours, and I get stuck doling out parking tickets for disobeying orders and sneaking you in here."

Doc waited on the porch steps, studying me with a frown. "What is it?" he asked and looked over toward the pines.

I searched the forest edge, but I saw only trees and shadows. "Nothing." I caught up to him. "I'm just seeing ghosts."

"Hi, Violet," Freesia Tender, owner of the Galena House, held open the screen door for me as I crested the top step. Her loose dark curls shimmied and waved in the cold breeze, catching in her long dark eyelashes. With her hair now past her shoulders, she didn't look as much like Halle Berry's twin anymore. But they could still be cousins, with Freesia being the more curvy of the two.

She welcomed Cooper and Doc after me, closing the door on the bone-chilling north wind. She looked warm and cozy in a thick cream-colored sweater, blue jeans, and thick slipper booties.

"It's good to see you again," she said, giving me a quick hug. She smelled like fresh baked bread. Normally, such an aroma might have spurred me to drool all over her neck, especially since I'd only nibbled on a protein bar for lunch. But the reason I had only nibbled was my stomach, which was still queasy from drinking too much rum last night.

Tequila was my usual drink of choice. My stomach and the blue agave-based liquor had developed a long and happy relationship over a history of sharing joys and heartaches. Pouring rum down the hatch, on the other hand, was like dumping holy water on the devil.

I should have known better than to try to hide it in Coca-Cola and sneak it past my stomach. What had gone down sweet and easy had come back up bitter and wrenching. After Doc had dropped me off last night and left to take Cooper home, poor Harvey had played nursemaid in addition to bodyguard, mopping my brow and stuffing bread down my throat to try to clog the leak my stomach seemed to have sprung.

"We've had a few walk-throughs over the last week." Freesia handed me a short stack of business cards. "They called ahead like the sign says," she said in a lowered voice, shooting a quick frown in Cooper's direction.

"So I had plenty of time to take down the police tape before they arrived."

The Galena House had been in Freesia's family for generations after her great, great uncle, Big Jake Tender, had built it with his own two strong hands. Jake had come out West after the Civil War and made a name for himself around the northern Black Hills as a skilled jack-of-all-trades. Tall tales of his feats still circulated at the senior center, some painting pictures akin to Paul Bunyan and Pecos Bill. Truth be told he was just a big man with an even bigger heart who had fallen in love with Ms. Wolff, the timekeeper I'd found dead and shriveled up like a raisin in her apartment at the Galena House last month. According to Doc, Ms. Wolff had been there at the time of Big Jake's demise, leaning over him as his heart slowed to a stop, holding his hand through it all. Unfortunately for both, their love was never meant to be.

There were many who whispered that Big Jake still roamed the halls of the Galena House where his true love had lived for so many years. Those many included Doc, who'd shared a moment in time with Big Jake during a séance we'd had in Ms. Wolff's apartment.

I pocketed the business cards, following Freesia down the hall toward Ms. Wolff's apartment. The police tape was there, crisscrossing the door again per Detective Hawke's orders.

"Bites from buyers are slow at the moment," I told her when we stopped in front of the apartment door. "But I've placed an ad on a few national websites."

She smiled, her brown eyes sparkling. "That's okay. I'm not in a big rush to leave town now."

I barely kept a groan from surfacing. For some crazy reason, Freesia had fallen gob smack into lust with Deadwood's own Abe Lincoln look-alike. One look at Cornelius and Freesia had started howling at the moon. Wait, did females howl at the moon? Maybe we just purred a lot. Anyway, while she lusted after Cornelius in plain sight, he seemed completely oblivious. I was beginning to wonder if his stovepipe hat was on too tight.

"I appreciate your patience with the selling process," I told her. That reminded me—I had good news for Detective Grumpy-pants as soon as he stopped gnawing on me for a moment. Rosy and I had swung by his place this morning for a walk through and she was even more enamored with his little blue bungalow. She was going to contact me with her official offer amount after she talked to her financial consultant and thought about it a little longer.

We came to a stop in front of Ms. Wolff's door. The little brass clock knocker was still there, reflecting the chandelier hall lights. Had that been a sign of sorts for those who came seeking help from the timekeeper? What kind of help had she offered? What purpose did all of those clocks play in the grand scheme of time? It certainly wasn't keeping up with the earth's daily rotation, because none of the clocks showed the same time, or the right time for that matter.

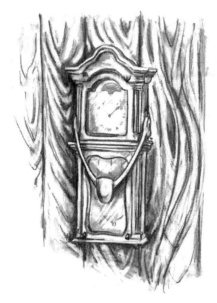

"Parker, hold up." Cooper stepped in front of me, checking the doorknob to see if it was still locked. It didn't budge. "Has anyone been in here lately?" he asked Freesia.

She shook her head. "Not that I've seen."

Doc's hand brushed my lower back, his touch reassuring.

"This is where you were standing when I saw you last time," Cooper said to me.

I nodded, my memory fine in spite of last night's rum disaster.

His steely eyes bored into mine. "And you said you could hear a cuckoo clock chiming from out here."

"I know what I said, Cooper."

He looked over at the door, holding his hand up to silence me when I started to speak. After several seconds, he turned back. "I don't hear anything. Do either of you?" he looked from Doc to Freesia.

Both shook their heads.

Cooper stared down at me again. "What about you?"

"What about me?"

"Do you hear a clock cuckooing?"

Doc and Freesia were watching me: one with a knitted brow, the other with wide, curious eyes.

"I don't hear one clock," I told Cooper.

"It must have stopped on its own then."

"You didn't let me finish, Detective." I reached out and tested the doorknob for myself. The door creaked open, the lock apparently not in effect for me.

"What the hell?" Cooper growled.

I frowned at him. "I don't hear one clock cuckooing, I hear two."

Chapter Seventeen

The sound of those two clocks cuckooing made my stomach tighten. The fact that nobody could hear them but me was unsettling enough, but add to that the detail Prudence had told me last month about what the cuckooing sound meant and my urge to tuck tail and run all of the way back to Aunt Zoe's place made my feet itch.

"Well, Parker?" Cooper stood inside of Ms. Wolff's apartment, holding the door for me to enter. "Are you going to get your ass in here or not?"

"I'd rather not." I took a step backward and collided with the solid wall of Doc's chest. I looked up at him. "Maybe we should come back some other time." Like when those clocks weren't cuckooing.

He placed his hands on my shoulders, turning me around. His brown eyes held mine. "I'll be right there with you."

"Yeah, but you can't hear the toll of the death bell." I used Prudence's words.

"The what?" Freesia asked.

I stayed focused on Doc. "What if you get dragged back into the past, and I can't get you out this time?" The last time he'd played medium in this apartment, Cornelius had thought we'd lost Doc for good.

"What's she talking about?" Cooper asked.

"Doc wouldn't wake up after the séance," Freesia explained from behind me. "Violet had trouble pulling him back out."

Freesia had been there with Cornelius, Doc, and me that night. It was her hand that had reached out to me through the mirror when I'd needed help finding my way out of the past and back to present day. I'd tried to figure out how that trick had worked for days afterward. It still left me scratching my head.

"I'll be fine. We all will. We're only going to take a look." Doc squeezed my hand and then pulled me over the threshold after him. Freesia brought up the rear.

"Are you sure your pal used the term *death bell?*" Cooper asked, locking the door behind us.

The two cuckooing clocks were louder inside the apartment. I cringed. How could the others not hear the commotion?

"Positive," I said over the racket. I stopped in front of the wall covered with wooden, Black Forest style clocks with unique macabre death scenes carved onto their fronts—some with animals of prey like bears and wolves, others had unrecognizable or distorted beasts hefting frightening weapons. There were several empty spaces on the wall where clocks used to hang. It looked like the same number were missing as the last time I had been in here, back on that day I'd heard the cuckooing coming from the mirror.

Cooper stood in the doorway to the bedroom, his arms crossed, his blue-jean clad legs in that wide-legged cop stance he did so well. "Did Prudence say why she called the cuckooing sound a death bell?"

Freesia moved up next to me. "Who's Prudence?"

"An old friend of Violet's." Doc walked over to the living room window that looked out at a stand of pines. They were the same trees in which I'd seen something on the way up the walk. He peeked through a slit in the white gauzy curtains, a deep V forming at the bridge of his nose.

I thought back to that conversation. "When I told Prudence about coming in this place and seeing the moving cuckoo clock in the mirror, all she said was that it was interesting I could actually hear the toll of the death bell. Then she commented that I was getting stronger."

"Does your friend Prudence know about Cornelius and the séance we did?" Freesia asked.

"No." I hadn't gotten around to telling Prudence about my battle with the ax-wielding juggernaut that night, or that I'd actually gotten sliced by his blade in the process of trying to escape from him. I didn't want to give her more to scoff about when it came to my skills and lineage compared to hers.

Doc turned away from the window, his forehead still sporting that deep V. "You ready?"

I shook my head, but headed toward the bedroom door anyway. Cooper stepped aside to let me pass. Ms. Wolff's bedroom also had a wall covered with creepy Black Forest clocks. A smattering of them were missing, same as the dining room. Whoever had broken in and stolen the clocks seemed to have done so with purpose rather than grabbing willy-nilly.

The commotion from the two cuckooing clocks was starting to make my head feel like it was going cuckoo, too. I skirted the bed, stopping on the other side in front of the tall mirror attached to the dresser. What would it mean if one of the clocks fell silent suddenly? I grimaced at my own reflection. Hell, I didn't even know for sure what it meant for them to be going off.

In the mirror, I could see Doc and Cooper standing in front of the clock-covered wall. Freesia's head poked around the door jamb, her usual smile missing as she stared back at me with worried eyes. Her paranormal experience prior to the séance we'd had included a Ouija board, a trip to a fortune teller, and a haunted house tour or two. We'd knocked her socks off that night with my mirror trip.

"Well?" Cooper asked. "Which ones are cuckooing?"

I glanced over my shoulder to double check that the ones I could see cuckooing in the mirror were actually attached to the wall in the real world.

"The one to the left of Doc and the one directly above your head." I watched in the mirror as Cooper took down the one over his head. In the reflection, it continued to cuckoo as he inspected it. I looked over my shoulder, making sure the actual clock he held remained silent. Yep, no movement.

Back in the mirror the little birdie kept popping out the window in spite of his hand being in the way. It was the oddest thing to watch, like looking at a pebble under rippling water.

A phone rang, loud and trilling.

That wasn't one of Doc's or my cell phone rings, and Cooper wasn't pulling out his phone, so it must be Freesia's.

After the fifth ring, I turned to where she now filled the doorway. "Are you going to answer that?"

She glanced to her right and left. "Are you talking to me?"

"Isn't that your phone ringing?"

Cooper frowned up from the clock. "What are you talking about, Parker?"

The trilling continued. "The phone that's ringing."

Doc's head cocked to the side. "You hear a phone?"

"You don't?"

He shook his head.

Oh, hell.

"So now you hear two clocks cuckooing and a phone?" Cooper asked, hanging the clock he'd been inspecting back on the wall. It continued to cuckoo in the mirror.

I nodded, kneading my hands together. "Am I going crazy?" I asked Doc.

"I think it's this apartment. I'm beginning to suspect ..." he trailed off, sending a quick frown in Freesia's direction. "Can you tell where the ringing is coming from?" he asked me.

I closed my eyes, letting my ears take over. I followed the sound around the bed, careful to swing wide enough. Doc's warm palm clasped my elbow, guiding me through the doorway to where the trilling sound was a bit louder. I turned and took several steps into the living room until Doc tugged me to a stop.

"It's the antique phone," he said.

I opened my eyes, finding myself in the corner where Harvey and I had found Ms. Wolff's wrinkled up body and severed head under the rocking chair. There was a Victorian style phone sitting on the end table next to the chair. It was the same phone that had been there the day Harvey and I had found Ms. Wolff. The very phone that Cooper had told me was not connected to a phone jack. We had figured it was for decoration. Turned out we'd been wrong, because it certainly sounded like it was ringing now. The trouble was, I was the only one hearing it. Had the cuckooing in this place finally broken my brain?

I pointed down at the phone. "None of you can hear this thing ringing?"

"No, Parker. Just like none of us can hear the clocks. But I'll humor you." Cooper nudged me back a step. He took a handkerchief from his jacket and grasped the receiver, lifting it to his ear.

The ringing stopped.

"Hello?"

I held my breath, holding Cooper's steely gaze.

"Is someone there?" he asked, his focus shifting behind me to Doc. "This is Detective Cooper from the Deadwood Police Department. If someone is there, you'd better start talking."

After a few more seconds, he placed the receiver back on the base. "Nobody," he told Doc. "Not even the sound of breathing." He looked down at me. "Are you sure you heard this phone ringing?"

"Positive," I told him.

"How can you be so sure it's not just in your head?"

"Because it stopped when you picked it up, and now it's ringing again." It had started seconds after he'd hung up.

I held out my hand. "Give me your handkerchief." I took it by the corner. "It's not used, is it?"

"Don't confuse me for Detective Hawke."

I wrapped it around the receiver and slowly picked it up, holding it to my ear. My hand trembled visibly.

It was only a phone, I reminded myself. It wasn't going to reach out and bite my head off, unlike the rigid-faced detective watching me with squinty eyes.

"Say 'hello,' Parker," he ordered.

I held my hand out to shut him up. I was building up to it, damn it.

"Hello?" I asked, my voice husky with uncertainty. "Is anybody there?"

"OPEN THE DOOR!" someone yelled in my ear.

I screeched and dropped the receiver back onto the cradle, hanging it up in the process.

"What did you hear?" Cooper asked.

"Someone yelling at me to open the door."

He tugged the handkerchief from my clenched fist. He wrapped it around the receiver and held it up to his ear again, listening with wrinkled brow. Then he shook his head and handed the receiver to Doc. "I don't hear anything, not even a dial tone. You try."

Doc took the receiver and listened. "Hello?" he waited, watching me without expression. "If someone is there who would like me to relay a message, I can open the channel for you."

He reminded me of the paranormal investigators I'd seen on television shows, only less bossy than some who demanded the ghosts talk back.

After several seconds of silence from the rest of us, he shook his head at Cooper and hung up the receiver. "Nothing."

The phone rang again almost immediately. I gasped, staring at it like it was a snake that had arched up and started hissing.

"Is it ringing again?" Doc asked.

I nodded, reaching for the receiver.

Cooper shoved the handkerchief in my hand before I made contact. "No prints, damn it. I don't need Detective Hawke knowing we were here."

Sheesh. He was going a little over the top if you asked me. Like Hawke stopped by every other day and dusted for new prints.

I wrapped the soft cotton around the phone and lifted it slowly to my ear, my eyes locked onto Doc.

"Hello?" I whispered into the mouthpiece.

"OPEN THE DOOR!"

A boom reverberated out from the bedroom.

I started in surprise but held onto the phone this time.

Doc looked over my shoulder toward the entrance to the bedroom, his brows wrinkling.

I covered the mouthpiece. "Did you hear it, too?"

"Hear what?" Cooper glanced toward the bedroom.

"I think I felt it more than heard it," Doc answered. At Cooper's glare, he explained, "Something hit the dresser mirror."

I swallowed my heart back down into my chest, making room for my tongue to come back to the forefront. "Who is this?"

Something growled on the other end of the line, sending a rash of goosebumps down my spine.

The boom echoed out from the bedroom again. I pinched my lips together, holding in a cry of alarm. Covering the mouthpiece again, I lowered the phone and told them, "I think someone or something is trying to come through the mirror."

Freesia let out a squawk and raced over next to me, staring with wide eyes at the doorway where she'd been a second ago. "Who is it?"

"I'm more afraid of what it is than who it is."

"What are you talking about, Parker?" Cooper walked over and stood with his shoulders framed in the doorway.

Doc turned me toward him, his gaze drilling into mine. "You're a medium. Focus on what you want to achieve."

What did I want to happen here besides the spooky craziness in this damned apartment to stop?

"There's nothing in the mirror," Cooper said from the doorway. I could hear the skepticism in his tone.

I sighed. "I want Cooper to hear what I do—the cuckooing, the mirror booms, the voice on the line."

"Okay," Doc said. "Now make it happen, medium."

Make it happen. I closed my eyes for a moment and pictured a candle flame flickering in a dark room. As the flame danced in my mind's eye, a calm settled over me. My trembling stopped. My fear receded into the darkness, away from the light, replaced by an ironclad resolve.

I raised the receiver back to my ear. "You want me to open the door?"

"Yes!" It sounded more like a snarl than an actual word.

"Not until you tell me why you want through."

"I can smell you, *Scharfrichter.*"

Great. Whatever it was knew my job description. Now we could focus on the *why* part of this call instead of *who*. "That doesn't answer my question."

Booming again.

I opened my eyes, focusing on the wall in front of me. The dancing flame still flickered in my thoughts.

"There it is again," Doc told Cooper, who'd returned to our huddle around the phone.

"What happens if I let you through?" I asked the caller.

The laughter that came through the line had a sharp, menacing edge to it. "All the better to eat you with."

I recognized the line from the Brothers Grimm. Was it role playing? "Who are you supposed to be? The big bad wolf?"

"My teeth are sharper."

Was this the other bone cruncher? The one I'd been warned about after executing its hunting partner? That sucker's teeth had been long, sharp, and wicked as hell. But I'd killed it just the same.

"Shall we see how your teeth stand up when I swing my war hammer at them?" Was whatever waited on the other side of the mirror the reason I would need that weapon soon?

"She has a war hammer?" Cooper asked Doc, sounding surprised.

"Open the door now!" The caller snarled again. The mirror rattled from the boom but held.

I looked at Cooper, but he didn't react. Damn it, how could I make him hear what I was hearing?

"Not until you tell me who executed the timekeeper."

Silence came through the line. In that moment of nothingness, I thought of Prudence and an idea hit me.

After a few more seconds, the caller spoke, "The *Scharfrichter*."

I reached out and grabbed onto Cooper's forearm, holding tight when he tried to pull away. "What about me?" I asked into the mouthpiece.

"*You* slew the timekeeper."

"You're mistaken. The door stays shut." I hung up the phone.

An ear-clanging crash came from the bedroom.

Freesia screamed.

Cooper yanked free, pulling out his gun with lightning speed.

Doc tucked me behind him, blocking me from anything that might step out through the bedroom doorway. I peeked around his shoulder in time to see Cooper disappear into the room, his handgun pointed up but at the ready.

"Holy fuck!" I heard Cooper say.

"What is it?" Freesia called out.

He rejoined us, holstering his gun. "The mirror shattered. There's glass everywhere in there." His gray eyes narrowed on mine. "I mean *everywhere*. What in the hell did you do?"

"Me?"

Cooper frowned toward the bedroom. "Jesus H. Christ, Parker! How am I going to hide this mess from the surveillance crew Hawke sends through here each week?"

"That wasn't me."

"Are you sure?" Doc asked under his breath.

No, not entirely. But there was no way I was going to take a single ounce of ownership for it while Cooper was on the warpath. He might put a bullet in me so I could share his pain.

"If it wasn't you," Cooper snapped, "who was it? And don't you dare tell me it was the big bad wolf."

I reached down and hoisted the receiver again. "Way to go, shithead," I yelled into the mouthpiece for a more dramatic effect. "You broke the damned door!"

* * *

Several hours later I was holding down the fort at Calamity Jane Realty alone, apart from any ghosts who might be keeping me company. My cup of coffee had grown cold for the second time since Doc had dropped me off at work after leaving the Galena House.

I had a gut feeling that Doc was right. I'd broken the mirror.

When I'd touched Cooper's arm, I'd tried to focus on that candle flame while willing the detective to hear the booming. Unfortunately, it appeared I'd cranked up the "volume" way too high. The pounding noise I'd been hearing had become a glass-shattering sonic boom.

Damn.

Such was my life. Whatever feat I attempted, I managed to overdo it and screw things up. Instead of accidentally getting pregnant with one child from Rex the rat bastard, I'd produced two. And though I loved them dearly, my accidental pregnancy had become twice the dilemma. While attempting to change careers, I'd become Spooky Parker, the ghost-loving real estate agent AND the lesser known—but more notorious across the realms—Violet Parker, Executioner Extraordinaire. I wasn't even going to touch my multiple slip-ups that involved Cooper and all of his murder cases. And then there was Doc ... actually I hadn't screwed that up yet, but our romance was still young and in the double-the-pleasure phase. With a little more time, I'd probably find a way to double up on the heartache in that arena, too.

The bells over the front door jingled. I blinked out of my daze as

Cornelius closed the door behind him. He was looking very presidential this afternoon in his stovepipe hat, long black wool coat, and walking stick. His pointy goatee appeared freshly sharpened. His round sunglasses hid his cornflower blue eyes.

"Thanks for coming down here," I said. "I wasn't in the mood to deal with Wilda today."

Cornelius lowered himself into the chair opposite me, his movements slow and stiff for a man I'd guess to be close to my age. "She has certainly had plenty to say about you today. Somebody needs to give that little terror a lollipop."

"About Wilda," I started, taking a sip of coffee and grimacing at how bitter it was as well as cold. Had Jerry switched coffee brands? "Doc wanted me to arrange an evening this week with you for the …" what was the word Doc had used? "For the extraction."

"Where is the tall medium?"

"He had an appointment down in Rapid this—"

"Shhh." Cornelius cocked his head to the side.

I waited. I'd played this game with him before. If asked, he'd tell me he could hear ghosts talking in the ceiling, walls, carpet, wherever. Only these days, he might not be as full of hot air as he used to be. Maybe Wilda was instructing him where and how to plant the letter opener I'd left sitting on my desk after going through the office mail.

"Hmmm," he broke the silence. "That's odd."

"What is Wilda telling you now?"

"Nothing. That's what's odd."

"Do you hear someone else?" Like my ex-boss, Jane?

"Only you. And me." He took off his sunglasses. I tried not to wince at how red-lined and dark-ringed his eyes were. "It's the first time in weeks that I've had peace and quiet." He sighed, his shoulders sinking deeper into the chair. "Now, what preparations have you made for the séance?"

Me? This was the Doc and Cornelius show. I was the special guest star. "None. But Doc may have stuff prepped."

"Who is this doctor you speak of?"

I rolled my eyes and switched to Cornelius's vernacular. "Doc is the tall medium."

"The tall medium is a doctor?"

"No. His name is 'Doc' Nyce." When Cornelius continued to stare at me with a wrinkled brow, I added, "He's a financial planner."

"A gambler? Hmm."

I was pretty sure my mouth had not said anything about Doc being a gambler.

Cornelius stroked his pointy goatee. "I wonder if he's ever spun a fortune wheel on a riverboat."

Because that was where all gamblers started their careers?

"You should ask him that when we get together for the séance." I brought the conversation back around to the reason I'd asked him to come down to the office this afternoon.

He eyeballed the mug of coffee on my desk. "What's that?"

"Coffee."

"Do you mind?" he asked, reaching for it.

"Uhhh, no." Nobody had ever asked to share my cold coffee before. "Go for it."

He picked up the coffee cup and stood, glancing around the office for Lord only knew what. Then he strode over to the front door, stepped outside, and dumped the coffee on the sidewalk.

"What the hell is he doing?" I whispered, standing to watch him through the plate glass windows as he placed the mug in the center of the spill. He stepped back, looked at the mug, bent over and turned the handle slightly, then nodded and rejoined me at my desk.

I stared quizzically down at him as he made himself comfortable. "Was my coffee bothering you?"

"Why would coffee bother me?"

"You know what? Never mind." I took my seat again. "What evening works for you to have the séance?"

"Thursday."

"Besides Thursday," I said.

"Thursday is ideal. The moon will be new."

"Thursday is Thanksgiving." I'd probably be down at my parents' place with the kids. I hadn't invited Doc to join us yet and wasn't sure I wanted to with Susan in town.

"Thanksgiving?" he said the word as if it were new to his vocabulary.

Surely he'd celebrated Thanksgiving before. He might be eccentric from the top of his hat to the tips of his pointy shoes, but he wasn't from Mars.

"Yes, Thanksgiving. You know, turkey, stuffing, pumpkin pie. According to my kids' history book, your favorite president was the one who made it a national holiday."

"My favorite president?"

"Abe Lincoln."

"What makes you think Lincoln is my favorite?"

Really, Mr. Doppelgänger? "I don't know, maybe your hat."

He took it off and frowned at it. "Kennedy is my favorite. He wore a similar hat back in 1961."

No shit. "My mistake."

"We'll have the séance on Thursday," he declared.

"Cornelius, that's Thanksgiving," I reiterated.

"Are you from Plymouth?"

I assumed he meant Plymouth, Massachusetts. "No."

"Are you a direct descendant of the pilgrims?"

"No." My lineage had a much darker history than sailing to new lands to form colonies. Although the pilgrims' history wasn't quite as rosy as they taught in elementary school.

"Are you a legitimate descendant of Wampanoag Indians?"

"The what?"

"Are you a fan of Sarah Hale?"

"Who's she?"

"She wrote 'Mary Had a Little Lamb.'"

"What does she have to do with Thanksgiving?"

"You don't know, Violet? Did you attend school in this country?"

"Of course."

"Have you hit your head hard lately?"

Not as hard as I'd like to hit it on the desk right now. "No."

"You'll need dried sage for Thanksgiving."

"For the stuffing?" My mom liked to make the dressing. She'd won first place for her recipe at the county fair three years in a row.

"Sage cleanses the air and purifies the energy. We'll need to burn it to create the proper space for the ritual to begin."

"Cornelius, you're not listening to me. Thursday is—"

The front door opened so fast the bells' jingle was cut short to a mere "jing."

"Violet!" Rex stalked inside, slamming the door behind him hard enough to make the plate glass windows rattle. His caramel colored suede coat hung open over his white sweater and gray corduroy pants. His blond hair was perfectly windblown. To any passerby, he looked like he'd walked off the cover of a men's magazine.

I took one look at the dark red blotches painting his cheeks and the vein pulsing dead center on his brow and stood to head trouble off at the pass. "We're closed." I pointed at the door he'd come through. "Get out or I'll call the cops!"

He ignored my threat, brushing past Cornelius's bony elbow in his rush to my desk. "I warned you about touching my car, you vindictive bitch."

"I didn't touch your precious car, Rex. You're barking up the wrong tree."

"You expect me to believe you had nothing to do with my windshield wipers disappearing?" He leaned over my desk, his eyes menacing. "You owe me a coat!"

I looked at the water spots darkening his shoulders, struggling to keep a smile from my lips. Natalie had been right about the coat. It was ruined.

"This sounds like a mystery," Cornelius spoke up. "I love a good whodunit."

Rex turned toward Cornelius, his brow scrunching as he took in the stovepipe hat and coat. "Who are you?"

Cornelius stood. With his hat back in place, he had a good six inches on Rex. "Cornelius Curion," he said with a slight bow.

The leer Rex aimed my way made me feel like I'd been slimed. "Is this kook your latest lover?"

I jammed my hands on my hips. "Rex, why do you assume every man you see me with is one of my lovers?"

"So you admit you have more than one."

"As a matter of fact, Violet and I do have a rather intimate relationship." Cornelius stepped up next to Rex, looking him over with one arched eyebrow. "What is your role in her life? You don't look like one of her preferred male companions, but you are acting the part of a jealous admirer."

"Preferred male companions?" Rex glared at me. "How many men are there, Violet?"

I wasn't going to dignify that question with an answer. First of all, it was absurd. Secondly, the professional philanderer could mind his own damned business.

"Sir." Cornelius fake coughed. "A lady's private affairs are never to be aired in public," he chastised. "Surely a gentleman such as yourself realizes that."

Rex's left eye ticked as he looked back and forth between Cornelius and me. "Listen, I don't know who you really are, Abraham Lincoln, or how you know Violet, but how about you step outside for a few minutes and give the 'lady' and me some privacy."

"Lincoln?" Cornelius tugged on the point of his goatee. "That is the second time I've heard his name this morning. I wonder if it's a sign that I should prep for a visit from his ghost."

Rex's upper lip curled. "Oh, you're one of *them*."

"Not yet," Cornelius said. "But in time I will be." He looked down over Rex's clothing. "Judging from your choice in outerwear, you must be Violet's tailor."

My tailor? Where had Cornelius come up with that? I opened my mouth to ask only to close it when he glanced my way. It didn't take a medium to read his mind—he was toying with Rex. I lowered myself into my chair to watch the show.

"Tailor!" Rex sputtered, apparently finding that choice of careers an insult. "I'm the father of her children."

I gasped. That no good, son of a bitch! I reached for the letter opener, eyeing his jugular.

"How does that work?" Cornelius asked, unruffled by Rex's claim to fame.

"How does what work?"

"Being her tailor?"

Rex growled. "I'm not her damned tailor, you clown."

"Sir, I don't understand this sudden hostility. There is nothing wrong with fitting clothing to individuals," Cornelius said, stroking his goatee as his cornflower blue eyes assessed Rex. "Although I find it odd that you clothe females. Normally the profession is based around men's wear." He brushed his fingers over the shoulder of Rex's suede jacket. "Your suede has water spots. Surely a qualified tailor such as yourself knows better than to allow such an expensive material to get wet."

"It's her fault." Rex fired another glare at me.

I held up the letter opener in the face of his malice.

"Ah, I see. She sprayed you with a hose." Cornelius shook his long, boney finger at me. "Violet Parker, you minx."

Rex frowned at Cornelius. "I didn't say she sprayed me with a hose, kook."

"That is incorrect."

"What is incorrect?"

"It's Cornelius. Although I understand why you'd be confused. K and hard C sound so similar."

"Are you calling me stupid?" Rex puffed out his chest.

"Am I calling you stupid?" Cornelius asked back. "The shape and size of your skull are similar to other normally intelligent homo sapiens, but without actually weighing your brain we can't be certain."

I bit my lip to keep from giving my opinion on Rex's brain.

That pulsing vein I'd seen in Rex's forehead when he entered the office had split into two pulsing veins. "I'll have you know I'm a renowned scientist."

"Indeed?" Cornelius shot me a crooked half-grin—his trademark smile. There was a distinct glint in his gaze. Was he enjoying this game with Rex as much as I was? "I was unaware that fitting clothing was now considered a scientific field of study," Cornelius continued. "I suppose you would need to understand the structure of the human body, along with potential friction points that would vary depending on girth and height." Cornelius patted Rex on the back. "Excellent, tailor. I have a whole new respect for your expertise. Have you set up a shop in town? I'm looking for someone to take in a few of my suits. The last couple of weeks have been hellish and caused me to drop several precious pounds."

Rex stared at Cornelius like he'd ridden into town on a two headed camel. "Are you insane?"

"On the contrary, I'm extremely levelheaded. Especially when a certain maniacal ghost isn't whispering assassination directives in my ear."

"Assassination directives?" Rex took a step back from Cornelius, raising his hands. "Maybe you should seek some counseling for that."

"Oh, I plan to as soon as Violet and I can arrange it. We were discussing that very topic when you joined us."

The front door jingled.

Cornelius blocked my view of the door.

"Welcome to Calamity Jane Realty," I said, standing so I could see around Cornelius.

"Why thank you, big sis."

My eyes nearly popped out of my skull at the sight of my sister, the ruthless, malevolent bitch. Several strands of her long, straight brown hair floated around her in the dry air, making her look even more witchy than she was.

What was this? First Rex, now Susan? Who would be joining us next at our fucked up family get together? "Susan, how'd you manage to slip past the demons guarding the gates of Hell this afternoon?"

She shrugged off her long coat, unveiling a pair of thigh high black boots, a skimpy black leather skirt and a very low cut glitter-infused sweater.

I scoffed. Where had she learned how to dress? A comic book?

"Hello, Rex," she positively purred, her focus zeroing in on him like she had a warhead ready to fire. "Long time no see."

Not long enough.

Then it hit me—Susan must have known Rex was here. Why else would she show up dressed like she was scouting for stripper poles to wrap her legs around? How did she find out he was in town? Had Natalie let it slip?

"Do you see a woman in black?" Cornelius whispered to me.

"Unfortunately I do."

"Did you bring her here from another realm?"

"No, but I'd like to send her to another universe."

"Ah, that hurts, big sis." Susan pouted, her red glossy lips puffing out for added effect. She leaned back against Ben's desk. Her skirt inched northward, showing off plenty of her long, pale thighs for Rex's benefit "And here I thought you'd see this as a potential *menage à trois* opportunity."

Ewww. "Now you're just being gross on purpose, Susan."

She giggled. "You know me well."

Way too well. "You'd prefer to steal him from me."

"It's more fun than sharing."

"She really means that," I told Cornelius.

He glanced back and forth between Susan and me. "I'm struggling to see the genetic similarities."

"Susan." Rex collected himself, his face darkening as he eyed her legs. "How did you find me?"

"Violet told me you were here." She pulled her shoulders back, shoving her perky mini-globes out for a better world view.

"That's a lie," I told Rex.

"She said you'd mentioned me, wondering how I was doing."

"Another lie." Although I did remember discussing something about Susan and Rex's history with the bastard.

"Ah ha! I've found it," Cornelius said. "You have the same mouth— heart shaped with the thicker lower lip."

"They kiss the same, too," Rex offered with a smirk.

"Nobody asked for your feedback, Professor Ass-hat."

Rex arched his blond brows. "Although I suspect Violet has more of a wanton, wild animal boldness during sex these days. You can see the passion in her eyes when she's angry at me, like right now."

All eyes shifted to me. My face heated about four hundred degrees in a flash. Talking about my sexual habits in front of Rex and my sister was torture enough, but having Cornelius witness my humiliation had me choked up on a ball of fiery rage.

"That's not passion," I spoke through clenched teeth.

"It looks more like stark raving madness to me," Cornelius said. "I once looked into the eyes of an angry hippo that appeared less hostile than Violet at this moment."

I sighed. Did he have to compare me to a hippo in front of my sister, the long-legged gazelle?

"Hippo," Susan laughed. "How appropriate."

"Sticks and stones, you stupid strumpet."

"Is that from a nursery rhyme?" Cornelius asked.

Susan lifted her chin. "Rex, maybe you need to run another experiment." She eyed my sapphire sweater dress with a wrinkled upper lip. "You already have a baseline with Violet."

I was a baseline? For what? Sex with Rex? That had been so long ago that ... Then it hit me. Susan somehow must have gotten the idea that Rex and I were back together.

I held my fist to my mouth, torn about current events. I wanted to laugh at the absurdity of Susan's confusion, but at the same time I was tempted to take a swing at her for coming to steal Rex from me yet again. Apparently one round of debauchery was not enough for the sadistic hussy.

"How did you know Rex was here in my office, Susan?"

"I didn't. I was coming to see you."

"In that outfit? Did your pimp send you here? Who's manning your street corner?"

"Tut tut, big sis. Jealousy does not become you. Neither does that color of blue, truth be told."

A red haze of rage blurred my vision. How becoming would I look when I jumped on her back and beat the hell out of her with my boot?

Wait! An idea bubble formed and popped in my head. Maybe there was a way to derail Rex while distracting Susan from finding out who was really sharing my bed. I had to try.

"There she is, Rex." I pointed at Susan.

"Your sister? What do you mean?"

"You were wondering who's been prank calling you and messing with your car, right? Susan's surprise visit here confirms it—she's your troublemaker."

Come to think of it, I'd lost track of his business card around the time she'd shown up at Aunt Zoe's front door and spent the night. Had she gone through my purse when I wasn't looking? I wouldn't put it past the scheming bitch. What else had she taken?

Susan's claws extended. "You lying fat cow!"

"She knows you've come back for me, Rex." I continued feeding the fire. "She's jealous."

History was repeating itself before my very eyes. Wasn't this a banner moment for all?

"She is?" Rex's mouth was catching flies.

"Yes, but Susan doesn't realize that you and I are not lovers." I stepped around my desk and latched onto Cornelius's arm. "That I've given myself to another man."

Rex's gaze narrowed. "I knew it!"

"As Cornelius said earlier, we have a very intimate relationship." We shared a terrorizing ghost who was bent on ending both our lives.

Abe Jr. looked down at me with one cocked eyebrow. "What about Thanksgiving, Violet?"

Dammit, he had me over a barrel and he knew it. Today had shown me something—Cornelius was clearly not as obtuse as he so often played.

I gave Susan a fake smile. "Good news! I won't be able to make it to Thanksgiving dinner this year. Cornelius has promised me a night to remember."

Chapter Eighteen

Sunday, November 18th

I was sitting on the edge of my bed the next morning, staring down at my hands, when Aunt Zoe's voice interrupted my worrying.

"Ten fingers and ten toes," she said from the doorway. "I counted them right after you came out of the womb."

That made me smile. Aunt Zoe had been there when I'd taken my first gasp of oxygen. She liked to joke that she'd been putting up with my screaming and hollering ever since.

"Willis has breakfast almost ready."

Harvey had played bodyguard from the couch again all night, snoring loudly enough to scare away any non-humans within a ten mile radius.

"What's he making?" It smelled sweet and lemony.

"A Dutch Baby. He says it's his momma's secret recipe, so he kicked me out as soon as I set the table."

I almost drooled. "Damn! I see another marriage proposal to the old buzzard in my future."

She walked over and joined me on the edge of the bed. "Another?"

"I asked Harvey to marry me last month when he made us meatloaf, but he turned me down. He said I was too nutty for him."

She chuckled. "You want to call Doc and have him join us?"

"No way."

Her forehead pinched. "Did something happen?"

"No, we're fine, but I don't want to share any of that Dutch Baby with him."

That made her guffaw. "And here I thought you were ga-ga for him."

"Oh, I am, but I draw the line at sharing a Dutch Baby until there's a ring on my finger." I leaned back on my palms. "How's the glass order coming? Are you getting close to being done?"

"Another day or two and I'll have everything ready. The money will make for a nice Christmas bonus."

Christmas. That reminded me of another holiday. "I have bad news." I winced in anticipation of her reaction. "I'm not going to Thanksgiving at my parents' place this year."

"Is this due to that silly stunt Susan pulled?"

As soon as I'd made it home from work yesterday, I'd raced out to Aunt Zoe's workshop, locking out the rest of the world while I'd ranted and raved about my sister and Rex in the nakedly conjoined position. Aunt Zoe had listened with first a look of disbelief and then anger on her face that mirrored my feelings.

"No, it's because Cornelius wants to have the séance to rid himself of Wilda on Thanksgiving night. It's a new moon, which he believes will give us a better chance of success."

"Did you remind him it's Thanksgiving?"

"Yes, but he informed me that since I don't share DNA with any of the pilgrims, my celebrating the holiday was an unnecessary extravagance, especially with his sanity on the line."

"I thought his sanity was long gone."

"Me too. However, after the way he helped me diffuse the Rex situation yesterday and then acted as my stand-in boyfriend to throw Susan off Doc's scent, I'm beginning to think his eccentricities may be part of an act."

"Why would he act so odd?"

I shrugged. "Maybe to keep a buffer between him and anyone who might get too close and become an emotional risk. With his paranormal history, he may prefer to keep his distance from most folks who might not accept him and his lifestyle."

"Could be," Aunt Zoe said with a slow nod. "What about the kids? Won't they miss you being there with them at the Thanksgiving table?"

"I don't know. I called Mom last night to get a lay of the land and she told me she has a surprise guest."

"Who?"

"Someone who'll make the kids' forget I exist for the day."

Aunt Zoe gasped. "Your brother?"

"Yep. Quint is flying home for a few days from whatever corner of the planet he's working in at the moment."

My brother's career as a freelance photojournalist for several well-known magazines kept him on the go most months. Both of my kids adored him and the trinkets he always brought them from his travels. The last time he'd come home had been March when he'd helped me move some of my stuff up to Deadwood.

"Isn't he heading down to Mexico soon? Seems like I remember your dad mentioning something about a Maya site."

"Not yet. I think he has some gig in Canada first."

"Your kids are going to be so excited to see him, especially Layne."

"I know." I sighed. "I wish I could see him, too, but I need to deal with Wilda."

She squeezed my shoulder. "You and I can pretend you are under the weather Thanksgiving morning, and I'll take the kids down without you. Maybe you can catch your brother before he flies out again."

"Maybe, if Wilda doesn't take me out of the game."

"Violet, you're an executioner."

"Executioners can have heart attacks. If you could see that melted clown doll of hers, you'd be worried about your ticker, too." I shuddered.

She took me by the chin. "Don't you dare let that little girl and her damned clown mess with your head. You are stronger and smarter than she is."

"But she's evil, and evil trumps strength."

"Maybe so, but executioners can outsmart evil. You need to listen to Doc, let him be your teacher, and whatever you do, *don't* leave his side this time." She released my chin and stood. "Now, are you hungry or not?"

I reached for my robe. "What are you going to say if Dad sniffs out the truth on Thanksgiving Day?"

"I'll explain that you have family business to take care of. After I add that what we've been waiting for all of these years has finally awoken inside of you, he'll understand."

I found it hard to believe my father would swallow that watermelon-sized announcement without choking on it. My face must have showed my doubt because she added, "He won't like it, but—"

The sound of a chicken squawking loudly outside of my window stopped her mid-sentence. We swapped frowns.

"Is that Elvis?" I rushed over to the window, pulling back the curtains.

Aunt Zoe was on my heels, her face pressed against the window next to mine. "What is that silly bird doing in the tree?"

No sooner had the words exited Aunt Zoe's mouth then Elvis the chicken flew-hopped up to yet a higher gnarled branch in the old cottonwood tree in front of the house. When the feathers stopped flying, Elvis was almost eye level with us.

"That damned bird must be a good twenty-five feet off the ground," I muttered. My gaze lowered. A growl followed. "What are those two barefoot children doing outside in their pajamas without coats? Don't they have a lick of sense?"

As I pounded on the window, trying to get Addy and Layne's attention, Reid Martin's red dually pickup truck pulled up in front of the house. He parked at the curb, smiling at my two nincompoops as he came around the back of his pickup.

Several unladylike curses flew from Aunt Zoe's mouth as we watched Reid lift a ladder out of the truck's bed.

"What's he ..." I started to ask, and then realized what was going on. "Oh jeez, he's come to save the chicken. Please tell me Addy didn't call 911 about this." The snickering and nicknames that would ensue would rival the jokes that flew my way when Jeff Wymonds's garage roof blew up during my open house.

We watched Harvey head out to meet Reid at the end of the sidewalk, pointing up at the chicken when he put his arm around Addy's shoulders.

"It wasn't Addy," Aunt Zoe said.

"How do you know?"

"Because only Reid showed up, not any of his crew. My money's on Willis. He must have called him to come over and play fireman."

"That's fast service. You were just down in the kitchen with Harvey not ten minutes ago."

"Reid always was Johnny-on-the-spot when it came to damsels in distress." She snorted, adding under her breath, "Especially when the fire he needed to put out was in my bed."

I didn't know what to say in response to that, so I kept my big mouth shut and watched as Reid extended the ladder and leaned it against the tree's trunk. He put his weight on the first rung, shifting around, testing the ladder's stability.

Aunt Zoe growled. "He's going to break his neck rescuing that chicken."

"Harvey's holding the base."

"Yeah, but Reid weighs more than Harvey." She stepped back from the window. "I'm going down there."

I threw on jeans and a T-shirt and followed her down the stairs, scooping up my red pea coat on the way out the front door. "Addy and Layne," I hollered from the top porch step. "Go inside and put on some warmer clothes."

"But, Mom," Addy whined, "Elvis may fall while I'm inside."

"Your chicken is going to be all right, sweetheart," Reid told her as he climbed the ladder. "I'll bring her down safe and sound."

"Go!" I ordered, pointing my thumb back toward the house. "Trust me, no chicken is worth frostbitten toes."

Grumbling something about my lack of love for her prized chicken, Addy led the way inside with her purplish-pink toes.

Layne smiled up at me as he passed. "Morning, Mom. Your hair looks wild."

Great. Layne was now channeling Cooper.

"Did you have a bad dream?"

"No," I lied. "I haven't combed my curls yet."

He didn't need to hear about my nightmare involving a ringing phone and an albino juggernaut who had broken the mirror in Ms. Wolff's bedroom on his way through. Especially the part about the ax that he'd planted dead center in my chest. Where had that dang war hammer been when I needed it most?

I leaned down and kissed his forehead. "Go inside and put on some warm clothes."

He raced inside after his sister.

I stepped down onto the front walk, watching as Aunt Zoe and Harvey held the ladder for Reid, who was working his way up through the bare branches of the old cottonwood tree. I held my breath as Reid leaned out, reaching for Elvis's yellow feet. A cacophony of squawks rang out in the cold clear air, followed by a fluttering of feathers, a yip from Reid, and a shout of alarm from Aunt Zoe. Then it was over and Elvis was stuffed unceremoniously into a burlap sack. The chicken squawked a bit more on the way down the ladder, quieting when a more warmly dressed Addy pulled her out of the burlap sack and nuzzled her wattle as she carried her back into the house.

"Why don't you join us for breakfast, Reid?" I offered as he carried the ladder back to his truck.

Aunt Zoe nailed me with a glare. "I thought you had dibs on that Dutch Baby," she said under her breath.

"That was before Reid rescued Elvis. Addy wouldn't have let me enjoy my breakfast if he hadn't shown up to save the day, so I owe him." I smiled at the fire captain. "Harvey made a Dutch Baby. You interested in a piece?"

"Or two," Aunt Zoe added, challenging me with her raised brows.

She probably didn't want Reid joining us for breakfast as much as I didn't want to share Harvey's cooking. But Addy's hero needed to be rewarded for his quick action and efforts.

"Sure. I haven't had one of those in ages."

"Yer gonna love my momma's recipe." Harvey led the way up the steps.

"I hope you made two," I muttered to the old buzzard as he held the door for us.

He had, thankfully, and I ate so much that I had to unbutton my jeans before I'd finished.

"Wow, Sparky," Reid said as Aunt Zoe cleared our plates. "That was impressive. I don't know that I've ever seen a girl eat that much in one sitting."

"A word to the wise," Aunt Zoe said over her shoulder on the way to the sink. "Don't come between Violet and Harvey's cooking. You could lose an arm."

His laugh was rich and deep. I saw Aunt Zoe scowl over her shoulder at him as she filled the sink with water. It wasn't the first scowl she'd sent his way since he'd arrived and wouldn't be the last, but in between her not-so-happy-glances I'd caught her staring at him with a look that was heated and hungry. Very hungry. And not for Harvey's food.

My cell phone rang. I looked down at the screen, expecting Doc or Cooper, maybe even Cornelius. Instead it was Mona.

"I'm sorry but I need to take this," I told Reid and Harvey, who were still lounging at the table with me, finishing up their coffee. "And I'm too full to move."

"Who is it?" Harvey asked.

I answered the call in response with, "Hello, Mona."

"Hi, Vi. Jerry wants me to let you know that we received a thumbs up from the company managing the Sugarloaf Building in Dominick Masterson's absence. We'll be filming tomorrow as planned, but only on the bottom floor. They don't want anyone upstairs."

Hmmm, that was curious. "Great." My tone didn't match the word.

"I know," she said. "But you're almost done."

"Did Jerry mention which outfit he'd like me to wear for filming at the Sugarloaf Building?" I looked across at Reid as I asked her the question.

His eyes snapped to mine, his brow creasing.

"He mentioned the white dress with red cherries on the bodice."

I squeezed my eyes shut. I'd have preferred the pink with white polka dots. The cherry one was right out of a 1950s women's magazine and suggestive as all get out with the low neckline and juicy red cherries. "Mona, can I borrow that red silk scarf of yours?" That would at least fix the low neckline problem.

"Let me guess—this one shows cleavage."

"What cleavage I can muster, yes."

She sighed. "He means well."

"I know. That's why I'll wear it."

"I have a short script ready about the building, covering its history and the rumors about it being haunted. I can drop it by later." Mona knew I hadn't planned on coming into the office today, needing a day off to prep mentally for tomorrow and enjoy some downtime with my family.

"I thought Ray was supposed to write that."

She chuckled. "He did, but I rewrote it. The man needs to stick with selling real estate."

"If you don't mind dropping it off, that would be great. I'll be home most of the day." I had hopes of doing something with Doc later but hadn't set anything in stone.

Mona hung up and I looked across at Reid. "I need to know what you saw in the Sugarloaf Building the last time you were in there."

"I really wish you didn't have to go in there." Aunt Zoe came over to the table, joining us as she dried a glass. "But at least you'll be there in the daytime."

"Does that make a difference?"

"If there truly is a *lidén* roaming the place, then it might. Usually they are night dwellers."

"It was well after dark when I was in there," Reid told Aunt Zoe. "We received a call that someone saw some flames in one of the upper story windows. We were the first firetruck on scene and didn't find anything, not even signs of a fire. I sent the guys back down to the rig and was double checking one of the back rooms when I saw something waiting in the shadows in one of the dark corners." He focused on me. "At first, I thought I was seeing things, but then I heard scuffling."

"Was it hiding from you?" I asked. If this thing was as bad as Aunt Zoe implied, I'd expect it to have shown itself to Reid without qualms.

"Actually, I had the feeling it wasn't hiding, just studying me. I can't explain why. When I spoke to it, asking who was there, the shadow started to move."

Harvey sat forward. "Are ya sure it wasn't some younguns up there messin' with ya?"

Reid nodded. "It didn't move like a normal shadow would. It sort of billowed out toward me. I stepped back and raised my arms to shield myself, and that's when that special watchband Zo gave me seemed to flash. It reminded me of the glare you see when sunlight reflects off glass."

Aunt Zoe sat in the chair between us, the lines on her face doubling at his recount.

"After that the shadow pulled back and seemed to vanish through the wall." He looked around at each of us. "When I shined my light on the wall, I could see a black mark where it disappeared."

"Did anything else happen?" Aunt Zoe asked.

"I didn't hang around to see. The next morning I came to my senses, figuring my mind was playing tricks on me. When I went back, I didn't see any signs of a fire or the shadow thing. Just an old empty building with plenty of cobwebs and creaks." He drained his coffee cup. "But that black smudge was still on the wall."

"Have you gone back since?" I asked.

He shook his head. "But I need to. We've had several more reports lately about weird sparks and lights passing by the upstairs windows. I have a feeling I'm not going to find anything up there when I go, but I can't file an official report until I pay another visit."

"Why doesn't Lead send one of their fire department guys in there?" I asked.

Aunt Zoe stood. "The two towns share certain services to save money, including a fire investigator." Which was Reid's other role in addition to being a fire captain for Deadwood.

I looked up at Aunt Zoe. "I need to go in that building."

She blew out a breath.

"Today," I added and asked Reid, "Do you think you can get me in there for a walk through? I don't want any surprises tomorrow during filming."

"But if this thing only comes out at night ..." Reid started.

"Violet might unintentionally draw it out, day or night," Aunt Zoe cut in. "She's a magnet for other world beings."

"I suppose I could do the walk through this afternoon and take you along, Sparky."

"I'm coming, too," Aunt Zoe said.

Reid's brow rose. "With me?"

"And Violet."

Wonderful. I really enjoyed squirming and blushing and wishing for interplanetary spaceships to beam me up while they shared intimate conversations about what had gone wrong in their past love life.

"We have to wait until dusk, though," she added. "Our chances of seeing the *lidérc* are better after the sun sets."

Harvey rubbed his hands together. "I'll get ol' Bessie loaded for bear."

As much as I appreciated my partner in crime by my side, especially to offset the sexual tension always crackling between Aunt Zoe and Reid, I needed Harvey's help with a more important task. "Harvey, will you stay here and watch over my kids?"

He snorted. "You need me to babysit the whippersnappers while you go huntin'?"

"Yes. Aunt Zoe needs to be there to teach us about this *lidérc* creature. That leaves my kids home and at risk. I can't focus on what I might need to do if I'm worrying about Addy and Layne. What do you say? Will you guard the kids instead of me?"

Grabbing a cookie from the Betty Boop jar, he sat back in his chair and took a bite, studying me. "Okay. But plan on talkin' the ears off this ol' mule when you return to cool your heels."

When? He was more confident than I was. I lived more on an "if" outlook when it came to the non-human population. Although having Aunt Zoe with me this time would help me feel less like I was blindfolded, swinging at piñatas.

Harvey looped his thumbs in his suspenders. "You can borrow Bessie if you'd like. She'll go to the well with you every time."

"A gun won't work against a *lidérc*," Aunt Zoe said.

"You know, on second thought," Reid said with a grimace. "I'm not sure this is a good idea today, Zo. I don't want anything to happen to you or Sparky on my watch."

"Don't you worry that handsome head of yours about us." Aunt Zoe patted him on the shoulder. "I know what I'm up against, and Violet will have her war hammer in hand."

I would?

"It's you I'm worried about," she continued. "It already knows your scent along with your weaknesses. According to what I've read, a *lidérc* will often assume the shape of a cherished, lamented dead family member or lover in order to lure its victim."

"What do you mean my *weaknesses*? I have only one Achilles' heel." Reid stared up at her, his point of vulnerability the object of his heated gaze.

One of her eyebrows lifted. "And that glass jaw of yours?"

"That's not a weakness, more of a hindrance, especially around a certain woman who comes at me swinging more often than not."

With a shrug, she walked over to the sink. "What can I say? You inspire all sorts of passion. Always have, always will."

I saw a small smile flit over Reid's face as he watched her backside. Then he looked my way and winked. "So why does Sparky have a war hammer?"

"She's a killer." Aunt Zoe let the water out of the sink.

I shot her a surprised glance. Was it wise to let Reid in on our sordid family secret? He knew a little about Aunt Zoe's charms, but the bit about my assassination predisposition wasn't exactly casual after-breakfast chatter material.

Reid chuckled at her explanation. When Harvey and I didn't join him, his grin faded. "Who does she kill?" he asked while focused on me.

I fidgeted under his sudden intensity.

"Here we go again," Harvey muttered, stuffing another cookie in his mouth.

"Violet kills all sorts of troublemakers." Aunt Zoe leaned back against the counter while drying her hands. "But mostly she executes boogeymen."

* * *

To his credit, Reid took the news about my family calling with only a slight widening of his eyes and a cough or two of surprise. I did notice that he shot me a few curious glances when he thought I wasn't looking. I couldn't blame him. Freak shows were meant to awe the crowds.

He didn't stick around for long after Aunt Zoe's announcement, mostly because she kicked him out and threatened to get her shotgun when he dallied. As soon as he drove away, she claimed to have a lot to do before tonight's visit to the Sugarloaf Building and disappeared into her workshop.

Harvey took off to pay one of his lady friends a visit since he was going to have to break their Sunday night date. I didn't ask which lady, especially after he got a wicked glint in his eye and informed me that he'd be "tied up" for much of the afternoon. I'd learned long ago with Harvey that those kind of comments weren't merely turns of phrase.

After I'd showered and tamed my curls into submission, I called Doc. He didn't answer, so I hung up and texted him that Aunt Zoe, Reid, and I had plans to visit a haunted building after nightfall. Twenty minutes later, he texted back that he'd be joining us.

Foolish girl that I was, his reply made me feel sunshiny on the inside in spite of having to face off with a devilish creature in a dark haunted building.

After Mona dropped off the script for tomorrow, I spent the afternoon playing games with my kids, ending with a rowdy game of

Twister that I figured might limber me up better than the boring yoga poses I'd been doing when they'd found me.

Doc arrived early, stepping into the living room while I was in a rather awkward position, my limbs tied up with Layne's.

I peeked out at him from under my armpit. "Hey, Doc."

His gaze traveled over my twists and turns. "Nice pose, Boots. Your boss should put a picture of you like this on that billboard out on I-90. It'd be sure to cause an accident ... or ten."

"Why do you call Mom *Boots*?" Layne asked from his crab stance down by my right knee.

Doc's brown eyes held mine, flirting. "I'm a big fan of her purple boots."

"You want to play with us?" Addy asked him, getting back into her much less pretzel-like pose on the dotted plastic sheet.

"You don't have to," I told him, not wanting him to feel stuck playing a kids' game with us.

"Oh, I definitely want to get in on this action." He took the spinner from Addy.

A laughter-filled half hour later, Aunt Zoe came in from her workshop. Her gaze twinkled as she took in the scene.

"As much as I hate to break this up, we need to get ready for our double date," she told me. "Reid will be back to pick us up soon."

I collapsed flat on my stomach, conceding my defeat to Doc and the kids, who were all twisted up around me. My downfall took Layne with me.

"It's a tie," Addy said. "Doc and I win."

"I don't think so," I told her and rolled against Doc's forearm, making him cave in on top of me, pinning me flat on my back. I grinned up at him. The tantalizing scent of his cologne made my breathing even more labored.

"That's cheating, Mother," Addy reprimanded, lecturing me from over Doc's head.

"Doc doesn't appear too put out, Adelynn." Aunt Zoe snickered and then headed upstairs.

"Count her down, Layne," Doc said, pinning my shoulders in place.

"Ten, nine, eight," Layne said, smacking the plastic next to me with each number.

"Come on, Mom," Addy switched to cheerleader in a flash. "You can shake him. Buck him off."

I wiggled under Doc's weight, shoving my hips up a couple of times to try to throw him. Doc's gaze focused in on my lips, his face dropping lower. "You're going down, sweetheart," he said above my mouth, our noses almost touching.

"Six, five, four," Layne counted down.

Without warning, I raised up and kissed Doc, tugging on his lower lip with my teeth.

His pupils flared, darkening. He kissed me back, sinking down onto me, his muscles loosening along with his grip on my shoulders. Before he could figure out my ploy, I wrapped my arms around his neck and pushed against him, urging him to roll onto his back. He complied, taking me with him so that I was on top. Then I straddled him and sat upright with a victory grin.

"Girls rule!" I shouted, holding my hand out for a high five from my daughter.

Both of my kids were glaring at me.

"You kissed him," Layne accused.

"I did." What was the big deal? I'd kissed Doc hello and goodbye in front of my kids before. This kiss had been less heated than one or two others they'd witnessed by accident.

"That's playing dirty, Mother," Addy said, her attention shifting back and forth between Doc and me.

I felt Doc chuckle under me. "Very dirty," he said, his hands resting on my thighs.

"Not really. Doc didn't have to kiss me back."

"Why did you kiss her back?" Layne turned his glare onto Doc and crossed his arms over his chest.

"I didn't want to hurt her feelings," Doc explained with laughter in his voice.

I snorted. "Please. Like you could resist my feminine wiles."

"What are wiles?" Addy asked.

"They're the charms your mom uses to make me follow her around like an obedient little puppy."

"You shouldn't have kissed her back," Layne was still bent out of shape.

"Do I have wiles?" Addy walked over to the mirror by the front door, standing on her toes to check her reflection for wiles. She smiled in the mirror, then took her glasses off and smiled again with a squint.

"Are you mad at me for kissing your mom, Layne?" Doc asked, suddenly serious.

My gut tightened. I'd hoped my kids were starting to get used to the idea of Doc and me as a couple, but maybe Layne wasn't so keen on the idea yet.

"Yes." Layne emphasized his feelings with a foot stomp.

"Can you see my wiles when I smile?" Addy asked the mirror, her glasses back on her face.

"Definitely," Doc answered Addy, but his focus stayed on Layne. "Why does it make you mad, Layne? I thought you and I had an understanding about my purpose here."

What was Doc's purpose here? I frowned back and forth between the two males in my life. I had an idea of the role I wanted Doc to fill, but curiosity had me licking my lips, wanting to ask for his take on it. However, I waited along with Doc for Layne's response.

Layne's chin lifted. "I'm mad because you let her win. I'm sick of the girls always winning in this house. How are we going to beat these girls at games if you keep letting Mom cheat?"

A hiccup of laughter edged with a small sob escaped from my lips before I could swallow it down. I blinked away a rush of silly tears of happiness before either Layne or Doc noticed them.

Addy rejoined us, clueless that her brother had finally conceded a place for Doc in our little family. "Doc, can I use my wiles on boys at school?"

I didn't give Doc a chance to reply. "Don't even think about it, Adelynn Renee."

"You know, Layne, you're right." Doc's hands skimmed up over my thighs to my hips, locking on. Before I realized what was going on, he spun around and had me lying flat on my back under him again. His knees and forearms had me bracketed in, his body weight holding me prisoner. "We should punish the cheater. Come on, you two. It's pile-up time."

I cried out as the kids climbed onto Doc's back and he pressed down enough to make me gasp and writhe. Squeals of laughter followed until I cried, "Uncle" enough times for them to let me up.

The phone rang as the kids climbed off Doc's back.

Doc pulled me to my feet, holding onto my hand even after I was steady on my feet. "You okay, cheater?"

"I think you guys popped my spleen."

Harvey stepped in through the front door, a pizza in hand. The kids yipped in excitement, following the whisker-covered codger into the kitchen like lemmings.

Doc tugged me closer. "Popping a spleen will teach you for seducing me."

"I thought you liked it when I seduced you."

"It's my undoing every time, *querida*." He lifted my knuckles to his lips, kissing them. "How are your sister and Rex today?"

I'd called Doc yesterday afternoon and filled him in on what had gone down at my office, insisting he stay away from Aunt Zoe's last night. I'd wanted him to wait to come over again until I was sure the coast was clear with no other Susan sightings.

"Nonexistent."

"Good."

"Violet Lynn," Aunt Zoe called down. "That was Reid on the phone. He's on his way over. Get your butt up here."

Doc turned me toward the stairs. "You heard your aunt, Killer. Go get your ass-kicking clothes on."

He tried to smack my butt, but I blocked him and shook my fist at him, threatening. Then I ruined my tough girl act by giggling all of the way up the stairs to my room.

Fifteen minutes later I came back down the steps. The war hammer was tucked away in a duffle bag Aunt Zoe had dropped off on her way downstairs.

Reid and Doc stood talking quietly in the dining room. Both quieted when I handed Doc the duffle bag.

Doc hefted the bag, hitting me with raised brows.

"My hammer." I patted him on the chest and then headed into the kitchen to kiss the kids goodbye.

Aunt Zoe had a bag of her own. She had it slung over her shoulder as she drank down a glass of water. Dressed in jeans and one of her well-worn flannel shirts, I'd never have guessed she was on her way to face off with some sort of Hungarian devil.

She handed me a glass of water. "You should get something to eat, too."

I shook my head. My stomach was tied up in knots. "I'm good. I had a ham sandwich earlier."

Both kids had Joker-like pizza sauce grins that spread wide onto their cheeks. I kissed the tops of their heads and threatened plenty of trouble if they didn't listen to Harvey.

When I got to the old boy, I squeezed his shoulder. "You be good, too."

"Don't you worry none 'bout us," he told me. "We're gonna hunker down and spin our spurs 'til it's time to hit the bedroll."

"Let's go, Violet," Aunt Zoe called from the dining room.

With one last, "Behave yourselves!" I left the kitchen.

Aunt Zoe held the front door for me. Reid and Doc waited outside for us.

"You ready for this?" Aunt Zoe asked as I pulled on my coat.

"Not really."

"Good."

"Why is that good?" I buttoned my coat. Shouldn't an executioner be revved up for battle?

She followed me onto the front porch. "In this game, being overly sure of yourself will get you killed every time."

I laughed. It sounded cold and brittle like the night air. "If that's true, this little chicken will live forever."

Chapter Nineteen

"Holy creepy-oli." I looked up at the Sugarloaf Building and its chain-locked, paint-peeling doors. "This is a dead-body-buried-in-the-basement moment just waiting to happen."

Reid had parked his truck so that his headlights spotlighted the front of the old two-story structure which otherwise stood alone in the darkness. It was well out of reach of the soft orange glow from the few streetlights spaced out along Washington Street below. For some reason, I had thought the building was down on Main Street, but Aunt Zoe informed me that I probably had it confused with the building owned by the Sugarbell family, as in one Tiffany Sugarbell.

Grrrr. Hiss.

Located on the hillside above State Rt. 85, the *Sugarloaf* Building had a clear view across the valley of Homestake's Yates Shaft headframe, along with the few remaining surface buildings left behind after the mine had shut down. It had stood at this vantage point, watching for decade after decade throughout the twentieth century as the Western Hemisphere's largest goldmine had sprouted and flourished ... and then floundered and faded.

Here it sat still, deteriorating one brick at a time while over on the opposite hillside the specks of gold no longer lured the fortune seekers and their mighty drills. Instead, deep down in the darkness, much more elusive particles danced just out of reach, tempting the knowledge seekers and their even mightier curiosity.

Aunt Zoe joined me in the cold evening air. "I had hoped to live my life without ever having to step inside this place."

"I can see why." I stared at the masonry walls that had been repaired over the decades with different colored bricks and in some places plain old concrete. The outside stairway had a roof sheathed with rust-spotted, corrugated tin while old boards were nailed every which way along the sides. "It's like a rag doll version of a building, patched together with spare scraps."

"Too bad its stuffing is rotten."

The upper story windows were dark, no sparks of light or flames or anything that would lead the average bear to think the Sugarloaf Building was anything other than a decaying piece of history.

"Maybe the flash of Reid's watchband scared the *lidérc* away," I said.

"Maybe," Aunt Zoe sniffed. "But you'd better get that war hammer out anyway."

"Ready, Zo? Sparky?" Reid asked, zipping up the front of his canvas coat.

"Lead the way, Martin," Aunt Zoe said, slinging her bag over her shoulder.

Doc walked around from the back of the old building, his pants swishing in the tall dead weeds, his flashlight skimming over the rocks and litter that filled the lot. He'd wanted to take a gander at the building from all sides before heading in. He joined us as we followed Reid to the front door.

"Did you find anything interesting around back?" I asked as we waited for Reid to find the key the fire department had been given to pop the padlock securing the chain.

"More of the same—torn pieces of tar paper, random boards and hardware, and some broken bricks."

"What's up the hillside behind it?"

"Mainly trees from what I can tell. The Open Cut is just over there." He pointed off to the side. He shined the light up at the crumbling cornices. "This building seems like it's in the wrong part of Lead. The only other brick structures up here belonged to Homestake, right?"

"Yes," Aunt Zoe answered. "They were part of the Homestake Electrical Department back in their heyday."

We'd passed the few remaining Homestake brick buildings on this side of State Rt. 85 on the way up here. They were in pristine condition in comparison to the ramshackle mess we were about to enter. Why Jane, Katrina King, or anyone else would be interested in this particular building was beyond me. It looked like a stiff winter wind could blow it over.

"Seems like I remember there being a conveyor belt that crossed above the road over to Homestake from somewhere around here," I said.

"There was. It transported ore across to Homestake." She looked out toward the gold mine turned research lab. "This area of Lead was mainly housing for miners."

"Of any particular ethnicity?" Doc asked. "Weren't there different districts of Lead where miners grouped depending on their background?"

"Sure." She focused on Reid, who had singled out a key and was holding it up in the glare from the headlights. "The Italians were on Railroad and Miners Avenues and Ridgeroad in the Sunnyhill area. The Slavs were mainly behind the Opera House in Slavonian Alley, and there were a bunch of Finnish who lived down in the Park Avenue and Parkdale region. Over here on Washington Street, the miners were mainly from Cornwall. That group brought pasties to Lead, and Ottó Sugarloaf apparently built himself a home amongst them."

She lost me at "pasties." Just thinking about those pastries filled with meat and potatoes had me licking my lips.

The clanking of chain links followed by creaky hinges brought our history lesson to a close. Back to Hungarian Devil Hunting 101.

"Normally I'd allow you ladies to go first," Reid said, blocking the doorway as Aunt Zoe tried to enter, "but not tonight."

"Reid, please step aside," Aunt Zoe spoke with a quiet firmness.

He pointed his flashlight at Zoe's chest. "Zo, don't you leave my side." His light moved to me. "As for you, Sparky, try not to burn this place down on my watch." His tone was light, but tension underlined it.

Aunt Zoe sighed. "Reid, forget about this macho crap and let me lead the way."

"You don't know the layout of the building."

"If there is a *lidérc* in there, knowing the floor plan won't make a difference."

"I'm the fire investigator here. I'm liable if something happens to any of you, so I lead. If you don't like my rule," he spoke directly to Aunt Zoe, "we can cancel this little field trip right now, and I'll put the chains and padlock back on these doors."

A growl came from Aunt Zoe. "Fine." She fished in her bag for a few seconds and pulled out what looked like a bundle of twigs. "Lead the way, Fire Captain Martin."

Reid stepped inside, disappearing into the thick shadows, followed by Aunt Zoe and me. Doc brought up the rear, closing the door behind us. I half expected it to lock on its own, barring our escape, but it turned out my imagination was getting ahead of itself.

Inside was one bigger room up front, a living area maybe or an office waiting room. As Reid led us through the thick layers of dust, pieces of plaster that had fallen from the ceiling, and critter droppings, our flashlights covered every square inch of the room ... especially the dark corners.

"When was the last time anyone occupied this building?" Doc asked.

"I'm not sure," Reid said, "but according to the paperwork on it, it failed inspection over a decade ago. It's not listed as officially condemned, but it needs some serious capital sunk into it to fix the flagged problems."

And some serious air fresheners. I stepped over to one of the plastic-covered windows, wishing I could tear the thick sheet away and let in a little Black Hills pine-scented air, even if it were freezing cold. The place reeked like the local wildlife had thrown a rave party in here.

I tried to see through the plastic. Its opaqueness along with years of built up grime and dust turned the street lights below into blurry orange-brown circles. It swished slightly as a breeze whistled through the old wooden window frame.

I heard the rustle of Doc's jacket as he came up behind me.

"Are you picking up anything?" I asked as my gaze blurred along with the street lights.

"If you mean signals from the next galaxy over," his voice was laced with laughter, "all I'm getting is static at the moment."

I looked up at him, sticking my flashlight under my chin with the beam aimed upward, giving him my best spooky face. "I mean signals from the dead." I tried to sound like Vincent Price, but imitations weren't my specialty.

"Who was that supposed to be?"

I stuck my tongue out at him and then lowered my flashlight.

After a quiet chuckle, his smile flat-lined. "There's a definite unnatural scent in the air, sort of smells sweet and citrusy, like Brylcreem or some other pomade."

"A little dab will do ya," I repeated the company's old slogan.

"But I'm not sure if I'm picking up something ectoplasm based or not. I haven't noticed any of the other usual signs."

"If it's not a ghost, what could it be?"

"Residual energy embedded in the building's bones."

"Is that something you come across often? Residual energy?"

He nodded. "Especially in buildings as old as this. But I'm not well-schooled in Paranormal Psychometry, so I notice it every now and then, but that's it."

Reid's light swung our way. "Paranormal Psycho-what?"

"Psychometry. It's the idea that an object may have an energy field that can be 'read' by certain mediums, giving information about the history or future of someone associated with that object. You've probably heard of mediums who use psychometry when working with police to help find missing people. The medium will hold onto the victim's personal belonging, like a teddy bear or hair brush, and employ a dose of precognition to determine a possible future location where the missing individual might be found."

Reid motioned for us to follow and piloted the way down a hallway that appeared to lead to several smaller rooms in the back. I counted five open doorways. The layout sort of reminded me of the floorplan in Calamity Jane Realty, only with a few more rooms in the back.

"Is this residual energy something you can sense with these medium abilities you were telling me about before we left Zo's place?" Reid asked, stopping in the dark doorway of the first room and glancing back at Doc.

Ah, so that's what they'd been murmuring about in the dining room when I'd come down the stairs.

I joined them, peeking between their shoulders into the room. It was empty except for plaster littering the floor below a hole in one of the interior walls.

"Yep." Doc waited for me and Aunt Zoe to step back before squeezing past Reid to enter the room. He shined the light into the back corner and sniffed a few times.

"Well?" Aunt Zoe asked from where she and I were peeking in again, watching him work his magic from the hallway.

He shook his head but wore a frown when he returned to the hall.

Had something else beeped on his sixth sense radar? Something that could morph into the shape of an ex-lover? I wrinkled my nose. Oh dear Lord, if that *lidérc* thing turned into Tiffany Sugarbell right before my eyes, I was going to use my war hammer as a meat tenderizer and flatten the hell out of its perky boobs and round little bottom.

Wait, Aunt Zoe had said a *dead* relative or lover. Damn! And here I was sort of hoping to have a shot at a Tiffany look-alike.

"What did you say this building was used for?" Reid asked Aunt Zoe as he led us further back the narrow hallway, pausing to shine his flashlight into one empty room and then the other directly across, lighting up all corners before moving onward.

"I didn't say, fearless leader." I could hear the challenge in her tone.

Reid gave her a brief glare. "Quit messing with me, Zo, or I'm going to kiss you right here in front of Sparky and Doc."

"Try it and I'll knock you on your ass again, Martin, and this time I won't need my glass block to get the job done."

He stared at her, our breathing the only sound. Then the creases on his shadowed face deepened and he laughed. "You're beautiful when you're mad, have I ever told you that?"

"Shut your big trap," Aunt Zoe mumbled and pushed past him, leading the way to the next room. "According to what I read about Ottó and this building, when he first had it built, he had a doctor's office down here with several patient rooms, and his living quarters were upstairs. But then it changed hands after he died and became a small hardware store, then a boarding house for single miners, and most recently it was split into two apartments, one upstairs and one down—that's when they added the outside stairway."

"That explains those then," Reid said, aiming his light at several boards nailed to the ceiling at the end of the hallway. He pointed at some heavy duty hardware still bolted to the wall. "There must have been a circular stairwell here that led to the upper floor, but they took it out when they made it into two apartments."

"And this room over here was the kitchen," I said, which was obvious by the ancient looking stove left behind to rot with everything else. When I stepped into the narrow room, I heard a scuffling sound in the rusted chimney pipe leading out through the wall. I could only imagine what critters I would find nesting inside the oven if I opened the door.

The last room in the far back corner, sharing an interior wet-wall with the kitchen, was a cramped bathroom with a dust and dead insect laden porcelain claw-footed tub and stained toilet. The sink was gone, leaving behind corroded galvanized iron pipes sticking out of the wall below a broken mirror that was hazy around the edges.

It reminded me of the mirror in Ms. Wolff's apartment and the questions returned about what my breaking that mirror meant. Was that doorway now forever open or closed? Had I screwed up something major or were there other doors to be opened elsewhere? Surely there was more than one.

I leaned my war hammer against the wall and stared into the mirror, listening to the sounds of the other three moving around in the hallway and kitchen, whispering to each other. *Okay Mr. Hungarian troublemaker, where are you?* I waited, watching the wall behind my reflection for a ghostly face to appear over my shoulder like I'd seen so many times in horror movies.

But nothing appeared.

Nothing pounded on the mirror's glass from "the other side" either, nor made it shudder or crack further.

I leaned closer, opening my mouth wide. Was anything lurking down my esophagus, waiting to show its fingers in the back of my throat as it crawled up and out? Or would my throat split open, showing a blinking, bulbous eyeball? Or something even worse that would freak the hell out of me?

Wait, what could be worse than an eyeball in my throat?

It didn't matter. Nothing was hiding in my mouth. My "dud-ness" was showing its plain old anticlimactic self again.

"What are you doing?" Doc asked.

I glanced over, slowly closing my mouth. He was leaning against the door jamb, watching me with one raised eyebrow.

"Looking for trouble."

"Can't you see it, Killer? It's staring back at you in the mirror, capital T and all."

"Very funny, Mr. Tall Medium." I used Cornelius's name for Doc and walked over to him, pretending to pull a punch.

He caught my exaggerated swing and spun me around, pulling me back against him, resting his chin on the crown of my head. "So, do you talk to mirrors often, my evil queen, or is that a side effect of your new career?"

"I've always talked to mirrors. The girl on the other side is the only one who understands all of my highs and woes."

"Clever, oh fairest of them all."

"We're heading back out front, you two," Aunt Zoe said from behind Doc. "Bring that hammer, Violet."

I grabbed the war hammer and followed Aunt Zoe out into the hallway. "I'm feeling a bit silly carrying this thing around. There's nothing to swing at in here but spiders and the dead morsels caught in their webs."

"We're not done here." She stopped and pointed her light at the ceiling.

"Wouldn't that thing roam both upstairs and down? Surely it doesn't need a stairwell to go back and forth between floors."

"Reid, you were upstairs investigating when you saw the shadow, right?"

"Yes, in one of the back rooms."

"And weren't the flames and weird lights that were reported said to be coming from the upper windows?"

"I believe so."

She looked back at me. "Like I said, we're not done."

"Yeah, but shouldn't I be sensing or hearing something from down here?"

"I don't know, Executioner. Should you?" She reached out and pulled the necklace she'd made me from my neckline, palming the glass charm. "Maybe you're not focusing."

She was right. I wasn't. "Do you want me to try to focus on it from down here or wait until we're upstairs?"

"I think you would be smarter to start down here. If for some unknown reason it only resides on the upper floor, then you might be able to hear it and give us a head start on what we're going to face."

"Okay." I led the way back out to the front room, feeling the need for more space around me. I used my boot to clear a spot in the center of the floor and sat down with my legs crossed, as if I were preparing to meditate.

"That's different," Doc said as he looked down at me.

I laid my war hammer across my lap, the handle within easy reach of my right hand. "My legs are shaky from playing Twister too long."

Pathetic but true.

He grinned and then backed up to give me more room.

"Here goes nothing," I told Aunt Zoe and closed my eyes.

I did the ol' flickering flame trick, focusing on that little fire as it danced and weaved in the blackness. When I opened my eyes, Doc, Aunt Zoe, and Reid stood by, watching and waiting.

I closed my eyes again and thought of Cornelius's humming as he did during our séances. His one horned Viking helmet. His cornflower blue eyes.

Focus, Scharfrichter, focus.

I opened my eyes again. Doc, Aunt Zoe, and Reid were still there, all staring down at me. Still waiting.

Damn it!

It was usually easier than this. Something was throwing me off.

I closed my eyes and this time thought about the bone-cruncher, its foul breath, its milky gaze, its long spikey teeth gnashing at me. I squeezed my eyes even tighter, thinking about Wilda's damned clown doll.

When I opened my eyes, Aunt Zoe was digging in her bag, Doc had moved over next to one of the plastic covered windows, and Reid was inspecting some wiring sticking out of the old fashioned, push button light switch in the wall near the doors.

I sighed. "Aunt Zoe, this isn't working. I can't seem to—"

Heavy footfalls clomped overhead, interrupting my whine.

My mouth went dry. My stomach churned, sudden nausea making me gulp until it passed.

I slowly looked up at the ceiling, following the loud clomping sounds from the front of the building toward the back until they stopped suddenly. I waited for the ceiling to fall in on our heads, but it held firm, not shedding even a flake of plaster.

"Uh oh," I whispered, locking onto the handle of the war hammer. I scrambled very ungracefully to my feet, my thighs wobbly, stumbling over my own boots until Doc caught me by the arm and held me steady.

"What do you hear?" Aunt Zoe asked, pulling a lighter from her bag along with another foot-long bundle of twigs.

Twigs? A lighter? These were her chosen weapons of defense? Was she going to offer the *lidérc* a marshmallow, some chocolate, and a graham cracker and then Kumbayah it to death?

"Violet Lynn," she grabbed my arm in a solid grip. "Answer me. What do you hear?"

I pointed up at the ceiling. "Nothing now, but I heard footfalls going across the floor up there, only they sounded like high heeled shoes. Or maybe hooves." I glanced at Doc. Seriously, if it took the form of Doc's former lover, dead or not, I could not be held accountable for my actions.

"That makes sense," Aunt Zoe said, aiming her light up at the ceiling.

"What makes sense?" Reid asked.

"A *lidérc's* footprints are said to be that of a horse."

"I didn't hear a thing, did you?" Reid's question was directed to Doc.

"No," Doc said, "but Violet can often hear things I can't."

"I thought you were the medium."

"I am, but so is she, and her toolbox is bigger than mine."

"That's not true," I told Doc, hefting the war hammer as I stepped toward the hallway leading to the back rooms. "You just have a smaller tool."

Complete silence followed my statement.

Ah hell. I winced as I continued down the hallway. That didn't come out right. Maybe nobody would notice my *faux pas*.

"Nyce?" I heard Reid ask. "Do you think your girlfriend meant that metaphorically?"

The low vibrations of Doc's laughter reached me as I tiptoed back to the end of the hall where the old stairwell had been boarded up.

I heard Aunt Zoe tell Reid to shut up and then a *thwap*, which was probably her hand smacking his coat.

Doc caught up with me at the end of the hall. We stared up at the boards separating us from whatever was upstairs. My heart throbbed fast and hard clear to my toes. Did Prudence know when the end had been near in her reign as the local executioner? Had she been drowning in doubt about her abilities to take out her next kill like I was at the moment? Would I be able to fill her shoes with as much finesse as she so often crowed about?

"Doc," I whispered for his ears only, wanting to clear the air before I went up to face this horse-hooved devil.

"What?" he matched my voice level.

"I have a confession to make."

He waited for me to continue, both of us looking upward.

"Tiffany said something to me recently that sort of has me worried."

I felt his gaze move to my face. "And what was that?"

"Something along the lines that any feelings you may have expressed for me might be disingenuous."

I kept staring upward, afraid to meet his stare.

"Violet, do you really think now is the time to talk about this? Here of all places?"

"Probably not, but if whatever is up there wins tonight, I sort of want to clear this up in my head before we climb those stairs."

"It's not going to win."

"We don't know that."

"Your Aunt Zoe is here to make sure you walk away when it's over."

"She's scared. I can see it in her eyes. There is no guarantee with each kill. You know that as well as I do. Besides, it's not me I'm worried about as much as *you*." I blew out a breath, brushing some loose bangs out of my face. "Well, and Aunt Zoe and Reid, too, of course."

"Are we going to compare tool sizes again?"

I shined my light at the dirt covered floor. "Sorry about that. Would it help if I wrote you a sonnet about my appreciation for your tool?"

In the dim light, I could see the corners of his eyes crinkle. "I think a limerick is a more appropriate style of verse for that particular object."

I cleared my throat and started with, "There once was a medium named Doc, who had an obscenely large …"

Doc covered his eyes, shaking his head.

"Would you like me to continue?" I asked, giggling.

Laughter acted as a magic elixir, calming my fluttering stomach, easing my fears about what I needed to face upstairs.

"Please don't, not here." He glanced around. "You can remedy the wound your 'small tool' remark inflicted on my ego the next time we're in bed."

"Deal."

"Now, about Tiffany's comment."

I held up my hand. "You know what? Never mind. I don't want to go there right now."

"You sure?"

I was rarely sure of anything when it came to him and me, but he was right—now was not the time for that conversation. "I'm sure."

He shined his light back up at the boards. "Heavy footfalls, huh?"

"Extremely. I expected the ceiling to give way."

"Christ, Killer. You sure keep life exciting. Come on." He grabbed my arm and led me back out to the front room. "What now, Zoe?"

"We go up."

The clomp-clomp-clomp of footfalls boomed again on the ceiling, heading back to the front of the building, making me flinch and duck as they thundered overhead. My fear came back in a tidal wave of goosebumps.

"That's a bad idea." I took a step away from Aunt Zoe.

"Violet, we are going up there."

"You're not hearing how big that *thing* up there sounds. Maybe I should go alone."

Or we could just go home and I could call in sick for the filming tomorrow, and the next day, and the next, until Jerry either gave up on me or fired me. Either was preferable to risking our welfare on some silly, Hungarian pest.

"I don't need to hear it." Her hand snaked out and locked onto my wrist. "My purpose tonight is not to hear but rather to help you destroy."

"It could be a good devil. Have you ever thought of that? Maybe we should just leave it be for another hundred years." I tried to tug free, but she was in badger mode. "I mean who are we to condemn it to death?"

"You're an executioner. You're going upstairs, Violet Lynn, and I'm going with you." She started towing me toward the front doors.

"Reid," I said, dragging anchor. "It's probably not safe to go up those stairs is it?"

He followed us out into the cold night. "Actually, the stairs are still in pretty good shape. It's the foundation that didn't pass inspection."

Thank you for not helping, Mr. Fireman.

"Okay, okay!" I tugged free of Aunt Zoe's grip. "I'll go, but I'm leading the way."

"No, I am."

"No, you're not," Reid said. "You know the rule. I lead."

Aunt Zoe glared at him. "Reid, you don't understand the first thing about what we're dealing with up there or how vulnerable you are now that it already knows your scent."

He held up his watch. The glass charm band sparkled in the bright headlights. "But I have your protection charm."

She sighed, lowering her bag to the ground. "All right. Come here." Reid moved closer. She grabbed him by the shoulders and settled him in front of her. "Doc, would you step over here for a second, please?"

Doc moved closer while I stayed off to the side, shooting fret-filled glances up the dark stairwell.

I could hear a clacking sound from somewhere at the top of the steps, reminding me of something from my childhood. What was waiting for us? Were those teeth gnashing? Was it another bone cruncher?

"Get in line behind Reid, would you?" Doc did as asked. "A little closer."

"What the hell, Zo. Why are you lining us up like school children heading out for recess?"

"I'll explain in a minute." She turned slightly to her right and took a deep breath.

"This better not be a game you're—" Reid started.

"Look!" Aunt Zoe pointed up at the sky. "A shooting star."

Reid looked up, so did Doc. I would have too, except I was preoccupied by that clacking sound, trying to place it in my memory. My distraction kept me staring straight ahead, so I had a clear view in the glow of Reid's headlights of the uppercut that Aunt Zoe delivered to Reid's jaw.

I gasped, watching wide mouthed as Reid fell backward into Doc, who managed to catch the fire captain as his knees gave out and he slid toward the ground.

"What happened to him?" Doc asked, hitching Reid up as best he could. Doc was strong, but Reid was no lightweight.

With a scoff, I rushed over to help Doc. "Aunt Zoe sucker punched him again."

"Again?" Doc gaped at Aunt Zoe, who was grimacing as she rubbed her right hand.

"Reid has a glass jaw," she explained, making a fist with a wince. "One solid blow in the right spot," she snapped her left fingers, "and he goes down every time." She leaned forward and lifted Reid's eyelids one at a time, shining her light in each. "He'll be fine in a few minutes."

"How many times have you done this to him?"

"A couple of times. But only for his own good. Mostly, anyway." She reached down and wiggled her left hand into Reid's front jean pocket. "Why don't you carry him to the pickup and lock him inside." She pulled her hand out and held up two sets of keys. She handed Doc the small ring that held the pickup keys on it. "You hold onto these in case something happens to Violet or me."

"You mean you're not going to knock out Doc, too?" I said, helping Doc lift Reid enough to get a better grip on the fire captain's limp body.

"Don't get smart, Violet Lynn," she chastised.

After Doc and I had returned from lugging Reid to his pickup and locking him inside, she explained, "Reid was the most vulnerable of all of us. The *lidérc* had already seen him. It would have gone for him first." She shined her flashlight up the dark, covered stairway. "Now we have the element of surprise on our side." As she started up the stairs, I heard her add, "I hope."

I hesitated, my foot on the first step of the iron stairway, the cold railing under my palm. This was what I was born to do. Shouldn't I feel more puffed up about facing yet another foe? Then I remembered Aunt Zoe mentioning that being scared would keep me on my toes, and I started up after her with Doc on my heels.

At the top step, I heard the jingle of keys.

"Here we go," Aunt Zoe said and the lock clinked. She unhooked the padlock and turned the knob. The door opened without a single creak oddly enough. Complete darkness waited for us on the other side of the threshold, along with whatever it was I could hear mouth-breathing inside. Sheesh, bulldogs rasped less.

Then the clacking sound started up again.

Damn it, how did I know that sound? A memory of climbing narrow wooden stairs flashed through my mind.

Aunt Zoe flicked her lighter, holding the flame under the bundle of twigs. It flared to life and then eased to a pungent, smoking glow. She stepped inside, leading with the burning twigs.

Doc followed me inside.

"Here." She handed him another bundle of twigs and lit those as well. "Keep this between you and the *lidérc* at all times."

"What is that?" I asked.

"Birch twigs mixed with some incense. Normally it's used to prevent a *lidérc* from entering one's dwelling, but I've also read you can use it to keep the creature at bay."

"Where's mine?" I asked.

"You don't get one."

"Why not?"

"Because, Executioner, you have a war hammer."

Oh, yeah. I lifted it, readying for battle. "Let's go."

"Which way?" she asked me.

Which way? I thought she was the fearless leader here.

Then I remembered that she couldn't hear it like I could. I pointed to a narrow hallway on the far side of the open room. "Back there."

Stepping aside, she nudged me forward. She shined her flashlight over my shoulder, lighting the way as we crept across the old wooden floor. It creaked unbelievably loud with every step, letting our host and probably half of the folks on this side of Lead know we were coming.

I followed the clacking sound down the hall, noticing a black spot on the wall at one point. That must be where Reid had seen the *lidérc* disappear.

Then I noticed several other black spots along the walls.

Or maybe it wasn't the place Reid had mentioned.

We passed three darkened rooms, pausing at the doorway of each to shine a light in them while Aunt Zoe sprinkled something along the threshold. One was an old kitchen, ancient looking sink and stove still in place. Another was the bathroom with an old chain-pull style toilet with the tank on the wall, no bathtub or mirror. The other had a broken down iron bedframe in it and plenty of dust bunnies and critter droppings. All of them smelled musty, full of stale air.

The clacking sound continued.

Dominoes? I used to play them a lot with my brother, building long trains of upright dominoes to knock down.

No, that wasn't it.

We stopped on the threshold of the final room, this one twice the size of the others. It was empty except for a wooden chair sitting dead center.

Had the *lidérc* somehow slipped passed us? Moved through the walls?

I focused, slowing my breath, closing my eyes, listening.

The clacking sound started up again, louder now. The rancid odor of rotting flesh wafted over my skin, making me gag.

It was right in front of us.

I opened my eyes, seeing nothing yet but that empty chair.

My grip tightened on the handle of the war hammer. "It's here," I said, not bothering to whisper. No use playing hide and seek anymore. "I can smell it."

I heard Doc sniff a couple of times. Was he picking it up, too? Or had he caught the scent of something else hiding in here with my prey?

"You need to call it out," Aunt Zoe instructed.

I'd sooner call this whole thing off and get her and Doc out of here. Instead, I obeyed like a good little killer.

"Show yourself, *lidérc*," my voice sounded a lot tougher than I felt at the moment. If only I could see what I was dealing with instead of feeling my way around its lair.

No sooner had that thought finished when I noticed movement in the far corner.

"Over there," I said, pointing it out to Aunt Zoe.

She swung her flashlight toward the corner, but the beam went dark before reaching it.

"Damn it," Aunt Zoe smacked it a couple of times.

"Doc, light it up," I said.

The clacking grew even louder.

A memory of shafts of sunlight shining through windows popped into my head.

Doc lifted his light, shining it toward the corner.

His flashlight died, too, leaving only an imprint in my mind of something huddled back there.

I heard more scuffling sounds. Was it coming closer?

"Fuck," I whispered, reaching behind me. "Aunt Zoe, your lighter. Now!"

Her handoff was quick. I flicked the lighter, the flame shedding a flickering light around the room. It was still empty except for the chair. How could that be?

From out of nowhere, a putrid breeze blew out the flame.

Aunt Zoe hauled me backward, stepping in front of me. In the darkness, I could see the embers in her bundle of smoldering twigs.

"What are you doing?" I asked, trying to pull her aside so I could get back in front.

She didn't budge. "Nice try, trickster," she said to whatever was hidden in the darkness. "You heard her, show yourself."

Light flared from something Aunt Zoe held up in front of her. It blazed white, turning everything pale gray, making me squint and shield my eyes for a second.

There was a low hissing sound that grew almost deafening and then stopped.

The floor creaked behind me. Doc's hand clamped onto my shoulder. At least I hoped it was Doc.

"*Scharfrichterrrrrrrrrr,*" I heard something say on a breath, followed by another putrid breeze.

Whatever Aunt Zoe had lighting up the room faded to a dim glow.

I squeezed around Aunt Zoe, leading with the war hammer as I stepped into the room. I flicked the lighter again. The flame painted the walls with a rippling yellowish glow.

The clacking returned, more rhythmic this time.

"I can hear it," Doc said.

"Me too." Aunt Zoe said. "It reminds me of your ..." I heard her quick intake of breath. "Give me the lighter, Violet."

I handed it to her. With smoldering birch twigs held out in front of her in one hand, the lighter in the other, she walked to the middle of the room and then stopped. Her eyes were wide, but her hands were steady.

"Show yourself," she ordered again, saying something in a foreign tongue that I didn't understand.

Back in the corner, something formed suddenly at the edge of the shadows. It was huddled low, its curved back toward us, a cloak shielding it from view. As it moved slightly, the clacking sound came again. Little white stones fell onto a black cloth next to its bare, dirty feet. The clacking stopped. I watched as long bony fingers snaked out, collecting the stones. Then the clacking sounded again.

White stones.

Wait! Not stones.

"Hidden danger," said a rickety voice from my past.

"Oh, God. No." My knees began to tremble, my breath coming fast and hard suddenly. "Not her."

The memory of climbing the narrow, wooden stairs played through my vision again, followed by a beam of afternoon sunlight streaming through the attic window. The clacking of rune stones, the scratchy sound of her voice, the rattling of breath in her lungs.

That's why I knew that clacking sound. It haunted my childhood memories, along with my great grandmother's yellowed nails and gnarled fingers.

"Come closer, child," Grandma-great spoke again from the corner in her rusty voice, her back still bent, shielding her from me. She cast the rune stones. Her gnarled fingers waved over them, picking up the one that had always shown in Merkstave when I was in the room with her.

"You smell of death, Violet," she whispered. She turned her head slowly toward me, giving me a glimpse of tendrils of gray hair, the edge of her craggy cheek, and the glitter of her eye.

Aunt Zoe's flame flickered out, pitching us into darkness.

Silence filled my ears like cotton balls.

And then someone shrieked.

Chapter Twenty

The shrieking stopped.

All was dark around me, except for the lone flame of a white candle that flickered and danced.

You smell of death. I heard the echo of those words fly past me in the darkness.

Then I realized my eyes were closed.

I opened them and found myself far away from the second floor of the Sugarloaf Building.

In front of me, dust particles swirled in the bright rays of sunlight shining in through an attic window. The air around me was warm, almost stifling, filled with the scent of stale varnish and musty cardboard. I was back in the attic I knew so well from my childhood nightmares.

And I wasn't alone.

Across the room, out of reach of the sunlight, my great grandmother sat huddled, her silver-haired head lowered, a black cloth at her feet. Her rune stones clattered as she shook them in her deerskin bag. Her breath rattled in her old lungs, extra loud in the quiet room. With her face veiled in shadows, she dumped the bag of rune stones onto the black cloth.

"What do the stones say, child?" Her long, gnarled fingers waved over them.

I didn't need to see those damned rune stones. I already knew. "They say that I carry hidden danger in my pocket."

Her narrow, watery eyes looked my way, glittering out from the shadows. Her silver hair hung loose around her face, helping to hide the craggy furrows in her age-spotted cheeks. Cheeks that I was always forced to kiss when she came to visit.

"Come closer, child. Let me comfort you."

A bark of laughter rang out through the room. My bark, laden with scorn. "You made a mistake," I told her.

"The rune stones are prophetic, child. There is no right or wrong in their songs."

"I'm not talking about the stones."

I took a step forward and stood bathed in the sunlight. There was no warmth in it. Just as there was no attic and no great grandmother. The *lidérc* was trying to woo me, only for some reason it had its wires crossed. This was my memory all right, but any grieving for this particular dead relative was done by Aunt Zoe, not me.

She stood and took a step toward me, which brought her partly out of the shadows. She opened her arms wide, urging me to bridge the distance and accept her parasitic embrace. "So young and so wise. You make me proud, *Enkelin.*"

My right hand gripped the war hammer handle, ready to swing if she lunged at me. "Your time here is finished."

"My time?" Her raspy chortle was spot on with that from my childhood nightmares. Goosebumps rose on my skin. "What do you know of my time, child?"

"I know that your clock is about to stop."

Her watery eyed gaze held mine. "You are no timekeeper."

"You're correct. I'm not the timekeeper." Then I thought back to that voice on the phone in Ms. Wolff's apartment and what it had told me. "I'm her killer."

I didn't believe that, but it sounded tough when facing off with a tricky Hungarian devil.

Her gaze widened, her pupils growing larger, her eyes filling with an empty blackness. Her gnarled hands rose in my peripheral vision, her fingers wiggling as if each hand were playing an invisible piano.

What in the hell was this? Part of the enchantment game used on prey? Or maybe a distraction technique.

"I've missed you, sweet child. Come to me."

"Your mistake, you old Hungarian asshole, was choosing the shape of the wrong dead relative." Without further preamble, I pounced, swinging the pointed end of the war hammer at her.

But she was faster. My hammer swooshed through the air where she'd been a split-second prior. A black shadow flew past me, sprinkling burning embers in its wake that died before hitting the floor.

She left me in a cloud of smoke reeking of the same odor I'd noticed earlier. Coughing, gagging slightly, I strode after the tricky devil. She hovered mid-air in the far corner, surrounded by billows of smoke. My great-grandmother's face morphed before my eyes.

"Dear sister," Susan spoke from the smoke swirls. "I've missed you so."

I had to give the *lidérc* credit where credit was due. It had nailed the image of Susan that I had stored in my memory, with her perfect body, bitter smile, and resentful glare.

"Well done," I said. "But wrong again. That bitch isn't dead." I lifted the war hammer. "But I'd love to take a swing at her."

She rushed me, surging forward exactly as Reid had described back in Aunt Zoe's kitchen. I dodged sideways, striking out when she flew past. The sharp point of my war hammer made contact with something in the smoke, snagging her. I held on tight and tugged while flaming embers fell around me, yet felt cold when they landed on my cheeks.

A high pitched shriek rang in my ears. It was the same shriek I'd heard when the lights went out in that second story room of the Sugarloaf Building, right before I'd landed back in this attic.

I tugged harder, but she slipped free, coming to a halt near the top of the stairs.

Choking up on the war hammer, I glared across the attic where Susan waited for me. Her head was lowered, her long brown hair shielding her face from view as the black smoke swelled around her, swallowing her whole.

"Your days of leeching are over," I said, trying to figure out where to land a blow that would knock the thing out of the air. "Ottó didn't deserve the years of hell you unleashed on him."

In the smoke, a face started to take shape. I frowned, trying to figure out who was next on this nut-ball version of *This Is Your Life*. I didn't have to wait long.

Rex stepped out from the smoke, only it was the younger Rex I had known back in college. The one who had shared my bed and left me pregnant with twins.

He held his hand out for me to take. "Sweet, beautiful Violet. My love for you will never die. Come to me. Let me hold you once again."

A howl of cynical laughter burst from my chest before I could stop it. "You picked Rex? Really!!?" I shook my head, flummoxed and chagrined at the same time. "I thought you were supposed to woo me, not piss me off."

The perplexed expression on Rex's handsome young face made me laugh again.

"Fine, I'll play," I told it. "Rex, you lousy piece of shit. I've been waiting for this moment for ten long years." With a battle cry, I rushed it, war hammer cocked back. It rose toward the ceiling, dripping sparks and burning embers onto the attic floor. But before I could get close enough to make contact, it flew down the stair steps, fleeing through the lower door.

I raced after it, shoving out through the attic door … and into the cold, shadow-filled Sugarloaf Building. The change in scenery made me skid to a stop, all senses on alert. Within the blink of an eye, I'd returned. I spun around, searching for the *lidérc*. More importantly, where were Aunt Zoe and Doc?

A soft orange glow lit the room, leaking in through the thick plastic covering the windows. Wind whistled a tune of cold loneliness. The place was empty except for me.

Hold up.

My gaze returned to the plastic. There'd been no plastic on the upstairs windows, only on the downstairs. I glanced around, getting my bearings. Sure enough, this was the level we'd checked out while Reid led the way.

As that thought sank in, footfalls clomped across the ceiling, followed by a shout of surprise. Was that Doc?

"Doc!" I heard Aunt Zoe yell. "Get back here! Hurry!"

Oh, shit!

I raced to the door, but it wouldn't budge. What the hell? We hadn't locked it when we'd left.

More shouting came from overhead followed by the heavy clomping of footfalls across the ceiling. Was it chasing them?

A deep, resonating roar thundered, rattling my heart along with the windows in their frames. Criminy! I had to get up there.

I looked down at the war hammer still clutched in my hands.

Well, duh.

Spinning it around so the pointed end faced the door, I took a solid swing. The steel tip pierced the weathered wood. I tugged it free and swung again, cracking the wood this time. With another tug, I freed the hammer and lifted it overhead. This time when I swung, the steel bashed through the door.

I stuck my hand outside, angling around for the door handle.

Someone grabbed my wrist.

I shouted in surprise and tried to yank my hand back inside.

"Sparky, it's me." A familiar voice said from the other side of the wood, holding tight.

Reid! "You're awake."

"Yeah, with one hell of a jaw ache thanks to your aunt."

Something slammed upstairs.

Crap! "Open the door!" I yelled. "Hurry! Aunt Zoe's in trouble."

He let go of me. The door rattled, the handle made a clanking sound, and then the door flew wide.

I raced past Reid, making a beeline for the second story stairway, not bothering with an explanation. There was no time.

Taking the iron stairs two at a time, I rammed my way into the upper apartment. A flashlight lay on the floor in the middle of the empty room, spotlighting the opposite wall. At the edge of the light was the hallway, a path into the darkness beyond.

All was silent except for the whistling wind.

"Aunt Zoe?" I called out, heading for the hallway opening.

"Violet!" Her voice came from the other end of the hall. At least I hoped it was her voice and not an imitation.

"Where are you?" I asked, easing along the wall next to the hallway opening, careful of what might be waiting in the dark.

"In the back room."

"Is Doc with you?" I needed to know who was where before I started down the hall with my war hammer poised to land a blow.

"Yes. I've sealed us within a grouping of defensive wards, but I don't know how long they'll hold it off."

I peeked around the edge of the wall. It was thick with shadows. There were too many places for the *lidérc* to hide between me and them.

Something touched my shoulder.

I ducked and spun around, my war hammer at the ready when I shot up to face off with my opponent.

"Sparky!"

"Damn it, Reid!" I blew out a breath in relief. "You really need to stop scaring me in dark buildings."

"Did I hear Reid's voice?" Aunt Zoe called out.

"I'm not talking to you, Zo!" Reid answered.

"Get him out of here, Violet! It's too dangerous."

"What's going on?" he asked me.

"The *lidérc* is somewhere up here."

He leaned over and took a look down the darkened hallway. His shoulders stiffened. "Something's on fire back there."

I nudged him back a step and peeked for myself. Sure enough, the smoky devil hovered at the end of the hall, dripping flames.

"Killer," Doc called out, warning me.

"I see it." I heard a shuffling sound behind me but didn't want to take my eyes off the slippery bastard.

While I tried to figure out the best plan of attack, it morphed into a middle-aged man I hadn't seen before. I squinted in the shadows. A man who looked a lot like Reid.

"Dad?" I heard Reid say from behind me. I looked around and found him leaning forward as if invisible strings were pulling on him.

"Reid!" Aunt Zoe yelled. "Close your eyes, dammit!"

"What are you doing here, Dad?" Reid's voice was higher than normal, full of awe. He took a step toward the *lidérc*.

I reached for him but then pulled back. I had an idea.

Peeking around the wall again, I looked at Reid's father's gaze. It was focused entirely on Reid as it billowed nearer, focused on its prey.

If I could get it to come a little closer, I could land a solid blow. I grabbed Reid by the belt, locking my fingers around the leather while wedging my boot against the wall. I held tight when he tried to step toward his father. He struggled against me, but I held him in place, dangling at the end of the hallway. My bait.

"Violet!" Aunt Zoe's voice was edged with panic. "Don't you let it near him!"

Reid tried to pull free again, reaching out toward his father as it billowed even nearer.

I risked a glance down the hall while fighting to hold Reid in place. "That's close enough," I whispered. Angling my war hammer down, I hooked one of Reid's ankles and yanked.

He fell sideways into the wall, which dragged me into the hall to face off with his father. I tugged my hand free of his belt and leapt over his legs, the war hammer raised and ready.

His father shrieked and sank back into the smoke, fleeing the other way. Burning embers swirled through the air around me as I raced after him, but I was too slow. He headed straight for the wall at the end of the hallway, the escape plan clear.

I stopped, pulled back, and threw the war hammer after it. In what seemed like slow motion, the hammer flew end over end through the air. It reached the *lidérc* at the same time a blast of flame exploded against the wall.

In a blink, it was gone, leaving yet another black smear on the wall in its wake.

I strode over to where it had disappeared along with my damned war hammer.

"What the fuck?" I said, slamming my hand against the black spot where both had disappeared. The wall was cool under my palm. "Where did it go?"

"Violet." Doc raced out of the darkness. He hauled me around to face him, touching my cheeks, then my shoulders and arms. "Are you okay?"

"No, I'm not okay. I'm freaking pissed, and I think I'm getting a blister from swinging my hammer like John Henry." When Doc remained silent, staring down at me, I added. "You know, the steel-driver?" He continued to stare. "This relationship isn't going to work very well, Doc, if you don't get my similes and metaphors."

He let out a scoff that ended as more of a laugh full of disbelief. "I know who John Henry is."

"And his race against the—"

"Steam-powered hammer. I got it, Killer, but you're missing your hammer."

Aunt Zoe stepped out of the dark room, holding her lighter up in front of the wall, frowning at the spot. "Why did you throw your war hammer at it?"

"Why did I ... " I jammed my hands on my hips. "I don't know, maybe to kill it."

Something rumbled low and deep, shaking the building enough to raise the dust around our feet.

"What was that?" Reid said from the other end of the hallway where I'd left him.

"We need to get out of here." Aunt Zoe pulled on my arm.

"But what about my war hammer?"

"It's gone, Violet. Come on. The *lidérc* will come back and now we're weaponless."

"Don't you have anything else in your bag of tricks?"

"Sure, more protection wards but nothing to kill it. That was supposed to be your job."

I followed her. "I didn't expect it to be so dodgy."

"You think it's lived this long by being slow and clumsy?"

Doc held out his hand to Reid, pulling him to his feet. The fire captain had a definite limp as he headed for the door. I watched him ease down the stairs, grimacing after him. That was my fault. Between Aunt Zoe's punch and my hammer trip, the Parker women had left him battle bruised.

Aunt Zoe yanked the door shut behind us. She slid the padlock back into place and clicked it closed before blowing out a breath of relief. "That was close."

Something thumped against the other side of the door, making us both jerk back. Several more thumps followed, but the door held.

"Let's get the hell out of here." I led the way down the stairs.

"The downstairs doors need to be locked," Aunt Zoe said.

I ran around to the front, but Doc was already there, padlocking the chains.

"What happened here?" He pointed at the hole I'd made.

I stared at the hole, remembering the surge of panic at that moment. "I was testing out my war hammer."

He grabbed me by my coat collar and pulled me close. "You scared the shit out of me when you disappeared in the dark."

I frowned up at him. "Trust me, that wasn't the plan."

"It never is. Where did you go?"

"Hurry up!" Aunt Zoe called from her open window.

"I'll explain after we're away from that thing upstairs." I jogged over to Reid's pickup. As I opened the back door on the driver's side, I looked at the upstairs windows. In the darkness behind the glass, I thought I saw a lone ember drifting down.

I shuddered and then climbed inside the pickup.

Reid lit out, sending gravel flying. I leaned back against the headrest, closing my eyes in the safety of the cab. I tried to make sense of what I'd seen, but my brain was too wiped from the adrenaline hangover to do more than sputter.

I reached out and found Doc's hand, lacing my fingers with his. He held the back of my hand against his heart for a moment, then let it rest on his thigh.

None of us said a word all of the way back to Aunt Zoe's.

When Reid pulled into her drive, he cut the engine and killed the headlights, but left the dashboard lit up. He looked across at Aunt Zoe. In the glow, I could see the lines on his brow. "That was my dad back there. He died twenty years ago. Lung cancer ate him up."

"No, Reid," Aunt Zoe's voice was low and comforting. "That wasn't your dad. It was a *lidérc* taking on the shape of someone you loved and lost, trying to lure you in close enough to latch onto you like it did Ottó."

Reid turned further in his seat, looking back at me. "Sparky, did you use me as bait?"

I squirmed under his and Aunt Zoe's stares.

She made a growling sound in her throat. "That was too risky, Violet Lynn. If it had gotten a hold of Reid …"

"A hold of me?" Reid interrupted her. "What if it had gotten through whatever barrier you'd set up around Doc and you?" He shook his head. "I shouldn't have let you talk me into taking you there tonight."

"We had to know what Violet was going to deal with while filming in there." She touched his shoulder. "Can you put a sign on the upstairs door in the morning before anyone else gets there? Something that says nobody can enter the upper rooms?"

"I'll put one upstairs and down, woman. That place is a slice of hell."

"The downstairs is safe. It can't leave the second floor."

The Sugarloaf's management representative hadn't wanted us to film upstairs tomorrow. Was it because of the *lidérc*? If so, that was a doozy of a secret someone was trying to keep locked away up there.

"How do you know it can't leave the second floor?"

"The exits were all guarded with wards. Whoever shut that thing upstairs knew what they were doing."

I hadn't noticed anything that looked like a ward, but then again, I hadn't been looking for those, only the smoky devil. "But what about when it goes through the walls?"

"It may be able to travel into different realms, but when it's here, it's stuck in that building on the second floor."

Doc unfastened his seat belt. "Do you think that was Ottó's handiwork, Zoe?"

Aunt Zoe shook her head. "I think it latched onto Ottó while he was alive, but after he died, someone else stepped in and trapped it."

"Why?" Reid asked.

"It's believed that whoever has control of a *lidérc* will be capable of extraordinary feats and will become extremely rich. Some even mistakenly believe it can offer immortality, but in truth it'd be like handing over your soul to a hell of its own making. I suspect what Ottó dealt with during his tortured life was something along those lines."

"I'm with Reid. I don't think anyone should go back in that building," Doc said. "Especially Violet."

Reid nodded. "It should be burned to the ground."

"No!" Aunt Zoe said looking from one man to the other. "That would set it free of its wards. Fire is not its enemy."

"Why doesn't it burn down the building itself?" Reid asked.

"The fire you see coming off of it is a visual effect only. It doesn't really burn things."

"I can attest to that." I told them what had happened in the attic after I'd disappeared, and then about being downstairs when I'd returned. I explained how the *lidérc* had dripped embers on me repeatedly without any effect.

"So, somebody is keeping that thing as a pet?" Doc asked.

"Maybe," Aunt Zoe said.

He looked at me. "Who owns that building?"

"Dominic Masterson."

"And nobody has seen him since he broke through the Opera House wall, right?"

"Right."

Aunt Zoe yawned again. "How about we finish this discussion inside?"

"I'm going home." Reid glared across at Aunt Zoe. "I need to ice my throbbing jaw."

I saw Aunt Zoe wince. "I'm sorry about that."

He pointed at her. "You owe me, Zo."

"For what? I already thanked you for taking us up there tonight."

She must have done that while Doc and I were chaining the front doors.

"For that punch. You lined me up and everything."

"I said I'm sorry. I didn't want you going up there. You were our weakest link. You saw what happened as soon as it locked onto you."

"Sorry is not going to cut it this time, Zo."

"Fine. I owe you." She pushed open her door, letting a blast of cold air inside. "What do you want in return?"

He stared at her for several seconds. "I think you know."

"No way. That's out of the question."

"I'm not asking. I'll call you when it's time to collect."

"I won't do it, Reid." She slammed the door on him and headed up the walk.

I thanked Reid, throwing out a quick apology for using him as bait, and then raced after her, catching her at the porch steps. "What does he want? Inquiring minds need to know. Sex?"

"If only it was just sex."

Just sex? Instead of analyzing that, I pressed, "What then?"

"He wants to take me on a date—dinner and dancing down in Rapid."

"How is that worse than sex?"

She watched him back out of the drive, deep lines emphasizing her irritation. "I'm afraid the son of a bitch is going to charm the hell out of me and sweep me off my feet again."

* * *

Monday, November 19th

I woke stiff and sore from swinging that damned war hammer. The rusted tin man would have made it out of bed and to the bathroom faster than I did. I crawled under the hot shower jets and let my brain replay last night's ending.

Doc, Harvey, Aunt Zoe, and I had stayed up until the wee hours, rehashing what had happened in the Sugarloaf Building, throwing out ideas on how to eradicate the troublemaker.

We came up with a few theories about why the *lidérc* kept choosing its various identities during my adventures with it in the attic. The one Aunt Zoe figured was most likely came from Doc. It had to do with my having an innate defense from such tricks due to my bloodline. It couldn't read my mind as clearly as others, grasping at straws when it came to me. Whatever the reason, I was proof that it was stoppable. It was merely a matter of figuring out how to snag it long enough for me to kill it.

Eventually, Doc had headed home to sleep in his own bed since Harvey had dibs on the couch and my bed appeared to still be on the outs with Doc. He didn't actually say that, but he had known there was a vacancy with his name on it and yet had chosen to drive home and crash in his own sheets. When he'd kissed me goodnight, he'd explained that he had a couple of appointments in Spearfish come morning and needed some sleep. I hadn't pressed him any further, wishing I'd felt as cool and collected on the inside as I'd sounded on the out when I'd wished him happy dreams and turned my back on him.

Surprisingly, I slept hard. Not a single nightmare had haunted my dreamland. However, that was probably why I was so stiff this morning. Ten minutes of hot water therapy on my shoulders and back made only a small difference. I was going to need to pop some ibuprofen to get up to speed today. I wrapped the towel around me, dragging my achy ass back to my bedroom and the white dress covered with red cherries that awaited me.

It took several more minutes to finally convince my legs to walk over and stand in front of the mirror. When I did, I cursed. I should have let the *lidérc* get me.

Old man Harvey had a heyday about my getup. "Howdy-doody, tooty-fruity! That fancy dress makes ya look built like a brick outhouse."

I wasn't sure if that was a good thing or bad. My knowledge of outhouses was limited, containing only tidbits about black widows living under the seats and slivers getting lodged in all the wrong places. I took the coffee he offered and slurped it down.

"I need your help getting the kids to school, Harvey. Jerry texted me this morning and wants me to come in early."

"No need for Harvey to drive them in," Aunt Zoe joined us in her robe. "Natalie called while you were in the shower. She's going to swing by and take them to school this morning."

"Why's that?"

"She said she has something for you."

"I won't be here."

"I'll send her down to your office. Unless that will cause you problems."

I shook my head. "We'll be going over lines before heading up to Lead."

"You're wearing your charms?" she asked.

"Every single one."

"Ya sure you don't want to take Bessie with ya?"

Actually, I did, but I'd probably end up shooting the real Ray instead of the *lidérc* version. "I'm sure, but thanks for offering."

Fifteen minutes later, the kids raced past me into the kitchen as I was heading for the door. After giving them kisses and warnings to keep out of trouble and have a good day at school, I saluted Harvey and then hugged Aunt Zoe goodbye.

"Be careful up there, Violet. If it figures out a way to escape its cage, it might come for you and the others."

"If it does, I'll introduce it to Ray."

She chuckled and ushered me out the door.

When I arrived at the office, everyone but the orange-faced baboon was there. I asked Jerry about Ray's whereabouts and learned that he'd called in sick. Damn it, there went my plans to infest Ray with a Hungarian devil.

I was standing outside the back door, practicing my lines in the cold morning air—which was an excuse to escape from Jerry's constant adjustments to my outfit—when Natalie came walking up to me, a brown paper sack in hand.

"That's some killer red lipstick, hot stuff," she said. "You been out sucking blood from the local population again?"

I grinned. "Thanks for taking the kids to school."

"My pleasure."

"Aunt Zoe said you have something for me."

She nodded. "I do."

"Is it another piece of Rex's car?"

"Nope, not this time." She looked around, acting suspicious, reminding me of when she was about to stir up some trouble back when we were kids. "It's this."

She lifted the sack and held it out to me to take.

I looked at the sack but didn't touch it. "Did you bring me some tequila to help me get through the day?"

"No."

"It's not a dead rat, is it?"

She snorted. "Why would I give you a dead rat?"

"I don't know. Because you're weird."

"No, you're the weird one, especially now." Her smile took any sting out of her words. "But I still love your crazy ass." She shook the sack. "Come on, take it."

I did. Whatever was inside was heavy, like glass. I opened it and peeked down in it. "What is this?"

"Careful," she said when I reached inside. "It's broken in a couple of spots and has some sharp edges."

I grabbed something cold and hard and smooth, slowly pulling it from the sack. I turned it right side up and froze, heart and breath and all ... except my brain, which fired up the nightmare furnace.

In my hands was the top of the clown cookie jar that had been in Wolfgang Hessler's kitchen. The tip of its yellowing pointy hat was broken off, and one piece of the ruffle circling its neck had taken a hit. Otherwise, the thick red sad lips, the black + signs covering the grayed out eye sockets, and the little button nose were still there. Only now, the lid was cracked and singed from the fire that had taken the rest of the house.

"No no no no," I suddenly realized I was saying it aloud.

"Vi? Are you okay?" Natalie reached out toward me.

The world around me tunneled as I stared down at the clown's ghoulish frown. All sound faded, replaced by a cackling laugh that made me want to find a closet in which to hide. Then the laugh died out, and I heard two words. They were breathed more than spoken: *Kill ... her.*

A screech flew from my throat, and I let go of the lid.

Chapter Twenty-One

Natalie caught the clown cookie jar lid before it hit the ground, her years of playing catcher on the school softball team still evident by her quick reflexes.

"Dang it, Vi. Don't drop it." She took the paper sack from me and slid the lid inside.

"Where did you get that thing?" I wiped my hands off on my coat, wishing I could as easily wipe away the memories that flashed back at the sight of it.

"I went to the Hessler house last night—well, what's left of it." She rolled the top of the sack closed.

"You went there at night?"

"I had to, otherwise someone would've seen me."

"Why in the world did you go *there*?"

"To sift through the piles of debris and ashes," she said, as if it should've been obvious.

I crossed my arms over my chest. "Is this what you do for fun at night now that you're not having sex?"

She grinned. "Well, I have to get my kicks somehow."

"What's next? Grave digging? Necrophilia?"

"You know what they say about necrophilia?"

I nodded. "It puts the 'fun' back in funeral?"

"And the 'rot' back in erotica."

I wrinkled my nose. "You're sick."

"But not as twisted as you." She held up the paper sack. "Anyway, I was reading one of Terri Reid's books and had an idea for our séance."

"Does Terri have a séance how-to guide in her books?"

"No. The heroine doesn't actually do séances because the ghosts come to her on their own, but in one of the books she's given a personal item by a ghost as a reward."

"So you want to reward me?"

"No, smarty-tart. I want to give you something personal from Wilda.

Maybe it will help draw her ghost to you."

I didn't like the sound of this one bit, but I let her finish.

"But since Wilda's been gone a long time, I had to settle for second best—a familiar object from her home."

Familiar? More like bone chilling. "That's probably a bad idea."

"Not according to Cornelius."

"When did you talk to him?"

She broke eye contact. "I ran into him."

"Where?"

"In his suite."

"You went to Cornelius's suite?"

Her gaze returned to mine. "I thought it would be helpful if I knew the lay of the land before we meet there for the séance. In another one of Terri's books—"

I didn't let her finish. "Nat, aren't those books about fictitious characters?"

"Yes, but I'm sure Terri did lots of research on the paranormal."

"But still, we're talking fiction." I pointed at the sack. "This shit is for real. I'm for real. You need to understand the difference."

"Trust me, after what I saw out at Harvey's place, I get the difference. But you need to be open minded. There are others who might be able to help you be more successful when you screw around in the past. Besides, this ghost business isn't even your line of work. Cornelius and Doc are the experts, and if Cornelius is on board with me bringing the piece from the Hessler house, you should be, too."

I frowned down at that sack as if it held a venomous snake.

"I'm only trying to help you, spaz."

"I know. I'm sorry. It's just that house really creeped me out. Seeing the lid to that spooky clown cookie jar brought those feelings back in full force."

The door creaked open behind me. "Violet," Jerry said, "they're heading out."

"Okay. I'll be there after I make a quick call to a client." I needed to let Katrina King know that whoever was in charge of the Sugarloaf Building had gotten back with Mona finally—the building was NOT for sale. I wondered if that decision had come from Dominick Masterson himself, wherever he was hiding, or one of his minions who was running his business in his absence.

After the door closed, Natalie asked, "You sure it's a good idea to go back up to that building so soon? Your aunt gave me the short version of last night's fun and games while the kids were rounding up their school stuff this morning."

"Hell no, but I need to be there with the film crew in case something goes south with that thing up there."

She leaned in and hugged me "Be safe, babe."

"That's rich, coming from a girl who touched the end of an electric cattle prod."

"That was your brother's handiwork. There's not much I won't do on a twenty-dollar bet." With a wink she left.

I went back inside and made the call to Katrina King, leaving the no-deal message on her voicemail. Then I grabbed my stuff.

"Here we go again," I muttered and headed out to my SUV to lead the way up to the Sugarloaf Building ... and whatever awaited us there.

* * *

Not much awaited us there except a lot of clomping around overhead. It was the same sort of song and dance I'd heard from the first floor last night. Since nobody else on the Paranormal Realty crew seemed to hear it, I was able to make it through several hours of filming without more than a few cringes at the heavy thudding moving back and forth across the ceiling, which almost sounded like pacing at times.

I had little doubt that the *lidérc* knew I was downstairs. At one point, it sounded like it was jumping up and down right over my head. But as long as it was locked up in its cage and nobody sneaked upstairs to explore its lair, I wasn't too worried about things going haywire.

Reid had made doubly sure no sneaky visitors would check in on the creature by installing an additional padlock on the second floor door. He'd also posted his official fire department DO NOT ENTER signs in a couple of key locations—the entrance to the outside stairway and the door at the top of the stairs. A piece of wood had been nailed over the hole in the downstairs' door that I'd made with my war hammer.

We were wrapping up and getting ready to head back down to Deadwood later that afternoon when my cell phone rang. I looked at the number not recognizing it, and stepped away from where Rosy and Rad were packing up their equipment to take the call in private.

"Hello?"

For a moment all I heard was breathing, mine and the caller's. A light went on in my head. Before the voice on the other end started to speak, I knew what was going to be said and a flair of irritation burned white-hot in my chest.

"We want what be—"

"Fine!" I was tired of this prank calling bullshit. I refused to let the game be played by someone else's rules. "You want the damned book, Caly? Come and get it, you spiky bitch. Tomorrow night at ten-forty-seven at the Sugarloaf Building." I took a chapter from Cornelius's book on down-to-the-minute rendezvous times to throw her a curveball. "Don't be late!"

I hung up on her, muted my phone, and returned to helping Rosy and Rad load up their stuff. I'd call Cooper later and let him know what I'd done, which I doubted would elicit any praise from him. He'd want to be the one to make the game rules, but I was not his pawn.

For the rest of the afternoon, I focused on showing a few houses to an older, soon-to-retire couple who'd stopped by on my return from the Sugarloaf Building.

Natalie joined Aunt Zoe, the kids, Doc, and me for supper. After Addy and Layne headed to their rooms to finish their homework, the four of us adults sat around the kitchen table, talking about the weather, work, my kids—normal stuff for once. The break from the insanity that was my current life warmed my soul, making me feel normal again.

Doc's fingers caressing the back of my neck reminded me that killer or not, I was still very much a girl who wanted someone to curl up next to every night. Someone without feathers or a beak who didn't leave non-golden eggs hidden throughout my room in the morning.

I thought about telling the three of them about the phone call from Caly and my response but kept quiet, wanting to enjoy this happy moment a bit longer.

"Where's Harvey?" Natalie grabbed a beer from the fridge.

"Another date," Aunt Zoe answered, opening the lid to her Betty Boop cookie jar. She pulled out a snickerdoodle and offered it to Doc, who shook his head. I on the other hand took it. I was not one to turn down sugar, especially when it was in the form of a cookie.

The cookie jar reminded me of another—one with a clown head on it that was in Natalie's possession. I turned to Doc. "Last night when we were in the Sugarloaf Building, you mentioned something about precognition."

He nodded once.

"Is that the same thing as someone using an object that was associated with a person when he or she was alive to lure their ghost after they are dead?"

"That would be more along the lines of a retrocognitor."

"A what?" Natalie asked.

"Precognition is used to determine a possible future. Retrocognition, on the other hand, is based on acquiring information from past lives. Some believe it can be used to prompt for events that happened between physical lives when the consciousness existed in a different dimension."

I let that soak in for a moment. "But not just any medium can use retrocognition?"

"Correct." His fingers stopped caressing. "What's with these questions?"

I looked over at Natalie, who'd returned to the table. She'd conferred with Cornelius about the lid, but I was curious how Doc would feel about her plan.

"Go for it," she said and took a swallow of beer.

"Nat talked to Cornelius about using an object from the Hessler haunt to help lure Wilda back during our séance on Thanksgiving night."

"What object?" Aunt Zoe asked.

"The burned and broken lid to a clown cookie jar that she found in the debris pile. My question for you is," I said to Doc, "as an experienced medium, do you think it's a good idea?"

He leaned forward, resting his elbows on the table, hands clasped. "I don't know." He looked at Natalie. "Cornelius approved?"

She nodded. "He said that items from the deceased are often used during séances."

"That's true."

"We used an old gun and the blonde babe sitting next to you to reach Harvey's Grandpappy. That seemed to work."

"But he wasn't a psychotic, snot-nosed brat," I said.

"What's your problem with this clown head?" Natalie asked, peeling the label from her beer. "It's not going to come to life and bite you."

"We don't know that."

She rolled her eyes. "You've seen too many scary movies."

Yes I had. My imagination was plenty fertile thanks to that.

"If Cornelius thinks it will help," Doc interrupted our back and forth, "then we can give it a try."

"You don't foresee any potential problems?" Aunt Zoe asked.

"There are several potential problems with exorcising a ghost from a living person, including some with fatal results." His gaze drifted around the table, landing on me. "But my answer to whether or not this object being present will have an impact on the success of the séance is still, 'I don't know.' I'm not as experienced in séances as Cornelius is." He looked back at Aunt Zoe. "I worked alone until I met Violet. My psychometry skills are pretty rusty."

"Psycho-what?" Natalie asked.

"A psychometrist is someone who can gather information from the energy of an object."

Layne ran into the room with his science book held open. "Doc, can you help me?"

Without waiting for Doc's answer, he set the book on the table between us and started asking about neutrons and protons, ending our discussion about clown head offerings and dead girls.

Aunt Zoe excused herself and headed back out to her workshop. I left Layne and Doc at the table and went upstairs to put on my warmest leggings and a flannel shirt. It was dark and cold outside, and the idea of sitting next to Doc on the couch while watching a movie with Natalie and the kids sounded like the perfect way to end our happy family night.

A few hours later the kids were in bed, Natalie was snoring in the recliner, and I was getting handsy with Doc under the covers on the couch. He was getting mouthy back, his lips on mine, heating me inside and out.

"Let's go up to my room," I whispered, moving over him, showing him why with my hand.

He groaned against my mouth. "We can't."

"Yes, we can."

"The kids."

"They're asleep."

"They could wake."

I stilled, frowning down at him. "They know you're my boyfriend, Doc."

He stared up at me, suddenly serious. "When's the last time they saw a man in your bed?"

That was an odd question to field while my hand was in his pants. "They've never seen a man in my bed."

"Never?"

I shook my head. "Since they came along, my dating life sort of dried up with sporadic squalls passing through over the years. I wasn't going to bring a man into their lives who might not stick around."

He stared up at me, watching me with an inscrutable expression.

"I mean a man who I didn't really want to stick around." I grimaced slightly. "Not that I expect you to stick around forever or anything like that."

His silence continued along with his stare.

"I'm not saying you're not the kind of guy who wouldn't stick around." Wait, did I use a double negative there?

"What are you trying to say, Violet?"

That I wanted him to spend the rest of his life with me. That's all.

The sound of a vehicle pulling into the drive made us both look over at the window where headlights lit the curtains for a moment before going dark.

"What time is it?" I asked.

He looked over my head. "Almost midnight."

"Harvey?" Nobody else would show up this late on a weeknight.

"That doesn't sound like his truck." He slid out from under me and stood, buttoning his jeans as he moved over to the window. "More like ..."

There was a knock on the door.

"Cooper's car," Doc finished, stepping back from the window. "Are you decent?"

I tugged my camisole back into place and collected my flannel shirt from the mess of covers. "I will be by the time you let him inside."

He walked over to the door and after a glance to make sure I was ready, opened it for Cooper.

I nudged Natalie awake. She woke up with a start, popping out of the chair like a hot toaster pastry.

"Hey, Coop," Doc said quietly as the detective closed the door behind him. "Everything okay?"

"No. I need to talk to Parker."

I joined the two of them in the dining room. Glancing up the stairs to make sure neither of my kids were standing there sleepy eyed and curious, I waved for them to follow me into the kitchen. Natalie trailed after us, rubbing the sandman's leavings from her eyes.

"We have a problem," Cooper told me, his face emphasizing the situation with its deep furrows. "I need you to grab your coat and take a ride with me."

"If you've found another dead body, I didn't do it," I joked.

His granite mask didn't soften even one pebble's worth as he stared at me.

"Oh, shit." I pulled out a kitchen chair and fell into it, my blood pressure spiking. "Who?" Please don't let it be someone that's going to make my heart hurt.

"Katrina King."

A breath of relief gushed from my lungs.

"What does Katrina King's death have to do with Violet?" Natalie asked, pouring herself a cup of cold coffee.

Cooper pulled out his little flip notepad that he often scribbled in during his interrogations. I was the protagonist on many of the pages in that damned pad of paper.

"Parker, did you leave Ms. King a message earlier today regarding the Sugarloaf Building?"

I nodded. "She was interested in purchasing the building, but I told her we'd heard back from the owner's representative that the building was not for sale."

"Did you tell her to meet you there tonight for any reason?"

I shook my head and then remembered the phone call I'd received earlier and my eyes widened.

"I know that look, Parker." Cooper pulled out the chair next to me, lowering himself into it, leaning forward until we were face to face. "Unless you want to spend the night in jail, you had better fess up."

I got the feeling he wasn't trying to intimidate me for once, just get closer to the truth.

So I gave it to him. "I got a phone call this afternoon while we were packing up after filming at the Sugarloaf Building. The caller started with that crap about wanting what belonged to them." I stopped to glance at Doc, who was watching me with a drawn brow. I should have told him about this before now. Focusing back on Cooper, I continued, "Before she could finish, I assumed it was Caly and told her to meet me at the Sugarloaf Building tomorrow night if she wanted the damned book."

"What book?" Natalie asked.

Another glance at Doc met with a taut jaw and pinched lips. He shook his head slightly.

"What book, Parker?"

"A history book." That was no lie.

"You're telling me that Wanda was killed over a history book?" Cooper wasn't buying any of what I was selling.

"It's a very important history book."

"And you have this book?"

I nodded. Well, Aunt Zoe did.

"Why do you have this book?" he pressed.

I pointed at his notepad. "Before I tell you anything else, Detective, you need to put that away. This has to be off the record."

He flipped it shut and tossed it and his pen on the table.

"You also have to promise not to tell Detective Hawke or any of your other pals down at the cop shop what I say."

His steely eyes bored into mine. "Jesus, Parker. What now? More kooky ghosts?"

I shook my head.

"Your friendly albino pals?"

I kept shaking my head.

"Another one of those creatures we killed in Uncle Willis's graveyard?"

"We?"

"I filled it with bullets."

"Which only pissed it off more."

He cursed in my face and then shoved to his feet, lording over me. "What's the deal with the book, Parker, and if you give me that 'history' bullshit again I'll make you go see Detective Hawke tonight alone, without me there to keep you out of jail."

"Why would I go to jail?"

"For murdering Katrina King."

I frowned. "I was here all evening." I pointed at Doc and Natalie. "I have alibis."

"They won't be enough to keep you out of jail tonight if I don't help you."

"You have proof pointing specifically to Violet?" Doc asked.

Cooper looked his way. "Unfortunately, yes."

"What?" Natalie stepped partially between us, running interference, her body stiff. "You need to explain that, Cooper, and if you give us that 'police business' blow off, I'll tear you a new asshole on Vi's behalf."

He looked her up and down, then nodded. "I've been informed by Fire Captain Martin that the murder weapon found on the scene will most likely have Parker's prints on it."

"What's the murder weapon?" I asked.

He took Natalie by the shoulders and shifted her to the side so he could glare at me better. "You go first. What's so special about this book that Wanda Carhart had to be killed to get it?"

"It's a book about a demon," Doc spoke up.

"A demon?" Cooper's squint was full of skepticism.

"It goes by the name of Kyrkozz," I explained. "I took it from Lila Beaumont after the fracas at the Carhart house that night."

Cooper's nostrils flared. "You removed evidence from the scene of a crime again?"

"That was my first time, so using 'again' in this case is incorrect."

"Parker!" His teeth actually snapped together.

"What? I didn't think you'd need it after that night since you had the killer behind bars."

"And this book can what? Raise this demon or something ridiculous like that?"

Doc shrugged. "I have a feeling it may contain more than that."

"Such as?"

"Instructions on how to control the demon."

Cooper's face scrunched up, thunderclouds rolling over his brow, mixing with lightning. I might even have glimpsed an F5 tornado on the horizon.

He hit me with a scowl. "This is so fucked up."

"Welcome to my world," I said. "Now it's your turn, Detective. What was the murder weapon used to kill Katrina King?"

"Your war hammer."

Chapter Twenty-Two

Tuesday, November 20th (just after midnight)

The loud crackling of police scanners blaring out code numbers and commands interrupted the silence of the cold night. Across the dark valley, the Homestake Mine Yates Shaft stood guard while Lead's finest nosed around the Sugarloaf Building, shining flashlights on anything that moved, including me.

"What in the hell is *she* doing here?" Detective Hawke strode over as I crawled out of Cooper's police cruiser. He reminded me of a pissed off bull, snorting and pawing at the ground at the sight of my red pea coat.

Cooper rounded the front of the cruiser.

"Screw this," I told Cooper and returned to the back seat of the car, pulling the door closed behind me. It was too late to face off with that brute and his thick sideburns. I was tired and wanted to return to playing hanky-panky under the covers with Doc on Aunt Zoe's couch.

Cooper yanked open my door. "Come on, Parker. Out!"

"I changed my mind. I don't want to do this tonight." I settled my gaze on Hawke, who'd shouldered up next to Cooper. Both cops glared down at me. "It's too cold and he's too big of an asshole."

"She has a good point," Natalie said from beside me in the back seat.

Cooper's glare broke. He turned away, clearly fighting a grin.

Hawke leaned down, looking in at Natalie. "Come again, Ms. Beals?" His voice was acid-free when he addressed her, friendly even.

"It's freaking cold out here tonight," she clarified, zipping her thick coat up to her neck. "I wouldn't be surprised to see snowflakes any minute now."

"They aren't calling for snow until next week," Hawke said.

"I thought there was a possibility for it this weekend."

"You've gotta be fucking kidding me." Cooper's glare was back, nailing Hawke this time. "You're really going to stand here and talk about the weather at a goddamned crime scene? Can we return to the task at hand,

Detective, so I can get the body removed before the sun comes up?"

Doc moved next to Cooper. "I think we need to take a little walk before Violet looks at the body."

"Looks at the body?" Detective Hawke turned to Cooper. "I didn't authorize Parker to be here, let alone view the victim."

"You didn't, but I did."

Hawke looked down his nose at me. "What in the hell are you thinking, Coop? Parker is probably responsible for this."

Damn it if the bunghole wasn't on the mark there. I kept quiet, sharing a small grimace with Doc.

"I brought her because she might be able to help us with this investigation."

"Help us? Shit-criminy, Coop. You've let the witch get under your skin."

Sheesh. How many times did I have to tell the bonehead I wasn't a witch?

I climbed out of the cruiser, adjusted the purple wool skirt I'd thrown on over my sweater leggings, and strode up to Hawke, forcing him to take a step back. "I'm not a witch, Rockford." Actually, that was an insult to the late, great James Garner. "And that," I pointed at Cooper, "is 'Detective Cooper' to you, especially while we're standing at his crime scene. You should show some respect to the one detective in this town who wants to close cases for reasons other than landing some stupid promotion."

Detective Hawke's eyes grew hard and beady. He loomed over me, threatening with his size. "Why are you really here tonight? Is it to make sure we don't find any evidence you may have left behind?"

Maybe, dammit!

Before I had a chance to answer, Doc stepped between us. "Back off, Detective. She's here to help."

"I don't need help from *her.*"

"Oh, really?" Doc asked. "So you have all of the information you need to find the killer and close the case then?" When Hawke grumbled in reply, Doc nodded. "Exactly. You need her. Trust me."

In truth, he needed Doc not me, unless he decided to go up to the second floor in the Sugarloaf Building. Then he needed both me and my war hammer.

However, the plan the four of us had concocted back in the kitchen after Aunt Zoe had agreed to stay home with my kids was to use me as the "medium." I'd distract the other cops while Doc, the real deal, checked for any signs of Katrina King's ghost. If he made contact with her, he would try to figure out who'd found my war hammer and where, and why it had been used to kill her. During my diversion, Cooper would lead the fake medium—aka me—inside the first floor of the building where I could listen for the *lidérc* and make sure it was still behaving itself upstairs.

Natalie had come along to throw Detective Hawke off his game whenever necessary, like when we'd arrived and he'd come at me barking and snarling. Cooper had not been thrilled at all about this part of the plan, citing several unconvincing reasons she shouldn't go along, and then clenching his jaw when Natalie had told him to quit being so bull-headed and drive.

Detective Hawke took a step back from Doc and me, whirling on Cooper. "And how in the hell did you figure she could help with this investigation?"

"She helped us find the body at my uncle's ranch, remember?"

That was Doc's doing, not mine, but I added for effect, "And I figured out who might have killed the guy and why."

Doc looked at me. "There is no 'might have' about it."

"This medium business is bullshit," Hawke said. "Come on, Cooper, can't you see she's just playing you, pretending she's a clairvoyant."

"Not clairvoyant," Doc said. "What we're talking about here is retrocognition, focusing on the past."

Hawke snorted. "It's one big hoax, if you ask me."

"But nobody asked you, did they?" I snapped. "And you want to know why? Because your head is buried so far up your own ass admiring the view that you're blind to everything else."

"Violet," Doc warned.

Hawke's shoulders pulled in tight, giving him a hunchback appearance. "Watch your mouth, Spooky Parker."

I rolled my eyes at his use of my notorious nickname. "Are you going to stand there making angry faces at me until someone else ends up dead or let me help find whoever killed Ms. King?"

"Don't you mean until you kill your next victim?"

I guffawed. "Is there even a brain in that coconut you call a head?"

"Mark my words, Parker," he bit out, "you're going down, and I'm not talking about your lipstick on my dipstick. Unlike Cooper, I'm immune to psycho blondes."

Doc moved lightning fast, going nose-to-nose with the big oaf. "You need to think twice about the next thing that comes out of your mouth, Detective. That badge does not give you the right to insult the lady."

Hawke took a step back. "Call off your hound, Parker, or I'll throw him in jail for assaulting an officer."

"Detective Cooper," Doc's focus stayed locked on Hawke, his body still taut, ready to spring. "If you don't do something about this cretin, I will. And I don't care if it lands me in jail for the night."

"Jesus, Hawke." Cooper stepped in, playing referee. "What's gotten into you?"

"It's her," he huffed. "I'm sick of seeing this condescending, frizzy haired, meddling blonde at our crime scenes."

"My hair is not frizzy." At least not tonight—I had my curls well-tamed.

"Trust me," Cooper said, giving me a flat stare. "I know how you feel about Violet ... and her hair."

I scratched the bridge of my nose with my middle finger.

With a slight shake of his head, he returned to Hawke. "But even more frustrating is the lack of answers in these murder cases."

Hawke jammed his hands on his hips, frowning across the valley at the Yates Shaft headframe. "This place is fucked up."

"Maybe, but using this all-brawn-and-no-brains tack isn't helping. We have to find the truth using whatever tools we can find." He pointed at me. "Tonight, Parker's a tool."

"You're the tool," I told Cooper.

He raised his eyebrows. "Is that all you got for me?"

"No, here's something else." I pulled my left hand from my coat pocket, giving the butthead another middle fingered salute.

His mouth curved into a grin, but only for a heartbeat or two and then his stony mask fell back into place.

"Fine, you can take Parker around the building," Detective Hawke said. "But I don't know that I'll buy anything she says." Hawke's scowl moved from me to Doc. "Why did you bring your roommate along?" he asked Cooper.

"He wasn't thrilled with me hauling his girlfriend up here in the middle of the night to look at a dead body."

Hawke turned to Natalie, eyeing her up and down. She smiled back at him, charming him with a flirty bat of her lashes. Instead of asking for an explanation of her presence, he said to his partner in crime-fighting, "Keep a close eye on Parker. I wouldn't put it past her to plant false evidence."

He was too busy walking away to see the karate kick I aimed his way.

Doc chuckled. "That's my scrapper."

"I like her windmill move better." Cooper pulled his notepad out of his pocket along with a pen. "It had more finesse." He pointed his pen at me. "Let's get this song and dance done. I have a shitload of paperwork to do on this murder."

I touched Doc's arm. "You ready to work your magic?"

One of his eyebrows lifted. "Which magic are we talking about, *Tish*?"

"Stop right there." Before I could reply, Cooper interrupted us. "Don't make me put a bullet in you tonight, Nyce. Now what's first? The Sugarloaf Building or the body?"

"The body," I answered. "Then we'll go inside."

"You sure?" Doc asked.

"I need to see the war hammer," I said for their ears only. "Make sure it's mine."

"Who else's would it be, Parker?" Cooper asked. "They don't sell war hammers at any hardware stores around here."

If he wanted my help tonight, he needed to drop the attitude. "I know that, Detective Pissypants, but whoever gave me one might be passing them out to others. I'd like to confirm if it's mine or not."

"It's Detective Cooper at my crime scenes, remember?" he threw my words back at me with a smartass grin.

I ignored him and looked at Natalie, who stood shivering next to Doc. "I need you to run interference for us. I don't need to deal with Detective Hawke while I'm trying to focus on the *lidérc*. One asshole at a time is plenty."

"I'm on it."

"Distract how?" Cooper caught Natalie's arm as she turned to leave, holding her in place.

She patted his cheek. "If I tell you that, Coop, you'll see through all of my charms. Then I'll have no chance of getting you under my wicked spell again."

I scoffed. "I doubt that."

Cooper glared in my direction.

Oops, I'd opened my big mouth again. "I say that because Cooper is not under any spell of yours … or any other woman's for that matter … at least none that I know of anyway." I pulled my head deeper inside of my coat, like a turtle retracting into its shell. "How about we look at that body now, Detective?"

With one last scowl in my direction, he let go of Natalie. "Be careful, Beals."

She saluted Cooper. "His bite can't be any worse than yours."

"I haven't bitten you … yet."

"Oh, I think you have, Coop." She fake punched his shoulder. "I learned my lesson well."

"Once bitten, twice shy," I threw out.

"Zip it, Parker." After watching Natalie walk away, Cooper led the way over to a tarp tented over what I assumed was Katrina King's body. "You sure about this?"

"It can't be worse than a decapitated body on the morgue's slab first thing in the morning, can it?"

"I hope not," Doc said.

"There might be another black wart for your viewing pleasure," Cooper said.

I gagged. "Thanks for that memory."

"Paybacks are hell." Without another word, Cooper flipped back the tarp.

I winced, but it was short-lived. In truth there wasn't much to see. Katrina had been wrapped up in the thick murky plastic that I recognized from the downstairs windows in the Sugarloaf Building. I could see a lumpy form with a pale arm sticking out. Clean cuts in the plastic around Katrina's face gave a clear view of her pale, lifeless eyes. The cops must have had to trim away enough to figure out who they had on their hands.

The thing that made me scratch my head was my war hammer—and it certainly looked like mine after a quick inspection. It had been buried into her chest through the plastic. Apparently, she'd been wrapped up in the plastic and then killed. Had she suffocated first? There was blood on the plastic. Would she have bled out like that if she'd already been dead? Probably not.

I heard a sniff behind me and looked around at Doc. Was that a sniff because he was cold or because there was someone here with us? "What is it?"

He was looking across the blue and red flash-filled yard at the Sugarloaf Building. "I thought I saw something move in the downstairs window."

All I saw was darkness.

"There it is again," he said.

"I didn't see anything," Cooper said.

Me either, but we were both duds when it came to ghosts. Well, mostly.

I pointed down at Katrina. "What's with the plastic?"

Cooper shrugged and covered the plastic-wrapped body with the tarp.

The war hammer's handle acted as the center tent pole. "This is how we found her. I was hoping one of you could help me figure that out, along with why your war hammer is stuck in her chest."

Those were good questions. I didn't think I'd be much help, but Doc might be able to provide a few key pieces of information.

A freezing cold gust of wind blew past us as we stood over Katrina's body, each focused on our own who and why.

"Let's go inside." Doc took my hand, pulling me over to the Sugarloaf Building.

Cooper followed. "Upstairs or down?"

"Downstairs first," Doc answered. "That will give Violet the opportunity to listen for any sounds from upstairs."

"Right, sounds from … what did you call it?" Cooper asked.

Earlier in his cruiser on the way up to Lead, I'd explained about our visit to the Sugarloaf Building last night with Aunt Zoe and Reid. Cooper had listened to our recount about the *lidérc* without a word. When it was over, he'd looked across the front seat at Doc and said, "This supernatural shit would go down better with whiskey."

"I'll buy you a bottle when it's over."

Unfortunately for Cooper, I had a feeling that bottle of whiskey would be a long time coming.

"If I need to head upstairs tonight," I said as we climbed the steps to the building, "I'm going alone." I shivered from the cold air along with the realization of what we might find inside.

"There's no way in hell that's going to happen, Killer," Doc tightened his hold on my hand. "Where you go, I go."

"This is my crime scene," Cooper joined us at the doors. "Nobody goes up there without me." His obstinacy reminded me of Reid.

I sighed. Didn't they realize how dangerous that thing upstairs was? I wasn't even sure I understood what we were dealing with, but Aunt Zoe had certainly made it clear that it was one hundred percent trouble.

I looked down at the door handles. Hold up. The chains holding the doors shut were gone. "Who took the chains off?"

"What chains?"

"The ones holding these doors closed."

"There was a padlock, too," Doc said.

"There were no chains or padlock when we arrived."

Had Katrina removed the padlock and chains? If so, they must be lying around somewhere in the weeds, unless someone else took them. "How did you find out about her? Did someone call it in?"

Cooper nodded. "A guy down the street was coming home from work and saw what looked like a roll of plastic lying here. Turned out to be Katrina." He pushed open the door. "Shall we?"

We crossed the threshold. Doc let go of my hand, walking deeper into the front room. There were no cops inside, but their bright flashy lights lit the place up with a flickering effect through the murky plastic covering all the windows but one. There were shreds of the plastic, which was now wrapped around Katrina King's body, still stuck to the nails.

Why the plastic mummy wrap job? What in the hell had happened here?

Doc inhaled a couple of times. "Someone is in here."

"We've been through this first floor a few times tonight, combing for clues, and found nobody."

"I'm talking about someone dead. I can smell something ..." he trailed off, moving over toward the hallway.

"Is it her?" I tiptoed after him.

"I'm not sure. Cooper, I need your flashlight." After Cooper handed his extra one off, Doc said to me, "Come on."

I followed very carefully, listening for the sound of our pal from upstairs but not hearing anything.

Doc stopped in the back bathroom where I'd made faces in the mirror such a short time ago.

"Is she in here?" I whispered.

"No."

"Then what are we doing back here?" Cooper asked from behind me. I hadn't heard him following.

"Violet needs to focus," Doc told him. "Those flashing lights might screw her up."

He was right. I hadn't realized it, but my concentration had been superficial out front. In here, though, I was somewhat sure I could close my eyes and sense what was going on upstairs.

"Okay," Cooper had a growl in his tone. "Get to it then."

I tried to, thinking of the candle, the dancing flame, the trail of smoke rising into the darkness. While focusing, I listened.

"Well?" Cooper asked a short time later.

"Could you breathe any louder, Detective?"

"Sure. I could huff and puff and blow your house down."

"You already did, and then you tossed me in the hoosegow."

"You need to get over that."

"I will if you let me break your nose again."

"In your dreams, Parker. I'll wait out front," he told Doc and walked away.

After he left, Doc stepped back to give me more space, his shoulders filling the doorway. "Okay, Killer, get to work."

I went back to it, this time reaching out into the darkness even though Cornelius usually warned against it. After several minutes of reaching, I opened my eyes. "Nothing."

"You want to try another room?"

I shook my head. "No. I mean I heard absolutely nothing. I can't feel any trace of it."

"Are you sure?"

"I will be after I go upstairs."

"You're not going alone."

"Damn it, Doc. That thing up there is not a ghost."

"I know that, but the ghost that was down here has disappeared. Unlike the *lidérc*, the wards your aunt talked about probably wouldn't stop a ghost from moving back and forth between floor levels, so I need to go up there, too."

"Fine, but I'm not Aunt Zoe."

"What's that mean?"

"I can't shield you up there like she could."

"You don't know what you're capable of, sweetheart." He stepped out into the hallway. "Let's go see if it's playing hide and seek again."

I led the way up the stairs to the second floor this time. Cooper insisted on coming along, unlatching the leather strip holding his gun in its holster as I paused at the top landing. The lock was gone from this door, too.

I had a bad feeling in my gut about this whole setup, so I took it out on Cooper. "You'd better not shoot me, Detective, or I'll sic that damned Hungarian devil on you."

"Just get your meddling ass inside."

The place was just as we'd left it last night except for one thing. There was no *lidérc* there waiting for us.

I walked the floor from front to back, using the few tricks I knew to call it out. All I found were shadows and empty rooms.

Doc followed me, sniffing and waiting for the ghost he was hunting to come his way.

"It's gone," I told him when we returned to the front room. "Any luck with your wispy pal?"

"No. There's something here, but it's hanging back."

"You think it might be shy? There's a lot of commotion outside?"

"No. I think it was here last night, too, and there were only four of us then. Shyness isn't holding it back."

If it was here last night, it wasn't Katrina King. Unless there were two ghosts he was picking up tonight on his radar. "Why didn't you say anything?" He had mentioned the smell of Brylcreem, come to think of it.

"Because nothing came of it, and I wasn't sure if I was picking up the *lidérc* or something else. With your prey gone, I know now that it was someone else."

"Shit." Cooper scrubbed his hand down his face. "Now what?"

"You bring me back tomorrow night," Doc told him, "without all of these other officers around. That will let things settle down a bit before I try again."

The detective frowned out through the windows, the flashing lights flickering over his skin giving his face a craggy appearance. "Fine. You want Parker along, too?"

Doc looked at me with raised brows. "That's up to her."

"Of course. I'm still not sure if that *lidérc* is really gone or just hiding somewhere out of reach."

"I have a feeling it's gone," Doc said.

"What makes you say that?"

"When you disappeared last night, Zoe showed me the six wards that she believed were holding it captive—one carved on each of the four walls, one on the ceiling, and one on the floor. It was essentially boxed in, like a prison cell." He pointed at the wall next to the door. "This ward has something smeared over it."

"It looks like it's supposed to be some kind of symbol," I said, walking over to it. "But it's hard to tell for sure with the paint drips distorting it."

Cooper came up next to us, shining his light on the symbol. "That's not paint, Parker. It's blood."

Chapter Twenty-Three

I slept like crap. No surprise there after viewing Katrina's pale face surrounded by plastic.

I dreamed that I was the one who planted the war hammer in her chest. The *lidérc* had used her as a host, and the only way to kill it was to kill her. So I'd swung and swung and swung, only there was no plastic mummy wrapping in my nightmare. When I'd woken, my hands were still clenched around the invisible war hammer's handle and my body was bathed in sweat.

Why couldn't I dream about petting puppies or swimming with dolphins? Something besides bludgeoning someone to death with a medieval weapon?

Breakfast was late after a longer than usual hot shower to steam away the kinks of a fitful night. Natalie had spent the night on the couch and was pouring a cup of coffee when I joined her in the kitchen. Aunt Zoe had taken the kids to school for me. Real life guardian angels like Aunt Zoe were few and far between.

I took the coffee Natalie offered me. "I meant to ask you last night how well your charms worked on distracting Detective Hawke." After we'd joined back up with her, the discussion had been about the missing *lidérc* and the bloody symbol, not her adventures with the big buffoon.

"He tried to get a little too handsy when we were behind the Sugarloaf Building."

My mouth fell open. "At a crime scene?"

She frowned. "Yeah."

"What'd you do?"

"Suggested that he remove his hand from my ass before I broke his nose."

"Seriously?"

"Yep, but he thought I was joking around until I twisted his arm and dropped him to his knees."

"Damn. Your days as a distractor might be over."

"Nah. He thinks I'm playing hard to get now. Said he likes women who are into rough foreplay."

I fake puked. "Wait until you show him one of your patented elbow jabs. That should really pop his willy."

She chuckled. "Ronnie showed me a new takedown move while I was in Arizona last month. Maybe I'll try that on Mr. Let's-Get-Physical."

"Don't you mean Claire?" Natalie's cousin had possessed a bruiser reputation since elementary school, but her older sister, Ronnie, was usually more refined.

"No, it was Ronnie. Turns out she's taken several self-defense classes over the last few years." She took a drink of coffee, looking over my thick black sweater, gray corduroy skirt, and black boots. "You look like you're going to a funeral this morning. Got a cold date waiting for you on the slab down at the morgue? Or is this a mood-enhancing outfit for another day in front of the camera?"

"No to both. We're done filming for now." Unless Dickie decided he didn't like the retake Rosy had filmed of Cornelius and me that was meant to replace the "missing" bit co-starring Wilda and her clown doll. "And Cooper's text this morning didn't mention the morgue."

"He texted you already?"

"I'm not sure he even went to bed. He was heading back to the station last night after dropping us off to work on that paperwork he kept bitching about."

"Was he sending you love and kisses in his text, telling you how he can't live without you?"

I chuckled and grabbed my phone, pulling up the detective's message, and read: *Parker, get your ass to the station at 9. Don't make me come find you and your crazy hair.*

"Ah, he was being funny, isn't that cute." Natalie's eyes sparkled. "You two are becoming real pals."

"I know, right? I wonder how he'd feel about exchanging friendship bracelets with me."

"I can see the inscription now—Cooper and Violet, Best Friends Forever."

We got a good laugh out of that one, then I checked the clock and decided I needed to take off so I could swing by work before heading down to see James Bond and Jim Rockford at the Deadwood cop shop.

Cooper was standing at the front desk waiting for me when I walked inside the glass front doors. I was right—he hadn't gone to sleep. I could see it on his face, which was covered in deep lines and blond stubble this morning.

"You changed your shirt," I said to him in lieu of a greeting.

"I keep an extra here." He eyed me warily. "You're not going to throw up on this one, are you?"

"I save my vomiting for your ties."

We exchanged a series of squints, then he led the way back to his office without another word. Before he opened the door, he said, "Detective Hawke is inside."

"Lovely. I can hardly wait to pinch his pudgy cheeks."

"Try to hold your tongue this morning, Parker."

"I'll hold mine if he holds his. Or maybe you should hold both of our tongues for us."

He didn't crack, not even a hairline fracture. "Detective Hawke hasn't slept either, and he's not as sweet as I am after an all-nighter."

I sighed. "Two sour grapefruits for breakfast. Makes me pucker up just thinking about it."

His forehead wrinkled more. "Don't fuck this up." Without further orders, he opened the door and ushered me into his office.

Detective Hawke looked not just worn, but wrinkled and stained, too.

"Sit, Ms. Parker."

I jutted my chin. "Listen, Detective, I'm not your dog. You don't get to order me around. If you want me to sit, you need to ask me nicely."

"Here we go," I heard Cooper mutter. He dropped into the chair meant for me.

"Fine, stand. I'm too tired to give a shit." Hawke picked up a manila envelope sitting on top of a messy jumble of paperwork on Cooper's desk and held it out to me. "Look at these and tell me what you see."

"Don't you mean tell you what I sense with my medium skills?"

He glared up at me through his bushy black eyebrows. "Just look at the damned pictures."

I started to argue, but Cooper cleared his throat and nodded his head at the pictures. His gray eyes were sagging at the corners, his exhaustion cracking his tough cop façade.

I took pity on him and grabbed the envelope, pulling out several pictures.

The first one was straight from my nightmares—Katrina King's face surrounded by the plastic from the window of the Sugarloaf Building. Her lifeless eyes looked doll-like, staring upward, fringed by eyelashes coated with mascara. Her lips were open, gasping her last breath maybe?

I glared over the top of the photo at Detective Hawke. "You could have warned me."

He shrugged. "I figured a so-called medium would be used to seeing dead people."

"I'm used to seeing living people, too, but your face still makes me angry."

Cooper cleared his throat again. He must have an extra large frog in his throat, one with thick sideburns and a corduroy jacket.

I returned to the handful of pictures. In the next, someone had cut the plastic back further, showing an open white coat covering a pink blouse with pearl buttons. Of course the blood staining most of the shirt front made it look more ghoulish than stylish.

"Expensive shirt," I said. Did Katrina King always dress to the nines when visiting haunted old buildings? "What kind of shoes did she have on? Were they name brand?"

"I didn't bring you in here to shop, Ms. Parker."

I scowled at Hawke. "Have you considered that her clothing might show if she came straight from the office? Most women don't wear such finery when sitting around the house in the evening."

"Leather high-heeled boots." Cooper yawned before adding, "Fancy looking. Some Italian name brand."

I nodded, thinking back to how nice she'd been dressed the day I'd visited her office. "I bet she came from work. Have you checked the phone records from her Lead office?"

"We're in the process," Hawke answered for Cooper. "Go to the next one."

I flipped to the next photo. Katrina's shirt had been removed but not her white lace-edged bra, giving a clear picture of the wound at her sternum. I grimaced at the dried blood spread down over her stomach. I could see the stainless steel slab of the morgue's work table under her bony shoulders. A ring of puncture marks marred the pale skin on her upper left arm. Was that a bite? Aunt Zoe hadn't mentioned that the *lidérc* would bite.

"She's over in Mudder Brother's basement?" I asked.

Cooper blinked slowly, like his eyelids were getting hard to lift. "Eddie is working on her as we speak."

I cringed, then did a double take. "Eddie's back on the job?"

Eddie Mudder had disappeared for a short time last month, landing me temporarily in hot water since I was the last one to have seen him before he'd skedaddled. Turned out he'd been scared off by one of my non-human troublemakers, thinking he was its next victim. Our little phone conversation where I cleared up that the killer was after me, not him, must have calmed him down enough to get him to come home.

"His mini-vacation is over," Cooper confirmed.

The next photo was a close up of her lower ribcage. There was some discoloration along the lower ribs, making it appear she'd taken a hit to the ribs prior to death. I could see the top of a tattoo barely sticking out above the lace waistline of her underwear. Once again, Jeff's girlfriend's tattoo-covered chest flashed through my memory. Damn it, was I going to need a lobotomy to get the image of those nipple rings out of my skull?

I flipped to the next photo and sucked in a breath. It was a close-up of the tattoo.

"What are you looking at?" Cooper asked.

I showed him the picture. "I've seen this tattoo before."

"In one of your trances?" Hawke asked, his sarcasm thick.

Ignoring him, I focused on Cooper. "Lila Beaumont had one just like it, remember?" So had Prudence's killers back in the late eighteen hundreds according to Doc, as well as whoever had sneaked into Wanda's house lately while Prudence watched.

He nodded.

Hawke reached out and snagged the photo from my hands, his brows crumpling into one wavy caterpillar as he stared at it. "What's that mean?" he said under his breath.

It meant Katrina was mixing with some not very nice people who were into raising demons so they could copulate with struggling, blonde single moms to impregnate the poor stressed-out women with their evil spawn. "It means Katrina probably wasn't in the Sugarloaf Building by accident last night."

Katrina had told me she was in search of immortality. Had she known about the *lidérc* being held in the building? Is that why she wanted me to help her acquire it? Was she under the assumption that connecting with the *lidérc* would win her immortality like the false theory Aunt Zoe had mentioned? Would it? For all we knew about the *lidérc*, maybe there was some way it would grant immortality. Although things certainly hadn't worked that way for Ottó.

Hawke handed me back the picture.

Then again, maybe Katrina was the one who had kept calling me about that stupid book. If she had shared the same tattoo, maybe she had been part of the same demon loving club as Lila. Maybe the book on Kyrkozz had been hers, not Lila's. Come to think of it, the second anonymous call I'd received had been in Katrina's office and she'd insisted I take the call.

But yesterday I had told Caly—or the caller I'd thought had been Caly—to meet me there *tonight* at ten-forty-seven, not last night.

"Do you have a time of death yet?" I asked, wondering if Katrina had gotten confused and showed up last night.

"Nothing concrete yet." The knowing look Cooper gave me told me he was running on the same track as I was about that anonymous caller.

"Explain the significance of that tattoo." Hawke's pen was poised above his notepad, ready to take notes.

I tried to act nonchalantly about the goat-pig connection, not wanting to give too much away to Hawke until I'd thought things through myself and had a chance to talk to Doc. "There isn't much to explain beyond the fact that Lila and Katrina seemed to be connected by more than just being involved sexually with Douglas Mann."

Detective Hawke scribbled something about Douglas Mann on his notepad. Good. With any luck I'd succeeded in sending him off on another tangent for now.

Cooper, on the other hand, was squinting up at me with more than tiredness in his gaze. I had a feeling he'd be wanting to hear Doc's take on this tattoo business, too.

I moved onto the final picture. It was a shot of the blood smear on the wall of the second floor near the door. I'd seen it in person and it looked the same in the photo, but I couldn't think of anything new to say about it.

I tucked the photos away in the envelope and dropped them on Cooper's desk.

"What did you pick up?" Hawke leaned back, his fingers steepled, his gaze skeptical.

"I need to think about it for a day," I lied. "You know, let my visions and thoughts sink in." I also needed to sneak up to the Sugarloaf Building tonight with Doc and Cooper to try to contact the ghost again and get more answers.

"Ha! I knew you were full of shit. You're just buying time to come up with more of your phony baloney."

I turned to Cooper. "This idiot really needs to work on his interrogation skills. Right now, the last thing I want to do is explain to the numbnuts what I saw in those pictures."

Cooper closed his eyes, squeezing the bridge of his nose.

"That's because you didn't see anything beneficial to the case that Coop and I didn't already note."

"Oh, really, Detective Know-It-All?" I grabbed the envelope and fished out the pictures again, singling out the picture with Katrina in her white lace bra. "Tell me what you see in this picture." I tossed the photo on his desk.

"She's not wearing her fancy silk shirt that showed she had probably come from her office."

I scoffed. "Tell me something besides what I've already schooled you on."

He leaned over the desk, frowning down at the picture. After a few seconds, he growled up at me. "I don't know and I'm too fucking tired to play games this morning."

Cooper picked up the picture, studying it for several seconds. "What else am I supposed to be seeing, Parker?"

I pointed at the red circle on her upper left arm. "Somebody bit her."

"I already know that," Hawke said. "You think this is our first dead body?"

I bet it was his first dead body with a war hammer planted in her chest. "Why would somebody bite her on the arm and then wrap her in plas ..."

I picked up the picture, taking a second look at that bite mark. Cornelius's voice played in my head: *What is wrong with you? Ouch! Oh, my God! Stop!*

Then I remembered sitting on the stage at the Homestake Opera House after Cornelius's and my run-in with Caly down in the old pool. Paramedics and cops had been milling around while Doc stood next to me as we waited for me to be cleared to go home. Cooper had come over and asked if I'd received any bites, telling me: *Your buddy over there had a nice chunk taken out of his arm. It'll leave an interesting scar.*

He'd been right. Caly's bite had left an interesting scar on his arm. And now Katrina had a bite mark on her left arm, just as Cornelius had.

Was it coincidence? Or had Caly been there last night? Was she the one who'd buried the war hammer in Katrina's chest? If so, why? And how had someone gotten hold of my war hammer?

"What is it?" Cooper asked.

"Nothing. I was just trying to see if I could figure out what brand of bra she's wearing." Dropping the photo back on the desk, I looked at the door, feeling the need to flee suddenly. "May I use the ladies room?"

Cooper's head tilted sideways, as if that helped him read my thoughts easier. "What aren't you telling us, Parker?"

"That I drank a big cup of coffee this morning and if you don't let me use the restroom soon, there will be a puddle on your floor."

"Go."

I didn't have to be told twice. I raced down the hall and escaped into the women's restroom. As soon as I'd closed the bathroom stall door, I leaned my head against it, my breath coming in pants.

Shit. Had Caly killed again? While there wasn't one hundred percent evidence of that fact, I had a strong hunch she'd planted that war hammer in Katrina King. She was certainly strong enough to deliver that kind of blow.

The question was, had the *lidérc* been inside of Katrina King prior to her being bludgeoned with the war hammer? Was that how it had escaped its prison? Had Caly known the *lidérc* was inside of Katrina? Was it part of some grand scheme or an accidental discovery? To what end? Why would Caly want to free the *lidérc*?

I blew out a breath, wishing I had some crystal ball to give me the answers to all of these questions.

I took my time in the restroom, washing my hands thoroughly as my brain raced. When I opened the door, Cooper stood waiting.

"You think I was going to make a run for it?"

One side of his mouth tilted upward. "Something like that." He grabbed me by the elbow and tugged me along, only we turned toward the front doors instead of his office.

"Where we going?"

"You're leaving. Detective Hawke is too tired to look at your hair any longer."

Thank God! "Yeah, well I'm sick of looking at his bushy sideburns."

Cooper made sure I walked outside without stopping to chit chat with any officers along the way. He glanced around us and then leaned in closer. "I'll pick Nyce and you up around ten tonight at your aunt's place," he said quietly.

"You're not joining us for supper?" I asked with false sweetness.

"I'm a little busy with this murder business of yours."

"This one wasn't my doing."

"I'm sure you're tied in here somewhere." He frowned out at the street. "What's with the bite, Parker?"

"I'm wondering if Caly was there last night with Katrina."

"You think she's the killer?"

"I wouldn't be surprised."

He cursed. "Another albino drive-by killing. Lucky me."

"At least she didn't go up in smoke."

"Not yet, Parker." He shook his head, looking ten years older in the harsh morning sunshine. "Not yet."

True to his word, Cooper showed up after I'd put the kids to bed. He looked less haggard but still frayed around the edges. In addition, he'd grown a large, bearded appendage with two gold teeth and a pair of suspenders—aka his uncle.

"You here to hang out with Aunt Zoe?" I asked Harvey.

"No way, girlie. I'm here to make sure nothin' happens to ya up in that ol' buildin'."

I looked at Cooper, who shrugged and said, "When I asked to borrow his pickup, he insisted on coming along and refused to get out even when I threatened to shoot him."

Harvey grinned. "I told ya Coop was all talk and no bite."

"I'd beg to differ," I muttered and grabbed my coat.

While Aunt Zoe made sure I was armored with her charms and wards and some small bundles of birch to burn if we needed to keep the *lidérc* away, Cooper filled us in on the current status of Katrina's murder, which hadn't changed much from the previous night. They had no definite suspects or motivations for killing Katrina.

The war hammer had been bagged and sent off to be examined. He couldn't confirm yet if there were prints found on it. Would Caly even leave fingerprints if she was the killer? If so, were they like human fingerprints or something else?

"I still think this is a bad idea," Aunt Zoe said as Doc opened the front door to leave.

Earlier at supper, Aunt Zoe had been full of reasons why Doc and I shouldn't go even after I'd told her that I hadn't picked up a single sign of the *lidérc*. She wasn't convinced it had escaped, worrying it may have found a deeper place to hide until I returned.

"The building is empty," I repeated. "We'll be fine."

"I hope you're right, Violet Lynn." After promising she would keep a close eye on my kids until I returned—and I would return, I assured her—she gave me a hug goodbye.

"Cooper." She made him hold up before stepping out the door. "Wear this while you're in that building or anyplace else you feel something isn't quite right."

Cooper's brows rose as she looped a leather string around his neck with one of her charms dangling over his chest. "So anywhere near Parker qualifies, right?"

Aunt Zoe chuckled, patting his chest. "Something like that."

I aimed a mock glare at her.

Her smile faded as she watched us pile into Harvey's Ford and back out of the drive.

Then we were off, heading up the hill to Lead for another round of ghostly fun. The only difference was this time Harvey had taken Natalie's place and Cooper's cruiser had been swapped for the old man's pickup, which Cooper explained would blend with the other vehicles on that street if any cops drove past.

Cooper parked about a block down from the Sugarloaf Building and pulled out three flashlights, handing out two—one to Doc and the other to his uncle.

"Where's mine?"

"I only have three."

"Then give me yours." His had a long handle, like those I'd seen on cop reality shows.

"Nobody touches my flashlight." He pointed his light at Doc. "You share with Nyce."

Maybe I'd just knock Cooper out and take his, like I took his gun back in Mudder Brothers months ago. How would the bossy detective like them apples?

Doc handed me the flashlight. "Light the way, Killer."

"You don't need your shotgun, Uncle Willis."

Harvey snorted. "I'd sooner leave my pecker behind than Bessie when it comes to that ol' buildin'." He held up the shotgun. "She's comin' with me along with those fancy charms Zoe gave me."

Grumbling about pain in the ass old men and blondes, Cooper stuffed the pickup keys in his pocket.

"You ready for this?" Doc asked Cooper.

"Shouldn't that be my question?" He led the way up the street toward the building.

"Upstairs," I directed as we drew near. "I have a feeling that's where the party started."

"The plastic came from downstairs," Cooper said, hesitating at the base of the outside stairway.

"Just humor me, Detective."

The four of us headed up the steps, Harvey bringing up the rear—my rear. "Don't shoot me in the butt," I warned him when Bessie bumped my backside.

"Don't ya worry yer pretty head. I'm saving my bullets for yer Hungarian devil."

Cooper removed the crime scene tape and unlocked the second floor door.

"Let me go first," I nudged him aside. "You're a sitting duck if it's still in there."

Amazingly, he obeyed. "Close the door behind you," he told Harvey after we were all inside.

We stood near the door, shining flashlights into the shadow-filled corners while the wind whistled through the old window frames.

I moved to the center of the room, closed my eyes, and tried to focus on the candle flame like before.

After several seconds of twiddling my thumbs in my mind's eye, I blew out a breath of relief. "It's not here." Although, that relief was short lived, because if it wasn't here where was it? Out there free? Hunting for a new host?

"The *lidérc* may be missing," Doc said, "but there's someone else here." He walked toward the dark hallway. "I think it's lurking back here. Violet, can you bring the light over here."

I did, shining the beam down the dark hall, seeing nothing but floating dust particles.

"Come on," he headed down the hallway, pausing outside the room with the chair where we'd found the *lidérc* Sunday night.

I held onto his arm as I shined the light around the room. The chair had been knocked over sometime between when we were here last night and now. "It's in here."

"What does it smell like?" I whispered.

He looked down at me. "A ghost." I could make out his grin in the semi-darkness.

"Do they make that as a candle scent, you think?"

"Sexy curves and a quick wit. Are you available for a drink after work tonight, hot stuff?" He walked over to the chair, setting it upright.

"One drink and that's it. I'm not easy, you know."

"I was hoping you'd be game to try some sex on the beach."

"Vodka isn't my liquor of choice. I'm more of a tequila girl."

"I wasn't talking about vodka." He looked over at me. "But you are my licker of choice, Boots."

Harvey snickered from the doorway. "I'm gonna have to try that one down at the senior center during the next luau night."

Doc sobered as he looked around the room. "I think the ghost in here is a man. The scent is older, reminds me of an old barbershop. Come here, tequila queen." He pointed at the chair.

"Am I sitting?" I asked, hesitating partway across the room.

He nodded.

"You're not going to tie me to that chair, are you? Because I've been tied to chairs in haunted buildings before, and each time somebody ended up dead."

Harvey raised the shotgun, aiming at the back wall. "Nobody is dyin' on my watch, girlie."

"Lower that shotgun, Uncle Willis, or I'm taking it away." Cooper's mug showed up over Harvey's shoulder.

"Spoilsport." Harvey lowered the gun, joining Doc next to me as I settled onto the chair.

"Why am I sitting? You're the mental medium."

"This ghost is playing hard to get. I need you."

"Can't you have Cooper threaten to shoot it if it won't come out to play?"

Doc squatted in front of me. "Stop being a chicken."

"But I don't like getting my feathers ruffled."

Nudging Doc's leg, Harvey snickered. "I'll bet that's not what she was sayin' the other night when ya showed her yer rooster."

I rolled my eyes. "Keep it up, old man, and I'll hire one of your sexy widows to choke your chicken for real."

"I've heard tell that near death experiences can double a man's—"

"Stop!" I glared at his toothy grin before looking at Doc. "What am I doing in this chair?"

"You're going under with me."

"Can't we go get ice cream together instead?"

He chuckled. "We'll do that when we're done here."

"You're not using me as blonde bait again, are you?"

"No. I have something else in mind."

"What?"

His hands warmed my thighs. "Close your eyes and trust me."

"This sounds like the beginning of a bad date."

"A blind date," Harvey corrected.

"Violet," Doc said, his thumbs stroking my legs through my jeans. "Focus on the task at hand."

I closed my eyes, enjoying the heat of his touch. "What task?"

"Materialization."

One eye opened. "Come again?"

"Making something out of nothing."

I cocked my head to the side. "How about I make like a chicken and fly away?"

"Chickens are lousy fliers," Doc said in a low, calming voice. "Now close that eye and let's start with a candle flame."

I did, only instead of one candle tonight, there were two right out of the gate.

That was different. Maybe my inner medium was drunk and seeing double. Oh well, I went with it and played with the two candle flames, entwining them together, watching their flames grow, doubling in size, flaring brighter before sinking down again as I pulled them apart.

"I need you to look into the darkness for whoever is here with us tonight." Doc's voice was velvety, calming me. "Bring the lurker into the light."

I was entranced with the fire, merging the flames then separating them, then merging again. Each time I brought them together, the flames grew taller and fatter, making small explosions of fire and sparks when they touched. I pulled them apart again, seeing small sparks flitter upward into the darkness. Then I touched them together. The explosion of light and heat made me shield my face for a second.

When I lowered my hands, a young girl was standing on the other side of the candles. Her eye sockets were blackened, like fire had burned out through her eyes, leaving nothing behind but singe marks. Her pink, heart-shaped mouth had a vertical fracture running down through it with a small triangle of color missing from the lower lip, as if it had chipped off. Her skin looked gray and cracked, like an antique doll with a porcelain face that had seen better days. Her blonde hair was parted down the middle with long braids draped over her shoulders, the ends secured with pink ribbons. Her dress was covered with a white apron, reminding me of the old Walt Disney cartoon version of *Alice in Wonderland*, only this girl's dress was pink instead of blue.

I recoiled thinking Wilda had found me. But then I realized this girl was older than the ghost I'd seen on Rosy's playback that day in Cornelius's suite. Nor was there any creepy clown doll in her hand.

"Who are you?" I asked.

"He doesn't want to talk to you." The sound of a child's voice seemed to come from the girl. She spoke English with a hint of something Slovak maybe? Her lips didn't move.

I focused on her pink, heart-shaped mouth, afraid to look up into the dark holes where her eyes should be. "Who doesn't want to talk to me?"

"The doctor."

What doctor? "Why not?"

"He is angry at you."

"What have I done?"

"Set him free."

Set who free? Was this girl somehow tied to Ottó? Hadn't Aunt Zoe said he was some sort of doctor? "Freedom is good, isn't it?"

"Many more will die now, just like the other yellow-haired lady."

Did she mean Katrina? "What happened to the other lady?"

"There had to be a sacrifice. Freedom comes at a cost."

"Tell the doctor I need to know who helped free the *lidérc*."

"She did," her voice lowered to a whisper.

"Who?" I matched her level.

"The visitor."

"The yellow-haired one?"

The girl's arm lifted jerkily, like someone was controlling her movements overhead using a set of wires. Her index finger lifted, bumping against her lips, shushing me.

I heard the sound of a door slam somewhere in the darkness off to my right. I looked and saw nothing; when I looked back, the girl doll was gone and a dark haired, middle-aged man with thick V-shaped eyebrows, heavy lidded eyes, and a handlebar mustache glowered at me. His brown jacket was worn with patches on the shoulder.

"You brought it back here." His accent was thick, turning *brought* into *BRA-oot* and adding a slight trill to the *r* at the end of *here*, making my brain flash back to Eva Gabor in *Green Acres*.

"Ottó?"

Footfalls clacked in the darkness, coming from the same direction as the door that slammed. "Go and take your *TRA-bull* with you *BE-forr* there is more blood spilled."

He faded into the blackness. Which trouble did he mean? Old man Harvey? Doc? The lawman?

"Ottó, wait."

The footfalls stopped. "Here, kitty kitty," said a voice I knew well from my nightmares. "I can smell you, my pet."

Caly!

"Run, Boots," I heard from the darkness. Then someone shoved me backward.

I gasped in surprise, falling into the dark, bouncing onto the cold, hard wooden floor. I opened my eyes, frowning up at Harvey and Cooper, who were both bending over me.

Harvey reached down and pinched my arm.

"Dammit, Harvey!" I smacked his hand away.

"How many fingers am I holding up, Parker?" Cooper made the peace sign in front of my face.

"Enough to poke each of you in one eye." I pushed his hand away and scrambled to my feet. "What time is it?"

Harvey checked his pocket watch with his flashlight. "Almost eleven."

"What time exactly?"

"It's ten-forty-six," Cooper said. "What's with the sudden concern about time? You late for something?"

"You didn't hear her?"

"Hear who?" Harvey asked.

The sound of the second story door slamming open echoed down the hall. Cooper drew his gun, whirling toward the darkened doorway leading to the hall. Harvey grabbed his shotgun from the floor next to me.

"Don't move," I whispered to both of them.

Footfalls clacked across the wooden floor out front, echoing off the tall empty walls. "Here, kitty kitty," Caly repeated. "I can smell you, my pet."

Déjà vu, I thought. Ottó must have been giving me a warning of what was to come before fading back into the ether.

"Who in the fuck is that?" Cooper said quietly.

"Caly. She's here for our ten forty-seven meeting." I'd forgotten about this meeting actually, thanks to the distraction of Katrina's death. But Caly hadn't apparently.

I glanced around at the shadow heavy corners in the room. "Where's Doc?"

"He left," Harvey said.

"What do you mean he left?"

"He told us to keep an eye on you while he went to find the other ghost."

He left me? Wasn't he the one who always told me not to go out on my own? And what other ghost? I'd talked to Ottó after that bizarre talking doll had disappeared.

"Come out come out wherever you are, my kitten," Caly purred. "You can bring your little friends along, too."

"Who's she calling little?" Harvey asked, taking aim at the empty doorway.

"Cooper, give me your gun."

"No way in hell."

"Harvey, I need Bessie."

"I'd sooner hand ya my right nut than give up ol' Bessie."

His right nut was his favorite, of course. I growled. "Your bullets won't do any good against her. Besides, if either of you shoot, the cops will come."

"I'm already here."

"I mean more cops, including Detective Hawke."

"If our bullets won't work, why do you want our guns?" Harvey asked.

For batting practice. But I could see that neither man was going to play baseball with me, so I changed my tactic. "Cooper, give me your knife."

"I don't carry a knife."

"Why not?"

"Because I have a gun. Why do I need a knife?"

Harvey's hand bumped mine. "Here."

I held my hand out under his closed fist. He opened his hand and a Swiss Army knife fell into my palm.

Frowning down at the red casing with the cross logo on it, I sighed. "This is all you have? I thought you always liked to travel prepared."

"I do. That puppy is eight tools in one."

I opened the knife only to find the blade broken in half. When I held it out toward Harvey with a scowl, he frowned. "Hell. I forgot about breakin' that blade when I was poppin' a lid off an old gallon of paint."

"Great. Now what? Am I supposed to clip her to death?" I held up the knife with the fingernail clippers sticking out.

"Beggars can't be choosers," Cooper said.

With a final glare at both stubborn men, I told them, "Stay behind me, but don't shoot me in the backside."

I tiptoed toward the hall.

It was time to face off with Wanda's killer, as Prudence ordered when she had Cooper's fingers digging into my thigh. In lieu of my war hammer or any other sort of medieval battle ax or samurai sword or plain old shotgun, I decided to lead with the Swiss Army knife's corkscrew attachment sticking out between my knuckles.

"What are you going to do with that?" Cooper said when we reached the doorway and paused.

"She's gonna screw 'er," Harvey answered.

Something like that.

A movement at the end of the hall caught my attention.

"Hello, kitten." Caly stood there, backlit by the orange glow of streetlights coming through the front windows. "Where's my book?"

Chapter Twenty-Four

W hat's the magic word?" I asked Caly, tightening my grip on the Swiss Army knife in my palm. I had a feeling this was going to turn ugly quick, and I was going to be lucky to make it out with only scratches this time.

Caly's chin jutted. She said something in a language so foreign to me I couldn't begin to place its origin.

"Did you get that?" Harvey whispered.

"Not even a little." I chewed on my lower lip. That had sort of backfired on me. What magic word had she spoken? Should I be worried now about something else besides her sharp teeth and claws, dammit?

"Yer 'bout as useless as a needle without an eye."

"Can it, old man," I muttered out of the side of my mouth. To Caly, I said, "I'm not giving you the book." Mainly because I didn't think to bring it with me tonight, but also because I highly doubted she wanted it for her late night reading pleasure.

"The book does not belong to you, *Scharfrichter*."

"It doesn't belong to you either, Calypso." I'd once heard Dominick Masterson call her by that name and she hadn't liked it one bit. Something told me making waves was a good way to keep her off her game and give me the upper hand.

I heard a hissing sound come from her end of the hall. Her eyes seemed to be more reflective tonight, almost glowing in the flashlight beam I had locked onto her. Had she shucked her contacts, freeing those snake-like eyes I'd witnessed in the Opera House?

"You have met your match, kitten" she stepped toward me.

That's when I noticed the short sword-like blade attached to her arm—the one I'd stabbed last time we'd battled. The withered stump that remained served as a hilt, the blade somehow secured to the flesh. "That's a fancy hand shaker," I told her, lowering the light to it.

"Give me what is mine or I will use it to remove your head."

Criminy. Did it always have to be about decapitation with these white-haired freaks? "Why did you kill Wanda?"

"She mewled when I came for the book. It disgusted me."

"What is your fetish with cats?"

Caly took another step closer. "We kill for sport." She hissed again, showing off her sharp canines. After all of the vampire love played up in movies and books these days, I wasn't impressed. Now if she could distended her jaw and flash a set of shark teeth, that would make me look twice.

"Would you stay on task, Parker," Cooper bit out behind me.

The bossy detective must have been reading my thoughts. Fine. I returned to Caly's most recent bloody deed.

"Did you kill Katrina King?"

Her smile looked positively ghoulish in the beam from my flashlight. "Maybe." She practically purred the word.

"Why?"

"Her hunger for immortality made her useful."

"Useful how? Did she know how to free the Hungarian devil locked up in this place?"

"She thought she did."

I had no patience for her games tonight. "Stop fucking around and answer my questions, Caly."

"Or what, *Scharfrichter*? You'll slay me?"

Her thick sarcasm made my gut boil. When I thought of the way she'd killed Jane, Helen, and Wanda, the urge to rip her tongue out made me tighten my grip on the knife even more.

"Oh, I'll do more than slay you," I stretched my neck from side to side, gearing up for battle. "I'll take your stupid blade, gut you, and cram your innards down your throat like a Thanksgiving turkey."

"Jesus, Parker," Cooper said from his seat in the peanut gallery. "Hawke's right about your violent streak."

"She started it." I glared at Caly, sick of her games. She reminded me of a spoiled child tearing the wings off butterflies because she was bored. "Before I kick your ass for murdering my friends, the lawman here wants to know why you killed Katrina? How about you humor him so he'll quit pestering me?"

"Her death was your fault," Caly said.

"My fault?" Sheesh, first the caller in Ms. Wolff's apartment and now Caly. Did anyone else want to step forward and blame me for more murders that I didn't do? Anyone besides Detective Hawke?

"We cannot have you execute the succubus," Caly continued.

Who was *we*?

"So I helped it to escape its bondage."

"And then you killed Katrina with my war hammer?"

"The weapon was offered to me as a gift in exchange for freedom. Of course I could not turn down an opportunity to kill a human," she said that last word with a sneer. "Especially with a weapon belonging to a *Scharfrichter.*"

"You set me up on purpose." Caly would make a good chess player, the Deadwood police department acting as her pawns.

"We want what belongs to us."

"Yeah, I heard you the first five hundred times you sent that message."

"Give me the book or I will tear your daughter to pieces before your eyes."

The mention of Addy sent a zing of adrenaline down through my arms and out of my fingertips. There it was—the gauntlet. Thrown down at my feet. I would now have to kill or be killed to protect my child. Prudence wouldn't hesitate. Neither would I but not yet. I needed to know one more thing.

"Let me fill 'er full of holes." Harvey bumped me aside, doing his version of a guard dog, snarling and growling.

I grabbed his shoulder and pulled him back. "Wait." I had another question for the hissy bitch first. "Why are you hanging human body parts in the trees around here?"

I wasn't sure Caly was responsible for the foot Layne had found in that tree back in July, or the hand someone else had found up on Mount Roosevelt, but she might know the guilty party.

She laughed, haughty like. "It's bait, of course. It's about the only thing these disgusting monkey spawn are good for."

"Bait for what?"

"You shall see, my kitten." She lifted her sword to her mouth, her tongue flicking out and slowly licking up the blade.

I winced, my tongue shrinking back into my throat.

"You will be easy prey for the hunters, *Scharfrichter.*" She pointed the sword at me. "If I let you live that long."

"What hunters?"

"Enough questions!" She sliced a Z through the air with her sword.

She must have some Zorro aspirations. Santa should leave her a black mask under the Christmas tree this year.

"Give me the book!"

Hmmm. I didn't like her tone much. I opened my palm, frowning down at the Swiss Army knife in my hand. "I believe it's time to put an end to your long life, Caly."

I just hoped I had the right tool and enough grit to follow through without ending my own life in the process.

"We need to prove your innocence," Cooper reminded me. "You can't kill her."

I turned my head partway toward him while keeping my focus on Caly. "You heard what she said about my kid. I'm not letting this bitch live long enough to deliver on her threat."

"We need a confession from her, Parker."

"You think you can kill me, kitten?" She snickered. "You are part human, remember? That makes you weak and slow."

What did she mean by "part human"?

Something moved in the darkness behind Caly.

"I will tear out your heart be—"

A black shroud covered her ghoulish face, cutting her off, sliding down over her shoulders. Then a pair of arms wrapped around her from behind, locking hers down before she could free her sword or claws. She stumbled forward under the weight, falling facedown onto the floor with a muffled shriek of fury.

It all happened so fast, I didn't notice her captor until he looked up while struggling to hold the spitfire under his weight.

My mouth fell open. "Doc?"

His face was tight with the strain of holding Caly prisoner. "How about a little help with this wildcat, Coop?"

That's when I put together that the shroud was actually his leather coat and that Caly wouldn't be kept down for long.

Cooper raced to Doc's aid with me right behind him. I wrestled to get a grip on Caly's legs as she kicked wildly, finally sitting on them in order to win. Doc moved off of her enough for Cooper to handcuff her wrist to her makeshift sword hilt behind her back.

Cooper shined his light on the sword. "What the hell is that?"

"Look." I pointed at the disfigured flesh above the hilt, what was left of her arm above the elbow joint after I'd stabbed the glass into her forearm at our last meeting. "That's what I was trying to explain to you that night at the Opera House."

He leaned closer for a better look.

"Be careful," I warned.

"She's cuffed, Parker. Relax."

I thought of the way Caly had kicked and clawed when Dominick

Masterson had held her up by the scruff. I didn't have a lot of faith in those handcuffs.

Cooper and Doc flipped her over while I continued to hold her legs. "Watch her," I told Doc as she twisted and turned her head under the leather still cloaking her face. "It wouldn't surprise me if she tore her way free with her sharp teeth alone."

He tied his coat sleeves around her extra tight.

"Where were you?" I asked him.

"In the front corner closet." He indicated the location with his head, still holding onto Caly's shoulders. She was bucking with her whole body now. I could hear her hisses and her teeth gnashing through the leather.

"You left me," I said more questioning than accusing.

"Your energy kept sending out these blinding bursts of light. I had to put some space between us in order to see well enough to open the doorway and slip over to the other side."

"But *you* left me. Aren't you the one always telling me not to go anywhere without you?"

"I only left physically. Mentally, I was there with you while you spoke with the old doll Ottó sent in his place."

I let that soak in, thinking back to my time in the darkness with the two candle flames. "Ottó showed up later." And so had Doc, telling me to run. He must have been the one who shoved me back out of the darkness and into the room with Cooper and Harvey.

"I saw. He came when he heard Caly approaching. He alerted me to her arrival so I had time to return. I waited in the closet until she'd passed and I could come up with some way to stop her."

"What're we gonna do with this hellcat?" Harvey asked, prodding Caly's shoulder with his shotgun.

Her head turned under the coat in Harvey's direction. I heard the clacking of her teeth again.

"I need to do my job," I told Cooper in particular, since he was the main objector to me removing Caly from the equation.

Cooper shook his head. "I told you, we need her to clear your name and close several murder cases."

"What? You think you're going to take her into the station and she'll cooperate without tearing you all to pieces? I'll refer you to the blade attached to her arm."

"We'll keep her well-secured." His voice was all matter-of-fact, his will unbending. The cop in him ruled on the topic, leaving no room for rebuttal. "Uncle Willis, go get your pickup and back it up to the steps.

Then get your ass up here with the rope you keep under the seat. We'll need your help carrying her down."

Caly was still struggling, making inhuman noises and growls, wrenching her shoulders back and forth in spite of Doc's attempt to keep her in place, showing no sign of weariness. If Cooper thought he'd just stroll her through the Deadwood Police Station, he must have been smoking happy weed while I was playing patty cake with Ottó's old doll.

Harvey leaned Bessie against his shoulder and hitched toward the doorway.

I was watching him step outside and close the door when Caly snapped the chain holding the handcuffs together. I looked around in time to see her pop upright with enough force to send Cooper backward into the wall.

Caly's struggle for freedom knocked Doc's grip on her loose, and her arms were suddenly untethered. She tore off Doc's coat and with a hiss whirled on Cooper, raising her sword as she turned.

Without thinking, I sprung forward, deflecting her sword with my left forearm as she swung it toward Cooper's throat. Then I spun around and planted the corkscrew into the side of her throat.

Her snake eyes widened and bulged as I twisted the corkscrew deeper, leaning into her, shoving her off balance into the wall next to Cooper. She regained her bearings faster than I expected and lunged forward, sinking her teeth into my arm when she couldn't free her sword blade from behind her. I felt the powerful clench of her bite through my wool coat as black smoke began to billow out of the hole where I'd buried the corkscrew.

With an angry cry, I drove it deeper, winding the corkscrew further into her throat. The need to put an end to her malicious reign filled my every cell. "This is for Jane and Wanda, you fucking bitch." I shifted my weight, gaining more leverage while she continued to lash out at me. "And Helen Tarragon, too."

A high-pitched humming noise came from her chest, growing louder as she thrashed under my weight. I jammed my arm deeper into her jaws, sacrificing my arm to keep her from biting at my face. I let go of the corkscrew which was now firmly planted deep in her neck and grabbed a fistful of her spiky hair. I yanked her head back.

Her hate-filled snake eyes were now lined with something cloudy and dark, almost black, along with the lower half of her face. Death was spreading through her, weakening her finally. I could smell it thick and heavy in the back of my throat.

"You've met your match, kitten." I threw her words back at her and yanked my arm free of her jaws. Her skin withered, looking shrunken, hardened, like a long-dried Egyptian mummy. "Your killing days are through."

"We will destroy you, *Scharfrichter!*" she croaked through blackened lips, her voice crackly.

Keeping a tight grip on her hair, I leaned in close. I wanted my eyes to be the last she saw. "Adios, Calypso."

Vein-like fingers of blackness spread across the rest of her face. She writhed, opening her mouth wide in a silent scream as her face distorted, her nose and mouth elongating, her teeth lengthening as her lips pulled back.

I knew from experience what was going to happen next and shoved away from her, turning aside. "Cover your eyes," I yelled to Doc and Cooper, shielding my own as a bright flash of light lit up the hallway followed by a searing blast of heat.

When the light faded and the heat dissipated, Caly was gone. There was nothing more than a wisp of smoke and a sprinkling of ashes left. A cold draft of air blew open the door and swirled through the room, whisking them away.

"Holy fuck," Cooper said. He ran his fingers through his hair.

Doc grunted in agreement, leaning back against the wall.

Cooper's beam of light searched the floor where Caly had been, roving over Caly's blade and the Swiss Army knife lying there with the corkscrew still sticking out. He cursed and aimed the beam at me.

"Oops," I said, squinting in the spotlight.

"Dammit, Parker," Cooper stood, holstering his gun and then bending to pick up the blade. "I told you we needed her."

"That was an accident."

"Right. You just happened to fall forward and accidentally ram that corkscrew into her neck, twisting it as you fell?"

"Yeah, something like that."

"I saw the whole thing, remember?"

"And did you see how I saved your neck at the same time?"

"She would've missed me."

"Whatever! While you were watching the whole damned thing, did you see her turn to ash and smoke? That's what I was trying to tell you about the other one at the funeral parlor."

Doc pushed to his feet and then leaned down to pick up the Swiss Army knife on the floor between us, folding the corkscrew back into place. He helped me to my feet.

"She bit you." He pulled back the sleeve of my coat and checked my arm. Purplish-red marks marred my forearm, but no blood. "It doesn't look like she broke skin."

"Good, because I think she was a tiny bit rabid, minus the mouth foaming trick of course."

With a sigh, he pulled me into his arms, holding me close for several seconds. "I know why she killed Katrina," he spoke over my head.

"She hated blondes?" I asked, pulling away so I could look up at him.

"Not quite. The only way to release the *lidérc* from the wards imprisoning it was to let it attach to a host. Caly convinced Katrina that the *lidérc* would impart the immortality she craved. After the joining occurred, Caly cut Katrina's thumb and used her blood to smear over the ward, telling her it was part of the process."

"That explains the cut Eddie noticed," Cooper said.

A cut? That was news to me.

"That allowed the *lidérc* to leave the confines of the building. However, it was still imprisoned in Katrina's body—until Caly freed it."

"By bludgeoning Katrina with my war hammer?"

"She pierced Katrina's heart to set it free."

"Did Ottó show you this?"

He shook his head. "The old doll did, or rather the little girl that Ottó killed while trying to remove the *lidérc* back in Hungary. She was using the doll, hiding behind the illusion of it. After Ottó killed the girl, the *lidérc* attached to him, but it held onto the little girl even after her death. She was a trophy of sorts is my guess."

But now it must have let her and Ottó go, since they were still here and it was gone.

"This is just fucking great," Cooper said, stalking out into the front room. He pointed Caly's blade at me. "Let me make sure I have this straight. We have two ghosts here, no *lidérc*, and the killer has turned to ash and floated away. This is going to look real fucking fine on paperwork, Parker."

"Try to see the upside, Mr. Glass-Is-Half-Empty," I snapped back at him. "I eliminated the one who killed Jane Grimes, Helen Tarragon, Wanda Carhart, Katrina King, and Lord only knows how many others over the years. There will be no more bodies on your case board thanks to Caly's handiwork."

"I know that and you know that," he glared at me, "but how in the hell am I going to convince Hawke and the Chief and everyone else that we got our killer?"

"I found yer pot o' gold, Coop," Harvey said from the doorway. He stood in profile with Bessie held at waist level, her double barrels aimed at something outside the door.

"What are you talking about, Uncle Willis?" Cooper sounded tired, defeated.

Harvey stepped back. "You first," he said toward the steps.

Doc moved in front of me, shielding me.

I heard the old wooden floorboards creak by the door. My stomach cramped, the sudden churning making me clutch my side and swallow fast.

"No fucking way," I heard Cooper say. "Where in the hell have you been?"

Who had Harvey found outside? Another albino? The juggernaut's twin? Swallowing down the nausea crawling up my throat, I peeked around Doc.

Holy cheeseballs!

Dominick Masterson stood in the doorway with Harvey's shotgun pointed at his back.

His gaze zeroed in on me. "Hello, Violet," he said in that whiskey smooth voice of his. "It looks like you've been busy."

* * *

Wednesday, November 21st

I slept like the dead. The non-ghost kind of dead, anyway.

When I woke the next morning, I was alone in my bed and for the life of me couldn't remember how I'd ended up there. I lay in my warm flannel sheets, replaying the pieces I remembered from the night prior.

After Dominick had arrived, Cooper had wanted to send Harvey, Doc, and me off in the pickup, leaving him to interrogate Dominick without me there to interfere. Cooper hadn't minced words on that. He was still pissy about my removing Caly from the picture.

I'd hesitated to leave him, expressing concern that Dominick had another wall-breaking trick up his sleeve, only this time he might break Cooper, but the stubborn detective assured me he had it under control.

So, while the control freak was busy giving instructions to his uncle and Doc, Dominick had waved me over to where he stood next to one of the windows.

Something about Masterson made me nauseated when I stood too close, so I kept a few feet between us.

"I won't hurt the lawman, *Scharfrichter*," he said quietly.

Aunt Zoe was right. There'd be no hiding who I really was anymore. My enemies knew I was in town and why—probably more than I did. "Why did you return, Dominick?"

"I had no choice."

"Because of Caly's latest murder spree?"

He smirked, at least I thought it was a smirk. In the orange light, the half of his face that wasn't hidden in shadows looked more ghoulish than usual. "She used to be so obedient. Then Katrina and the others started putting ideas into her head."

"Like killing Jane?"

He nodded. "And Helen."

So, Katrina had been behind those two murders? "Why? What did they do to her?"

"They did nothing." His dark gaze swung my way. "Katrina wanted me, but I refused to take her as a lover. Helen, however, intrigued me. When Katrina learned of my interest in Helen, she ordered Caly to eliminate her. Jane was working as Katrina's agent at the time, helping her negotiate for the purchase of this building from me even though I'd repeatedly refused to sell. She overheard the order to have Helen killed, so Caly murdered Jane on the spot." He sighed and turned back to the window. "All of this death for what? Jealousy? Lust? Humans can be so juvenile."

"Katrina told me she wanted to be immortal. Could you have made her one of you?"

He scoffed. "There is no immortality for humans, nor my kind for that matter."

"So you came back because of Caly and Katrina?"

"No." He wrote something on the window with his fingertip, a symbol of some sort that burned deep orange before fading. "I came back because of you."

"Me?"

"We need you."

There was that *we* again. "For what? And if you say you need to impregnate me with a demon's spawn, I'm going to tell you to go blow a goat-pig, or whatever that thing is on the tattoo Katrina and Lila had."

"*Caper-sus.*"

"Come again."

"It's a form of Latin. The creature's name. It originally symbolized a mixture of spiritual ambition and power or strength, but Katrina's group has given it a much darker meaning." He glanced behind me. I followed his gaze. Doc was watching us, his eyes narrowed and his mouth tight as he looked at Dominick.

"You've assembled a team." He smiled at me, his white teeth reflecting the orange coming through the window. "You're smarter than most expected. That will work to your benefit when the hunters come."

Who were these hunters Caly and now Dominick spoke of? Executioner hunters? Bounty hunters?

Before I could ask, Dominick continued. "The enemy of my enemy is my friend."

"Who's your enemy?"

"You are, *Scharfrichter*. I've been ordered to come back and help you."

"Parker!" Cooper stalked over to us with a face full of surly scowls. "Get out of here before you kill another key witness."

"Caly wasn't a witness," I corrected him. "She was a murderer."

Cooper turned to Doc, who walked up behind him. "Get her out of here, Nyce, before I arrest her for pissing off an officer of the law."

"That's sweet," I said to Cooper as Doc took my hand and began to lead me away. "This is the thanks I get for saving your life. Next time, I'll let any crazy psycho bitches in the area slice you in half."

"Good," he snapped back. "Then I'd be out of my fucking misery instead of neck deep in another one of your messes."

I hissed at him, taking a card from Caly's deck. "That man needs counseling," I told Doc.

"His stress level is out the window," Doc said. "Remember, he's only recently come to see the paranormal world. That's tough on someone who's used to seeing things in black and white."

"Coop may have his horns out at the moment, but he's as smart as a bunkhouse rat," Harvey said. "If he wants you out of here, it's because he is tryin' to save yer bacon." He held open the door for Doc and me. "So let's vamoose before any other badge-toters show up fer the party."

Harvey had dropped me off at home where Aunt Zoe waited for me. Doc wanted to go home, shower, and crash. With Caly no longer in the game, there were no worries about playing night guard on the couch for me and the kids, so I sent him on his way along with Harvey.

Aunt Zoe listened to my tale between my yawns, then I must have fallen asleep on the table. I had a hazy memory of her walking me up the stairs but nothing else.

Now with the morning sunlight peeking through my window, I felt renewed and ready to face a day full of Jerry, Mona, and Ben. Hell, even the séance to kick Wilda from Cornelius's life tomorrow night didn't dampen my outlook since the weight of Caly's threats had been removed from my world.

I checked on the kids and headed to the shower. I took my time, enjoying the hot water until it began to turn cold. When I returned to my bedroom, my phone chirped. Someone had sent me a message.

I picked up my phone expecting Doc, maybe even Jerry, hoping it wasn't Cooper with a first thing in the morning ass chewing. Or worse, Hawke.

The sight of Tiffany's name made me frown. I tapped on the message to read the whole thing: *If you're under the delusion that Doc is your Prince Charming, ready to rescue you and your children with his castle and money, think again, Cinderella. He will see soon enough that the glass slipper is too big for you.*

Due to a lack of caffeine after a freak-filled night, I had to read her message two more times before it sank into my foggy brain. Then I threw my phone on the bed and covered it with my pillow, pretending it was Tiffany I was suffocating.

Criminy. Why couldn't Doc have had sport sex with a non-demented chick with droopy boobs and a flabby ass?

I dropped onto the side of my bed, sitting with my head between my knees until the blood started pounding in my temples for a reason other than rage.

If I showed Doc the message, how would he react? Would he believe her?

I had been pretty pathetic when we'd met with barely any money in my bank account and not a sale to be found. As Tiffany had said, he'd stepped in and played Prince Charming, buying his house from me and keeping me from losing my job. But then I'd gone on to sell the hotel to Cornelius without Doc stepping in to help. If anything, Mona was playing the heroine in my world, helping me land sales and sharing commissions with me. Doc was more often there to pick me up emotionally and dust me off, giving me someone to lust over … and someone to love who didn't share my bloodline.

A clucking sound came from my closet. I lifted my head, looking over at my closet door as it inched open. Elvis's beak pushed out, then one wing, nudging the door open further until she could slip through the opening. Ignoring me completely, she strutted past me all the while clucking to herself and exited through the crack I'd left in my bedroom door.

I stood and walked over to my closet, opening the door wide. Inside, she'd left me an egg on the floor between my purple cowboy boots, which were slightly crushed and dusted with tiny white down feathers.

I bent down and picked up the egg. It was still warm.

Palming Elvis's parting gift, I stared down at the boots, my heart picking up speed in my chest.

I knew what I needed to do.

I grabbed my boots.

Chapter Twenty-Five

The Picklemobile was in the parking lot when I arrived at Calamity Jane Realty. Instead of heading into the office, I veered and stepped inside Doc's back door.

"Doc?" I called out, giving him a heads up that I was there.

"Out front."

I could smell his woodsy aftershave when I passed by the open restroom door. He must have hit the gym this morning. And here I'd thought just making it to the shower had been an accomplishment after our go around with Caly last night.

I found Doc sitting behind his desk in the front room. Papers were spread out across the desktop next to his open laptop. His green, long sleeve T-shirt and faded blue jeans were all about comfort, not impressing clients. His hair still looked damp from the shower.

I set my tote on the floor next to his desk without saying a word and walked straight to his door, flipping the Open sign to Closed and twisted the lock.

"Am I closing up shop?" he asked.

I didn't answer. Instead, I lowered the blinds covering the door and the front windows, shutting out the world. When I turned around, he was leaning back in his chair, watching me intently in the darkened room.

"We need to talk," I told him, returning to stand across the desk from him. I turned on his desk lamp to shine some light on our situation.

One of his eyebrows rose. "Is this about last night?"

"Nope." I pulled my phone from my pocket, selecting Tiffany's latest message, and held it out for him to see.

The other eyebrow lifted. "Did Cooper text you already this morning?"

"Not Cooper."

He took the phone and looked down at it. The room was silent except for the old heat radiator ticking by the window as he read Tiffany's message. When he finished, he lowered my phone to his desk. His jaw was rigid. Frown lines fanned from the corners of his eyes. I hoped that anger was meant for Tiffany, but I wasn't going to play any guessing games this time. No more dancing around the truth.

"Before you say anything," I started, swallowing the fluttering sensation that was inching up my throat. "I have something I need to say."

I wiped my sweaty palms on my dark blue corduroy skirt and straightened my purple sweater, dredging up some courage as I squirmed.

He watched me, his gaze guarded.

"Tiffany thinks I'm in this relationship for your money." My heart pounded in my chest, making my voice vibrate slightly. Oh man, I was going to bungle this if I didn't get a grip.

"Violet, you know Tiffany—"

I stopped him with my raised hand. "I'm not done yet."

He frowned but held his tongue.

"Tiffany is wrong." I thought about the commission check I'd received for Doc's house. "Sort of."

He leaned back in his chair, his focus one hundred percent locked on me.

"You see, I've gone and screwed things up a few times when it comes to you and me. With us. I mean in regard to our relationship."

Hells bells! This was why I had decided years ago to stick to sex with no strings. This deep, emotional shit was for the birds.

I swallowed in spite of the dry patches in the back of my throat that were making my voice sound raspy. "But I need to make it clear here and now that I don't expect you to play Prince Charming and rescue me and my kids." As much as I wanted to look down at my boots, up at the ceiling, anywhere other than into his dark brown eyes, I held course. "We've bumbled along for almost a decade now, and I expect that we'll continue to bounce and rattle our way through the next decade."

His forehead wrinkled.

I licked my lips. "But that doesn't mean I'd object if you wanted to bounce and rattle with us for however long you'd like. I just don't want you to ever feel obligated when it comes to us."

"Violet," he started again, but I shook my head.

"Give me a minute. I'm almost to the reason I've come here this morning." I pressed my palms together and held my hands up to my lips, praying to Aphrodite that I didn't botch this up royally. "I don't want your money, Doc. It's true that I've had my fair share of financial struggles, and I expect to brave those rough waters again from time to time in the future, but for now the kids and I are doing okay." Thanks to him, Cornelius, and Wanda, of course.

Lowering my hands to his desk, I continued with my bumbling message. "The reason I came here today and showed you Tiffany's latest text is not to have you give me a hug and reassure me that you and I are doing 'fine' as a couple. You have made it clear over the last four months that you find me attractive and enjoy my company."

A smile ghosted his face, but after searching mine, he sobered again. "Then why are you here?"

My knees trembled. I started to answer twice, only to stop each time and regroup.

"For Christ's sake, Violet." He stood, clearly sharing my agitation. He crossed his arms over his chest. "Just spit it out so we can deal with Tiffany's bullshit."

"Fine!" I jammed my hands on my hips. "I've fallen in love with you, damn it. But just because I told you how I feel doesn't mean I expect you to spend the rest of your life taking care of me and mine. And I'm certainly not thinking about wedding dresses or diamond rings, so don't go getting antsy about me bringing up the M word."

Okay, maybe I was thinking about the M word a teeny tiny bit, but that was my secret until death did we part or he up and left, whichever came sooner.

Doc stared across his desk at me without a smile or frown, not saying a word in response to my big announcement. I felt my cheeks warm. "I wanted to tell you how I feel before Tiffany comes along and whispers her lies in your—"

"Say it again."

"The part about Tiffany?"

"No. The other part."

I felt a drop of sweat roll down my back. "I love you, Doc. But I don't expect you to marry me or adopt my kids or any—"

"Did that hurt?" His lips twitched ever so slightly.

This wasn't going anything like I'd hoped or imagined. I fidgeted with a pen lying on his desk. "Did what hurt?"

"Finally saying that aloud?"

I slowly spun the pen in a circle, mirroring the way I felt at the moment. "It did a little, in a jumping off the high dive and getting water up my nose sort of way."

A trace of a grin appeared on his face. "You should keep practicing. The jump will get easier."

"How do you know? You've only said it to me once."

"And you said nothing in return."

"I thought you might be playing the part of Gomez again. Then we were interrupted and the moment was gone."

He smirked. "Gone and not to return for a whole damned month."

"It wasn't a whole month."

"It felt like twelve to me." He stuffed his hands in his pockets. "I wasn't playing Gomez when I told you that."

"You could have said it again after that night."

"And risk sounding like a fool? I jumped off that high dive first, remember?"

I looked him up and down, tapping the pen on his desktop. "You could say it again now."

He came around his desk and took the pen from my nervous fingers. Clasping my hand, he rubbed his thumb over the back of my knuckles. "You have me so turned around that I don't know which way is up anymore."

I pointed at the ceiling. "It's that-a-way, along with the stars." And my head probably if he'd say the actual words again.

He leaned closer, his lips touching mine, stealing my breath along with another piece of my heart. I closed my eyes, sinking into him as he returned for a second kiss, longer this time and deeper, hungrier.

"Open your eyes," he said when he pulled away.

I raised my eyelids, meeting his dark gaze.

"I'm in love with you, Violet Parker."

There went my head, floating up past the moon in record speed. It'd reach the Hubble telescope in no time at this rate.

I wrapped my arms around his neck. "I love you, too, Dane R. Nyce." He was right, it was an easier jump this time.

He kissed me again, only harder and with more intensity, blasting my heart high into the sky after my head.

"I have something for you," I said when his mouth slid over my cheek.

He chuckled and pressed against me. "I have something for you, too, Boots."

Good, we were on the same page. I pulled free from his arms and extracted a small paper sack from my tote. "A gift just for you." I held it out for him to take.

He looked at the sack but didn't touch it. "You brought me lunch?"

"Not lunch. Breakfast." I shook the bag. "Take it. It's one of your favorites."

He obliged, opening the sack enough to peek inside. "What did you …" He reached inside and pulled out a pair of red satin panties.

They matched the bra I had on under my sweater.

"You said I owed you breakfast." I plucked my underwear from his hand and tossed them onto his pile of paperwork, then I hopped up on the desk next to both. "Well, here I am."

Capturing his hands, I placed both on my bare knees under the hem of my skirt. Then I pulled my sweater off over my head so he could admire the matching bra.

He stared down at my chest. "Is this really happening?"

"I can pinch you again if you'd like proof."

"Hell, no." His attention moved to my lips. "I've been on the receiving end of your pinches before. The bruises last a week."

"Ahhh, poor boy." I reached down and unbuttoned his jeans, sliding my hand inside his waistband. "How about if I hurt you in a good way instead?"

"I'm yours for the taking, vixen."

His breath hitched when I did just that, taking him in hand while seducing his mouth with mine. I didn't stop until he'd gone to the moon and back. By then, I was all hot and bothered as well.

"I want you now." I hauled his hand under my skirt and showed him where and how.

"You're going to have to give me a minute to catch my breath, Boots."

I was normally a patient woman but not this morning, not after the promises he'd made while I'd worked him into a heated lather moments ago.

"Or we could try something else that might speed things up a bit for you." I slid onto the floor and turned around so my back was to him.

"What are you doing?"

"Watch." I unhooked my bra, letting the straps slide down off my shoulders with a provocative shrug. Then I let the satin fall to the floor at my purple boots.

"Damn."

"There's more." I leaned back against him, sliding my arms up around his neck so I could pull his head down and kiss along his jaw while I pressed back into his hips.

His palms slid over my bare skin, his touch hot. "You're so soft," he whispered in my ear, nipping at the lobe as his fingers grazed my breasts before sliding down to explore the bare skin hidden under my skirt. I moaned, my body spiraling as his fingers worked their magic on me.

I'd almost come undone when he stopped. "Put your hands on my desk," he ordered, his voice gravelly with need.

"You sure you want to mess up all of this paperwork?" I teased.

"Now, Violet." He hiked up my skirt, nudging my legs apart.

I obeyed, shoving papers and folders aside.

His hands blazed a trail up the back of my legs and over my hips, cupping my breasts before grazing down over my stomach and upper thighs—almost touching where I wanted him most, but not quite.

I was panting and trembling when he pressed against me.

"Remember when you teased me about frisking you against my desk?" he asked.

"Yes." I moaned in anticipation.

"And then bending you over and making a mess of my paperwork?"

"God, yes!" My body throbbed. I moved against him, trying to ease the ache.

"I haven't been able to stop fantasizing about you and me here in my office." He gripped my hips. "About doing this."

I gasped at how fast he slid inside of me. For a second, he held still, his breath steaming the back of my neck as he waited for my body to adjust to him. Then I moved against him, wanting more, and he was all over me, caressing and kneading, stroking and teasing until my back arched and I cried his name. Pleasure rolled clear through to my fingertips and toes.

He wasn't long after me, holding me tight, praising me in a throaty, lust-filled voice that gave me another rash of goosebumps. When the last of our groans and moans faded, all that was left was our heavy breathing.

"You are incredible, Violet." His forehead rested between my shoulder blades. "The sight of you bent over my desk in those boots is something I'll never forget." He kissed his way up my spine.

I sighed under his tender kisses. "You've been teasing me for weeks. I was ready to go supernova on you at the slightest touch."

"I noticed. Oh man, did I notice." He kissed the nape of my neck and then stood, moving away. "Thanks for breakfast, Boots," he said, buttoning his jeans as I turned around.

"You're a big tipper." I collected my red undies and the matching bra, slipping both on as he watched with rapt attention. "That went better than I'd hoped."

A snort of laughter came from him. "You expected a different outcome after giving me a sack with your panties in it?"

I shrugged, straightening my skirt. "Tiffany worked hard to fill my head with unhappy thoughts."

He handed me my sweater. "I warned you about her."

"I know." I slipped my sweater over my head. "But she's so pretty and perf—"

"She's not you." He pulled me close, his kiss sweet and gentle this time. "I want you and only you, Violet. It's been like that from day one."

I smiled up at him with big hearts in my eyes. Little bluebirds flapped around my head, tweeting in happiness. All that was missing were Bambi and Thumper at my feet. "That sounds like a sickness to me."

His chuckle was low, sexy. "You're a regular heart attack."

My phone started playing the Globetrotters' theme song. "That would be Jerry."

Doc leaned in for one last kiss, and then he handed me my phone. "You'd better take that."

I did. Jerry told me to meet him and the others at Bighorn Billy's for a filming wrap-up. When I hung up, Doc was straightening the mess we'd made on his desk.

"I have to go." I stuffed the phone in my tote.

"I heard." He half sat on the corner of his desk. "When is Zoe taking Addy and Layne down to your parents?"

"Tomorrow morning."

"Do you want alone time with them tonight?"

I smiled, appreciating his unspoken offer. "We've had alone time for almost ten years, so if you feel up to spending the evening with us, I'd like that."

"There's a PBS special on this evening about the engineering behind some of the well-known Maya temples. Layne asked me to watch it with him."

"Okay, but you're stuck with Addy and me, too, and probably Aunt Zoe as well." She'd finished with the glass order for Denver and had it all ready to ship off after the holiday.

"I'm cool with all of them except for you."

"Oh, yeah?"

He nodded. "With you, I'm always hot." He fanned himself and pretended to swoon. I grinned, lightly slapping him on the shoulder before kissing him goodbye.

I headed back out to my SUV and down the road, my head still floating in the clouds all of the way to Bighorn Billy's.

* * *

Thursday, November 22nd (Thanksgiving Day)

Doc spent the night at Aunt Zoe's.

This time, instead of the couch, he slept in my bed with the kids snoozing right down the hall.

And he slept with *me* in the bed next to him under the sheets all night long. Apparently, those three words I'd told him earlier in his office had acted like a golden ticket for him to enter my *boudoir*.

My camisole and underwear ensemble had earned me plenty of ogling and touching from him, but in spite of sharing a bed we hadn't done more than get handsy under the sheets. It was more of a test to see how our slumber parties would go over in the future while Aunt Zoe and the kids were within hearing distance. Although, there'd been a moment shortly after the sun had risen when I'd teased him awake with my mouth and he'd almost finished me with his tongue. But then the kids had started fighting in the bathroom so I'd had to hit the pause button and go play referee.

I gave both Addy and Layne a technical for fouling up my chances of early morning nookie. Only I didn't use those exact words and instead threatened to ground them if they acted like rotten brats at their grandparents' house while under Aunt Zoe's care. All the while I had to pretend I wasn't feeling well, staying in my bathrobe to go along with the ploy Aunt Zoe and I had planned as my excuse for not attending Thanksgiving at my parents. This turkey day would be spent with an ectoplasmic rotten brat and her creepy clown doll instead of my own sweet monsters. Lucky me.

The kids didn't seem to notice that Doc had slept in my bed instead of on the couch since he was dressed in his jeans and a flannel shirt when they made it downstairs, and I didn't make a grand production of it. We'd cross that bridge when they caught him in my sheets some other day.

After a quick breakfast of cereal for the kids, I fake swooned and held my stomach while I kissed each of them goodbye. "Remember," I warned, "you two need to be good for Aunt Zoe and your grandparents."

"Yes, Mother," Addy said, slipping her arms into her coat. "Don't forget to feed Elvis and let her outside a few times to air her feathers."

"I won't. Don't believe anything your Aunt Susan tells you."

"We know, Mom," Layne said while looking from me to Doc, who stood in the kitchen archway, and back again. His little forehead wrinkled.

"And give your Uncle Quint a big hug and sloppy kiss on the cheek from me," I added.

"I can't wait to see Uncle Quint," Addy's voice was high pitched and giggle-filled as she zipped up her coat. She pulled open the front door and skipped outside. "Hurry up, Aunt Zoe!" Without a backward glance, she was gone.

My brother had a way of making females act silly like that.

Layne dragged his feet even though I knew he was just as thrilled to see his uncle. "You could come to Thanksgiving later after your stomach starts feeling better."

"We'll see, sweetheart. In the meantime, don't worry about me and have fun. Your grandfather told me last week on the phone that he wants to have an Indiana Jones marathon with you today."

That lit my son up like a Vegas marquee. He bounced toward the door, glancing back at Doc long enough to say, "Take care of Mom. She needs lots of crackers and soup when she's sick."

Doc saluted him. "I'm on it, chief."

After one last worried frown at me, Layne followed his sister.

Aunt Zoe trailed the two of them, carrying a box filled with a container of chicken salad and a dish of green bean casserole, along with two pies, both cherry. I was sad to see them go—the pies and Aunt Zoe. I wondered if she'd notice if one of the pies disappeared before she left the house.

"Focus on what you need to do tonight, kiddo." She leaned her cheek out for a kiss from me. "And remember, be careful not to let anything else come through when you open that doorway."

I nodded. "You sure you need that second pie?"

She laughed. "Your brother is in town. He requested one cherry pie all to himself, and you know I can't resist Quint when he's being sweet and charming." She sobered and turned to Doc. "Watch over her for me, Doc."

"I promise."

"Let me know when it's over so I can sleep tonight," she told me over her shoulder and stepped outside.

"Be careful around the bitch from Hell," I warned from the porch as she walked down the steps. "She's been known to bite." Much like Caly, now that I thought about it.

"She only bites you, dear."

Grumbling about Susan's sharp teeth under my breath, I waved goodbye to Aunt Zoe and the kids as she drove away. My heart felt cloudy with a chance of rain when I closed the door. Then I looked across the room at Doc and the sun came out again.

"Cornelius called earlier while you were helping the kids pack," Doc told me from where he still stood in the archway, his shoulder against the wall.

"Let me guess, he wants me to bring double D batteries tonight and two pints of bat's blood."

"Double D?"

"Don't ask." I patted him on the chest on the way into the kitchen, needing coffee and something to eat now that I didn't have to pretend I had a stomachache anymore.

Doc stared at me, his expression mirroring Layne's before he'd left. "Cornelius didn't mention batteries or blood."

"Then why are you looking at me like that?"

"Because he changed his mind about where he wants to hold the séance."

"If he wants to go back up to Wild Bill's grave, I'm out. It's too damned cold."

"Not Mount Moriah."

I finished pouring the coffee and set down the cup. "Where?"

"The Hessler property."

My hand went to my chest in surprise. "But that's burned down."

"Not the house. The root cellar."

No! I took a step back, my butt bumping into the stove. No way. That was not going to happen. Not even drunk on a bet.

Last night, I'd had plain old dreams floating through my head while I slept. Happy dreams. There might even have been a unicorn and a rainbow in one of them. Not one nightmare had shown up to ruin my sleepy-time. But if I went down into that root cellar, I had a feeling I'd regress to waking up screaming and bathed in sweat for another month.

"Cooper will never go along with that location," I told Doc, thankful for once that the detective was such a stickler for rules and his off-limits, "police business" mantra. "Besides, that would be trespassing, wouldn't it?"

"Cornelius said he'd already contacted Coop and cleared it with him."

"No. Fucking. Way."

He nodded. "I called Coop to confirm it, and it's true. Apparently, Coop hasn't closed the Hessler case yet. He'd been told to wait and see if any other local missing children reports could be tied to Hessler. So the police still have the keys to the lock on the root cellar door, and access has to be cleared through Cooper."

"What about Detective Hawke?"

"Any possible related kidnappings are supposed to fall under Cooper's jurisdiction, so he is the sole detective in charge."

"But why would he agree to letting us go down there? That's not like Cooper." His first reaction was usually to reject such a request; his second reaction was to shoot whoever asked. "You think the *lidérc* has latched onto him?"

Doc raised his brow. "Are you looking for another excuse to beat up poor Coop?"

"I don't need an excuse when it comes to that bossy mule." I lifted my coffee, taking a sip and making a face.

"You forgot sugar." He grabbed the jar off the table and held it out to me, but then pulled it back when I reached for it and snagged me by my robe belt, reeling me in. "I could use some sugar, too."

"I'll trade you." I untied my belt and let my robe fall open, making room for his hands. "One sweet for another."

He placed the sugar on the counter, his hands sliding inside of my robe as he backed me into the counter. "After abstaining all night with your curves pressing into me, I'm going to need more than just one sweet." He kissed me. "You taste like coffee."

I took the jar of sugar and sprinkled some onto my tongue. "There. Now I taste like sugar."

He chuckled and kissed me again, skimming his palms down over the curves that had pressed into him throughout the night. "How about we go upstairs and make your bed creak?"

"What about tonight in the root cellar?"

"Well, I prefer your bedroom. It's warmer and has a soft mattress. But if you're into sex in creepy places, I'll give it a whirl for you."

I playfully pinched him. "You know what I meant."

"First, come upstairs with me and let me take your mind off of tonight for a while."

"Then what?"

"Then we'll take a field trip down to what remains of the Hessler house and take a look around, get a feel for the place, see if we can get Cooper to join us and unlock the root cellar door for a peek inside."

"You sound like you're game to have the séance there."

"It makes sense. That's where I first met Wilda. It's her home turf."

"But root cellars are creepy. What if Wilda is one of many ghosts that we run into down there?"

"That's why I want to go check it out. I'd like to try to be more prepared."

I leaned my forehead against his chest. "I'm afraid that if we have the séance there, Wolfgang will show up. I don't know if I can keep it together if he joins us."

"You're much stronger now than you were when you met him." He rubbed his chin on the top of my head. "You'll kick his ass if he tries to tell you how you're his one true love and woo you into the afterworld."

That made me chuckle. I looked up at him. "You're just jealous that he beat you to the punch," I teased.

"Maybe," he played along. "Or maybe I didn't like the way he looked at you."

"With his dreamy blue eyes?"

"Dreamy, huh?" He laced his fingers through mine. "He bugged me from the start. A golden boy with diamonds up his sleeves. With him in the picture, I didn't have a chance with you."

"*Au contraire, mon amour.*"

"Tish, that's French," he mimicked Gomez.

I held out my arm for him to play along and kiss. Instead, he lifted me up and threw me over his shoulder, heading for the staircase with me laughing all of the way. When we got up to my room, he peeled off my robe. My camisole and underwear followed shortly and then his briefs. My laughter ebbed, lust taking over.

"Doc." I pushed him down onto the bed and crawled on top of him. Skin on skin, I rested on his chest, our legs tangling.

His hands roamed down my ribs and over my hips. "What, Boots?"

"Don't leave me tonight."

His dark eyes met mine. "I'll be right there in the root cellar."

"I wasn't talking about at the Hessler house. I mean afterward, if we make it out alive and still sane."

"You want me to spend the night here again?"

"Yes, please."

"Is this going to become a habit?"

"Maybe."

His smile strummed my heart strings. "Good, now kiss me, woman."

I hovered over his lips. "One more thing."

One eyebrow lifted.

"I like your sexy brown eyes way more than Wolfgang's dreamy blue ones."

"You sure?"

I nodded. "They're like dark chocolate, very tempting, making my mouth water."

"You don't say?"

"Definitely." I straddled his hips, brushing against him, teasing. "And I *really* love chocolate."

"Show me, Violet." His dark gaze held mine as he guided the way, sliding inside of me in a slow, smooth move that made me moan and want more.

I took over then, showing him several other things I loved about him, and forgot about creepy ghosts, haunted houses, and annoying cops ... for a little while anyway.

Chapter Twenty-Six

Later that night …

Natalie picked up Cornelius from his hotel and met Doc and me an hour before midnight in front of the Hessler house. We'd parked a block away in different directions in case Detective Hawke or any officers from the Thanksgiving skeleton crew decided to drive past the place.

For the second time today, I skirted the remains of the house, its stone block foundation littered with charred wood and twisted metal. Doc and I had visited earlier in the daylight, checking out the ruins. In the dark, I could barely make out the front porch with its steps going up to a partially collapsed floor. The burned remains of the back porch looked even more ominous in our flashlight beams. The footing pillars stuck up like round teeth through the debris.

I looked away from the blackened mess, trying not to think about what I was about to do here tonight so my legs would keep moving toward the root cellar instead of turning and sprinting all of the way back to Aunt Zoe's place.

The air was still, like the cooler room in the makeshift morgue at Mudder Brothers. I could smell a tinge of wood smoke in it. The tall dry grass crackled as we walked, dead weeds grabbing at our pant legs. The world around us was heavily shadowed, the garage and root cellar door outside the reach of the nearest streetlight's orange glow. The lack of moonlight made it feel as if someone had covered Deadwood with a thick bolt of black velvet bedazzled with starry diamonds. Every now and then a dog barked further up in the Presidential district, the sharp sound echoing off the steep walls of the gulch.

Cooper was waiting for us, stepping out of the shadows from behind the old garage that had survived the fire thanks to Reid and his crew. "I took off the padlock," he said, leading the way over to the root cellar, which was partially hidden by dried grass. He reached down and flipped open the door.

We hadn't bothered him earlier to let us inside the cellar, deciding to explore the place on our own without the tension he might add. Now as I stared down at the dark, gaping mouth daring us to enter, I sort of wished we had.

Doc went first, ducking under the low headframe, leading the way with his flashlight. I followed into the cramped, eight-by-ten room. Shelves lined the brick walls from floor to ceiling. I sniffed, detecting an odor mixed with the musty dirt, something rotten. Then I noticed the small pile of salt chunks in one corner and a wave of revulsion made me grab onto Doc's coat and swallow fast several times.

"You okay?"

"I can smell them."

"Ghosts?" His voice was laced with surprise.

"No. The dead …" I couldn't say it, the memory of their decomposing faces still too clear.

Doc picked up on what I was saying and put his arm around me. "It's in your head, Killer. I can't smell anything."

"Smell what?" Cornelius asked, joining us. He carried a hard shell suitcase, which he immediately unsnapped and started unloading onto the cobwebbed, dusty cellar shelves. He set out several fancy-looking meters and two EVP recording devices that he'd used in Harvey's barn. Last was a bundle of dried sage and a video camera.

He knew my feelings on being recorded during a séance, but I reiterated my lack of love for the camera in case he'd had a brain fart.

"Brains do not emit methane gas, Violet," he told me while stabilizing the camera on a tripod. "I'm surprised you weren't aware of that."

"Shush it and hurry up, ghost whisperer. The sooner we get this show on the road, the closer we are to me going home and watching some Bogart and Bacall from under the covers." With Doc, I didn't add, but patted his backside as he helped Cornelius set up his equipment.

Natalie came down next, carrying that damned, creepy clown cookie jar top. "Where should I put this?" she asked Cornelius.

"Bend over and I'll show you," I told her.

"Parker," Cooper said from midway down the steps, "what is your fixation with shoving foreign objects into body cavities?"

"I don't know." I glared up at him. "It probably comes from getting the shaft from the Deadwood cops so many times."

Natalie laughed. "You have to admit, Coop, that was a good answer." She set the clown head on the shelf next to one of Cornelius's recorders. I frowned at it, cursing that dang author, Terri Reid, under my breath for filling Natalie's head with new ways of terrorizing me.

"I have a feeling it's going to be a wild night in Deadwood," she said, dusting off her hands.

"More like a wild fright," I muttered.

"Shut the door," Cornelius told Cooper.

A mewling sound seeped out of my mouth before I could clamp my lips together.

Natalie looked my way. "Did you swallow a cat on the way here?"

"More like a chicken." I took a deep, calming breath, making a face at the hint of decaying flesh I swore I could smell even if Doc said otherwise. "Do we really need to close ourselves down here?" I asked Cornelius. "What if someone locks us in here?"

"Nobody will lock us in," Cooper said, leaning against the support beam next to the steps. "Besides, if they do, I'll shoot a hole in the door and then put a bullet in them."

I crossed my arms over my chest. "I thought we agreed there'd be no guns here tonight."

"You insinuated no loaded guns. Mine's not loaded at the moment."

Before I could argue further with Cooper, Doc pulled me over to one of the corners, his back to the others, giving us a sliver of privacy. "Listen, Killer, I know you are hell on wheels in other realms, but ghosts are my specialty. This could easily take a bad turn and career over a cliff if we're not careful, taking Cornelius with it."

I nodded, my anxiety coating my skin with a layer of sweat. "How do we keep any careening from happening?"

"Don't let Cornelius leave your side."

"What are you talking about? We're all in here, packed together like pickles in a jar."

"Pickles?"

"Yeah, it's a root cellar, so jars of pickles came to mind."

His grin was short lived. "You're going to leave the root cellar during the séance."

"I am?" At his nod, I asked, "Are you a fortune teller in your off time?"

"No, a fortune seeker." He glanced over my shoulder, nodding at someone and holding up his finger for them to wait. "After we get started, I'm going to open the door for you."

"The root cellar door?"

"No, the door between now and then, where you'll need to take Cornelius to find Wilda."

"Shouldn't we have discussed this plan before now?"

"You would have overthought it and made it tougher for me to do my part."

"But aren't you supposed to be the one freeing Cornelius from Wilda?"

"This is not a job for one medium, Violet. We have to work together."

"Okay, so keep Cornelius with me. But how do I get rid of Wilda?"

"Cornelius says that'll become evident once you two are in there."

"In where?"

"The Hessler house."

I shook my head. "Don't make me go in there again." The mere thought of returning to that house of the dead made me almost pee my pants.

He placed his hands on my shoulders. "You can do this, Violet. You've destroyed far more dangerous things than Wilda." He kissed me on the forehead and then stepped back.

"Okay." I gave in, but my heart wasn't really in it. The beating organ had locked itself in a closet inside of my chest and refused to come out until I stopped doing such foolish stunts.

When he stepped away, Cornelius turned to me and held out his broken-horned Viking helmet. "Put this on."

"Are you serious?"

"It will make it easier for you to connect with Wilda."

"I don't want to connect with her. I want to boot her out of your life." And mine.

"Just put the damned helmet on, Parker," Cooper said, "so we can get this over with. I have work to do yet."

"It's Thanksgiving night," I reminded him.

"Exactly. Nobody will be at the station to bug me."

"Fine, but I draw the line at holding that stupid clown cookie jar top, so don't even go there." I put the broken helmet on my head. "Now what?"

Cornelius lit the end of the dried sage bundle, waving it around in the air and then handed it to Natalie. "Smother that," he told her and took a seat in the center of the dirt floor. "Violet, sit with your back to mine."

I did, leaning back against his black coat. The coolness of the packed dirt seeped through my jeans.

"Close your eyes, Violet," Cornelius directed. "And this time, instead of picturing one candle, picture two."

Two? I had recently done that very thing and along had come Caly.

Maybe two was a bad idea.

"Use the flame of the first candle to light the second, then set them a hand's width apart and focus on the dark center between the flames."

"You don't want me to pair the flames?"

"No. Not unless you want to catch an entity in the web the pairing creates."

Oops! Was that why Caly had come looking for me? Or was the doll ghost or Ottó the result of my pairing? Or had something else come forth that I hadn't realized with the distraction of Ottó, the doll, and Caly?

Shaking off my worries for another middle of the night toss-and-turn festival, I closed my eyes and maneuvered the candles. Then I stared into the blackness, the flames flickering in my peripheral mind's eye. After what felt like several minutes, I opened my mouth to ask Cornelius if I was doing something wrong, when he came walking out of the darkness and picked up one of the candles.

"Ready?" he asked.

"You didn't do your humming thing," I said, suddenly realizing that fact.

"I didn't want to call her to us. We're going to her."

"We are?" That's what Doc must have meant about my going back to the Hessler house.

"Grab that candle, Violet. I need you to lead the way since I haven't been where we need to go."

When I reached out and touched the candle, a wave of dizziness swept over me so strongly that I had to cover my eyes for a moment. When I lowered my hand, the candle was gone and I was standing outside under the starry night sky. In front of me, on the other side of a wrought iron gate, loomed the Victorian style Hessler house.

I stared up at the two-storied dwelling that had been the setting of so many of my nightmares. Even in the darkness, I could tell the house was different this time. The structure before me was younger and sturdier, the precursor of the dilapidated house I'd first seen back in July. A soft glow of light poured out through the windows on both floors, beckoning me inside out of the cold.

But I lingered, shivering with cold and dread, looking around for an option other than stepping inside Wilda's lair. Wasn't there a door number two? Another showcase on which I could bid?

The wood smoke in the air was thicker than before, the barking dog now silent. The street lights glowed white instead of orange, the street empty of any signs of life. The windows in the neighboring houses were all dark, shuttered, uninviting. In the distance, instead of lights dotting the hillside, there was nothing but blackness. That's when I realized that I hadn't stepped back in time but rather I'd entered the twisted world in which Wilda now lived.

"What are we waiting for?" Cornelius asked, joining me in front of the Hessler house. "We can't remove her from here."

At least I wasn't alone. "I'm working up to it," I told him, glad to have him by my side.

The front gate didn't creak even a little. It was well-oiled apparently. We climbed the porch steps, the crunch of snow underfoot seemed muffled.

I raised my hand to knock.

"There's no need," Cornelius pointed at the door. "It's already open."

Was that Doc's doing? Was he here somewhere, watching over us?

I pushed open the door and we stepped inside, shaking off the cold and snow from our shoes—a force of habit, even in dreamland. I looked over at Cornelius. "What now?"

The door slammed shut behind us, making me jump.

I shook my fist at it.

"Did you do that?" Cornelius asked.

The lights went out before I could answer.

Again, I wasn't entirely surprised. Nor was I pleased about this. Walking through a well-lit haunted house was heart-stopping enough.

"No," I told him. "I didn't kill the lights either."

I heard the sound of shoes scuffing the floor near the half-closed pocket doors that led into the dining room. When I squinted into the dark in that direction, I thought I saw the shape of a head in the darkness peeking around one of the doors. A giggle followed, then the shape was gone, the footfalls leading deeper into the house.

"There's our little pest. I'm sure she's the one responsible for our sudden lack of lighting. Let's see what else she has in store for us." I led the way toward the dining room, banging my knee on a table that hadn't been in the sitting room when I'd gone through the house as Wolfgang's real estate agent. "We need a flashlight."

One appeared a moment later in Cornelius's hand. He handed it to me.

"Where did this come from?"

"My pocket." He pulled out a second flashlight.

"What other tricks do you have up your sleeve?" I jested.

"I've come prepared, Violet."

I turned the light on him. "What do you mean?"

He reached into his coat pocket and pulled out a chicken foot, handing it to me.

Next came a black feather.

"Raven or crow?" I asked.

"I can't believe you're asking me that."

Then came a pair of fuzzy dice with seven dots on each side.

"Fuzzy dice?"

"I bought those from a guy in Vegas who practices a new age style of voodoo. He swore they'd protect me from unhappy gremlins."

"Are there actually happy gremlins out there?"

"Sure. Gremlins have gotten a bad rap in the media."

Next came a quarter-sized ivory heart, then what looked like a shark's tooth with symbolic carvings on it, then a vial of bones.

I should've brought the alligator tooth that Zelda had given me. "What are these?" I held up the vial. "Baby bird bones?"

He scoffed. "Why would I have bird bones?" He shined his light on the vial. "Those are the bones of a Siberian pixie faery."

I squinted at the tiny vial. It looked like a bunch of tiny twigs and a pebble to me. How much did a vial of Siberian pixie faery bones cost on the free market these days?

Before I had a chance to ask, he pulled out a horseshoe, well-scuffed and scratched, then a tiki doll carved out of obsidian, then a ...

"Okay, stop," I told him, handing him back all of his protection trinkets. "I think you've covered all of our bases."

He stuffed them all back into his wool coat pocket, which didn't even bulge when he'd finished. "I told you I've come prepared for battle."

"Oh, yeah? Then where's your cannon?"

"In my pants."

I did a double take. That comeback wasn't Cornelius's style, more like Ray's. "I can't believe you said that."

"It's true." He reached into his pants' pocket and pulled out something, holding it toward me. I shined the light on his open palm. A miniature brass cannon from the Civil War era sat there, ready for battle.

"It's my lucky cannon," he explained and pocketed it.

I should have known better than to ask.

Through the narrow doorway to the kitchen, I heard the sound of another giggle, then footfalls running away again.

"Come on." We started to follow Wilda toward the kitchen, but suddenly she was behind us in the entryway where we'd stood moments before.

I strode back through the sitting room in time to hear a door upstairs slam closed. Standing at the base of the oak stairway, I glared up the steps into the darkness. "I'm not going to play hide-and-seek with her in this haunted house." I'd been there and done that with her brother, and frankly, the idea of going up into the violet wallpapered room turned my feet into anvils. I looked over at Cornelius. "How can I get her to come to us?"

"I don't know that you have that ability, but I do."

"Get her down here so we can finish this and get the hell out of here."

Cornelius started chanting under his breath.

Then I remembered that I was wearing his Viking helmet. I took it off. The horn was no longer broken. "Wait," I said and switched hats with him, plopping the Abe Jr. hat on my head. "Okay, go."

He sat down on the second step and started again, chanting, humming, calling the ghost to him.

I stood next to him, squinting up the stairwell into the dark, waiting for Wilda to appear.

I heard no footfalls.

No doors slamming.

No giggles.

Something poked me in the back.

I looked down and around.

A garish clown face looked up at me with a ghoulish grin, scaring me so badly that I almost swallowed my tongue.

"Roses are red," Wilda's high-pitched child's voice filled my head. "Violet is blue. Mother is mad. She's coming for you."

God, I hated that stupid poem!

My hand snaked out, latching onto her arm. "Gotcha, you little shit! What do we do now, Cornelius?"

He kept humming and chanting, lost in his own rhythm.

Wilda let out an ear-piercing shriek. She started tugging to be free, but I held tightly, stronger by far.

"Cornelius!" I yelled in the midst of the frenzy, but he continued to sit there, unaffected by the cacophony.

Wilda kicked out at me and then twisted in my arms, her teeth gnashing, trying to take a piece out of me. Why was everyone so into biting these days? I struggled to hold her, turning her around so her back was to me and bending down to lock her in a bear hug.

She stilled so suddenly that for a moment I thought I'd squeezed her to death. Then she whimpered, "Let me go."

"Not until you let Cornelius go."

"No. I won't. And you can't make me."

Criminy, it was one thing to discipline an obnoxious kid in real life, but how did you make a bratty ghost child obey? I was at a total loss on what to do next.

Doc.

I closed my eyes and pictured two candles, one lit, one not. Following Cornelius's earlier instructions, I used one to light the other and then focused on the black space in between them, trying to conjure Doc this time.

Nothing happened, at least not with Doc. Wilda on the other hand, began struggling again. After several seconds of fighting her and finally subduing her again, I closed my eyes and this time took the candles and held them together, merging the flames. Little bursts of light billowed up, then I pulled them apart again and stared into the black space. Come on, Doc.

Still nothing.

Damn it. I opened my eyes.

Cornelius was gone.

I looked up the stairs and all around us, but he was nowhere to be seen. "Where did he go?" I asked Wilda.

"I let him go."

What? Had I somehow spurred her to free him with my candle trick? "Why?"

"I got what *we* wanted."

There was that royal "we" again.

My stomach dropped. Oh no. She hadn't somehow killed him, had she? "What's that?"

"You."

Suddenly, my strength ebbed and I could no longer hold her. She pulled free of my grasp and turned, her garish clown face had a sad smile painted on it now.

"Violet, the one that I love," Wilda said, only her voice sounded more like her brother's.

I took a step backward, stumbling as another wave of dizziness washed over me, Cornelius's stove pipe hat fell to the floor. I bent to retrieve it and when I lifted it, I saw something shiny inside the black silk lining. I stuck my hand inside the hat and pulled out the top of the clown cookie jar.

What the hell?

Wilda cried out and snatched it out of my hand. "Where did you get this? Mother is going to be very angry. This is her favorite cookie jar. Nobody is supposed to touch it."

A loud slam boomed from overhead, making the whole house shake. The sound seemed to rumble for several seconds, echoing throughout the house. It sounded like the Fourth of July fireworks earlier this year over the Open Cut in Lead.

I took a step back, aiming the beam up the stair steps. "What was that?"

Wilda's clown face turned toward the stairwell. "Uh oh," she said and giggled nervously.

My flashlight went dark. I banged it on my leg but had no luck. "Shit." Now what?

Footfalls creaked across the floor up on the landing. I cringed with each step, squinting into the shadows. They stopped at the top of the stairs.

"You've done it," Wilda whispered.

"Done what?"

"Woken Mother."

I heard another *creak* from the top of the steps.

"You're the one who kept screaming," I told the brat.

Wilda let out a whimper and hid behind me.

Wait a second. Why was she hiding? It was her mother.

Silence stretched, wrapping around me, trussing me up like a mummy. My focus tunneled, centering on the thick shadows at the top of the stairs. My pulse was pounding so loud the partiers down at the Purple Door Saloon must have heard it.

I saw the shadows shift, sort of ripple even, but I couldn't make out anything definite in the darkness.

A warm fetid breath of air puffed against the right side of my face, heating my skin. Then I heard what sounded like a low-pitched, inward scream in my right ear, growing louder and steadier with each beat of my heart, which was busy trying to break land speed records. The whole right side of my body tingled, goosebumps spreading from head to toe.

Wilda's mother was beside me. I could feel her energy making my hair stand on end like static electricity.

Gulping, I slowly turned my head to the right … and stared straight into Mrs. Hessler's face.

Her cheeks were paler than in the picture I'd seen of her months ago up in her bedroom. Her chin was unnaturally long, as if she were being stretched. Her nose looked more pointed, her eyes black, bottomless pits. Her hair seemed to float in water around her, alive even though she was long dead.

The inward scream stopped. Her thin lips pulled back from her teeth, reminding me of a partially decayed body I once saw in Layne's archaeology books. "Child killer," she snarled, her teeth chattering like wind-up teeth.

Her hand lifted, long bony fingers reaching toward my face. I wanted to pull back. I needed to pull back. But I stood frozen, my eyes widening as her fingertips came closer, blurring.

The front door banged open behind us.

Mrs. Hessler's head whipped around, her mouth gaping extra wide. Then she was gone and she took Wilda with her, flying out the door with a banshee scream that scraped over me like fingernails on a chalkboard and rattled the windows.

I ran after them out into the cold, fresh air, tripping on a charred and broken board and falling to my knees. When I looked up, I was back in the here and now. At least I figured it was present day since Cooper was sprawled out on his back on the grass below.

"Cooper?" I pushed to my feet and scrambled down to where he was slowly sitting up, shaking his head as if to clear it. "Are you okay?"

"What in the fuck was that?"

"Did you see her?"

"See who?"

"Mrs. Hessler. She just flew out of …" I looked back at the house that wasn't there anymore, only the burned remains.

"What are you talking about, Parker? There was nobody here but you. Then this wind came out of nowhere and slammed into me, knocking me down." He rubbed the back of his head as he got to his feet. "I think I blacked out for a second there."

"I don't think that was wind." I reached out to steady him and he batted my hands away. "It was a ghost."

The creases on his face deepened. "Christ. You really don't expect me to believe that, do you?"

After the crazy shit he'd already witnessed, yes, but I bit my tongue rather than try to convince Cooper otherwise. Now was not the time, and I had a feeling we had bigger problems to juggle than his continued skepticism.

"Hell." He winced while rolling his left shoulder. "Watching your back is hazardous to my health."

He should try dodging an ax-swinging juggernaut. "Where're the others?"

He jammed his thumb over his shoulder. "Still underground. You took off again, so I followed."

"What did I do?"

He looked toward the burned pile of rubble that had once been a house. "You walked around the foundation like you were in some trance, then climbed the porch steps and turned into a statue."

"Until that wind blew," I said, replaying that last bit in my head. I shuddered at the memory of Mama Hessler. "Did Cornelius follow me?"

"No, you acted alone."

So, I must somehow have brought Cornelius along mentally? Or had I made that up with him and his pocket full of tricks? I scratched my forehead. This ghost business fit me like a pair of wooden shoes, all clunky, slippery in the muddy spots; whereas playing executioner felt as natural as running barefoot through the sand.

"Is Doc okay?" I asked.

"Besides his infatuation with a crazy-haired troublemaker?" When I glared at him, he shrugged. "He was more cognizant during this run than when we were at Uncle Willis's ranch."

"Violet?" Natalie called in the darkness.

"We're over here, Nat."

She jogged over, giving me a glance over and then focusing on Cooper. "What happened to you?"

"Nothing, why?" His tone was surprisingly terse. He usually saved that level of snappiness for me.

"Wow." She turned to me. "Is my head still attached or did he bite it clear off?"

Cooper sighed, pinching the bridge of his nose. "Sorry, Natalie. It's been a long week."

I almost felt sorry for him. Almost.

"Apology accepted." She crossed her arms over her chest, her back still stiff when she faced him. "Anyway, Doc told me to find you and make sure you were okay. He said something about you'd been caught in the blast zone."

"Doc's coherent already?" I asked.

"He and Cornelius both are. You kicked them out early."

"I did?"

"According to Doc you did. Cornelius opened his eyes first, then Doc shortly afterward. He didn't wake up happy either, saying something to Cornelius about you opening the channel too wide and something else coming through."

Mrs. Hessler.

"Crud! That was my doing?" I sank both hands into my hair, tugging it away from my face. Aunt Zoe had warned me about doing that very thing. "Double crud! Now what?"

"Well, if it makes you feel any better, Cornelius said you were successful in removing Wilda's hold on him."

So the little terror hadn't lied when she'd claimed to have let him go. "I have a feeling her haunting him was a ruse."

Cooper scowled. "What are you saying, Parker? That Cornelius was screwing with us all along about that ghost? For shit's sake, do you realize the risk I'm taking by letting you down in that root cellar?"

"Relax, Cooper. Don't go busting any blood vessels until you hear me out." I growled at the ornery detective for good measure. "I'm talking about Wilda being the trickster. She was playing me all along, baiting me with Cornelius."

"Why would she do that?" Natalie asked.

"So that I'd bring back her mother."

Chapter Twenty-Seven

Friday, November 23rd

I woke up in an empty bed. The sky outside my window was gray, sleet pelting the glass. With a groan, I pulled the covers up over my head.

I'd screwed up big time last night ...

Natalie had run Cornelius home after he'd finished packing up his gear. He'd been jovial in spite of the new mess I'd caused freeing him from Wilda. He told Doc he'd call him today after he woke up from what he hoped would be a long, quiet night with no trouble from ghosts for the first time in over a month.

Cooper had locked up the root cellar after us and threatened to throw me in jail if I called him within the next twenty-four hours. He strode back to his car and headed toward the police station without even blowing me a kiss goodbye.

"What a grumpy bear," I told Doc.

He chuckled and put his arm around me, leading me toward the Picklemobile. "Cut him some slack. He leads a tortured life."

"Fine, but he doesn't have to use his thumbscrews on me."

A short drive later, during which I texted Aunt Zoe that we were all fine and dandy at the moment, we were back in her warm, bright kitchen. I recounted what had happened in the Hessler house to Doc while we waited for Natalie to return from dropping off Cornelius. While I planned to share my ghostly adventures with Natalie, there were details that I wanted to work through with only Doc, such as the candle flame game I'd played while we were under. I needed to find out where he thought I'd screwed up and opened the channel too wide, and I didn't really want an audience during that discussion.

Unfortunately, Doc didn't have any concrete answers. According to him, in the paranormal activity business, there were different strokes for different folks, depending on the medium's abilities. Since his specialty differed from mine, he was able to sense when the channel had opened wider but could only surmise that it happened sometime after Cornelius got involved with his humming routine. It was shortly after that when I'd somehow managed to boot both Cornelius and Doc from the whole show, which was an experience that had not happened to Doc before tonight.

Natalie's return spurred a rerun of the night's events. We each took turns speculating about the cookie jar lid and how it played into the whole shebang. Each of our theories included Mama Hessler's appearance, making me wonder if Wilda had somehow played Natalie by offering up that lid from the burned ruins.

After Natalie called it a night and went upstairs to crash in Aunt Zoe's bed, Doc and I moved to the couch. We both downed a bottle of beer while lost in our own thoughts as Humphrey Bogart smoked and rattled off one-liners on the TV screen. Halfway through the movie, Doc stood and held out his hand for me, pulling me after him up the stairs.

I took a quick rinse shower, wanting to wash away the rank mustiness of that root cellar along with Mrs. Hessler's foul smell from my skin before crawling under the sheets. Doc was already asleep when I closed the bedroom door and eased in beside him. He woke enough to pull me close and nuzzle my neck and then went out again. Much to my surprise, I followed his course within minutes, snuggling into his body and forgetting about garish clowns and terrifying ghost mothers.

Unfortunately, with the morning light came another reckoning of my royal fuckup. I hid deeper under my covers.

I was in the midst of beating myself up again when I heard the bedroom door open. Familiar footfalls crossed the floor. The mattress shifted next to me.

Doc peeled the covers back, grinning down at me. "Hiding from the world again?"

I blinked up at his unshaven face, noticing the damp ends of his hair, catching a whiff of my shampoo. Showered but not shaved. Hot damn. "How do you do it?"

"Lie next to you all night long without ravishing your body?"

"You didn't quite make it all night on that score."

"Oh, but I did score, Boots."

Yes, he had early this morning. Or rather I had. Actually it'd been more of a tie on the scoreboard. "How do you battle ghosts at night yet look fresh as a daisy come morning?"

"You fought the battle last night, not me. I just facilitated transitions for you." He combed some curls back from my face. "Besides, I wasn't the one who looked Wilda's mom in the face up close and personal."

"Thanks to you all I did was look."

When I'd met up with Cornelius and Doc as they were coming out of the root cellar last night, Cornelius had told me that after I'd booted the two of them back to the present, Doc had gone back under in order to shield me from whatever harm Mrs. Hessler had intended. He'd been the reason the front door had banged open, saving me from her touch. Unfortunately, that move had given Wilda and her mom an escape route, something for which Doc took full blame. Never mind that I was the one responsible for Mrs. Hessler showing up in the first place.

"Come on." He pulled the covers down further. "Harvey is here. He made bacon and waffles. That'll make you feel better."

I sat up and pulled my shoulders back in a big stretch.

Doc watched me, his eyes locked south of my chin. "On second thought," he reached for me, "forget breakfast."

I dodged his hand and rolled off the other side of the bed before he could catch me. "Bacon trumps sex, buster," I told him, stepping into a pair of pajama bottoms and slippers. "Especially when Harvey's working the spatula." I put on an old sweater and chased him out the bedroom door.

He detoured toward the bathroom while I headed for the kitchen. Cooper was sitting at the table when I stepped into the room. He welcomed me with a scowl.

I stopped short. "Who let you off your leash already?"

His steely eyes narrowed, moving up to my hair. "It's even worse first thing in the morning."

"How about some coffee with a splash of hemlock to start your day, Cooper?" I walked over to the fridge to get some creamer, poking Harvey in the ribs on the way.

"Thanks, Parker, but your venom is deadly enough."

"Jeez." Natalie stumbled into the kitchen, rubbing her eyes. "Do you two wake up thinking of ways to insult each other?"

Harvey snickered. "They're both mean as bulldogs on gunpowder diets this mornin'."

She joined me at the coffee pot, not noticing that Cooper was checking her out, from her tousled hair to her faded Lead-Deadwood Golddiggers T-shirt and black yoga pants to Aunt Zoe's smiley sunshine slippers.

Doc strolled into the kitchen, his face clean shaven, his boxer briefs and bare chest covered with jeans and a black thermal. I couldn't decide which I preferred.

He handed me a thick book.

I looked down at it. Make that *the book*, as in the family history book that had gone missing while I was sick.

"Where did you get this?"

"Layne called while I was shaving. He wanted me to check for a library book under his bed. He'd forgotten it's due today."

"Why didn't he call me?"

"He did, but you didn't answer."

My phone was still up in my bedroom. I held the book close to my chest. "This was under his bed?"

Doc nodded. "Is that what Zoe was talking about?"

"Yes." So Layne had it all along. Cripes, how much had he read? Did he have any clue it was our family line?

"We'll find out after he comes home," Doc told me, apparently reading my mind. "You should probably put that somewhere safe."

"Right," I said and disappeared into the laundry room for a few seconds. When I returned, Harvey looked at me with raised brows, but I shook my head.

"What's going on, Coop?" With his coffee in hand, Doc took the chair across from the detective. "I thought you were heading out to the shooting range this morning to blow off some steam."

"I am but I needed to swing by and pick up Natalie. She owes me a trip to the range."

"Food first, then guns," she said, joining him at the table. "I should shower, too, or you may feel like shooting me."

Cooper watched her take a drink from her mug before turning back to Doc. "I also need to talk to Parker about something."

"Did you look at Rosy's offer?" I'd dropped it off at the front desk of the cop shop Tuesday afternoon in a manila envelope with his name on it. He'd been busy in a meeting and I was happy not to bother him.

He shook his head. "I'll get to it later today or tomorrow. She gave me plenty of time."

A week to be exact, due to the holiday. So, if not Rosy's offer, then what? "If this is about Katrina King, I plead the Fifth." I stirred sugar in my coffee, needing to sweeten up if Cooper was staying for breakfast.

"It's not."

"You mean Detective Hawke didn't send you here to threaten to put me in jail for Katrina's murder?"

"No. Dominick Masterson has written up a statement that clears your name, sharing information that ties Katrina in with some shady dealings in the past, listing several possible suspects who might have wanted to take her out of the picture."

That gave me pause. "And how are Dominick and you going to explain his exit from the Opera House in September and subsequent absence until now?"

"We're still working on that mess of yours."

I subdued the urge to snap back at him by pouring coffee down my throat.

In my silence, Cooper continued, "Something else happened that saved your ass when it comes to Katrina's death."

"What's that?" Doc asked.

"I learned this morning that the war hammer disappeared in transit. It never made it to the lab for further examination."

I fell into the seat next to Doc. "What? How?"

"That's what I came to ask you."

"I had nothing to do with that," I lowered my coffee cup. "I was with Doc all day yesterday and the night prior."

"I know that, but Detective Hawke has a different idea."

"What? He thinks I hijacked it during transport?"

"No. He suspects one of your henchmen swiped it for you."

"I have henchmen? Damn, if I'd known I had henchmen working for me, I would've had them help with getting the kids back and forth to school, bullying Ray when he was being an extra big asshole, and threatening Rex to leave town."

"Cute, Parker, but Hawke is determined to pin something on you, so try to keep your nose squeaky clean for a while."

"There you go again, obsessed with my nose."

"At least I'm kind enough not to break yours."

"Do I need to put ya both in separate stalls for breakfast?" Harvey asked, threatening us both with his spatula after setting down a stacked plate of waffles.

"Sorry," I told the old buzzard as he dropped a couple of pieces of bacon on my plate. "I'd just like to enjoy a day without the police crawling up my ass."

"Great, tell Coop that, not me."

I turned to our not-so-friendly detective with a sigh. "Is there anything else you needed to tell us, Cooper?" I asked in my nice Realtor voice.

He fidgeted with his fork, which was unusual behavior for the gritty detective. He looked up at me and then Doc. "I have a question for you two."

"About last night?" Doc asked.

He shook his head. "About ghosts."

That was more Cornelius and Doc's department than mine, but I kept my lips closed.

"I went into work extra early this morning and found something." He hesitated, his gaze concentrating on his fork.

I looked at Doc, who shrugged back. He prompted. "What'd you find?"

"A prisoner in one of the jail cells."

I lowered my cup of coffee. "It wasn't Cornelius was it?"

"No." He set down his fork. "The guy had a rope around his neck. When I asked him where he'd gotten the rope, he walked into the wall."

"Was he drunk?" Natalie asked.

"You don't understand. He didn't walk into the wall and fall down, he walked *through* the wall and disappeared."

In the silence that followed, Cooper's steely gaze dared each of us to challenge him.

Doc spoke first. "Last night, you said a wind came out of nowhere and knocked you down."

Cooper nodded.

"That wasn't wind, Coop. I'd opened the door to help Violet escape the trap Wilda had set, only Violet wasn't the only one to use that door."

"What are you saying, Nyce?"

"While we are all born with the ability to see beyond our everyday world, not everyone develops that ability." He raised one finger. "Some of us are born with our sixth sense cranked all of the way up from the get-go, which was my case." He raised a second finger. "Some know they have the ability but need to work at it, building the muscle if you will, before they can see."

"Like Cornelius?" I asked.

"I guess, but I don't know his full history." Doc raised a third finger. "And some people get blasted wide open by an event in their lives—it could be spurred by extreme stress, by a near-death experience, or by a particularly powerful ghost."

Cooper set his fork down, his gaze locked on Doc. "You're saying that a ghost blasted me open when it knocked me down?"

"Maybe."

"Hell hath no fury like a woman scorned," I mused. In this case, there were two women—Wilda and her mom.

Child killer, I heard Mama Hessler's accusation in my head. Chills peppered my back.

"Shut up, Parker." To Doc, he said, "And that's why I saw what could've been the prisoner who hung himself in that jail cell years ago?"

"Possibly."

"Could you be any more ambiguous?"

"Sure, if you'd like to have a longer, more detailed discussion on psychic abilities and using your sixth sense, I'll make your head spin." Doc grinned at Cooper's curses. "Time will tell for you, Coop. Until then, all you can do is keep your mind open to the possibility that you may not be seeing or hearing or sensing something real in the usual sense of the word."

The doorbell rang before Cooper could swear some more. Natalie hopped up to get it since she was closest to the door.

At the sound of her cry of surprise, I lowered my fork. I was in the midst of standing to go join her when my brother came striding into the kitchen with Natalie on his heels, her face split by a wide smile.

Quint had a cherry pie in one hand and a long, brown paper package in the other. He set the pie on the table and the package on Nat's empty chair, and then shucked his coat and hung it over the back of the chair. "I brought you some get-well pie, outlaw Curly Bill," he said, using the nickname he'd given me as kids after we had watched a show about Tombstone.

Everyone stared at him in surprise, including me. I hadn't seen Quint in months. His dark, wavy hair was longer than usual, brushing his collar. He looked more buff in his T-shirt than I remembered, but his smile was as infectious as ever.

Natalie took his coat, poking him in the ribs playfully and giggling when he tickled her back, the same screwing around type of fun they'd shared since childhood. Cooper watched with a masked expression, but his eyes soaked up the whole show, his face rigid.

When Natalie took Quint's coat to the other room, Quint glanced around the table, his eyes alight with questions when they settled on me. "Are you going to give me a hug hello or just sit there with your pie hole hanging open?"

"I'm gonna pop you in your pie hole, knucklehead," I said and rushed into his open arms, giving him a loud kiss on the cheek. He smelled good, like fresh air and laughter-filled memories. "I can't believe you're here."

"Aunt Zoe said you really wanted some pie, so I thought I'd share it with you." He glanced over my head. "But it looks like you already have company."

I made introductions, saving Doc for last. "And this is Doc Nyce. He and I are ..." I searched for the appropriate word. *Boyfriend and girlfriend* sounded juvenile and *lovers* seemed too dramatic.

"Playing doctor," Harvey supplied.

"More like playing house," Natalie said, her face alight as she focused on Quint. She'd been in our lives so long Quint was practically her brother, too.

"Ahh," Quint shook Doc's hand. "Now it makes sense."

"What's that?" I asked.

He released Doc's hand and crossed his arms over his chest, his gaze still locked on Doc. "Aunt Zoe told me that you weren't feeling well but not to worry because you had a doctor making house calls."

Doc's face turned a shade of red under Quint's scrutiny. "Yes, well, I'm happy to report your sister is in excellent form."

Harvey hooted, smacking the table.

"Good." One of Quint's eyebrows rose. "And you'll make sure she stays that way, right?"

"I'll do my best," Doc said, giving me a look that made my heart almost as happy as the sight of that cherry pie. "But she does tend to run headlong into trouble now and then."

"Only now and then?" Quint winked at me. "You must be out of practice, Curly Bill."

I stuck my tongue out at him and hauled him over to the chair next to me. "Join us for breakfast. I want to hear all about your latest adventures." It would be refreshing to hear about something besides ghosts, murders, and all of the other gruesome topics ruling my life lately.

"What's this?" Natalie asked him, holding up the package he'd left on her chair.

"It's for Violet."

"That's heavy." She passed it to Doc, who handed it to me. His eyes narrowed slightly when they met mine.

I hefted it. Something about it felt familiar. "What is it?" I asked Quint. "It's too heavy to be another pair of purple boots."

He chuckled. "Isn't one pair enough?"

"No," Doc answered before I could.

I winked at Doc and started unwrapping the package. "What did you bring me? It's too early for Christmas."

Quint dished up a waffle on the plate Natalie handed him. "It's not from me. I found it on the front porch."

I froze in the midst of tearing off the thick paper. My gaze met Doc's and then Harvey's. "You did?"

"It was leaning against the wall under the doorbell." He pulled an envelope from his back pocket. "This was next to it."

My name was written across the front, the handwriting familiar. I tore open the envelope and pulled out a piece of paper.

If you want to survive, Scharfrichter, try not to lose this again.

"What's it say?" Doc asked.

I gulped. "Happy Thanksgiving," I lied, not wanting to drag my brother into my messy life if I could help it, and handed the paper to Doc to read for himself.

Cooper apparently sniffed out my anxiety. He lowered his cup, his eyes on the prize. "What's in the package, Parker?"

I had a feeling I knew the answer, but didn't want to find out if I was right. "How about we finish breakfast. I'll open it later."

"Come on, have at it," Quint said, stuffing a piece of waffle into his mouth, appearing none the wiser to my acting. "Now you have me curious."

With a frozen smile, I tore off the rest of the paper and exclaimed in mock surprise at the contents.

"Is that real?" Quint took the war hammer from me, touching the pointed tip.

I was pretty sure it was, especially since the last time I'd seen it that very point had been buried in Katrina King's chest.

Quint's pocket rang. He pulled out his cell phone and looked at the screen. "It's Jeff Hughes."

"Jeff from high school?" I asked.

"Yeah." He handed the war hammer to me and scooted back from the table. "I need to take this. I'll be a minute or two," he said and headed into the dining room. "Hey, Jeff," I heard him say, and then the front door creaked open and thudded closed.

With Quint out of earshot, I held up the war hammer. "Did anyone see the stork who left this baby on the porch again?"

Doc lifted the war hammer out of my hands, taking a closer look at it. "The leather's been cleaned and the point sharpened."

Natalie aimed her fork at it. "That thing is going to come in handy, you wait and see." She winked at me and said in a sing-songy voice, "*Ex'srays arcay.*"

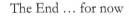

I shot her a warning look, glancing over at Cooper to see if he'd picked up on her Pig Latin translation of "Rex's car."

"Goddammit, Parker." Cooper shoved his plate away, apparently too busy being pissed off to have heard Natalie's words. "If Detective Hawke finds out that weapon is back in your possession, you're seriously fucked."

"You got a flood of trouble comin' yer way, girl. Five foot high and risin'." Harvey picked up a piece of bacon and took a bite, his eyes gleaming. "Looks like yer gonna need bigger waders to keep yer powder dry."

The End ... for now

About the Author

Ann Charles is USA Today bestselling author who writes award-winning mysteries that are splashed with humor, romance, paranormal, and whatever else she feels like throwing into the mix. When she is not dabbling in fiction, arm-wrestling with her children, attempting to seduce her husband, or arguing with her sassy cat, she is daydreaming of lounging poolside at a fancy resort with a blended margarita in one hand and a great book in the other.

Facebook (Personal Page):
http://www.facebook.com/ann.charles.author

Facebook (Author Page):
http://www.facebook.com/pages/Ann-Charles/37302789804?ref=share

Twitter (as Ann W. Charles):
http://twitter.com/AnnWCharles

Ann Charles Website:
http://www.anncharles.com

BONUS READ from Ann's friend: NYT Bestselling Author Robyn Peterman!

Fashionably Dead

Book One of THE HOT DAMNED Series

by
Robyn Peterman

Prologue

I drew hard on the cigarette and narrowed my eyes at the landscape before me. Graves, tombstones, crypts ... she didn't belong here. Hell, I didn't belong here. My eyes were dry. I'd cried so much there was nothing left. I exhaled and watched as the blue grey smoke wafted out over the plastic flowers decorating the headstones.

Five minutes. I just needed five minutes and then I could go back ...

"That's really gross," Gemma said, as she rounded the corner of the mausoleum I was hiding behind and scared the hell out of me. She fanned the smoke away and eyed me. "She wanted you to quit, maybe now would be a good time."

"Agreed. It's totally gross and disgusting and I'm going to quit, regardless of the fact that other than you, Marlboro Lights are my best friend … but today is definitely not the day," I sighed and took another long drag.

"That's pathetic," she chuckled.

"Correct. Do you have perfume and gum?"

"Yep." She dug through her purse and handed me a delicate bottle.

"I can't use this. It's the expensive French shit."

"Go for it," she grinned. "You're gonna need it. You smell like an ashtray and your mother is inside scaring people to death."

"Son of a … " I moaned and quickly spritzed myself. "I thought she left. She didn't want to come in the first place."

"Could have fooled me," Gemma said sarcastically, handing over a piece of gum and shoving me from my hiding place.

"Come on," I muttered, as my bossy best friend pushed me back to my beloved grandmother's funeral.

***

The hall was filled with people. Foldout tables lined the walls and groaned under the weight of casseroles, cakes and cookies. Men and women, most of whom I knew, milled around and ate while they gossiped. Southern funerals were a time to socialize and eat. A lot.

As I made my way through the crowd and accepted condolences, I got an earful of information I could have happily lived without. I learned that Donna Madden was cheating on her husband Greg, Candy Pucker had gained thirty pounds from eating Girl Scout cookies and had shoved her fat ass into a heinous sequined gown, *for the funeral no less,* and Sam Boomaster, the Mayor, was now a homosexual. Hell, I just wanted to leave, but I had to find my mother before she did something awful.

"I loved her." Charlie stopped me in my tracks and grabbed my hand in his old gnarled one.

His toupee was angled to the left and his black socks and sandals peeked out from his high-water plaid pants. He was beautiful.

"Me too," I smiled.

"You know I tried to court her back in the day, but she only had eyes for your Grandpa." He smoothed his sweater vest and laid a wet one on my cheek … and if I'm not mistaken, *and I'm not*, he grabbed my ass.

"Charlie, if you touch my butt again, I'll remove your hand." I grinned and adjusted his toupee. He was a regular in the art class I taught at the senior center and his wandering hands were infamous.

"Can't blame a guy for trying. You have a nice ass there, Astrid! You look like one of them there supermodels! Gonna make some lucky man very happy one day," he explained seriously.

"With my ass?"

"Well now, your bosom is nothing to scoff at either and your legs … " he started.

"Charlie, I'm gonna cut you off before you wax poetic about things that will get you arrested for indecency."

"Good thinking, girlie!" he laughed. "If you ever want to hear stories about your Nana from when we were young, I'd be happy to share."

"Thanks, Charlie, I'd like that."

I gave him a squeeze, holding his hands firmly to his sides and made my way back into the fray.

As I scanned the crowd for my mother, my stomach clenched. After everything I had to put up with today, the evil approaching was just too much. Martha and Jane, the ancient matriarchs of the town and the nastiest gossips that ever lived were headed straight for me. Fuck.

"I suppose you'll get an inheritance," Jane snapped as she looked me up and down. "You'll run through it like water."

"Your Nana, God bless her, was blind as a bat when it came to you," Martha added caustically. "I mean, my God, what are you? Thirty and unmarried? It's just downright disrespectable."

"I'm twenty-nine, happily single and getting it on a regular basis," I said, enjoying the way their thin lips hung open in an impressive O.

"Well, I've never," Jane gasped.

"Clearly. You should try it sometime. I understand Mr. Smith is so vision impaired, you might have a shot there."

Their appalled shrieks were music to my ears and I quickly made my escape. Nana would have been a bit disappointed with my behavior, but she was gone.

Time to find the reason I came back in here for … I smelled her before I saw her. A waft of Chanel perfume made the lead ball in my stomach grow heavier. I took a deep breath, straightened my very vintage Prada sheath that I paid too much for, plastered a smile on my face, said a quick prayer and went in to the battle.

"Mother, is everything alright?"

She stood there mutely and stared. She was dressed to the nines. She didn't belong here … in this town, in this state, in my life.

"I'm sorry, are you speaking to me?" she asked. Shit, she was perfect … on the outside. Gorgeous and put together to a degree I didn't even aspire to. On the inside she was a snake.

"Um, yes. I asked you if … " I stammered.

"I heard you," she countered smoothly. "If you can't bother to comply with my wishes, I can't be bothered to answer you."

"Right," I muttered and wished the floor would open and swallow me. "I'm sorry, I meant Petra. Petra, is everything alright?"

"No, everything is not alright," she hissed. "I have a plane to catch and I have no more time or patience to make chit chat with backward rednecks. It was wrong of you to ask me to be here."

"Your mother died," I said flatly. "This is her funeral and these people are here to pay their respects."

"Oh for God's sake, she was old and lived well past her time."

I was speechless. Rare for me, but if anyone was capable of shocking me to silence, it was my mother.

"So, like I said, I have a plane to catch. I'll be back next week." She eyed me critically, grimacing at what she saw. "You need some lipstick. You're lucky you got blessed with good genes because you certainly don't do anything to help."

With that loving little nugget, she turned on her stiletto heel and left. I glanced around to see if we'd been overheard and was mortified to see we had clearly been the center of attention.

"Jesus, she's mean," Gemma said, pulling me away from prying eyes and big ears.

"Do I look awful?" I whispered, feeling the heat crawl up my neck as the mourners looked on with pity. Not for my loss, but for my parentage.

"You're beautiful," Gemma said. "Inside and out."

"I need to smoke," I mumbled. "Can we leave yet?"

Gemma checked her watch. "Yep, we're out of here."

"I don't want to go home yet," I said, looking around for Bobby Joe Gimble, the funeral director. Where in the hell was he and did I need to tip him? Shit, I had no clue what funeral etiquette was. "Do I have to … ?"

"Already took care of everything," Gemma told me. "Let's go."

"Where to?" I asked. Damn, I was grateful she was mine.

"Hattie's."

"Thank you, Jesus."

**

Hattie's sold one thing and one thing only. Ice cream. Homemade, full of fat, heart attack inducing ice cream. It was probably my favorite place in the world.

"I'll have a triple black raspberry chip in a cone cup," I said as I eyed all the flavors. I didn't know why I even looked at them. I was totally loyal to my black raspberry chip. My ice cream couldn't talk back to me, break up with me or make me feel bad. Of course, my love could extend the size of my ass, but I wasn't even remotely concerned about that today. Besides, I planned a very long run for later. I needed to clear my head and be alone.

"Sorry about your loss, Sugar," Hattie said and I nodded. Her big fleshy arms wobbled as she scooped out my treat. "Do you want sprinkles and whipped cream on that, Baby?"

"Um ... " I glanced over at Gemma who grinned and gave me a thumbs up. "Yes, yes I do."

"Me too," Gemma added, "but I want mint chip, please."

"You got it, Sugar Buns," Hattie said and handed me a monstrous amount of ice cream. "It's on me today, Astrid. I feel just terrible I couldn't be at the funeral."

"That's okay, Hattie. You and Nana were such good friends. I want your memories to be of that."

"Thank you for that, Darlin'. Ever since my Earl died from siphoning gasoline, I haven't been able to set foot near that goddamn funeral parlor."

I swallowed hard. Her late ex-husband Earl had siphoned gasoline since he was ten. His family owned the local gas station and apparently, as legend had it, he enjoyed the taste. But on the fateful day in question, he'd been smoking a cigar while he did it ... and blew himself to kingdom come. It was U-G-L-Y. Earl was spread all over town. Literally. He and Hattie had been divorced for years and hated each other. It was no secret he had fornicated with over half the older women in town, but when he died like that, he became a saint in her eyes.

I bit down on the inside of my cheek. Hard. Although it was beyond inappropriate, whenever anyone talked about Earl, I laughed.

"Astrid totally understands." Gemma gave Hattie a quick hug and pushed me away from the counter before I said or did something unforgivable.

"Thanks," I whispered. "That would have been bad."

"Yep," Gemma grinned and shoveled a huge spoon of ice cream in her mouth.

"Where in the hell do you put that?" I marveled at her appetite. "You're tiny."

"You're a fine one to talk, Miss I Have the World's Fastest Metabolism."

"That's the only good thing I inherited from the witch who spawned me," I said and dug in to my drug of choice. I winced in pain as my frozen ice cream ass-extender went straight to the middle of my forehead.

"Are you okay?" Gemma asked.

I took a deep breath and pinched the bridge of my nose. God, I hated brain freezes. "No, not right now, but I've decided to change some stuff. Nana would want me to."

My best friend watched me silently over her ice cream.

"I'm going to stop smoking, get a real career, work out every day, date someone who has a job and not a parole officer, get married, have two point five kids and prove that I was adopted."

"That's a pretty tall order. How are you gonna make all that happen?" she asked, handing me a napkin. "Wipe your mouth."

"Thanks," I muttered. "I have no fucking idea, but I will succeed … or die trying."

"Good luck with that."

"Um, thanks. Do you mind if we leave here so I can chain smoke 'til I throw up so it will be easier to quit?"

"Is that the method you're going to use?" Gemma asked, scooping up our unfinished ice cream and tossing it.

"I know it seems a little unorthodox, but I read it worked for Jennifer Aniston."

"Really?"

"No, but it sounded good," I said, dragging her out of Hattie's.

"God, Astrid," Gemma groaned. "Whatever you need to do I'm here for you, but you have to quit. I don't want you to die. Ever."

"Everybody dies," I said quietly, reminded that the woman I loved most had died only a week ago. "But I've got too fucking much to do to die any time soon."

For more info on Robyn Peterman's FASHIONABLY DEAD and her other fun books, check out her website at: www.robynpeterman.com

The Jackrabbit Junction Mystery Series

Bestseller in Women Sleuth Mystery and Romantic Suspense

Welcome to the Dancing Winnebagos RV Park. Down here in Jackrabbit Junction, Arizona, Claire Morgan and her rabble-rousing sisters are really good at getting into trouble—BIG trouble (the land your butt in jail kind of trouble). This rowdy, laugh-aloud mystery series is packed with action, suspense, adventure, and relationship snafus. Full of colorful characters and twisted up plots, the stories of the Morgan sisters will keep you wondering what kind of a screwball mess they are going to land in next.

The Dig Site Mystery Series

A headstrong and determined archaeologist

A tall, dark, and unwelcome photojournalist

Both are trying to unearth secrets that have been long buried, but an ancient Maya curse threatens to destroy them …

Unless they can learn to trust each other enough to make it out of the jungle alive.

Made in the USA
Columbia, SC
22 November 2023

26550024R00233